The Forbidden Path
Dragonfly Series: Book 3

Gloria W. Nye

Spiral Press

Spiral Press
www.spiralpress.ca

Spiral Press Logo by Ken Coward,
Holy Cow Communication Design Inc
.www.holycowcom.com

Cover Design by Robin Ludwig Design
www.gobookcoverdesign.com
Cover Photos:
38123949 © Alanpoulson | Dreamstime.com
8049072 © Selenka | Dreamstime.com

Dragonfly Brooch made in Scotland by Ladycrow Silks,
www.ladycrowsilks.co.uk
Photo of Dragonfly brooch by Stuart Mccannell
Poem For You Who Cries by Ruth Cunningham,
www.selftoself.com

ISBN 978-0-9951914-5-7

For You Who Cries[1]

For you who cries into the night
a frantic heart engulfed by fright,
injustice sparks the demon's ire
into the dragon's vengeful fire

You only need recall your name
to slay that dragon-demon Blame
and douse your fiery frights and fears
with loving Self's forgiving tears

You only need unleash your mind
your open eyes are not so blind
they cannot see past heaven's edge
to self's reprieve above time's ledge

You only need reject pain's witch—
such spell can never mend and stitch
your heart's desires from twice-torn truth
such lies cannot withhold love's proof

You only need return your heart
to Self's sweet purpose, source and start
of living's lesson, life renewed—
accept your strength—self's fortitude

Supported by time's buoyant care
that shapes your days to dream—to dare
pursue your wiser vision's glance
and choose to live beyond fear's chance

---

[1] From Mystical Verses by Ruth Cunningham   www.selftoself.com

Other books written or edited by Gloria W Nye

DreamQuest Cards
DreamQuest Dictionary
DreamQuest Journal

Compiled and Edited
Stories of Prayer and Faith

Edited
A Walk in Fields of Gold: An Anthology
from Headwaters Writers' Guild

Compiled
Limericks from the Animal Kingdom
Written by Mary Hackney, Illustrations by Carly Hatton

Compiled and photographed
Realms of Metaphor
Poems by John Millard Hughes

Co-editor for
Fifty Shades of Natural Grey:
Spicy Stories for the Seasoned Woman

Dragonfly Series
The Hidden Vow: Book 1
The Broken Promise: Book 2
The Forbidden Path: Book 3

Buried Treasures:
19 Short Stories

The Forbidden Path
Dragonfly Series: Book 3

Gloria W. Nye

Spiral Press

For my Sisters with love
Alberta (aka Lady May)
Louise (Lou Lou)
Barbara (Big Bully Barbara)

Chapter 1

On that late August day in rural Germany, 1652, restless villagers grumbled and groused. Crops were poor again and food stocks low. Hungry men and women looked for something—or someone—to blame. Whispers grew louder, stronger, and angrier. "She's not one of us." Men raised their fists and women pointed fingers. "She's a foreigner." "She doesn't belong in our village." Faces turned to one person.

Anne Farber, an English woman, and her eight-year-old daughter Emma lived alone in a modest fieldstone house a mile from the village. Six years ago, her husband Helmut Farber, a blacksmith, had been killed by a spooked horse.

A fat carrot, a fist-sized turnip and an onion lay on the table ready for the evening soup. Root vegetables from their kitchen garden had been stored snugly in barrels of straw. Earthenware jars held salted cabbage while bouquets of dried parsley and rosemary hung from the rafters. They had plenty to get them through the cold winter months.

With rhythmic chops, Anne sliced the carrot into even rounds. Orange discs piled up on the wooden cutting board. Emma, perched on a high stool at the pine table, held her rag doll Molly on her lap. She straightened its calico dress, which matched her own. Scraps of material, stuffed with cotton, formed the doll's body while coloured embroidery thread made a pink mouth, blue eyes, and a brown nose. Red wool, dyed from the Madder root, fringed the forehead, and a fat plait fell from each side.

"Mama, why—."

"Shush, child." A cold wind crashed the door open, swirling in a thick dank smell. Anne's heart beat faster. She held the knife aloft. Eyes alert, she stared toward the creaking door. A tangle of cinnamon hair tumbled over her forehead. Unlike the women of the village, she wore neither bonnet nor scarf to cover her free-flowing hair. Many had frowned at such a disgrace.

Outside the small cabin, swaying branches groaned, and a hundred leaves fluttered in fear. Anne continued to hold her breath, putting every ounce of attention on listening, sensing, and feeling the touch of evil the wind had carried in. She shivered.

"What is it, Mama?" Emma's eyes darted from the doorway to her mother's tight mouth and stern gaze and back to the empty doorway.

Her mother raised her other hand." Be still." The moment stretched long and silent. The breeze settled down.

Anne let out her breath and released her shoulders.

"Mama, what's wrong? Molly is scared." The wide-eyed little girl pressed her rag doll to her chest.

"I think it's time for us to go to England." She handed her daughter a wooden bowl. "Put the carrot pieces into this."

Emma propped her doll against a fat candle holder on the table and scooped up the orange circles. She popped a piece into her mouth.

The main room served as a kitchen, eating, and living area. At one side, under three windows, stood a hand hewn pine table with two wooden stools drawn up to it. Shelves on the opposite wall held books, small boxes, and packets of dried herbs. Outerwear clothes hung on a row of pegs near the front door. Three padded birch chairs, each covered with a woven blanket, faced the hearth. Several branches of sweet honeysuckle filled a jug beside the chimney.

Emma cradled the bowl on her lap. "Mama, I want to go to school like the village boys do."

"But I have taught you your letters and numbers at home as my mother taught me. And you speak perfect English and a lot of German."

"I want to learn more."

Her mother turned to the wood stove behind her. Above it hung an iron pot, a saucepan, and a pewter ladle. She hoisted the heavy stew pot off its hook, placed it on the table, and reached for the turnip. A long white apron covered her outer skirt to the floor. She wore natural linen next to her skin rather than the coarse and scratchy wool that the pious German women favoured.

She picked up the paring knife and a long curling strip of purple peel soon dangled over the cutting board.

Emma pulled at one of her doll's braids. "Why can't I go to school and learn like the boys do?"

Her mother sighed. "Boys become men and need to know much to do the work of the village and in the towns and great cities."

"But I want to learn and do work too." She punctuated the last word with a firm nod of her head, making her walnut curls bounce.

Her mother cut the turnip into chunks. "We have many books."

"I want to learn more. I want to learn about the stars and how clouds make rain and why leaves change colour and—"

"When the time is right, I will teach you more." She lowered her voice. "Things that boys do not learn in school."

"What sort of things, mama?" Holding onto Molly, she leaned toward the table.

"You have watched me make herbal potions for the village women: mustard plaster for a chest cold, St. John's Wort for melancholy, and a tincture for the lovelorn."

"I want to learn that too." She tilted forward on her stool, nearly tipping it over.

"Careful, my dear." She put out a hand and steadied her slanted daughter. "All in good time." She moved the onion to the cutting board. "You can already distinguish many healing plants. That is more than most boys know."

"Yes, but—"

"Stop!" Anne sucked in her breath. Her heart thumped wildly, and for the second time on that early August evening she held the carving knife straight up in the air like a spear ready to strike.

She stood very still and silent.

Chapter 2

A small animal—a mouse or mole—scurried back into its hole.

Anne opened her hand, letting the knife drop. It glanced off the iron pot with a dull clank. "We must go. Now."

Her mother's scary voice leaped at Emma. She tightened her muscles and squeezed Molly.

Anne rushed into the back room. Their bedroom held two single beds, a trunk, a chair and a wall of shelves. She grabbed a leather bag and pulled clothes off a shelf and stuffed them into it.

Emma stood in the doorway, squishing her doll to her chest. "Mama, what is it?"

Her mother pulled Emma's bag off a hook and tossed it at her. "Quickly. Pack a few warm clothes. We must leave right away. Now!"

Emma grabbed the bag and ran to her shelf. She picked up a flannel nightgown and stuffed it in. Stocking and a woollen hat followed. "Mama, what's the matter?" Her voice quavered.

Her mother ran to a table in the front room and swept packets of herbs, powders, and gemstones into her bag.

A chorus of raucous voices came closer. Emma squeezed her doll.

Her mother slung her leather bag over her shoulder, grabbed Emma's hand."Quickly. We must get to the forest grove—"

Howls and shouts of screeching voices loomed closer.

Anne took a piece of black root from her pocket and put it into her mouth. She and Emma raced down the path toward a thicket of trees. More shouts and stamping feet reached the bottom of their lane.

They had gone a metre when the crazed mob bore down on them. Men and women, friends and neighbours, surrounded them. Red angry faces. Screaming mouths. With fists and arms raised, they shook farm tools and walking-sticks high in the air.

Fleischer, the butcher, his eyes flashing, rushed at them with a shout. "Get her!

Frau Bäcker, her apron white with flour, waved a stout stick over her head. "Stop her!"

And gentle Erich, face now red and mottled, cracked the air with a horsewhip. "Seize the heretic."

Twisted faces and tearing hands grabbed Anne. Emma huddled against her mother's skirt, but a calloused hand thrust her aside. She fell to the ground, losing her grip on Molly, who tumbled away and a thick boot stomped on it. Emma's chest thumped and blood oozed from her scraped elbows.

Herr Schmidt, who gave her sweets in town, and another burly man held her mother fast. Scattered clothes lay crushed in the dirt, kicked aside, or stomped on. Packets, stones, and herbs were strewn from her mother's leather bag.

Emma sprung up and leaped toward the assailants, pounding and scratching at whoever or whatever she could reach. "Let my mama go!" Iron hands grabbed her again and threw her to the hard ground. She scrambled up, bound forward and flung her arms around a brute's knee. He easily shook her off.

"Run," her mother called. "Go to your Uncle. You'll be safe—"

The yells and cries of the swarm smothered the rest of her words. Emma rolled away from the heavy boots. Rough skirts scraped her face. Her head pounded and heart raced.

"Mama!" She staggered to her feet, coughing and spluttering dirt. "Mama!" With knees bloody and hands stinging, she stumbled after the terrible people taking her mother away.

The shrieking hoard hauled her mother down the path toward town. When Emma got close, a hand or stick would knock her away. Her mother's beautiful soft leather shoes were scraped and dirty.

With trembling legs and a throat hurt from screaming, Emma scrambled to her feet to chase after their crazed neighbours.

Chapter 3

The vicious horde reached the centre of the village where more twisted faces met them. So many people, shouting and shaking sticks. Emma dodged past thrusting elbows and stamping feet but could not see her mother through the clambering crowd. She climbed on top of an overturned rain barrel leaning against a tree and peered over the throng of lurching heads and swinging hoes and rakes.

Farmer Bauer, who sold them flour, held her mother against a post in the middle of the square and yanked her hands behind it. She did not struggle. Her eyes were closed, but her lips moved. Emma clung to the tree, her face pressed against its ragged bark. Tears of fear and confusion streaked her muddy face. "Mama." But no one heard her cries.

Her body shook, and she pushed her fist into her mouth.

Franz Bäcker threw a hairy rope to the butcher. He and another man wound it around her mother's waist and ankles, fixing her to the post. Two youths, Helmut and Konrad, piled faggots and twigs at her feet. Dirt streaked her white apron, its hem torn and ragged.

Emma quivered on her perch. *I have to help Mama.* She leapt off the barrel and bolted toward her mother. "Mama, Mama!" She squished past a screeching woman and a jabbing fist. Weaving through churning arms and waving hands, she staggered from the blows. Shouts and cries swamped her as she continued to push through the writhing mob. "Mama!"

She reached the pile of sticks and scrambled up the sliding mound. Clambering to her mother's feet, she grabbed the edge of her skirt. Rough rope secured her ankles. Emma tore at the cords, pulling chunks of skin off her hands. "Mama!"

Her mother opened her eyes and stared into the child's wild face. "Emma." Her voice rang clear and commanding. "Leave this place. Now. Go to your Uncle Albert."

Emma stopped her frantic yanking for an instant, wanting to obey her mother, but a greater power welled within her. "No, no!" And she tore anew at the unyielding rope, ripping more skin off her fingers.

Her mother spoke again in a controlled and even voice. "Emma. Listen to me. I am all right. I will be with you in dream time."

Emma looked up into her mother's piercing eyes.

Her strong and fearless voice commanded. "My dear child. You must go. Now. I love you."

Tears streamed down Emma's dirt-streaked face. "Mama!" She held fast to her mother's skirt, tearing it further.

A rough hand, smelling of rotten fish, snatched Emma off her mother and threw her aside.

Gudrun, the baker's wife, yelled, "Burn the girl too."

Others joined the chorus.

"Burn Satan's child."

"She's bad blood."

"Burn them both."

Emma lay stunned on the hard ground. She lifted her head. Warm liquid dripped from her forehead and trickled down the side of her face. She wobbled to her feet and the smelly man grabbed her again. With a vice grip on her arms, he tossed her like a piece of firewood, onto the tangled pile at her mother's feet.

She landed with a thump, rolled over on her stomach and again tore at the sliding sticks. Her mother inches away. Her feet slipped and skidded on the treacherous mass which shifted beneath her. Scratching wildly with feet and fingers, dirt, tears, and blood, streaked her face. "Mama, Mama!"

Herr Kruger, the innkeeper, stepped forward. He was holding a bundle of burning rushes.

He yelled over the crowd. "The child is no matter. She has no power." With his other hand, he grabbed Emma and pulled her off the pile where she rolled to the ground. A fresh upsurge of shouts and screams from their once-friendly villagers drowned out the child's cries.

She lay in the dirt, crumpled and dazed. A whoosh of hot air swept past her face. Farmer Bauer threw the blazing torch onto the stack. It fell beside a freshly cut log, sizzled and spit itself out. Another flaming torch flew through the air and hit a pile of dried sticks. In seconds, flames shot up.

Winding streams of black smoke coiled into the air as more sticks caught and crackled. Larger pieces joined, simmering and bubbling with fire.

Choking white trails rose from a smouldering log, writhing and twisting higher, joining the black clouds of stinging smoke that shrouded her mother's face.

Chapter 4

Anne's body slumped over. The black root she had taken had deadened the pain, but she could not stop the burning smoke from searing her lungs. She had used all her will power to speak her last words to her dear daughter, commanding her to leave that ugly place. From the moment those savaged hands had grabbed her, she had called with inward voice to Albert to come for Emma. Albert, her older brother by minutes, would hear for they had shared unspoken communication since children.

For two weeks, signs of unrest had rippled through the village and when the Fleischer lad under her care had died, it triggered the people to their terrible mission.

With lips barely moving, she whispered her last prayer upon the wind. "Albert. Save my child." She released her last breath, and as it softly left her numb body, her consciousness slipped into the spirit world—a world she had visited many times in dream time and meditation.

Albert, you can hear me clearly now. Come for Emma.

Her body sagged further; the coarse ropes holding it to the post while her spirit soared, jubilant in that new space and way of being.

All is well. Albert will save my daughter, and I will never leave her.

* * *

Emma crawled along the hard ground, making her way back to the monstrous pile of terror. The fire licked at her mother's skirts, and the crowd roared as flames danced from stick to stick. Blankets of swirling smoke wrapped her mother in a thick white shawl.

"Mama!" Crying and coughing, Emma reached the bottom of the pile when strong arms picked her up and swept her away from the frenzied mob.

"No!" she screamed. "Let me go." She scratched and bit at the arms and hands that carried her off.

"Mama needs me."

The man held firmly and strode through the throng to his waiting horse he had hastily tied to a tree. Emma screeched and twisted, stretching her arms in the direction of her bound mother.

The man kept walking, holding the squirming child tightly. "Emma. Stop. I'm your Uncle Albert. You're safe."

She stopped struggling and with a frown, stared at the face of the man holding her. "Uncle Albert?"

His dark hair, conspicuous in a country of fair heads, hung long to his shoulders. His deep-set eyes blazed with barely controlled rage and with shaking arms, he gathered his niece close. "You're all right, my sweet. You're safe."

"They're hurting Mama."

"We must leave this evil place at once."

"But Mama. We can't leave Mama."

"Your Mama is in safe hands now. I promise you."

They reached his horse, and he lifted the child up and pulled himself up behind her. "Hold tight." He deftly coaxed the skittish animal to turn away from the fire—away from the ruthless shouts and hideous laughter.

Behind them, amidst the bedlam, a cold and mighty wind swirled in, lifting capes and tearing hats from heads. People cowered and shrunk back from the icy blast, grasping flapping jackets and waistcoats to themselves.

As suddenly as the fierce wind blew in, it howled to a stop over the flames and out of that unearthly silence, a torrent of rain fell. A gush of water pounded over the burning mass, making hot sticks hiss, splutter and steam.

Following the cascade, came a gentle summer shower, washing the woman's face clean. Her eyes were closed, and on her lips, a peaceful smile. At the bottom of the wretched pile of death, rivulets of black water bubbled toward the startled mob, standing frozen at nature's fury.

Frau Bäcker crossed herself as snakes of slithering water reached her boots. "We are damned."

Farmer Bauer threw his hoe to the ground. "The witch will haunt us from the grave." With face stricken, he backed away. Thrashing his arms and falling against his neighbours, he turned and ran.

Two others stumbled after him, and soon all the terrified villagers slipped and slid in the mud as they scuttled away from the obscene wooden pillar erected in the centre of their town.

Chapter 5

Emma's elbows, knees, and hands stung; her arms ached, and her throat burned. Her chest thumped fast and loud. She twisted around on the galloping horse and begged her uncle. "Uncle Albert, we must go back and get Mama."

He held one arm tightly around the wriggling child. "Your mama is with God."

"No." Emma wailed—her eyes dark circles. "Bad people took her. They're burning her." She flattened her hands on his chest and pushed.

Albert pulled the horse up. "Emma. Listen to me." His eyes glistened, and his jaw tightened. "Your Mama did not suffer. She is at peace."

The child's eyes grew large. "No, No. We have to go back." She pushed again, her arms straight as she leaned back.

"We have to leave now. Your Mama wants you to be safe."

She held his gaze and collapsed against his chest, sobbing.

He urged the horse on again, and galloped past the last hut in the village. The exhausted child continue to whimper and when they came to the crossroads to her house, she lifted her head. "Where are we going?"

"First to my cabin for a few things and then far from this ghastly place."

Her voice quavered. "Can I get Molly and mama's precious things."

"We should not tarry."

Tears filled her eyes, and dried mud streaked her face. "Please, Uncle Albert. We're so close."

"All right, but we must be quick." He turned the horse and in a few minutes reached his sister's cottage. He pulled up, slid off and lifted the child down.

Anne's leather bag and Emma's small canvas one lay strewn at the end of the path. They hurried to them and gathered clothes, herbs and packets, shoving them into the large bag. Emma picked up her small one. Her rag doll lay in the dirt where it had fallen. She grabbed it, brushed it off and ran back to her uncle. He took her hand, and they started to walk back to the horse when she stopped.

"Wait!" She dropped his hand and ran back. "It must be here." She looked to where her mother's belongings had fallen.

Albert strode to the horse. "We must hurry."

"There it is." She dove to the ground. Beside a clump of wild forget-me-nots, lay her mother's pewter dragonfly brooch. She stretched her hand toward it, and a dark figure stepped out from behind a tree. A manure-covered work boot stomped on the dragonfly.

Emma screamed. Albert turned and dropped the bags. He raced toward his niece and the man looming over her.

The ruffian snatched up the dragonfly. "I'll take this. And the brat too." His muscular arm encircled her waist and yanked her up.

"Put me down!" She flailed at him, punching, scratching and kicking his shins.

Albert, his face a mask of fury, took two swift paces toward him. "Let her go."

The brute slapped his other hand over Emma's mouth and nose. "Another step and I'll break her neck."

Albert stopped. The child's eyes grew frantic as she fought for breath. In the next moment, her eyes rolled up, and she went limp. Albert's dark eyes narrowed, and he stared at the man, compelling him to release the child.

The man's mouth twisted. "Those demon eyes don't scare me."

Albert pointed three fingers, like a fork, toward the brute. "Let the child go, or I will curse you with Leviticus." He took one step forward. "Hideous terrors will come upon you. A wasting disease will destroy your sight and drain your blood from every limb."

The man's eyes widened and his brow furrowed, but his hold tightened.

Albert's voice rose on the wind. "Boils will cover your entire body. Putrid pus will blister from them and eat into your flesh. Blood will drip from your ears." He bent his elbow and drew his hand back, like a viper ready to strike.

The man stumbled back, dropping Emma onto the hard ground. He flung the dragonfly after her and fled into the trees and the field beyond.

Albert rushed to her. She lay in a heap beside a sharp rock. An ugly gash streaked her forehead. He picked her and the dragonfly up, collected the bags and slung them over his shoulder. Holding his precious cargo, he marched back to his horse.

The full moon gave plenty of light as they rode steadily on toward his own nearby cottage. He held the limp child in front of him with a firm hand. The scratches on her hands and knees had stopped bleeding, but her forehead needed attention. He'd have to wrap that wound.

A wave of grief over his dear sister's death flooded over him. Anne, the sister he'd shared a womb with. Closer to him than lover, parent, or comrade. He stifled a sob and pulled Emma to him. "Help me now, Anne. Help me live without you and to care for Emma."

He shook his head to clear it. Grief would have to wait. Right now, they had to get away. Burning one person may not have been enough for the unruly pack. They would be after the brother who read the devil's books. He urged the horse to move faster.

With bad crops again that year, his sister had been an easy target for superstitious and ignorant villagers. Neither a heretic nor a devil worshipping witch, she believed in the ancient wisdoms, as did he.

He raised a fist and made a vow to himself and his sister. "They will not take Emma. We will flee this wretched country."

His friend Otto would hide them for a night, and on the morrow, they would start on the long journey back to England, back to his native land.

The last six years had sped past. He did not regret leaving his homeland to help his sister and her young child. After her husband died, they would have returned to England but civil wars still raged. No country was safe for anyone with a questing mind but at least in England, one could have a trial and if found guilty, would be hanged and then burnt.

In the distance, the roof of his thatched cottage poked high above the bushes. He turned his horse and followed the path. His niece had not wakened since the brute had thrown her down. He would have to bandage her head and put ointment on the many scrapes and cuts on her arms and legs. In another two miles they would reach his friend's house. Would the mob come to find the witch's brother that night to burn him or his cottage? He stopped the horse at the front and slid off, holding Emma tightly. Perhaps one burning had appeased them and the downpour, smothering their monstrous inferno, had frightened them off.

He reached his door, and another wave of grief hit him full force. His body shook and his legs buckled. "My dear, Anne" He kicked the door open, staggered in and fell to his knees. He gently laid Emma on the thick rug, and as his bags slid off his shoulder, he wrapped his arms around his trembling body to keep it from flying apart. His insides screamed as he gasped aloud. "My darling, Anne. The other half of me. How could those monsters—." He crouched like a dying animal, grasping his chest as deep sobs engulfed him. "Why didn't I get to you in time? "

At fourteen, he had taken a self-proclaimed oath to protect her always, and now sorrow and guilt flooded him. He pounded the floor. "I failed you. I will never forgive myself." He squeezed his head in a vice hold and rocked back and forth, but the terrifying scene continued to burn through his tortured mind. A long agonizing howl tore from his throat. He yanked at his hair, crying, weeping, raging, and sobbing in a nowness that never ended.

After a long time, he lay curled and still in an empty ball of silence. A soft voice drifted around him. *There is Emma to care for. Look after my child.*

He opened his eyes. W*as that my voice or Anne's?* He looked around, dazed. "Where am I?"

Emma lay where he had placed her. "She's safe, Anne." He pulled himself up and put her in his large armchair. "I will take good care of her."

The instant he'd heard his sister's cry of alarm inside his head, he'd raced to the village centre and when he'd burst upon that horrific scene, his body had taken over. All his instincts had screamed to save his sister, but at the same time he knew he was too late.

He covered his niece with a blanket. "But I did save Emma."

He washed his face at the water basin and took a cloth and gently dabbed the angry slash on Emma's forehead. Slowly, he cleaned blood and dirt off the wound. She would have a scar. He went to his sideboard and scooped out a spoonful of raw honey from an earthenware jar. Holding the edges of the cut together, he patted the sticky substance over it and tied a clean bandage around her head. Frau Weber would have some yarrow salve for the smaller cuts and scrapes. She lay so still.

He could come back in the morning to pack up his books and papers and other choice possessions, but he needed one thing now. On a shelf by a window, the moonlight shone over a row of crystals. *Which one?* He passed his hand over them and stopped at a double-terminated clear quartz which he put into his pocket.

He gathered the child in his arms and took a quick glance around. "Tomorrow, we shall leave this vile country. Forever." He stepped out the door and closed it firmly behind him.

Chapter 6

A solitary owl hooted his presence and a scurrying night animal scuttled under a bush. In the quiet night, the horse plodded along the little-used road toward Otto's house.

Albert's mind flooded with sights of twisted faces and wild cries. He shook his head to force the ghastly images away. He had to protect Emma. He had no fear of dying himself; he had done it many times and would many more. In reverie, he had retrieved memory of three of his past lives and deaths. But the child had hardly begun this one. She must live to fulfill her destiny—whatever that was, for we each have a purpose in life. The distant light from the weaver's cottage flickered through the thick foliage.

He rode on, with Emma tightly held in front of him. She was still senseless from the blow on her head when the brute had dropped her, but her strong little heart beat against him.

They arrived at the clearing, and with one hand on the reins, he pulled the horse up. He dismounted and with Emma cradled in his arm, he walked up the curved stone path. He knocked on the door.

A moment later, a stout man with a wild bush of white hair opened it. "Ach du meine Güte! What have we here?"

"We need refuge, my friend."

"Ja. Of course." He stepped back.

Hilda, his wife, a short, wide woman, came up behind him, drying her hands on a kitchen towel. She flipped the cloth over her shoulder and stretched out her arms to take the child. The woman's head barely came to Albert's elbow. "Otto, give him some dumplings and hot stew while I look after the little one." With chubby arms, she gathered the sleeping child to her cushiony bosom. Dried blood and dirt still streaked one side of her face and her hands and knees. Frau Weber drew in a quick breath. "I'll have you cleaned up in no time. Why the angels would not know you with that dirty face." She disappeared into a back room.

Otto lifted a jug from the sideboard and poured beer into two wooden mugs. He handed Albert one and gestured toward the kitchen table. "Sit, my friend. You look as if you need some sustenance."

Albert dropped the bags and scraped a chair out from under from the table. A pot of butter, a salt cylinder and a tub of freshly chopped garlic sat on a woven mat. From a high shelf, the soft rays of an oil lamp lit the small cottage. He sat down and swallowed a mouthful of warm beer.

Otto placed a soup spoon and a bowl, filled with steaming cabbage stew and dumplings, in front of Albert. He sat opposite. "What has happened, mein Freund?'

Albert leaned over the bowl, breathed in the life-giving smells, and picked up the spoon. In a low and faltering voice, he spoke the wretched words, telling what had happened.

Otto thumped the table, making the salt jump. "Verdammt! Superstitious idiots. Can they not think for themselves?" He clenched his fist. 'They are like blind sheep without a wit of sense."

"It is the worst it can be, but I cannot dwell on it. I must take Emma to safety—to London. I need to do that for Anne." Albert's eyes glistened in the lamplight. "Will you help me?"

"Ja, of course. What do you need?"

"A little food. I have money and can pay for lodgings on our way. We will stay at monasteries and respectable inns." He put his hands to his head. "But first, I must bury my dear sister. I cannot leave her with those monsters."

"Is that safe?"

"I think they've had their fill. I threatened one with a curse, and the rain put the devil's fear into the others." He looked at his friend. "I have to do this. Tonight."

Hilda Weber came into the kitchen, a fresh towel over her arm.

The men looked up.

"Emma is still sleeping. I washed and rewrapped that nasty head wound. The yarrow salve will help with the scrapes and scratches."

Otto nodded. "It is best she sleeps. She can eat when she awakens."

The woman brought several thick slices of bread to the table and sat down. "Eat up, Albert. You must stay strong for the child and yourself. And for Anne." She gulped back a sob. "I could not help but hear your horrendous words as I tended to Emma."

Albert looked up. "Thank you, my friends."

They finished eating, and Hilda insisted he lie down. "Just for a little while." She steered him to a cot and covered him with a quilt. "I will see to Emma when she wakes up. Do not worry."

Chapter 7

Albert slept fitfully, and nearing midnight, he awakened. Otto had the horse and wagon ready. He splashed water on his face and joined his friend. The full moon hid behind a cluster of clouds.

Otto shook his head. "Let us hope the clouds linger. Men may be watching for you to claim her body."

"I fear not. Any not scared off by the rain would be drunk from mob madness. After killing Anne, they would have filled their addled brains with beer until they couldn't stand."

"A stupid bunch. What would set them off to carry out such an unspeakable atrocity?" Otto tightened a strap on the horse.

Albert shook his head. "Crops have been bad, and last week the Fleischer boy died of fever. Anne did what she could, but angry words flew about blaming her." He placed a thick blanket in the back of the wagon. "I told her not to tend to the boy, but she insisted."

"Women are fine care keepers." He put a hand on Albert's shoulder. "I can do this alone. Why don't you stay here and prepare a place for her? She loved the back meadow by the edge of the forest where the wildflowers grow."

"Thank you, my friend, but I must do this. I should have gotten there sooner to prevent that horror." He pounded his fist on the wagon. "The least I can do is be sure her body is properly laid to rest."

Otto climbed up and grabbed the reins. "Then we go."

The horse moved steadily through the night, past fields and darkened houses into the centre of a now quiet town. Long fingers of scuttling clouds separated, and the full moon peeked through, exposing an ugly silhouette. A lone figure slumped on a post on an unruly pile of sticks.

Albert gagged. "Dear God."

Otto pulled the horse up, and they got down. With shaking hands, Albert took the blanket from the back and strode to the abomination. *It is only her body. She is not here. Give me strength.*

Silently, they untied the crude knots, and Albert lifted her away and wrapped her in the blanket. He placed her in the back of the wagon on a bed of fresh straw.

A shout rose from a nearby building. "Who goes there?"

Otto climbed onto the wooden seat. "Let us be gone."

"No." Albert stepped toward the voice. "I am Albert Lewis."

A fat man stumbled out, holding his protruding belly. "Who?"

Albert strode to the man. Ernst Brewer had obviously been drinking an excess of his wares. Albert glared at him. "I am Albert Lewis. Anne Farber's brother."

The brewer stepped back, almost losing his footing and slurred, "I don't know you, and I don't know any Anne Farber." A loud belch and a bubble of foul breath burst from him. "What are you doing here? Are you robbing someone?"

"I am robbing no one. Only taking what is mine." He grabbed a handful of the man's shirt and yanked him up. "You miserable cur. You killed my sister." He drew his other fist back.

Otto shouted from the wagon. "No, my friend. Do not lower yourself. He is drunk. You could kill him."

Albert's fist quivered. "I would happily kill him."

The man's eyes widened while he blubbered words of innocence and mercy.

"Speak not." His voice shook. "You are a worm. A slithering excuse for humanity. May your blood boil and urine burn. May insects crawl in your nose, and bugs hatch in your ears." With a final yell of damnation, he threw the man to the ground who lay whimpering on the cobblestones.

Albert stormed to the wagon. "Let us leave this vile place."

They were silent during the trip back to Otto's cottage. Clouds had covered the moon again, but Otto well knew the way.

They reached the cottage, passed it, and Otto turned the wagon toward the meadow, Albert shifted in his seat. "She would have taken Rosemary leaves or Valerian root to aid her in separating her mind from her body. With her senses deadened, she could concentrate on calling me to save Emma and focus on departing to the next world."

Otto did not answer. He guided the horse toward the edge of the forest.

Albert continued. "I'm sure she called the rain to her as well."

"Your sister was a wise woman."

"She is indeed a wise woman."

Otto stopped the wagon several yards from the trees and got down. He lifted two shovels from the back and handed Albert one. A small stream gurgled nearby as it wound its way across the meadow and down the hill.

Albert looked around. "This is the perfect place for Anne. Near trees and water and flowers."

He struck the shovel into the hard ground. With each thump, the soil loosened more and the pile of earth grew higher beside the deepening hole. They slid into it to dig. Each thud and toss of dirt resonated with the beat of Albert's heart. When the depth reached the height of his head, they climbed out.

Albert lifted the precious bundle out of the wagon and laid it on the ground beside the newly formed hill of earth. He knelt on both knees and tenderly opened the blanket. Her torn and burnt skirt exposed patches of blackened legs. The killing smoke had streaked her blouse and stopped her breath but the downpour had smothered the blaze before it had gotten any further. A halo of cinnamon hair encircled her rain-washed face and her lips graced a hint of a smile.

Otto gasped. "She looks like an angel. How can that be?"

Albert stroked her cheek. "Because she was—and is—an angel." He curved the soft blanket around her face. "Her serenity must have confused the brutes, and when the rain interrupted their madness they ran—afraid of her power even after death."

Otto stuck his shovel into the pile of earth. "One day, they will know the truth. I have learned much from you and dear Anne. About life and death and how we live many lives. Of course, I speak to no one about such things."

Albert folded his sister's hands on her chest, and placed the small crystal from his pocket into them. "This is only your body—your beautiful empty body. Your essence has flown elsewhere, and you are free." He kissed her cheek for the last time and covered the blanket over her. "Goodbye, my love. My other self." He lowered himself into the freshly dug hole and lifted her in. "May mother earth hold you in her arms and father sky shine upon you." He laid her down and stood for a long moment. He climbed out and picked up a shovel. Otto crossed himself and picked up the second one.

The clouds slid away from the moon, giving them full light. They filled the hole, patted the earth flat and dragged fallen brush across it. Otto placed a large rock at one end and Albert laid branches crisscrossed as if they had blown there.

Otto stood back. "The wildflowers will spread and cover this sacred place." He cleared his throat. "And I will check it often to see that it is undisturbed."

Albert pointed to a small oak a few feet away from its fully grown parent. "Its roots will surround her and hold her close." He gestured to the nearby stream. "And the running water will refresh her."

They threw the shovels in the back of the wagon, climbed on and Otto headed the horse home.

Clouds played hide-and-seek with the moon, giving glimpses of light while a far-away owl hooted in the silent night.

Every step tore at Albert's heart. *I know it's only your body laying back there.* But the pain in his chest eclipsed that truth. Unbearable sorrow swamped him, and he gulped for air in a world where every breath he took without her seared his throat. *You live on. I know you do.* But the hollow space of her absence filled him. *My dear one. Where are you?*

And as they moved along on that dark night, the clear notes of a nightingale broke the silence with its bid of Auf wiedersehen.

Chapter 8

Albert awoke with a start. He swung his legs over the bed and stood up, only to stagger and fall back onto the cover. He lay there a moment. His head pounded, his chest and stomach hurt as if he had been kicked by a wild horse. He closed his eyes to the unspeakable memories of the last night but the horrific scene remained etched in his thoughts. He held his stomach and took in a long breath. But as many as he took, it did not wipe away the hideous pictures or fill the empty space inside him.

He rose again, washed his face at the basin of water left on the side table and joined Otto and Frau Weber in the kitchen.

She looked up. "Sit my boy and eat. Emma is sleeping."

Albert frowned. "I will wake her. We must be away as soon as possible." He took a step toward the back room.

She touched his arm. "Let her sleep. She awoke in the night and I took her to the privy. She fell asleep right away. Do not worry." She motioned to the table where she had placed plates of sausage, eggs and fat slices of oat bread. "Sit and eat. You need your strength."

Albert sat beside Otto and picked up a fork. "You're right. I must be strong for Emma." He speared a piece of sausage. "I will not let Anne down again."

They ate in silence. He pushed his empty plate away." Thank you, Frau Weber. I needed that." He scraped his chair back. "I need to fetch my books and papers."

Otto wiped his mouth and slid his plate away. "How are you planning to take boxes and the child all the way to London? It took me twenty-one days to reach Calais on my last spring trip. And a good part of a day for the channel crossing plus another two days ride to the city."

"I have my horse. We will be fine."

"You cannot travel all that way, holding the child in front of you and carrying supplies. Nein, that is impossible." He shook his head. "You must have a wagon."

Albert stared at his friend for a long moment. "You're right. I will go to town and buy one."

"It is not safe for you to go anywhere near the town. I have a small wagon I do not use anymore. It is yours."

Albert clasped his arm. "Thank you, my friend."

"It will hold food supplies and your boxes of books. And Emma can sleep on the way." He headed for the door. "I will bring the wagon to the front."

Emma walked into the room, rubbing her eyes with one hand and clasping her doll to her chest with the other. "Uncle Albert?" Her borrowed nightgown touched the ground. "Where am I?"

Albert rushed to her, picked her up and took her back to the table where he sat her on a chair. We are at our friend Otto's and Frau Weber's house." He sat beside her. "And you're a whisker's breath in time for breakfast."

Frau Weber busied herself making up a plate.

Emma settled her doll, now washed and with mended braid, on her lap. "I don't remember coming here." She touched the bandage on her head. "My head hurts—outside and in. What happened?"

Albert patted her arm. "We came late last night. It was dark."

She looked around. "Where's mama?"

Frau Weber plunked a plate in front of her. "Eat up now, my dear."

She picked up a fork and dropped it. "Ow. That hurts." She turned her palms up. "I've scraped my hands. How did that happen?"

Albert took her hands in his. "Yesterday, you fell several times."

She sighed. "I do that. I fell out of the apple tree once and bumped my head bad. Mama wrapped a cloth around it then too."

Frau Weber sat down beside the child. "Do you want me to feed you?"

Emma laughed. "No. I'm not a baby." She curled her hand around the fork." It only hurts a little. I can do it."

She took a mouthful of scrambled egg and a long drink of milk. "Is Mama still sleeping?"

Albert cleared his throat. "Your mama is resting in another place."

"What do you mean? Why isn't she here? Mama would never leave me."

He took a sharp breath in. "Emma. My dear." He gulped and took her hand. "Your mama is with God."

Emma tilted her head. "Mama says we're always with God."

"Her way of being with God is different now."

She frowned and held her head. "My head is thumping inside. I don't understand." She looked up with large, questioning eyes. "Is Mama hurt? Did she bump her head too?"

He swallowed hard. *How can I tell her she lives on in another realm.* "Your mama will visit you in dream time."

"But I want her now, not only when I dream."

"I know, my dear. So do I." Hot tears filled his eyes. His body ached for her physical presence.

Otto opened the door with a bang and stepped into the kitchen. "I brought the wagon around. We only have to hitch it to your horse for your trip."

Emma looked up. "Are we going on a trip?"

Otto glanced at Albert and back at Emma. "Yes, you are. You and your uncle."

"Where are we going?" She took a bite of egg.

"To a big city called London. It's far away from here. Many days ride."

"Will we leave Germany?"

Albert slapped the table. "Absolutely. We're going to England. Back to your Mama's home."

Emma took another bite. "Mama will like that. Where is England?"

"It's a beautiful country across the sea. You'll like it."

"Will we take a ship?"

"Yes, a ship from France to Dover and by wagon on to London. The largest city in England."

"That will be fun. Mama has told me stories about England." She finished her milk.

Frau Weber, only a few inches taller than the child, picked her up. "Come, we'll get you dressed and ready for your journey."

Emma held Molly to her chest and leaned her head against the soft bosom. "We have to get mama first."

Albert watched them go, his mouth a tight line. His chest burned and daggers pierced his heart. "May she never remember that hideous night."

Otto grimaced.

Albert lowered his head into his hands. *Will I ever hear Anne's voice again?* Grief and pain had closed his connection to where he could sense her being.

Otto touched his shoulder. "Come, my friend. We will ready the wagon."

Albert rose and on wooden legs, followed Otto out. He had to get the child safely out of that abominable country, where he would have time to settle his mind and let Anne in. He prayed he could.

Chapter 9

Otto hitched the horse to the wagon. He had already placed two empty wooden boxes in the back for Albert's books.

Albert climbed up on the seat. "What's that folded on top?

Otto patted the cloth on top of the box. "That my friend is going to save your books from seawater and England's persistent rains."

Albert lifted an eyebrow.

"A few years ago, on a trip to England, I discovered a way to protect my fabrics from the rains."

"How is that?"

"From working with wool, I remembered how the water ran off my hands from the natural oil, so I tried rubbing the wool onto a piece of canvas. I let it dry and rubbed a second coat, and I ended up with a length of oiled cloth that resisted moisture. It was simple enough to poke holes along the edges so I could string twine through and tie it."

"Well thought, my friend."

Otto patted the cloth again. "I gave you some extra pieces to cover the top of the ties."

"My books and I thank you."

The front door opened. Emma ran down the steps. "Wait for me."

Albert picked up the reins. "I'm only going to my place to pack a few things. I won't be long."

"I'm a good packer. I can help." She lifted her arms up.

"All right. Come aboard."

Otto hoisted her up. Albert settled her in the seat and the horse moved down the lane. Mourning doves cooed their greetings, and a red squirrel darted under a bush.

"Is Mama waiting for us at your cottage?"

Albert turned the wagon onto the road. "Do you remember what we talked about at breakfast?"

"No."

"Your Mama is far away now. She can't come with us."

Emma frowned. The light bandage on her forehead slip a little. She pushed it back. "I don't understand. Where is Mama? Why can't she come with us?" She stuck the end of a doll's braid into her mouth.

The horse moved steadily on.

"Uncle Albert. Where's my Mama?" With her mouth full of woollen braid, her voice came out garbled and strained.

Albert stopped the horse at the side of the road and turned to his niece. "Your mama is with God."

Emma's chin wobbled. She pulled the soggy braid out of her mouth. "That's what Mama said when my cat died." Tears welled in her eyes and her voice shook. "Is my Mama dead?"

He reached for her, but she pushed his hand away as tears spilled down her cheeks. "I know what dead means. It means you bury their body, say a prayer and never see them again."

She crumpled against him, sobbing. He held her, smoothing her hair while his own tears fell. Small animals darted across the path and birds twittered morning calls. However, the man and child heard nothing over the sounds of their own crying.

After a while, Emma, still leaning on her uncle, hugged her doll to her chest. "Why did Mama die and leave us?"

His arm tightened around her. "Your Mama loves you and always will. She did not want to leave you." He looked into her eyes. "She is in the spirit world now but can still hear you."

"But I want her here. I can't see her in the spirit world." A fresh bout of tears sprung forth while nature boisterously lived on oblivious to the shattered world of an eight-year-old girl and her uncle.

Squirrels leapt from swaying branches, birds trilled their morning songs, and the wind shook dried leaves loose, spinning them merrily to the ground.

Chapter 10

They wept in a time not measured by a sundial and sat in an expanded space of quiet for a long while.

Albert picked up the reins in one hand, and with his other arm around the bereft child, he started the horse forward on their new journey together.

At his cottage, he pulled the horse up. No one lurked about, and the front door was still closed the way he'd left it. The brute who had grabbed Emma and the drunk in the village would have spread their frightful stories, putting the devil's fear into the townspeople. He and Emma would be far away before anyone dared venture after them.

He lifted her down and took the first box with its special cloth out of the wagon. Hoisting the box under his arm, he took Emma's hand, and they walked up the path. He pushed the door open. "We must be quick."

He set the box down, knelt and faced her. "I have to pack my books and a few things. Would you like to help?"

Emma clutched her doll in one hand and held his hand with her other. "Yes." She sat Molly in Albert's reading chair. "You have a lot of books."

"I do, but we can't take them all. Otto will fetch what's left." He opened the cloth and lined the box with it, folding it along the bottom.

"What are you doing?"

As he pushed the material into place, he explained Otto's ingenious method of making the cloth oily to protect his books from getting wet.

"What protects the books from the oil?"

"That's a good question, but the oil has dried and will not hurt the books." He went to one of the shelves, took a stack of papers from it and placed them in the bottom of the box. His eyes flitted across a row of books, and his hand stopped at *The Emerald Tablet*. He put it into the box. Two more followed. *The Composition of Alchemy* and *The Hermetica*. If any of those were found, they would be immediately burned and probably he as well.

Emma, close by his side, pointed to the next book he had in his hand. "What does—" she sounded out the letters, *Opus Majus* mean?"

"That's Latin for Great Work.

"Mama taught me some Latin words. Will you teach me more?"

"Of course, as soon as we reach England. But now, we must cover these books." He fetched a shirt, breeches, and hose from the back room, and Emma folded them and placed them on top of the forbidden books.

Albert stepped toward the door. "I'll get the next box."

"Wait for me." Emma fell over her feet trying to reach him.

"Be careful. You don't need any more bumps. I'll be right back."

She rubbed her knee. "I can help." She took his hand.

"Of course you can." And they walked out together.

She helped him line that box with the special cloth, and put papers on the bottom, and books and clothes on top. They covered it with a nightshirt and a jerkin, tucked the oiled cloth over everything and nailed on the wooden lid. He opened the hinged lid of the box he used for a footstool, and they fitted it out with the treated cloth as well. He added papers and more books, the last one being the Holy Bible. However, he'd hidden the book that questioned if the Bible was history or not. Even Protestants might have trouble with that.

Emma never moved more than a foot away from him. She climbed onto a nearby stool and gazed at a row of crystals and semi-precious stones lined along a window sill.

Albert handed her a shirt. "Why don't you pick out some of those and wrap them in this."

"They're so pretty. Can we take them all?"

"I think we'll have room for all of them."

She placed a pink crystal on the corner of the shirt and folded the cloth over it. She continued with each piece and brought the lumpy bundle to her uncle. "I made sure they wouldn't bump into each other."

"Thank you. They wouldn't like that." He tucked it beside the Bible, stuffed a thick winter scarf on top and tied the special oiled cloth over everything. Emma stayed close beside him as he stowed each box in the wagon, and held his hand as they walked back and forth. Words were not enough to reassure her that he wasn't leaving her too.

He handed her a leather bag. "We may as well take what food I have."

While she packed biscuits, bread and apples, he took a long look around his home of the past seven years. Eager to leave, he had to admit he would miss some of what Germany offered. There were his friends, Otto and Hilda Weber, and he would not forget rambunctious Greta who visited him when her husband was in München. Her carnal thoughts, flying ahead of her galloping horse, would alert him to her swift approach, and he would have enough time to close his book and pour a mug of beer. When she arrived, she would find a lonely bachelor staring out the window, most grateful for her attention.

"All finished." Emma cried.

Albert took his woollen cape off its hook and flung the leather bag of food over his shoulder. "Let's go."

Emma put her hand in his and held Molly in the other one. "I'm ready."

He closed the door behind him and didn't look back. He lifted Emma onto the wagon, climbed up beside her, turned the horse around and set off down the road.

They would travel as father and daughter to avoid suspicion of anyone looking for a young girl and her uncle. However, he didn't expect the villagers would follow them. They already had their scapegoat. He looked at his niece. *Dear God. Make me a good father. Help me to help her get through this.*

The horse plodded on through the familiar German countryside. Albert missed England, and looked forward to being home. At least the civil war was over but with Charles I executed, and his son Charles II exiled, England was now a commonwealth. *How will the country fare without a monarch?*

Somehow, he had to build a new life for him and Emma. Danger loomed for anyone who questioned the church or studied the 'black arts.' People were afraid of things they didn't understand and called it magic or witchcraft. When he continued with his studies in England, he would have to tread carefully to keep him and Anne's daughter safe.

Chapter 11

When they arrived at the Weber's house, Albert lifted Emma down. He rushed to Otto. "Thank you, my friend. We must pack and be on our way."

"No, you're not." Hilda Weber, almost as wide as she was long, appeared in the doorway. "It is well past midday and you need something in your stomachs and a good night's rest. You can get an early start in the morning." She took Emma's hand. "Come, child. You can help me wash the potatoes."

Albert and Otto shrugged and went outside to attend to the horse.

Emma finished her chore in the kitchen and sat cross-legged on the rug. She shook out her mother's bag and her own small one. Clothes and packets of herbs fell out. She reached for her mother's woven shawl and brought it to her face.

Frau Weber came over and started picking up the mud-stained clothes. "Let's wash these."

"Not this one." Emma held the shawl to her chest. "It smells like mama." Tears slid down her cheeks.

"Of course, my dear." She put the rest of the clothes in a wicker basket. Several small canvas packets lay scattered on the rug. "Why don't we take these herbs to the kitchen?"

"This one's not for cooking." She put it to her nose. "It's a healing herb." She picked up another one. "My Mama's healing herbs." More tears fell as she piled them on the shawl on her lap. She gathered the whole parcel up and hugged it to her chest, sobbing.

Frau Weber took the basket of clothes to the wash pump at the front of the house and called for Albert to come.

He rushed over. "What is it?"

"Emma needs you."

He ran into the house and swept his niece and the bundle she held into his arms. He carried her out of the house and over to a wooden seat under a large oak tree where he sat and rocked her until her tears —and his own—stopped.

Frau Weber came over, holding something in her hand. "I think this might be important." She handed him Anne's dragonfly brooch.

"Yes, indeed. Thank you."

Emma lifted her head as Frau Weber walked away. "That's Mama's dragonfly." She stroked a wing with one finger.

"Yes, it is."

Emma wiped the back of her hand across a wet nose and sniffed. "Where is my Mama buried? Behind the town church?"

He tightened his hold on the dragonfly. "No. She is buried in a special place."

Emma looked up at him. "Can I see it?" Her chin wobbled. "I never got to say goodbye."

Albert patted her hand. "Of course you can. Let's put your Mama's herbs in a safe place and wash our faces, and I will take you there." He lifted her down, and they walked back to the house. She held his hand and cradled the bundled shawl in her other arm.

They put the herb packets and coloured stones back into the large leather bag. Albert put the dragonfly on the wooden counter by the kitchen pump. "Let's wash this off, shall we?" He tapped her nose. "Along with our mucky faces."

Emma climbed onto a stool beside him, and they each took a cloth and washed their faces and wiped the encrusted dirt from the dragonfly's wings and back.

"Can we take the dragonfly with us to say goodbye to Mama?"

"Of course, my dear. That's a splendid idea."

Emma wrapped the shawl around her shoulders. It dragged on the ground, so Albert folded it in half, and it fit perfectly. Holding the dragonfly in one hand, she took her uncle's in the other, and they set off to walk to where her mother was buried.

A cool autumn air rustled the trees and orange, brown, and red leaves crunched under their feet. In fifteen minutes, they had crossed the meadow and started up a small hill. At the top, a burbling stream splashed nearby, and a large field maple tree grew a foot from a mound of freshly dug earth. A few resistant leaves still clung to upper branches, but the rest had made a thick mat around its base covering the fresh mound in red and burnt orange. Several yards away, a stand of spruce and pine trees formed a protective green border.

Emma walked over to the curved pile of earth and knelt on both knees. She brushed the leaves away from the large stone standing at one end.

Albert knelt beside her and put his arm around her. They stayed that way for a long, quiet time until an insistent wind urged them on. Emma pulled the shawl around her shoulders and stood up. "I'll see you in dream time, Mama. I love you." She took a step away and stopped. "We'll look after your dragonfly." She took her uncle's hand, and with silent tears and slow steps, they walked down the hill and through the meadow.

Chapter 12

As they neared the Weber house, Albert stopped. "Let's sit here." He indicated the seat under the oak tree in the glow of the late afternoon sun which washed over the trees and distant hills.

Emma held the dragonfly in her lap. "When did Mama get the dragonfly?"

"What did your mama tell you?"

"She said it was a birthday present."

"It was. Would you like to hear the whole story?"

"Yes, please."

"It was the day of our fourteenth birthday." He gazed into the distance. "It was springtime, and the daffodils were out. We were rolling hoops in the back garden when our Mama and Papa called us in."

"They gave you the dragonfly?"

"No. They gave us each a card with the drawing of a horse."

"Were the horses a birthday gift?"

"Yes, and we were very excited. Your Mama and I ran to the livery stables but just the regular horses were there. The stableman said our horses were in the east meadow, so off we went to find them."

"Was it a long way?"

"Yes, but we didn't care, and we raced off. However, about halfway along, in a shaded glen, we received the best gift of all."

"The dragonfly!"

"Yes."

"How? What happened?"

"The narrow valley was dark and we slowed down. When we were almost through, a voice said our names. We turned around, and a man in a flowing white cape stood before us. He had long white hair and a long white beard and wore a white pointed hat. It was the wise man who people called the Wizard of Wiltshire. We'd heard of him but had never seen him."

Emma's eyes grew big. "Was he scary?"

"On the contrary. His eyes were bright blue and sparkled like a sunlit lake, and the corners of his mouth curved up. He held a package out, and said in a strong wizardly voice, 'This is for you.'"

Emma drew in a quick breath. "The dragonfly!"

"Yes, but we didn't know it then. We took the white package and stared down at it. When we looked up, he had disappeared."

She lifted her eyebrows. "You mean in a puff of smoke, like a genie?"

"There was nary a puff. We looked this way and that but he was gone. We never saw him again."

"Maybe all he came to do was to deliver the dragonfly."

"I think you're right. We were probably wondering about that parcel for longer than we thought, and Wizards can move quickly." He looked down at his little niece. She was staring at the dragonfly in her lap. *She is Anne's daughter—her wisdom is showing already.* Emma should have the dragonfly. Its energy and love would bring solace to her. Anne told him that whoever possessed the dragonfly before had added their touch, their passion, and their essence to it. He often pondered who had it first. Who made it? And why? He may never know, but it was safe now and in good hands.

Emma patted the dragonfly and looked up. "I like that story."

A warm breeze caressed their faces and lifted their hair. A voice came with it on the wind. *We were only guardians until Emma could take the Dragonfly.* A sob caught in Albert's throat as a whisper of Anne's essence enveloped him, and a wave of love rippled over the wretched wound in his heart.

Emma looked up at his brimming eyes. "I'm sad too, Uncle Albert. Mama says it's good to cry when you're sad." And her tears joined his.

The scrape on his niece's forehead had scabbed over a little. Another whisper rose around him, or was it within him? *Console my daughter. Teach her the way.* On hearing his sister's voice, he couldn't hold back a sob. Emma leaned against him, and he squeezed her hand.

Of course, my dear Anne. I will look after her. A sharp, stabbing pain of never seeing his sister again shot through him.

Emma put an arm around him, her hand sliding over the soft linen shirt that her mother had woven for him. "Uncle Albert. Please don't die. Don't ever leave me."

Albert looked at the dragonfly lying in Emma's hand on Anne's shawl. "I won't, my dear. We have to look after the dragonfly, don't we?"

Chapter 13

Early the next day, the men ate a hearty breakfast and packed the wagon. Albert's three boxes, woollen blankets, pillows, and the bags, left just enough space for Emma to sleep. Hilda Weber had also prepared a package with bread, hard cheese, dried sausage and a half dozen late fallen apples. A bottle of wine for Albert and beer for both would suffice when they couldn't find clean water. She tucked the last parcel into the wagon and handed Emma her Mama's shawl.

Emma, standing beside the wagon, beamed "Thank you, Frau Weber. I thought I had packed it."

"You did, but I took it out."

Her eyebrows went up. "Why?"

"I made it into a jacket for you. I thought it would be easier for you to wear that way."

Emma held it up, letting the material unfold. "A jacket?"

"Yes, but you can take the stitching out, and it will be a shawl again. But now it has sleeves so it won't fall off your shoulders." She stepped up. "Let me help you."

Emma held her arms out as Hilda Weber slid them into the wide sleeves. "The front overlaps and I made a tie to hold it together." She crossed them over each other and tied a striped belt around it.

"Did you make that?"

She nodded. "Just for you. I had some scrap wool left over. I hope you like it." "

Emma stoked her hand over the red, yellow, blue and brown stripes. "I love it. Thank you." She wrapped floppy arms around the stout woman. "Now, I can wear my Mama wherever I go."

Albert picked her up and sat her on the wooden seat where Molly was waiting for her. Emma sat the doll on her lap, and he jumped up beside her. "All set?"

Emma hugged her arms around her new jacket. "All ready." She waved goodbye. "Auf Wiedersehen."

Hilda waved a towel with one hand dabbed at her eyes with her other. Albert clucked his tongue, and the beast moved forward. Light glinted off the jiggling metal of the harness.

They followed the path to the main road and turned onto the first branch to take a side road to the next county. It would add another hour to their journey, but they would miss that detestable town. A town he never wanted to see or think of again. With steady going, they could cover forty miles their first day. *The faster out of this damnable country, the better.*

When they got to Calais, he would have to   find a ship large enough to take the wagon. He could not lose his books and papers—objects that sailors did not value and would find sport in throwing overboard. They came to the intersection where they would turn onto the main road. Questions pushed to the surface of his mind. He glanced at his niece. *Can I be a good parent?* Anne had allowed the child freedom to express herself even when the German hausfrauen cried. "You are giving that child too much rein." "Children must be made to mind." "Too much imagination is bad." But despite what they called lack of discipline, Emma was a delightful child, full of play and wit and questions—interminable questions and now was no exception.

"Are we there yet?" "How far away is it?" "What is England like?" "How big is London?"

He took a deep breath and answered each one. "We have a long way to go. It's many nights away. England is bonny and you'll love it. Thousands of people live in London."

Many dangers abounded on long-distance travel—roads washed out, outlaws in forests, and thieves in towns. However, dressed as peasants they shouldn't arouse suspicion, and he had hidden his books and papers well under his clothes with the Holy Bible on top.

On the first night, they stopped at a small inn Albert leaned down to her. "It would be a good idea if you called me father."

"Why? You're my uncle."

"People might not understand why an uncle and his niece are travelling together. They might think I've kidnapped you."

"Oh my." She took his hand. "All right father. Lead the way." Before he could say they wanted a room, she announced in a loud voice. "This is my father."

The next day, he folded a blanket and placed it on the seat beside him. Other than when she slept in the back, she sat up front.

In four days, they reached an inn outside Stuttgart. The plague had killed half the population, leaving a hundred and twenty souls. Better to stay away from crowds as an outbreak could happen again.

It took another six days to make their way to France, where they stopped at St. Glossinde, a monastery in Metz. Albert had lodged there on his way to Germany, although the brothers did not remember him. Day after day, the horse plodded on. Every morning, Emma climbed up on the front seat and sat close beside him, holding her doll in one hand and her Mama's dragonfly in the other. Sometimes she kept the dragonfly in her pocket. On some days, she wasn't her usual smiling self and didn't ask a barrage of questions except for two recurring ones. "Are we there yet? "How much longer?

It would take another seven days to get to Lille and another two or three before they reached Calais and the Channel. That night they stayed at a convent where a curious Emma had many questions about the black-robed women. Most of the nuns were sweet and ever so helpful, except the one showing them to their room. Her tight mouth curved downward, but when Albert gave her some coins, she managed a toothless grin and brought a basin of water for them to wash in.

The next morning, one of the nuns walked up to Emma. "That's a very colourful belt on your jacket."

"My friend made it from my Mama's shawl."

"Where is your mama now?"

Emma's mouth quivered. She held Molly to her chest. "My Ma—Mama d–died, and she's—buried in the ground."

The black-robed woman crossed herself. "Oh, my poor child. Did she die of a sickness?"

When Albert overheard Emma struggling to talk, he strode over and glared at the woman. "Yes. She died quickly of a terrible sickness." He took Emma's hand.

The wretched woman continued. "I do hope she had a Christian burial with proper payers and God's blessing." She gestured toward the chapel. "Come. We will pray for the forgiveness of her sins and for perpetual light to shine upon her soul."

Albert tightened his hand on Emma's. "That is not necessary. Her mother had a beautiful burial. She is at peace." He walked swiftly away, still holding tightly to Emma's hand.

Emma scrambled to keep up as he strode through the arched doorway of the convent. He threw their bags into the back of the wagon, lifted her onto the seat, and climbed up. The horse clattered over the stones and through the gate. Emma leaned on her uncle's arm, resting her head against him.

At noon, Albert turned the horse off the main road under a stand of birch trees. He laid a blanket on a grassy slope and brought out a block of cheese and a loaf of bread the toothless nun had given him.

He took out the quarter bottle of wine and two mugs and cut chunks of bread and cheese.

They ate quietly for several minutes.. "The boys in the village said mama was bad and needed God to forgive her sins." She looked up, tears in her eyes. "What does sin mean?"

Albert put his mug down. "you know your mama was not bad."

"I know."

"The word 'sin' is an archery term. In Hebrew and Greek, it means 'to miss the mark.'"

"You mean when the arrow misses the bullseye?"

"Exactly."

She frowned. "But what's archery got to do with God and being bad?"

Albert took a deep breath. *Now is as good a time as ever for a theology lesson.* "If the archer misses his mark, it means his arrow did not go straight. Straightness—or righteousness—is an important concept in the Bible."

"What does concept mean?"

She is so like Anne. "It comes from the Latin word conceptum." He scratched his head. "I'll start again. Do you remember when your Mama and I would tell you stories, and you would make pictures inside your head?"

She grinned. "Yes. I liked that."

"And all those different pictures gave you a feeling. Like when you hear a story of someone helping someone: feeding them, or holding their arm to cross a river, or hugging them when they're sad. Or a mama cat carrying her kittens to safety. You might call those feelings 'kindness' or 'love.' Well, those words are concepts. Words that describe thoughts or feelings. Things you can't see."

Emma furrowed her brow.

"Think of it this way. If you can't put it in a wheelbarrow, it's a concept. For example, you can't put love in a wheelbarrow."

Her eyes lit up. "I could if I filled it with strawberries or kittens. Or Mama's blueberry pie." Tears welled in her eyes. "Or Mama."

He put his arm around her. "Your mama would love to ride in your wheelbarrow." He handed her his handkerchief.

She blew her nose, dried her face, and stared at him with a questioning face. "Does everybody learn the same meaning for concept words?"

"No, and that can be a problem. The same word can have different meanings to different people and at different times."

"But how do people know what other people mean?"

"They often don't and words are powerful. They can cause misery, fights, and even wars."

"Like when I was mad at those boys. They said the priest called my Mama sinful." She scrunched up her face. "The priest must have thought sin meant bad instead of missing the bullseye."

He hugged her. "You're a clever girl. You've just learned what some people take years to understand. And some never do."

Chapter 14

The next few days passed uneventfully. Emma sat quietly and would fuss when he went too far from her side. It took many reassuring words and hugs to convince her he would be right back.

It had been a long day, and Albert welcomed seeing the inn in the distance where they could stay the night. A light breeze wafted the essence of Anne over him. He breathed her in, smiling with her.

That night he had a vivid dream of his twin sister—so vivid he would swear she was physical. She wore a blue dress, a clean white apron and a smile. 'Look after Emma. Teach her.'

Albert embraced her. 'I will. I promise.' He kissed her cheek, and she dissolved into a mist.

Several days passed and they stopped outside of Lille. It would take two or even three more to reach Calais, where they would take a ship to Dover and those beautiful white cliffs that shone in the sun or by the light of a fully rounded moon.

The next morning Albert happily answered Emma's one recurring question. "We're very close now. Only a few days to the ship."

"Have you ever been on a ship, Uncle—I mean, daddy?"

"Yes, I came across the channel on a big one. It's quite exciting if the waves are high."

"We can pretend we're explorers sailing to the new world."

"We can."

"Will there be pirates?"

"I wonder." He jiggled his eyebrows and she laughed.

Activity on the channel had settled down after the May battles and the war between the English and the Dutch now raged farther north.

The early September sun still offered a little daytime warmth. That night, far from an inn or a monastery, they slept in the wagon, rolled up in itchy blankets. The next morning, Albert untwisted cramped legs, stepped over the edge of the wagon and toppled to the ground.

"Uncle Daddy," Emma cried as he disappeared over the side. She peered over. "What happened?"

He groaned and wobbled to his feet. "My muscles aren't awake yet."

She laughed. "You have floppy legs."

They breakfasted on hard white cheese, rye bread and a little red wine to wash it down.

They packed up the leftovers, folded blankets, and set off for the day, the wagon bumping over the rough road. Emma's questions changed to, 'where do we go when we die?' or 'what does it feel like to die?' He did his best to answer in a way to comfort her and leave her room to think for herself. As young as she was, she had an inquiring mind and a lively interest in learning.

On their last night before reaching Calais, Albert couldn't sleep. It would take a good part of a day or longer, depending on the vessel and conditions, to cross the channel to English soil—to the land where he and his sister were born. The narrow bed squeaked and he didn't want to wake Emma in the small cot next to him, so he rose and sat in a chair by the window. In the quiet of the night, that horrible scene of Anne in the village square tore through him like a hot blade. His rush to save Emma and his anguish at leaving his sister to die, burned like a fever within him. Thank God Emma's crack on her head had submerged that unspeakable night of horror.

"Oh, my dear Anne. I miss you terribly. I can't hear or sense you when I'm awash with grief." He held his head and steadied his breathing. "You don't dwell in that emotional place, so I will do my best to be happy for you and to meet you in your sublime state."

He would continue his and his sister's passion and quest to discover more about the mysteries of life. It would be a few years before his niece would be ready to broach such esoteric subjects. He thought of their discussion about words. Perhaps it won't be too long.

He still had to be careful who he talked to. The Catholics and now the Protestants, especially the Calvinists, were quick to accuse one of blasphemy. He would certainly be tortured if his papers were found. He had taken further protection of copying passages from the Bible and placing them among his own writings. If anyone had a cursory look, he would assume the pile of papers to be those of a pious man. He had to stay safe for Emma. He looked at the small mound under the covers. I will take good care of her.

He went back to his cot and pulled the scratchy blanket over him. The quiet breathing of his niece finally lulled him to sleep.

On their last day before the sea voyage to Dover, Emma climbed up on the seat, her doll in one hand and the dragonfly in the other. Albert headed the horse out.

Emma sat her doll on the wooden plank beside her. "I wish Mama were with us. She would love to see England." She held the dragonfly in her lap.

He tightened the leather reins in his hands as he guided the horse and wagon over the rutted road. The wheels rocked one way and another over or around the deep holes. "Hang on."

The surface smoothed out, and at that precise moment, a strong and unmistakably sweet scent of honeysuckle filled their noses. "Mama!" Emma raised her hands. "It smells like Mama."

A large bush of honeysuckle bloomed above the ditch on the side of the road. Anne's favourite scent. Albert pulled the horse up, jumped off the wagon and slid down the incline. He returned with an armload of reddish-pink flowers and handed them up to her. "Here you are."

She gathered them to her chest and pressed her face into them. "Mama. They smell like Mama."

Albert climbed aboard and flicked the reins. Emma plucked a blossom, put the narrow trumpet end into her mouth and sucked the nectar from it as her mother had shown her. Invisible arms wrapped around her as she placed another pink blossom on her tongue.

Chapter 15

They entered Calais where a stronger—and to Emma an unknown —aroma met them.

She wrinkled her nose. "What stinks?" She craned her neck, looking. Wagons, horses, and people pushing cards filled the roadway. Wooden or stone buildings lined each side while packs of squawking birds dove and strutted about. "What are those noisy birds?"

"Those are gulls, and what you smell is the sea. That, and dead fish."

At a little after four in the afternoon, Albert headed the horse to the docks. The ships sailed with the tide at night, and he needed to arrange passage for that evening.

Emma's eyes grew into large circles as they rumbled closer to the noise and bustle of the harbour where the tall ships were being loaded. Burly men, with huge loads on their shoulders, snaked their way up swaying gangplanks.

The first ship had no room for a horse and wagon. At the second, he found a captain who, after haggling over a price, consented to take them. The square-rigged caravel had ten wooden horse stalls, complete with canvas slings. Albert paid the man and guided the horse and wagon up the rickety ramp. Emma sat perched on top of a wooden box and peered one way and another. People shouted, boats creaked against the dock, and men and women in travelling capes and hats walked up the crowded plank. She grasped the edge of the swaying wagon and leaned over. Water sloshed against the wharf's pilings, trapping seaweed around the tar-blackened pillars. Dark trailing leaves wafted to and fro with the rhythm of the sea.

Albert unhitched the horse. "Stay where you are while I take this beast to its stall and strap it in." He walked off.

She swivelled her head about as he led the horse out of sight. So many people in this strange place. So many smells and noises. She swung her feet over the side and started to climb down when Albert came striding back. He lifted her down. "Where's your doll?"

"I packed her and my dragonfly in my bag and tied it tight. I don't want them to fall overboard."

"Good idea." He grabbed the front of the wagon. "I need to move this into place."

"I can help." She pushed and grunted as he wedged the wagon between two barrels and a stack of wooden boxes. A few yards away, a scruffy man and a pretty woman in a ruffly crimson dress sat on a bench for walk-on passengers. Her lips were bright red and cheeks a rosy pink.

Emma pointed to the empty bench across from them. "Can we sit with those people?" She had never seen anyone with paint on their face, other than the Gypsy clowns or when she and her mother would play dress up.

Two men and a youth rushed to the bench, slapping their knees and making silly faces. Emma had seen boys in the village act like that when they had too much cider.

Albert lifted her into the wagon. "I think we should stay with our belongings."

"And close to our food." Emma looked over her shoulder and pointed. "Can we walk up that way a little?"

"A short way." He lifted her out, and they walked between a row of barrels chained to the deck and a stack of boxes wrapped in oiled cloth. Someone else had discovered Otto's secret. They stopped at two giant coils of thick hemp rope, and she leaned over the railing where sailors were on-loading. A swarthy man with dark curly hair and a barrel on his shoulder strode up the ramp. Empty-handed sailors brushed past him as they went down for more cargo.

The curly haired man looked at Emma. "Ah, Bella," he shouted and blew her a kiss.

She waved back. From then on, when coming and going, he would shout bella, and Emma would answer with a wave.

"Uncle Daddy, what does 'bella' mean?"

"It's Italian, and it means beautiful."

Emma tilted her head. "Mama says sunsets are beautiful, and daffodils are beautiful, and herbs are beautiful." She paused. "Am I beautiful?"

"Yes, you are. Most beautiful."

The pile of boxes and rows of barrels on the dock grew smaller. The dark-haired sailor hoisted the last one onto his shoulder and hiked up the slanted boards. He dumped it on the deck and headed toward them.

"What is your name, my princess?" He displayed a set of white teeth and stood close to Emma.

Albert, on the other side, put an arm around her shoulders.

"Emma Farber—I mean Emma Lewis."

"The princess does not know who she is?" He spoke in a shouty kind of laughing voice.

Albert answered. "Her father was Farber. I am her stepfather, Albert Lewis."

The dark man leaned forward and stuck out his hand. "Ciao, I am Dominic. Welcome to The Aurora."

Albert took his hand. "Thank you."

The foreign man put his hand on Emma's head and ruffled her hair. "You are like my little Maria, the light of my life. She will be nine years next week, and I will be on this cursed ship instead of at her party."

Albert let his shoulders down and relaxed his hold on Emma.

She pointed to a tangle of ropes hanging far above them. "What are those for?"

Dominic roared a laugh. "That line controls the sails and that one —" he pointed to a thick cord attached to a rope ladder, "that is the ratline that leads to the crow's nest."

She wrinkled her nose. "I don't like rats. Why is there a nest for crows on your ship?"

Dominic bellowed another laugh. "The rats do run up and down it, but the crow's nest is not for crows. A crewman climbs the ratline, and when he is high up in the crow's nest, he can see straight out over the sea." His arm stretched forth, ending in a pointing finger. "To where we are going or—" He spoke in foreboding tone. "What might be coming our way."

Her face lit up. "You mean pirates?" Her mother had told her many tales of such ruffians.

Dominic's mock stern mouth turned upward, followed by another burst of laughter. "Nay, there are no pirates in these waters." She didn't see him cross his fingers behind his back, for guns were always at the ready and watchmen alert in the channel for pirate attacks. A shout from the captain called him away. "I see you later and tell you more. Ciao."

Emma waved at his receding back. She took Albert's hand, and they walked to the wagon away from bustling shipmates. Albert lifted her up and jumped in after her. He opened a parcel and took out a chunk of dark rye and a block of old cheddar. They had been replenishing their supplies as they went and would have enough for the crossing and a day on the road to London. They leaned against the back of the wagon and washed the sharp cheese and dry bread down with cups of ale. When they finished, Emma had more marine questions that Albert couldn't answer. He reassured her that Dominic would no doubt be back to tell her more about ships and sailing.

No matter how hard she held her eyes open, Emma succumbed to sleep, and by nine-thirty, the wind had picked up. With loud commands from the captain and a scurry of activity, casting off lines and raising sails, they eased away in the dark. Timbers creaked as the ship scraped along the dock, and when the rocking increased, Emma stirred and sat up. Men shouted back and forth, pulling on thick ropes. A wiry lad scrambled up the ratline, and the black sails puffed out.

Emma, fully awake now, rushed to the side of the wagon and stuck one leg over.

Albert sprang after her, and grabbed her arm. "Where are you going?"

"I want to stand by the rail to see better."

"We can see fine from here." He sat down with her in the front of the wagon. "There's too much activity going on with booms swinging and sails unfurling. The sailors would not appreciate having a little girl underfoot."

With a favourable wind, they moved swiftly out of the harbour and into the starlit night. A waning moon gave some light.

Emma leaned her arms on the edge of the wagon. "How do they know where to go in the dark?"

Albert pointed. "The stars guide them."

She looked up. "There's Orion with his belt and the evening star and— ."

"You are quite the stargazer."

"Mama taught me the stars, but I never knew ships sailed by them."

A loud call of "ciao" rang out, and Dominic with a wide grin, bounded toward them. He hitched himself up on the side of the wagon and, teetering on its rim, steadied himself by placing a high booted foot on a nearby barrel.

"So, what do you want to know, ma Bella?"

"Why are the sails dirty?"

Dominic's ready laugh boomed out again. "They're not dirty. They've been dyed with bark dye."

"Why? They would look so pretty if they were white."

"If they were not dyed, the salt would rot them." He pointed to the topsail. "See that piece on top."

"Yes."

"That's the bonnet. It can be removed if the skipper wants to shorten a sail."

"Why would he want to do that?"

"In case of a tempest or to simply slow down." He showed white teeth.

Emma wrinkled her nose. "Why does it stink so?"

"You think my ship stinks?" He waved a hand. "I'm used to it." He laughed again. "What you smell is the ballast."

"What's ballast?"

"That is weight to stabilize the ship. We use harbour sand, which stinks of port wastes." He frowned. "Do not go near it. It has fleas, rats and all kinds of vermin."

Albert had a question. "Do you still sail by the stars?"

"The channel is an easy sail. The old sailors use the stars on the open sea, but now the skippers use an astrolabe and an almanac."

Emma's face brightened. "Mama had an almanac. She said the stars and planets can help us find our way in life."

Dominic shrugged. "I don't know about that, but at night the captain sights by the North Star and by day, the sun."

"What if clouds cover the sun?"

His eyes grew big and his mouth made an O. "Then, we get lost." He lowered his voice into a hoarse whisper. "And we never make it to the shiny white cliffs."

She took her uncle's hand. "You don't scare me." She grinned. "I have another question."

"You ask a lot of questions, ma Bella. What do you want to know now?"

"Why are the cliffs white?"

"They are white because they are made of chalk." He jumped off the wagon. "Now, I have to eat and drink. Have a good voyage." He threaded his way to a group of sailors sitting around a metal box. A trail of wavering smoke rose lazily from it.

Emma yawned, and Albert settled her amongst pillows and blankets, silently petitioning pirates to keep their distance on that dark and starless night.

Chapter 16

Hours later, Emma awoke. Her bed moved, and a vile smell assailed her nose. She coughed from the stench. Her uncle stood beside the wagon, and most of the barrels around it had been removed. The ship rocked gently in the dark. A misty light glowed faintly in the distant sky as dawn stretched and peeped through sleepy eyes.

She yawned, crawled to the side and leaned on the top edge. "Where are we?"

Albert turned to his dishevelled niece. *She has been through so much, and still she greets the day with wonder.* "We're in England." He put an arm around her. "We're home."

By the time Albert turned the wagon around, and hitched the horse, daylight had washed away the night and opened Emma's eyes wide. The chalky cliffs of Dover, high and white, gleamed in the rising sun. Their wagon rattled off the gangplank amongst sailors coming and going and passengers walking or leading a horse off. The red-lipped lady passed, and Emma smiled. The lady smiled back, and the man beside her yanked her forward. Emma looked for Dominic among the busy sailors. Their wagon creaked to the end of the ramp and, with a bump, landed on solid ground. A yell erupted from behind them.

"Ciao, my friends."

Albert pulled up. Emma sat up front next to him and Dominic leapt into the back of the wagon. Emma turned, and he plastered a kiss on each of her cheeks. His strong fish smell made her cough.

"Ma Bella." He hugged Albert, kissed him the same way and jumped off. "Arrivederci, my friends. Be well." He turned and ran up the gangplank to join his mates in more offloading.

Albert started the horse moving again and glanced over at Emma —her face alight with anticipation. A good beginning for their new life in England.

On the first day of their two-day journey to London, it rained all morning on and off but Albert, happy to breathe English air after nearly seven years, didn't mind getting wet. It had let up by noon, and they stopped to eat the last of their bread and cheese. They stayed longer than he'd meant but the horse had a good rest, and they enjoyed sitting on a thick blanket on soft ground instead of the hard seat of a bouncing wagon.

Evening crept up, and a sleeping Emma lay tucked in the back of the wagon. They had already passed Sittingbourne—the halfway point with plenty of inns and beer houses. Perhaps they should have stopped there, but there had to be more inns along that much-used route. The road had been passable, until they headed into a rutted and rough stretch. A tired Albert, only wanting a good night's sleep, slowed the horse over deep and muddy puddles, threatening to trip it. Up ahead, a chunk of the road had been washed away, leaving a dangerous slope. Slowing even more, he attempted to maneuver around the broken side, but the horse, unsure of its steps, shied. Albert groaned. He'd have to get out and walk the beast through. He gathered the reins in one hand and leaned sideways, ready to swing his legs over the edge. At that moment, the back wheel slipped, and he slid off into the ditch. He grabbed onto the side of the wagon and pushed his shoulder against it. Skidding hooves slashed at the mud, and the wagon jerked toward Albert. The iron axle smashed against his head, knocking him face-down into the mucky ditch. The horse reared and plunged forward and when his feet hit firm ground, he bolted down the road and into the black night.

Chapter 17

The frantic horse raced over the uneven ground, flinging Emma side to side. She awoke with a start and flailed about. Boxes, bags, and blankets slid and careened into each other. She covered her head and curled into a ball. The wagon hit a deep rut, and a box bounced over the side and tumbled into the night. She yelled at the horse to stop, but she couldn't hear her own voice over the wind and the rattle of runaway wheels. After several chaotic minutes, the horse finally slowed and stopped at the side of the road, his flanks heaving. Emma unwound herself from the blanket and climbed onto the seat. She was breathing hard too and took a minute to calm down.

Her heart thumped, and her head ached. "Uncle Albert. Where are you?" She looked around in the dark and up at the sky. The stars would tell her how to get back to him.

She reached for the flapping reins and after a second try, grabbed hold of them. With a pull she signalled the horse to turn and they headed back in the direction of the North Star.

She peered into the darkness. *How far did we come? Where's Uncle Albert? What happened to him?* "I'm not afraid." Her voice quivered. Her mother had taught her about angels, wood fairies and plant devas. She only had to call, and they would come to her assistance.

"Angels of the Road. I need you now." Her voice disappeared into the wind.

On a walk in the forest once, she had glimpsed a wood nymph, and another time, playing in a patch of wildflowers, she caught sight of a hovering plant deva out the corner of her eye.

Mama. You know how to find Uncle Albert. "Help me find him."

Horse, wagon and child continued along the road. The waning moon, a sliver now, gave little light. If only she could find her uncle, all would be well.

She called into the wind. "Uncle Albert. Uncle Albert. Where are you?" But under the rattling wheels and the steady drum of hoofs, her cries disappeared

Tightening her grip on the reins, she forced her eyes to see through the darkness. Each bush and tree looked like a man. Her eyes stung, and she blinked hard. "I won't cry. I will find you."

In the distance, a bent figure crawled out of the ditch onto the road —one hand on his head, the other lifted high.

She gasped. Please be Albert and not an outlaw.

The wagon drew closer, and the man looked up. She let out a breath of relief. "Uncle Albert." She pulled the horse up and ran to him.

He smothered her in his arms. "Emma, Emma."

"I'm all right. But you're hurt. You're bleeding."

"It's only a scrape." He looked around. "Where are we?"

"I don't know." Now muddy herself, she hugged him again. "But we're together."

Leaning on her, he struggled to his feet and climbed onto the seat. When he reached for the reins, he flopped over. Blood ran down his temple into his eye and met up with a bleeding cheek.

Emma took the reins from him. "I can do it."

He didn't object. He grasped the back of the seat with one hand and held his head with the other. "There must be an inn along this road. It's the main passage to London."

"I didn't see one." Muck and blood dripped off his hair and face and clothes. "You smell like a cesspit."

"The ditch was filthy."

They continued on into the night. Emma peered for an outline of any kind of building. *Please, road angels. Show us an inn.* The moon crept out from under a cloud, and on the left, a little way off, a light flickered.

Chapter 18

"Uncle Albert. I see a light." She squinted into the distance. "It is a light." She let out a breath. *Thank you, road angels. Thank you, Mama.*

He lifted his head. "Thanks be to All That Is."

She turned the horse toward a small building on the left. A sign swayed under a flickering lamp. Peeling letters spelled, 'The Dog and Bull,' or was it 'The Bog and Bell' Only a local pub, not a coaching inn for travellers, but hopefully, it would have a room or two available. She guided the horse to the side of the building where a door opened, and a scrawny boy of about twelve walked toward them. He grabbed the bridle and stroked the horse's nose. Emma helped Albert down.

He groaned. "Our things. My papers." He turned to the boy. "Lad, bring everything in."

The boy lifted his eyebrows. "Everything?"

"Yes, everything. Fetch it all."

Albert leaned on Emma and limped to the side door. A stocky woman, drying her hands on a towel, came out. She tucked it into the waist of her apron, took Albert's other arm and led them through a narrow hallway to the kitchen. A wooden table, four chairs and a backless bench, sat in the centre. On the wall over a large oven, hung pots, pans, ladles, forks, and serving spoons. The room smelled of garlic, onions, and chicken. A thick soup simmered in an iron pot hanging on a hook over the stone fireplace.

She guided Albert to a chair. "Sit here." She filled a basin with water and placed it on the table. With a flick, she pulled the cloth from her waist and immersed it. After a few dabs at Albert's face, the water turned rusty red. The twelve-year-old, who had tied up their horse, stood at his mother's shoulder. She pointed to a bucket near the door. "Simon, fetch me some water from the pump."

The boy ran outside while she continued to wipe Albert's face with dirty water. "You're a bit of a mess."

The boy returned and set the slopping bucket on the floor. His mother handed him the basin. "Toss this out."

He scampered out, spilling water as he went, and his mother turned back to cleaning up Albert. As more dung and mud fell away, a gash appeared.

"That's not a big cut, but if you swallowed any of that muck, you'll be sick in the stomach for a time."

Emma held Albert's hand. "He'll be all right, shan't he?"

"Your father should be fine." She turned to Simon and a younger lad who had joined him. "Simon, you and John take him outside and strip his outer clothes off. He's not staying inside, smelling like that."

Another boy, a few years older, appeared. The youngest boy she had called John ran ahead while the older boy and Simon took each side and helped Albert out the back door. Emma started to go with them, but the woman stopped her. "Don't worry. The boys will tend to him. What's your name child?"

"Emma—Lewis."

"Where's your mother?"

"She's—dead."

"I am sorry. Where are you from?"

Simon walked in, holding a canvas bag in each hand. "Where do these go?"

Emma reached out. "Those are our clothes and possessions. And my unc—father wants the boxes brought in too." The people seemed nice enough, but she wished her Uncle Albert would come back.

The woman gestured to the boy. "Put them in the back room upstairs. There's a cot in that one for the girl." She turned to Emma. "You must be hungry, child. I'll get you some victuals."

Emma followed her into a large main room off the kitchen. A long table stretched against one wall, with three smaller ones in the centre. Two men sat on a bench at one side of the long table, and four men—

drinking and smoking—sat around one in the centre. They put down their mugs of beer and watched as the woman pulled a table closer to the fire. "Sit here dear and get warm."

Emma sat at the side furthest from the fire and the men went back to eating and talking.

The woman brought a plate of bread and beans. Emma looked at her blood-streaked, muddy hands. "Please, may I wash my hands."

"Aye, you are a bit of a mess." She led her back to the kitchen where Emma washed smears of blood and muck from her hands and face and swiped at the mud on her dress. She turned to leave when the door opened. A man in baggy breeches tied with a rope stood in the doorway. The bottom of his pants flopped over a pair of giant rubber boots. An oversized shirt flapped at his waist, and a grey bandage encircled his head and over one cheek.

Emma's mouth dropped open. "Are you my—?"

He stepped toward Emma. "I am and I'm fine."

The woman laughed. "I see my tribe of ruffians fixed you up but you must eat." She shooed them to the next room.

A moment later, she arrived with another plate of beans and stringy chicken and two mugs of home-brewed beer. The older boy walked in, carrying a box from the wagon on his way upstairs to their room.

Albert touched his arm as he passed by their table. "Did you bring everything in, boy?"

"Yes, sir. The wagon is empty."

"Thank you, young man, and bring me the contents of my pockets."

"Yes, sir."

A few moments later, the boy returned.

"The pockets were empty, sir."

"Empty? But I had coins."

"They musta dropped out when you fell."

Albert looked at him for a long moment. "Yes, maybe they did."

The boy left and Emma bent close to her uncle. "He's lying."

"Yes, but it's of no mind. There were but a few coins" He tilted his head. "How did you know he was lying?"

"I don't know. But he was."

"You're right, my child. He was lying. That is a good thing to discern, but it's even better to know how you know."

"How do I do that?"

"Ask yourself what made you think he was lying. How did you feel? Did he do something or look different from a person who wasn't lying?"

Emma glanced up. "His voice sounded funny, and his eyes kept moving."

"Anything else?"

"Mostly, I got this feeling in my stomach to be careful."

"That's your best compass. Always go by your feelings. They can tell you everything you need to know about a person or situation."

"Why did you agree with him and not demand your money?"

"It was but a few coins, and I cannot prove him right or wrong." He took a drink. "Worry not. Our money is well hidden in our belongings. We should go now and check them out."

Upstairs, the back room contained a narrow bed, a metal cot, a small table with a cracked washbasin, and a chair with a wobbly leg. A small window opened onto the back of the inn. One wooden box sat on the chair and the other on the floor beside their canvas bags. The parcels, still tied, looked as if they had not been tampered with. Albert handed Emma her bag and put his own on his bed. "Wait a minute."

"What's the matter?"

He glanced around the room, looked under the bed and behind the two boxes.

"What is it?"

His face turned white. "A box is missing. The one with my secret writings. It especially must not fall into the wrong hands."

Chapter 19

"Are you sure a box is missing?"

"Without a doubt. It also contains my diary—which should not be found or read by anyone." He dashed from the room.

Emma raced after him—down the stairs, through the kitchen and to the shed and the stabled horse. Albert leaned over the edge of the wagon and peered in. The moon offered sparse light showing nothing but twigs, leaves and the blanket-covered board seat,

Albert reached in and pushed a small branch aside. "Did anything fall off when the horse bolted?"

"I don't know. Everything was sliding and bouncing around."

"It must have been thrown out." His shoulders dropped. "We won't find anything in the dark." He put a hand to the cloth bandage on his head. "We'll search in the morning."

Emma changed and after finding her doll and dragonfly in her bag she crawled into her cot and quickly fell asleep.

Scuffles and shouts from downstairs awakened them. Were the boys fighting or playing? A slap and yell from their mother, followed by a door slamming, momentarily stopped the commotion. Albert groaned, and Emma threw off her light blanket and stepped over to his narrow bed.

"Are you all right, Uncle Albert? You don't look good." His grey face matched the bandage wrapped around his head. Spidery red lines crawled down his cheek and over his neck, disappearing into his nightshirt. "You're bleeding again."

He put his hand to his face, but no blood came off on his fingers as he touched the thin red tendrils lacing a downward path under his skin.

Emma frowned. "You're bleeding inside. Mama says that's not good."

"I'll be all right."

"I'll find you something to eat." She pulled on her shoes and slipped her outer dress over her sleeping clothes. She crept along the hall, past closed doors, and down the stairs. *A herb drink would be good for my uncle.* Did camomile grow by the roadsides in England as it did in Germany?

Mrs. Burke, the helpful lady from last night, stood at the sink washing dishes and pans. The familiar smell and plopping sounds of porridge came from the iron pot on the stove.

"May I have some food for my unc—father?" *Father, father.*

"Of course, my dear." The woman dried her hands and took down a wooden bowl. "How is your father this morning?"

"He is well." *Please, God make it true.*

The woman slopped a spoon of cornmeal porridge into the bowl and handed it to her.

"Thank you. Could I also have some water to wash my father's face?"

"You want to wash him again?"

"Yes, ma'am."

"All right. Take the small pail and ladle some from the bucket, but it seems like a waste of good water."

Emma filled the pail, and Mrs. Burke set four more bowls, brimming with hot porridge onto the table. She yelled out the door, "Ethan, boys."

The boys from last night came bounding in, yelling, pushing and shoving to get to their chairs, nearly knocking Emma over in their rush. A muscular man, even taller than her uncle, thumped in after them. Arms and legs as thick as trees bulged against a black shirt and black pants. Emma steadied her pail.

The man spied her and snarled. "So, you're the latecomer from last night."

She backed away, and with a quick nod and a firm grip on the pail, she picked up the bowl of porridge in her other hand and fled from the room. A bellow of laughter followed her.

Albert sat on the side of the bed with his elbows on his knees, and holding his head in his hands. He did not look up when she came in. Swaying crookedly, he muttered something in a low voice.

She put the pail down and placed the bowl on the side table. "What did you say?"

"Must find my papers—my writings—important."

She bent closer and patted his hand. *I wish you were here, mama.* Her small hand covered only half of his. "We'll find them. You have to rest and eat. Then we'll look for them." She'd held her voice steady, but her insides shook.

Albert looked up at her with a long gaze. His eyes cleared, and his lips moved into a suggestion of his old smile. "Yes. That would be good."

She handed him the bowl and spoon and made sure he had a grip on them. The steam rose lazily to the angry red line on his cheek. "I'll see if I can make you a hot drink."

She hurried downstairs to the kitchen. The boys had left and Mrs. Burke was clearing off dishes and putting them into the washbasin. The dark man rocked back on two legs of his chair. He gripped a massive mug of ale in one hand and a long willow cane in his other. He whipped it through the air, slashing at a flying insect that darted about his head.

Emma sidled over to Mrs. Burke at the sink. "Do you have any dried herbs I could use?"

The woman lifted an eyebrow. "I have some mint for the lamb chops. Whatever do you want with them?"

"I need to make a hot drink for my father."

The man slammed the front legs of his chair down and glared at her. "Can he not come and get it, lass?"

Her chin wobbled but she held his gaze. "He's not well."

Mrs. Burke picked up the kettle. "Stop teasing the child, Ethan, and get me a handful of mint from the shed."

"I'm busy, woman. I have to feed the horses." He stamped a heavy boot on the floor, scraped his chair back, and whipped the stick against his thigh. With a snarl, he thumped out the door and Emma jumped when the door slammed behind him.

The woman poured hot water into a mug. "Don't mind Mr. Burke, child. He's used to rough boys." She reached for a small bowl on a shelf. "I may have a few mint leaves here. Ah, yes. Here they are." She handed Emma the bowl and the cup of hot water. "I'v never heard of drinking mint."

Emma took the bowl and cup. "Thank you, ma'am. It's good for when you're sick." She hurried out of the room and headed upstairs.

Chapter 20

The next day, Albert's body shook alternately with fever or chills. No matter how many blankets Emma piled on him he continued to shiver. She touched a clammy hand. The red trailing line on his cheek had grown longer, and he breathed too fast. She put her head to his chest. His heart thumpety-thumped like a run-away horse. The words he spoke didn't make sense, and he didn't know where he was. He raised his head. "Anne, Anne. Where are you?"

Emma eased him back to the pillow and stroked his forehead. "It's all right. Mama is with us." Her voice quavered. "You must get well." She let her tears fall. "Please get well."

He'd lie quietly for several minutes and then rave about missing papers. What else could she do? Mama's dragonfly! It would help. She ran to her cot and brought it back to her uncle. She placed it on his chest, and put her small hand on top. "Please get better, Uncle Albert." She laid her head on his chest. "Please don't die."

Mrs. Burke helped. She fed Emma well and brought porridge and bread to Albert. However, he ate little and slept a lot. Later that day, he sat up and called for Emma.

"I'm right here, Uncle Albert." She uncurled herself from the chair under the window and came to his bedside. "What is it?"

"I need my quill and a little ink." He swayed and held his head.

"You need rest to get well."

He pulled his pillow up behind him. "I must write a letter. Find my paper and quill." He leaned back.

Emma ran to his bag and dug into it. Clothes, a small book, more clothes, a crystal—no paper or quill. She stuffed everything back. "I'll ask Mrs. Burke." And she raced off.

She returned in a few minutes with a tray. On it lay a wrinkled piece of paper, a ragged quill pen and a small pot of black ink. "It was all Mrs. Burke had. She only writes notes for the butcher."

Albert sat up. "That will do."

She put the tray on his lap, and he unstopped the small bottle. The dull point made scratches as he wrote. Sometimes a blob of ink would escape from the poorly trimmed quill.

Emma pulled the chair up beside him. "What are you writing?"

The red trail on his pale face stood out like a wandering tree root. His eyes were dark hollows and his voice weak. "I'm writing to Mr. Edwards in London. You'll be safe there—money in trust for you." He dipped the quill and slowly scratched its nib over the rough surface.

When he reached the bottom of the page, he placed the bedraggled pen on the tray, closed his eyes and leaned back on the pillow. Emma put the tray on the chest at the foot of the bed. She corked the ink. At the top of the paper, he had written 'Thomas Edwards, Solicitor', and a London address underneath.

She couldn't read the rest of it. It wasn't Latin but the letters didn't spell real words. It was one of his secret codes. 'To be deciphered by only those who know it,' he had said. He'd taught her a simple letter replacement code but she didn't know this complicated one. She folded the paper and put it into the bottom of her bag.

The next morning, Emma gasped to see her uncle grey and barely breathing. She stumbled down the stairs and rushed to the kitchen and up to Mrs. Burke stirring porridge on the stove. "He needs a doctor. Please send someone for a doctor. We can pay."

"Oh, my dear. You startled me." She put the spoon down.

"Please, fetch the doctor."

Mrs. Burke shook her head. "It's a half-day ride there and back. And it may well be too late."

Emma glared. "No, it will not be too late. He will not die. He cannot die." She blinked back hot tears. "We must try." She tugged at the woman's skirts. "Please."

"Let's have a look." They went upstairs. One look at the man in the bed and Mrs. Burke said, "I'll send Luke with the cart to fetch Doctor Morris. He's the eldest and knows the way."

In the afternoon, Albert opened his eyes and smiled weakly at Emma.

She patted his hand. "I know what will help. Stay there." She ran downstairs and dashed out. No comfrey, but lavender grew behind the shed and she brought handfuls into the kitchen. Mrs. Burke looked on in wonder as she pounded the stems and leaves, added a little warm water and made a poultice the way her mother had taught her.

It would soothe the wound but her uncle needed more than soothing. She raced upstairs and held the damp pack on his cold cheek. She shivered and tucked a heavy blanket up around his neck. *Don't leave me.* The dragonfly sat on the table beside him.

He stretched a hand out of the covers. "Emma..."

"I'm here." She took his hand and bent close.

"There's money—"

"Don"t talk, Uncle. All is well."

"Money—in my pouch. Pay someone—to find the missing box— my books." He took a breath and lay with eyes shut.

She held his hand, beseeching her life force and a host of angels to invigorate him.

His eyelids fluttered, and his voice faint. "Give letter—Mr. Edwards."

"Uncle Albert. You'll be all right. We'll go to London together. The doctor is coming."

Albert closed his eyes and lay still. Emma picked up the dragonfly and crawled on top of the covers and curled up beside him. She lay the dragonfly on top of the blankets over his chest, and put her arm across him. "I'm here. Be warm. All is well. We'll be all right."*Mama, I need your help. Send us your Healing Angels. Please make Uncle Albert well.* She had to be strong, but tears kept coming.

Chapter 21

Doctor Morris arrived at sundown and Mrs. Burke showed him upstairs. A little girl lay curled up beside his patient, her hand half covering a large dragonfly on his chest. A snaking red line slithered over the man's ashen face, down his neck, and disappeared under his nightshirt.

He stepped up to the bed and touched the man's forehead. "He doesn't have long. Take the child away."

The woman picked up the sleeping child. Emma opened her eyes and tightened her hand on the dragonfly as Mrs. Burke lifted her up. As they headed out of the room, Emma woke fully and struggled to get down. "Let me go. I need to stay."

Mrs. Burke took a firmer hold. "Come, my child. Your father will soon be with God."

"No!" She flung herself about, flailing at her captor. "He can't die. God can't have him."

The woman ignored her pleas, taking her downstairs to the kitchen. However, she would not be calmed. Mrs. Burke offered soup and even whisky to quieten her down, but Emma refused them and bolted for the stairs every chance she got.

Again, she stumbled up on weary limbs and met the doctor coming down. He picked her up. "Child. Your father is very sick."

"I must stay with him." She twisted and pulled to get away.

He held her tightly. "He's in God's hands now."

She collapsed in his arms. Her herbs hadn't worked. Angels hadn't saved him. Maybe God would help the doctor. She laid her head on his chest. "Please make him better."

A rumble of wagon wheels awoke her. A sliver of light shone on the dark horizon. She rubbed her eyes and pushed on her elbow to sit up. "Where am I?" She blinked and took in a deep breath of cool air. "Where are we going?" She sat up. Her uncle's boxes were beside her along with his leather bag and her small one. *He must be better, and we're on our way to London.* She pushed the blanket off and climbed onto the front seat.

"Uncle Al—" She stared. The doctor sat beside her.

"Glad to see you're awake, my dear. I had to give you something to sleep, and I feared I had given you too much."

"Where is my—father, and where are we going?"

"Your father was deathly ill, my child. I'm sorry. I did what I could, but I was too late."

She pounded on his arm and grabbed one of the reins. "No. We have to go back."

The doctor pulled the reins and stopped the horse. He turned to her. "Listen to me, child. I could do no more and I had to return. You will stay with Mrs. Morris and me for a day or two until I can arrange a ride for you to London." With a click of his tongue, the horse moved on.

Emma's mind darted this way and that. *Uncle Albert can't be dead.* A rising sun peeped over the rolling hills, streaking the sky in pinks and yellows. The horse moved steadily on. She sat stone-still, hardly breathing. *Why did God take you too?* She pressed her hands to her chest, holding the broken pieces of her heart together. *I need you.*

Doctor Morris patted her hand. "We're almost at my house."

Emma stared at the brightening sky and lifted a trembling chin. She climbed into the back and dug out dragonfly. Holding it tightly, she curled up in the blanket like a wounded snail. Over the crunch and creak of the wagon wheels, only the wind heard her sobs.

When they reached the doctor's thatched cottage, he drew the wagon into a side lane and stopped in front of a tool shed.

Emma slowly unwound herself and woodenly climbed down.

The doctor picked up his bag. "Come, child. Your things are safe here."

"I would like my bag, please."

He took out her small bag and handed it to her.

She tucked the dragonfly inside. "And my—the large one too."

He lifted that one out. "Can you carry both?"

She slid the strap over her head, and picked up hers. "I can manage." She followed the doctor up two stone steps to the door and trudged in, the heavy bag weighing her down. The house smelled of cinnamon and fresh bread baking. An archway on the right framed a large room where a fire blazed in the grate under an oak mantle. Two oversized stuffed chairs faced it, and a fat marmalade cat lay on a blue and yellow rag rug on the hearth.

A plump, smiling woman, her hair pulled back in a bun, came out of the kitchen on the left. She hugged the doctor and kissed him on the cheek, "Come in, luv."

The doctor stepped aside, and the cheery faced woman looked at Emma. "And who is this young' un?"

"This young lady is Emma Lewis." He put a hand on her shoulder.

The woman raised her eyebrows. "Are you all by yourself?"

The doctor shook his head ever so slightly. "She's on her way to London, where a good friend is waiting."

The doctor's wife put a soft arm around Emma. "Come in, my pet. I have some porridge and biscuits for you." She steered her to the fireplace room and pointed to a padded chair. "Sit there, my dear."

Emma let the bag slide from her shoulder and onto the floor. She dropped hers beside it and climbed into the big armchair. Her feet dangled over the edge and no sooner had she got settled when the orange cat leapt onto her lap. She stroked its warm fur, and within a minute, a low rumbling started.

The doctor's wife came in carrying a tray of two hot scones, slathered with melting butter, and a steaming bowl of porridge. "I see you've met Marmalade." She put the tray on a small table. "Eat up, and I'll bring you some warm milk."

Emma's mouth watered and her stomach gurgled in anticipation. She put a spoonful into her mouth. The sweetness tickled her tongue— sweeter than any porridge she had tasted. She took another bite and picked up a scone. So many raisins. She licked the butter off her fingers.

She looked around the room. Her uncle would like this house. Two shelves of books filled one wall, and an oak desk sat in the far corner with rolled-up papers stuffed into small compartments. Her Mama would love the long table with all those potted plants on it. The early morning sun sparkled through the window, dancing past green leaves and through a tangle of colours as it made its way across the room.

A bent-over man shuffled into the hall and passed by the doorway where Emma heard the doctor ask him to unhitch the horse and lock the wagon in the shed. Doctor Morris came in. "Your boxes will be safe there, my dear."

"Thank you." She looked at the wall of books, the dancing fire, and the purring cat. *Maybe I can stay here and wait for my Uncle.*

"You will stay, my dear, until we can find a reliable person travelling to London."

Emma slapped a hand over her mouth. *Did I say that out loud?* She looked up at the doctor. "I—I don't mind waiting."

The doctor's wife came in with a mug of warm milk. "Here you are, luv."

All morning, the doctor busied himself writing messages and reading a thick book, and after lunch, he left to visit sick people. Emma and the doctor's wife, Mrs. Morris, spent the day picking plums, washing and stewing them, and packing them into jars for the winter.

That evening they sat down to a feast of mutton, boiled potatoes and turnip. Emma ate her fill, and Mrs. Morris took her hand. "Come, my dear. You must be tired. I'll show you where you'll sleep."

Emma picked up her doll and bags and followed her to the back of the house. Mrs. Morris pushed aside a heavy curtain to reveal a small crowded room. A single cot lay squeezed in a corner beside a tall row of shelves packed with boxes and folded clothes. Framed paintings covered one wall all the way to the ceiling while coats and dresses hung on a line of pegs on the opposite wall. A pile of hats teetered on a high shelf.

She smiled. "It's a little crowded. It's become a storage room now but I cleaned off the bed for you."

Emma inched her way in and put her bag and doll at the foot of the bed.

Mrs. Morris hugged Emma. "Sleep tight, my dear." She backed out through the curtain, lifting it like a sail in full wind. As it settled back, wavering lines of light from the living room oil lamp peeked through the edges. Emma untied her bag and pulled out her nightdress. She changed into her nightclothes and, holding her doll in one hand and her dragonfly in the other, crawled under the covers. In that quiet room, with her heart crying for her Mama and Uncle Albert, she finally fell asleep.

The next morning, over a breakfast of toast and eggs, the doctor said he'd met a businessman at a patient's house. Mr. Johnstone, required transportation to his home in London and would be willing to accompany her. From there, he would take her to Mr. Edwards.

Emma put down her spoon. "Please, could I stay here?"

Mrs. Morris slid another piece of toast slathered with plum jam on Emma's plate. "We'd love to have you stay, luv, but Mr. Edwards will be waiting for you."

Emma nodded solemnly and finished her breakfast. All morning, she helped Mrs. Morris. They washed and dried dishes, watered potted plants, swept floors and made up her little cot. Near lunchtime, the doctor called her into the sitting room. A tall, bony man in a long black coat stood in the shadow of the doorway. He had a sharp chin and tiny teeth. Emma remembered seeing a rat that had teeth like that. She shivered.

The doctor gestured to his guest. "This is Mr. Johnstone who will take you to London."

Emma took the doctor's hand and leaned against him. "Maybe I could stay here a little longer?"

Chapter 22

The doctor and his wife walked Emma out and put her bags in the back of the wagon. He handed the child a letter with his waxed seal affixed. "I have written a note for you to give to Mr. Edwards."

"Thank you." *Maybe Uncle Albert didn't die. Maybe the doctor wrote   that he's sick and he'll soon be better.* She put it into her pocket, hugged the doctor and his wife goodbye, and climbed onto the wagon, sitting as far away from the black-coated man as she could. With a jerk, the wheels rolled forward. She clutched her doll and turned and waved until the two smiling faces became a blur.

Emma turned to the front and patted her pocket, where she had tucked the note and her dragonfly. She hugged her mother's jacket-shawl around herself. Her uncle's horse plodded on toward the main road, rocking Herr Weber's wagon side to side. *Does it know my Uncle Albert is not holding the reins?*

Mr. Johnstone snapped the reins. "Don't worry, child. I'm a good driver."

His oily voice slid over her and his mouth twisted. She shivered, and pulled her sweater/shawl closer around her. She glanced behind. Her parcel and her uncle's two boxes and his bag were alongside the man's black bag. The movement of the wagon had jiggled her against Mr. Johnstone's skinny pant leg, and she pushed herself over to the farthest edge. She closed her eyes and envisioned herself suspended in a bubble of light, the way her mother had taught her.

They stayed overnight at an inn. They could have made it to London, but Mr. Johnstone said he needed to rest. He told the man at the inn that he was her father, although Emma refused to address him as such. They ate in silence and retired to their quarters. An alcove at the far end of the room, held a cot where a tied-back curtain could be pulled across for privacy. She put her canvas bag on the bed and immediately undid the sash, letting the curtain fall. She poked her head around it. "May I get a drink of water?"

"Of course," came the greasy reply.

She went to a side table to a pitcher of water and two mugs.

Mr. Johnstone gave a little cough. "The good doctor told me you have some papers and books of your father's."

"Yes." She poured herself some water.

"What was his vocation?"

"He *is*—" The cup nearly slipped from her hand. "He was a writer."

"Pray, what did he write?"

She looked away from the squinting eyes. "I do not know. He never showed me. Something about the Bible, I think." The new King James' Bible was an acceptable topic of conversation, and she took a chance the nasty man was not a staunch Catholic.

"Was he a clergyman?" The man picked at a scab on the back of his hand

"No, he thought and wrote about the mysteries of life." She caught her breath. She shouldn't have said that much.

The man's thin eyebrows rose, and his sharp chin listed to one side. "Curious. Did he dabble in the dark arts?" He wrinkled a blotched forehead.

The last words her uncle had spoken to her were about his papers, and he would not like Mr. Johnstone knowing about them. "My father was a philosopher. He read many books, including the new Bible and met with scholars to discuss it. He was a Protestant."

"Of course." He stared at her, his hollow eyes willing her to say more.

Emma held his gaze for a long moment. "Good night, Mr. Johnstone." She picked up the mug, walked to the alcove and ducked behind the curtain, pulling it shut. She lay down in her day clothes and, holding her doll and dragonfly to her chest, whispered. "Don't cry, Molly. Maybe Uncle Albert is not really dead." She patted her doll. "Everything's going to be all right. Mama and the Angels are with us." She buried her face onto the wet pillow. "They will help."

Mr. Johnson slept in, and after a late breakfast, they resumed their journey. They arrived at the outskirts of London at mid-afternoon. Emma had been to München once, but she had never seen so many people and buildings in one place. Two-story houses, crammed against each other, pushed their neighbours into a threatening slant. High overhead, wooden sections stretching across narrow spaces, hung over a maze of alleys and tunnels below.

Their wagon twisted through the winding streets and Emma's ears prickled from people shouting, hooves hitting cobbles, wagons creaking, dogs barking, and children yelling. Her nose smarted from the pungent smells. A stream of slops rained past her shoulder, hit the side of the wagon and splashed onto the mucky ground. The horse plodded forward, and another shower missed them. She looked up to see a woman shaking the last drops from an under-the-bed pot. As they passed one rickety house, a string of curses burst out and a woman's shriek. A man's roar and a thump followed. Emma leaned away when a gush of brown liquid missed their wagon and landed on the shoes of a well-dressed man. He lifted his cane with a howl of protest and shook it at an upper window, which clanged shut. The wagon stopped, blocked in traffic and Emma gagged, covering her mouth and nose from the surrounding stench of human wastes. She clung to her doll with the other hand, glad she had stowed the dragonfly in her bag for safe-keeping. The horse moved forward through the foul smelling streets and Emma pinched her nose and took short breaths through her mouth.

Mr. Johnstone guided the horse through the narrow twisting streets as they gradually moved away from the odd-shaped wooden buildings. The street widened to where the houses were not so tall, but still wooden and some had thatched rooftops. Half-way along, he slowed in front of a row of houses, joined together side by side. At the last one, he turned off the main road and into an alley and a narrow lane behind the houses. He stopped the horse at the back of the third dwelling and pulled the wagon up.

"Come in, child. Tomorrow we'll find this Mr. Edwards."

Mr. Johnstone's house looked like him. Tall and sparse and squished in at the sides. She tucked her doll into her bag. "I need my uncle's bag. And his boxes."

He frowned but handed the large bag down. "Nathan will bring the boxes in."

She looped the larger bag over her shoulder. As she followed the skinny man along the weedy walkway to the back door, she encircled herself with a layer of white light as her mother had taught her.

When they reached the back stoop, Mr. Johnstone turned to her. "I live alone except for my manservant and an orphan boy. He helps with the garden."

Emma had not seen any gardens at the front of the houses and they passed none at the back.

They entered and Emma pulled her sweater around her. No fire had been laid in the living room or kitchen. Mr. Johnstone pointed to a hard chair for her to sit on and ordered Nathan, his manservant, to tend to a fire and bring the boxes in from the wagon. Nathan looked like a kindly grandfather that her mama had described in bedtime stories. He knelt down and set two sticks afire, but little heat or light reached into the cold room. He and the long, thin man left. Emma shivered. Mr. Johnstone's cheerless house matched its owner. The small hairs on the back of her neck stood up—a sign to be watchful, her mother had told her, and it confirmed her suspicion to not trust that man.

Nathan set the boxes down inside the door. "Are you all right, miss?" He lit a candle from the meagre fire, making tall shadows waver from the sides.

Emma sat on the straight-backed chair. She dropped the bags, took Molly out from the top of hers, and held it to her chest with shaking hands. "I'm fine."

Nathan set the candle in its holder on the mantle. "It's chilly in here. I'll get more kindling and a log." On his way out, he passed Mr. Johnstone coming in, who ordered him to bring bread and cheese.

Mr. Johnstone sat in a stuffed chair beside Emma in front of the struggling fire.

Nathan returned with a bundle of sticks and two pieces of split wood. He bent to the fireplace.

Mr. Johnstone frowned. "What are you doing?"

"Making a warm fire for the young one." He layered the sticks on top of the small flame and crisscrossed the logs on top.

"I never told you to do that."

"No sir." He picked up the bellows and the sticks soon caught.

Mr. Johnstone's thin lips turned even tighter into a rigid line. "Bring the food."

Nathan left, and flames licked over the first log and the second. The fire grew larger and brighter, chasing the shadows out of their corners and through the door.

Emma sat her doll in her lap. "Will the orphan boy be joining us?"

Mr. Johnstone scowled. "No. He's eaten already."

Nathan returned with a tray and set it on a low table in front of their chairs. He handed Emma a plate with a large chunk of cheese and a doorstep slice of dark bread. He turned and left.

The tall skinny man and the young girl sat by the growing fire and ate. As her stomach filled and her body warmed, Emma lowered her shoulders a bit.

After a slow and silent supper, Mr. Johnstone called Nathan in. "Show the child to the back room." He turned to Emma. "You are to stay there. Do not go wandering about."

No fear of that. "May I have my uncle's boxes with me?"

Mr. Johnstone's mouth twisted in a sneer. "Are you afraid I'll open them?"

She backed away from his fetid breath. "I promised I'd look after them."

He growled at Nathan to take the damn boxes to the room. She followed him and after he brought the second box in, she closed the door. It wouldn't lock, so she pushed the heavier box against it and took a deep breath. *Angels of protection, look after me tonight.* She opened her bag and checked its belongings. Her clothes, her own small purse with a few coins and her dragonfly had been untouched. Her uncle's bag was also as she'd left it when she had shoved everything back after looking for quill and paper. She knew about the hidden compartment where her uncle kept his money pouch, and she turned the bag over. On the bottom where the leather ties were, a small string dangled under a large knot. With a tug, she released a side pocket, slid her hand in and pulled out a small leather pouch. She patted it and pushed it back into its safe hiding place.

No friendly sounds came from the kitchen. No meowing, no conversation, just still and dark as if no one lived there. She took her dragonfly from her bag and placed it and her doll on the bed. "We'll be all right, Molly. Mama's angels are with us." She lay on top of the covers in her day clothes and patted her doll. "You don't have to be scared, Molly." *Mama, Uncle Albert. I wish you were here.* And for the third night in a row, she cried herself to sleep.

Chapter 23

In the middle of the night, she awoke with a start. Someone had pushed the box aside and now stood in the open door way. A dark figure—a little taller than she. Not the oily man. *It must be the orphan boy*. He stood rock-still and stared at her. The clouds drifted from the moon, and in the dim light, they looked into each other's eyes for several long minutes—his deep blue; hers, jade green. The clouds shifted and the night grew dark. She blinked into the blackness. The boy was gone.

The next morning, Nathan took the boxes and bags to the wagon. Emma followed, clutching her doll and the paper with Mr. Edward's address. Nathan lifted her onto the seat. "Have a good journey, Miss."

"Thank you, Nathan."

Mr. Johnstone hurried out and climbed up. The ride to the Westminster address of the solicitor that her uncle had written on top of the folded letter took a half hour.

They stopped in the middle of a row of two-story brick houses and went to the door with the designated number. A manservant showed them to the front room. Mr. Edwards—an old man, at least fifty, with a lined forehead as if he'd been thinking too much— greeted them.

Mr. Johnstone executed a small nod of his head. "I believe you know an Albert Lewis?"

"I do indeed. And who are you?"

Mr. Johnstone inclined his head and, in a sticky voice, said, "Only a messenger. I did not meet the man, but I bring his daughter to you as charged."

"His daughter?" Mr. Edwards stared at Emma. "I have been in contact with Mr. Lewis over the years and he never mentioned a daughter."

Mr. Johnstone gave a smirky twist of his mouth. "Ah, well, we know how that can be."

Emma liked Mr. Edwards right away. He had crinkles around his eyes and he wasn't even smiling. When Mr. Johnstone left, she would tell him that Albert Lewis was her uncle. Meanwhile, she kept her lips closed.

Mr. Edwards motioned to his man standing by the door. "Benson, bring in her things while we sort this out."

Benson left and Mr. Johnstone rubbed his palms against each other. His watery gaze went to Emma and the canvas bag she held. "A matter of our contract?"

At the doctor's house, they had agreed on the price. She took her small money purse out of her bag and counted the coins. "Thank you, Mr. Johnstone." She dropped them on his open palm without touching him.

He counted them, and with a slippery grin, walked toward the door.

Mr. Edwards looked at Emma and called to the departing man. "A moment, please. I need more information before you go."

Mr. Johnstone turned. A greasy strand of hair fell over his forehead and his lip curled. "That is all I know. She's your problem now." And he left.

Benson returned with Albert's leather bag. "I have unloaded everything from the wagon. Where shall I put it?"

"Leave it in the hallway for now. I will take the bag." He led Emma into the main room. "Why don't you sit here, my dear." He indicated a chair fitted with padding, covered in a navy fabric. "And we will sort this out." He put the bag down and sat in a matching chair beside her. "Now, my dear, tell me what this is all about."

Emma took a deep breath. "Albert Lewis is my uncle. My father died when I was little. My mother is Uncle Albert's twin sister, Anne."

"Anne! So you are Emma. I see that now."

Tears trickled out the corners of her eyes.

"Has something happened to them?"

Her mouth trembled as she handed him the crumpled letter. "My uncle wrote this for you." She blinked, but her tears fell anyway.

Mr. Edwards smoothed out the paper. "Let's see what he's written." He patted her hand. "I'm sure this will explain why he and your mother are not with you."

As he read, Emma sniffed and rubbed the side of her hand across her nose.

He finished, and with head bent, lowered the paper to his lap.

"Did he tell you my mama died of a terrible sickness?'

He put a hand to his head and didn't speak for several minutes. When he did, his voice cracked, and each word came out slowly. "I am so sorry—so dreadfully sorry."

Benson appeared. "Can I get you anything, sir?"

"Yes, Benson. Bring me a whisky—and milk for the child."

"Right away, sir." He left.

Mr. Edwards folded the letter and pressed it shut. His voice trembled and his hand became a tight fist. "Where is Albert now? Why is he not with you?"

Fresh tears bubbled in Emma's eyes. "He had a terrible fall." She reached into her pocket. "I have a letter from Dr. Morris for you." *Please let it say that Uncle Albert is only sick.* She pulled it out and handed it him.

Mr. Edwards ripped it open and read quickly. 'Domine mi, Puer mortuus est pater et febricitantem. Et sperent in te curam sui. reverenter, Morris Dr.' He dropped it on his lap, and Emma leaned over.

Her mother had taught her a few Latin words. *Mortuus means dead and pater means father.* "NO." She yanked the letter from his hand and ripped it into pieces. A searing pain cut through her chest and she crumpled.

Mr. Edwards caught her and held her tightly, soon losing his own battle with tears while the child wailed in his arms.

Chapter 24

Upstairs at the Dog and Bull Inn, Mrs. Burke covered the feverish man with another blanket. "Shivering one moment and sweating the next. God bless him, he's a fighter."

He opened his eyes and flung his head to one side and the other as if looking for someone. "Anne, where are you. Anne." His eyes darted wildly. "Emma. I'll look after you." He sat up, swayed and fell back. His cries turned to mumbles, mumbles to mutters, and mutters to gasps of shallow breathing.

She wiped his forehead with a damp cloth. "Rest, my lad. Only God and his holy angels can pull you through this." She went downstairs to make him a hot mint drink.

Simon rushed into the kitchen, carrying a bucket. He dropped it onto the floor, sloshing water over the sides. "Got some more leeches for you."

His younger brother John followed him in and snatched a fat one out of the bucket where it curled into a tight circle.

His mother slapped his hand, making him drop it into the water. "Leave that go. I need all of them. That poor man upstairs is dying of bad blood." She grabbed the bucket. "Off with you. I have work to do."

Simon picked up a sharp knife from the kitchen table. "I can help. I saw Dr. Stanley cut old Mrs. Sanderson's arm last year to let the bad blood out. That works faster than leeches."

"Get off with you. You're not a doctor. You could kill him. The leeches will be enough."

The boys ran out, pushing and shoving each other, and Mrs. Burke took the bucket of slugs upstairs. The man lay quiet, as close to death as she'd ever seen anyone. She peeled away the layers of blankets and one by one, placed the black greedy creatures onto his arms, legs, and chest.

The boneless, fat worms latched their strong, sucking jaws into his skin, each one sinking three hundred razor-sharp teeth, eager to do their part of cleansing his blood from the evil humours that had overtaken him.

Chapter 25

At Mr. Edwards' house, the housekeeper, Mrs. Thorpe, settled Emma into the spare room, making much of Molly and helping the child as best she could.

After three hours of sleep, she came downstairs, clasping her rag doll in one hand and a large dragonfly brooch in her other. She walked into the living room where a warm fire blazed in the grate.

Mr. Edwards looked up. "Come in, my dear."

She sat on the chair beside him. "Mama told me that when we die, we go and live with the angels."

"I hope she's right."

"Do you believe she is?"

"I'm not sure. But I'd like to."

Benson entered, and Mr. Edwards introduced Emma to him and, he to her. "I think a little something to eat is in order, Benson."

Benson went off and Emma hugged her doll. She put the dragonfly on the doll's lap. "I believe my Uncle Albert is with mama and her angels. Once he's settled, he'll talk to me." She touched the wing of the dragonfly. "I miss him terribly."

"I will miss him too, my child. He was a dear friend."

They sat in silence for a few moments, staring at the crackling fire. Mr. Edwards looked at Emma. "Your mother loved that dragonfly."

Emma looked up, eyes wide. "Did you know my mama?"

"Oh, yes. I remember when she and your uncle were born, and the birthday they received the dragonfly."

Benson entered with a tray and put it on the low table beside them. It held two cups of ale and two plates, each with a meat pie and two biscuits.

"Thank you, Benson. And do thank Mrs. Thorpe."

Between bites and swallows, Mr. Edwards told Emma many stories of her mother's and uncle's childhoods. Tears and laughter followed, as moment by moment, two bereft people got through the long evening.

Mrs. Thorpe tucked Emma in. Not a mother herself, she had seen her own mother tend to her younger brothers and sisters. "Sleep well. God bless and don't forget to say your prayers."

Emma lay in the dark, holding her doll and dragonfly. A spatter of moonlight splintered through the small panes of window, splashing dashes of light on her covers and scampering over the blankets like mischievous fairies. Her heart lifted, and she thanked them for coming but too soon they left, moving on to light up someone else's life. Even the moon hid and the dark room filled with emptiness. Emma pushed her face onto the pillow and cried herself to sleep.

The next morning, she had a serious talk with herself. She must be brave and learn how to live with two holes in her heart. Everyone had been so kind to her. Mr. Edwards had a lot of books, and Mrs. Thorpe and Benson were nice.

She dressed and went down for breakfast. Mr. Edwards sat at the table with a full plate in front of him. The sideboard offered platters of scrambled eggs, toast, biscuits, and slabs of pork.

He looked up. "Do you need any help, my dear?"

Emma put her doll on a chair. "No, I can do it." She filled her plate and sat at the table.

"I went through your uncle's box of books and papers. I'm glad you managed to bring it."

Emma frowned. "It? There should be two boxes."

"Benson said there was only one in the wagon."

Emma put her spoon down. "We had three boxes. One was lost in the ditch, that left two." She scowled. "We definitely packed two in the wagon. That horrible man stole one." She gasped. "And what about Herr Weber's wagon and my uncle's horse. He stole those too."

Mr. Edwards shook his head. "This is a serious affair. Albert's books and papers must not get into the wrong hands. Mr. Johnstone is obviously a scoundrel."

"What shall we do? How will we get Uncle Albert's books and his horse back?"

Mr. Edwards sighed. "I'm sure the horse and wagon are sold by now but the books are another matter."

Benson stood in the doorway and Mr. Edwards signalled to him. "Benson, have a look in the brass tray at the entrance."

A moment later, he returned. "Mr. Johnstone did not leave his calling card."

Emma hugged her doll. "What shall we do? I could never find my way through those twists and turns to his tall, squished house."

"Do not fret, my dear. I'll keep searching for the elusive Mr. Johnstone."

A week passed and Mr. Edwards had no further information about Mr. Johnstone. Meanwhile, he'd also been looking for a suitable placement for Emma.

That evening they sat at the dining room table while Mrs. Thorpe filled their bowls with hot stew. She added another spoonful to Emma's. "Eat up, child,"

Mr. Edwards picked up his spoon. "I think it would be good for you to live in a house with children and their mother and father."

"Can I not stay here?"

"Living with a crusty old bachelor is no place for a little girl."

"You're not crusty and I like it here."

"You need other children to play with and people who can be like a mother and father to you."

Emma picked Molly up from the chair. Tears filled her eyes. "My Uncle Albert was my father to me. He still would be if he hadn't—if he hadn't—." She lowered her head as tears fell.

Chapter 26

The leeches had somewhat helped the poor man, and Mrs. Burke continued to tend to him despite her husband telling her to leave him to die.

When she returned to the kitchen after seeing to Mr. Lewis, he yelled at her. "You're wasting your time."

"Stop your noise. I'm feeding you as well aren't I? And the boys." She plopped a fat ladle of pottage into his bowl.

He grumbled and picked up a spoon. "Where are the boys? They never miss a meal." He dug in.

"They'll be back soon. They've gone on another hunt for the poor man's missing box. The young lass left some money for the one who finds it."

He swallowed and looked up. "I found it."

"You found it? What do you mean?"

"I might have found it. The morning after they got here, I was working at McPherson's farm and I spied a wooden box stuck in the mud. I threw it in the cart and tossed it in the shed."

"Didn't you know the girl was frantic to find it?"

He took another spoonful and shook his head. "Nobody told me."

His wife slammed the pot on the stove. "You stupid man. The girl has left and her father is dying. How will we ever get it to her now?" She plunked down at the table. "And what about the boys? They've been looking for two weeks."

"Give them the money. They can split it."

"You don't know your boys." She got up and filled their bowls. "Here they come. You tell them."

Mr. Burke waited until after lunch, and after much yelling, punching, and hitting, the boys were satisfied with the coins handed to them. Fortunately, the amount divided evenly three ways.

Another week passed with the poor man upstairs thrashing about. That evening, the fever finally broke, and Mr. Lewis ate his first food in a long while.

He sat on the edge of the bed and took a sip of watery stew. "Where's Emma? How long have I been sick?"

Mrs. Burke placed a cup of hot mint water on the side table. "You're lucky to be here, lad. It's been almost three weeks and Emma's gone to London. She thinks you're dead."

"No," he cried, trying to stand up. "I must go to London." His legs wobble and he fell back.

Mrs. Burke stepped beside him. "You're not well yet. You have to rest before you're fit for travel."

He held his head in his hands.

Mrs. Burke patted his shoulder. "You're a lucky man. Thanks be to God and all his saints you're still with us."

Chapter 27

Three days after Mr. Edwards had put inquiries at his club, he announced to Emma. "I have found the perfect home for you not too far away. You will be living with Mr. and Mrs. Cameron and their two daughters."

She looked up from her book.

He continued. "The name of their house is Hollyhock."

"I like the name. But I don't need another home."

He patted her hand. "Hollyhock House is only an hour from here, so you can visit me often. I think you'll like living in the country with fresh air and playmates."

The next morning, Emma said goodbye to Mrs. Thorpe and climbed into the carriage beside Mr. Edwards. Her bag and her uncle's had been stowed behind them with the dragonfly and Molly safely packed in hers.

Neither spoke as they moved slowly through crowded streets to the outer boroughs of London. Soon hedge rows, fields and manor estates filled the English countryside.

Emma peered out the window. "Can I come and visit you?"

"Of course, my dear. I would like that." He patted her hand.

"Will you look after my uncle's box and keep looking for that horrible man who stole it."

"Absolutely. I will keep in touch with you and let you know the moment I find him."

In the next few minutes, the carriage slowed and pulled onto a curving lane lined with flowering bushes. The circle straightened out and the horse walked over cobblestones up to a rambling three-story house. Emma had never been that close to such a large house and never seen so many hollyhocks in one place. They covered the front stretching above the lower window sills on each side of a carved door.

In Germany, she'd decorate mud pies with hollyhock blossoms or make skirts for a family of stick people. "I wonder why they're called hollyhocks?"

"I thought you might ask. Last night, I looked it up in my horticultural book. Hollyhock plants were used to make a salve for the Crusaders' horses' hind legs or hocks when they were injured while travelling to the Holy Land."

"Books are so wonderful. What would we do without them?"

He drew the carriage to a stop, and helped her down. He hoped he'd chosen the right family for his best friend's niece. Mr. Dwight Cameron, a successful litigator, worked long hours in his London office. His wife Mildred kept busy handing out pamphlets for her latest protest or demand for social justice.

The door opened, and a girl stood at each side of a smiling butler. They wore long dresses that touched the ground, pinched in at the waist and topped with a white lace collar. Beatrice, eleven, and tall for her age, towered over seven-year-old Catherine. Mrs. Cameron came up behind them.

The taller one stepped forward and took Emma's arm. "I'm Beatrice. I'll show you your room." She pulled Emma into the house.

Catherine ran after them. "Wait for me."

Their mother wore a sensible grey linen dress with a small white collar. She put out her hand. "Mr. Edwards, do come in. My husband is in London but you're welcome to wait."

"I can't stay long, and I met Mr. Cameron at the club."

"Oh, yes. He told me. Where is my head? Sometimes there's so much in it that things fall out the side. I declare, facts and figures regularly tumble out of my ears."

They walked into a large sitting room where Mrs. Cameron gestured Mr. Edwards to a chair with a brocaded seat and thick carved legs. She sat opposite in an equally brocaded one. A small oak table, with matching carved legs, sat between them. Sunlight from tall windows and a white plastered ceiling brightened the room. Tapestries hung on two of the panelled walls while the other two held large framed portraits.

A young woman in her late twenties appeared in the archway entrance. She wore a long black dress, and her blonde hair secured by a thick coiled braid at the nape of her neck.

Mrs. Cameron motioned her in. "Francesca. This is Mr. Edwards. He's brought Emma to us."

The woman entered and bowed her head. "How do you do?"

He opened his mouth to speak but Mrs. Cameron chimed in. "Francesca is my third arm and second brain. She keeps everything running smoothly and will take good care of Emma when I'm in town." She frowned. "We must get that dreadful Cromwell man out of power. He will be the ruin of England." She looked up as if surprised to see someone standing there. "Francesca, have Twin bring us some pound cake and white wine—and milk for the girls."

"Yes. Ma'am." She walked briskly away.

The three girls bounced in with the Cameron sisters talking over each other and dragging a smiling Emma with them.

Francesca returned with a small tray of glasses of wine and milk. She put the tray down and Mrs. Cameron introduced her.

Emma looked up at the blonde woman. "Are you Italian?"

"Yes, I'm from Milan. Why do you ask?"

"You have an Italian name, but you are blonde."

"I am from Northern Italy where most people have light hair and blue eyes. Have you ever been to Italy?"

"No, but I love to read about many things."

Mrs. Cameron clapped her hands. "You will be a good influence on my girls. They'd rather play games all day."

A young girl of about eighteen, wearing a grey dress and a white apron, came in carrying a platter of cut-up pound cake.

Mrs. Cameron looked up. "Twin, this is Emma. She'll be staying with us."

Twin bobbed a curtsy and Emma asked, "Why are you called Twin?"

Beatrice laughed. "That's a good story. She and her sister help Mrs. Hudson in the kitchen. They're twins and look exactly alike and no one can tell them apart. Well, no one except mother and that's a mystery."

Catherine continued. "We got tired trying to figure out who was Twin Mary and who was Twin Marie, so we called them Twin One and Twin Two."

Beatrice completed the story. "But that was silly because we still didn't know One from Two, so now they're both just Twin."

Emma looked up at Twin. "Do you mind being called Twin like your sister?"

"I like it. We can be ourselves or each other and no one knows the difference." She winked at Mrs. Cameron. "Almost no one."

"My uncle and my mother are twins. But they don't—didn't look anything alike."

Mrs. Cameron slapped her hands together. "All right, everyone, eat up. Mrs. Hudson made her special pound cake for you."

Francesca and Twin left, and the girls sat politely, having their milk and cake. They managed to sit still for another five minutes until Beatrice begged for them to be excused.

Granted freedom, she jumped up. "Come. We'll show you the backyard." All three girls raced out.

Mr. Edwards watched the girls leave. "Thank you for taking Emma. She needs a family right now."

Mrs. Cameron waved a hand. "It's our pleasure. I called everyone for a special conference and the vote was one hundred percent and you saw from my girls, she's part of our family already." She patted his hand. "She'll be cared for and well-educated."

Mildred Cameron, determined her daughters should have as good an education as any boy, arranged for private tutors to come to the house five days a week. Not only would Emma have a mother, a father and two sisters, but her mornings would be filled with reading, sums, and Latin.

He stood to take his leave. "Do keep me informed of her progress, and if there is anything extra you need over her monthly stipend, let me know and I will gladly cover anything she might need." He tipped his hat.

They walked out and Mrs. Cameron called to Twin, who hovered in the background. "Mr. Edwards is leaving. Please find the girls as Emma will want to say goodbye."

They had reached the waiting carriage when three figures ducked through an arbour in the side garden. A flowering vine scrambled over it, and beyond that, a layer of fallen pink honeysuckle blossoms carpeted the ground.

Emma ran to Mr. Edwards. "Thank you." She buried her face in his waistcoat.

He patted her head. "I'll come to visit, and you are welcome to come back anytime and have some of Mrs. Thorpe's chicken soup." He climbed into the carriage and waved goodbye as two excited girls pulled Emma away to new adventures.

He sighed. He would miss the delightful child and her unanswerable questions. At least he could set up a trust fund from Albert and Anne Lewis's estates, and on her eighteenth birthday, she would receive a comfortable inheritance.

He returned to the house and Benson met him at the door with a letter marked Urgent. "This came soon after you left."

He recognized the handwriting and ripped it open. His knees buckled and he staggered to the hall chair. He didn't bother to hide the tears smearing the words written so recently by his dear friend Albert Lewis.

Chapter 28

Mr. Edwards, usually a calm and methodical man, sprang from the chair. "Benson, where are you?"

Benson, a few feet away, stepped up. "Right here, sir."

"Ah, yes. There you are. Benson, find a man right away with a fast horse who will take a letter to Sittingbourne."

"Yes sir, but the regular post could take it."

"No, no. That will be far too slow. Find a man while I write a letter."

"Yes sir."

Ten minutes later, Benson returned and Mr. Edwards handed him a sealed letter and a small purse of coins. "That will cover his journey to and fro. Tell the man to wait for a reply, and start back as soon as his horse is rested."

Benson left, and Mr. Edwards rushed along the hall. "Mrs. Thorpe, where are you? We need to fix up a room for Albert."

The next day, at mid-afternoon, Benson entered with the return mail.

Mr. Edwards ripped it open, pleased to find that Albert had given explicit directions to the Dog and Bull Inn, a few miles before the hamlet of Sittingbourne. He raced along the hall. "Benson, have my carriage brought around immediately."

In ten minutes, he scrambled in, holding the parcel of food Mrs. Thorpe had packed for the late journey home.

Thomas Edwards and Albert Lewis, although corresponding regularly, had not seen each other for seven years. When they met at the Inn, a handshake quickly moved into a hug and Mrs. Burke settled them in the dining room to enjoy her chicken stew.

The ease of personal conversation comforted them as they shared memories of Anne and current news of Emma. In two hours, they were ready for the journey home and horse and driver had had a good rest too. The Burke's boys tied Albert's wooden box securely to the back of the carriage.

Albert leaned back in the seat, still weak from his bout with poisoned blood. "I think we should wait before telling Emma I'm alive. She needs to have time to get used to her new home."

"When she hears the news, a team of horses couldn't hold her from rushing right back." He chuckled. "And living with two bachelors is no place for a child."

"Thank you for finding such a good home for her. With only an hour away, we can visit Hollyhock often."

"Of course, my boy. Together, we'll look after Anne's daughter in the best of ways as Anne would have wanted."

Several minutes passed. The horse's hooves continued their steady beat, marking off the miles to Westminster. The men resumed their conversation, catching up on lost years of friendship. They arrived in the early hours of the morning, tired but looking forward to the future

Albert settled comfortably into the Edwards household. He waited a week before he wrote his first letter to Emma, and chose his words carefully. It would be a shock for her, albeit a happy one, that he was alive. He assured her several times that he was all right. He just needed more rest and Mrs. Thorpe was taking good care of him and no need for her to rush over.

Chapter 29

The moment Emma received the post, she raced to Francesca in a flurry. "Where is Mother Cameron? I need to speak to her at once."

"Calm down, my dear. Mr. and Mrs. Cameron have left for the city."

Emma waved the letter in the air. "I need to leave. Right away. Get a carriage. I'll pack my bag." She ran upstairs, her feet falling over each other.

Beatrice raced after the disappearing Emma. "What's in that letter? Where are you going?"

Francesca followed the girls upstairs to the bedroom. "Stop, child. You cannot go. I have no authority. You must talk to Mrs. Cameron first."

Emma dropped the letter on the bed and grabbed her bag and tossed clothes into it. "I can't wait to speak to Mother Cameron. I have to leave now."

Beatrice stuck her arm out, but Emma ducked under and snatched her nightdress from under her pillow.

Catherine rushed into the bedroom. "What's going on? What's Emma doing?"

Beatrice pointed. "She's packing to leave us."

Emma stopped for a brief moment and looked up at the three questioning faces. "My uncle is alive. I must go to him."

Catherine took Emma's hand. "You can't leave. You're our sister now."

Beatrice picked up the letter, smoothed it out and read out loud. "I am fine, my dear. I just need a little more rest and I will see you as soon as I can." She sat on the bed and patted the comforter. "Come and sit. Mother will be home soon. Let's hear what she says."

Emma shook her head. "No. I have to go." Tears spilled out.

Francesca put an arm around her. "Your uncle is safe and wants to see you." She guided her to the bed. "You will see him soon."

Emma sat on the edge, clasping her half-packed bag to her chest.

Catherine plunked on the other side. "Please stay with us. We don't want you to leave."

Mrs. Cameron arrived home later than usual that night, having spent the day on her feet, handing out pamphlets. She held up a hand and assured the babble of voices that she would attend to their requests after her supper. She informed Francesca that Mr. Cameron had stayed in the city for an early morning appointment, so it would be dinner for one that night.

Emma popped her head around the dining room door every five minutes until Mrs. Cameron had finally finished. One or both Twins made two trips to remove the dishes, after which the girls rushed in, all talking at once. Mother Cameron put up her hand at the onslaught of words thrown at her. "Slowly, girls, slowly. One at a time."

Emma took the lead. "My uncle is alive. He's alive. I must go to him right away. I'm already packed." She ran out of the room.

Mrs. Cameron stood up. "Come with me, girls. We have some convincing to do."

It took many more words, hugs, and reassurances to persuade Emma that her uncle was well looked after, but he needed to rest a while longer. She reluctantly agreed to stay one more night at Hollyhock.

The next day, a repeat of the same arguments for and against immediate departure continued. Emma acquiesced to writing a letter, but only if Mr. or Mrs. Cameron would deliver it directly.

That evening, Emma waited at the window for Mrs. Cameron's carriage to arrive. The minute it turned in, she ran to meet it and hardly gave Mrs. Cameron a moment of peace until she held her uncle's return letter in her hand. It, too, reassured her he was well but needed rest and that he was pleased she had found new friends. She looked up. "He said he will come to see me as soon as he can."

Mrs. Cameron removed her cape. "That's splendid, my dear. Now let us eat."

A minute after supper, Emma sat down and wrote another letter. How was he really? How did he get to London? How was Mr. Edwards and Mrs. Thorpe? Did the boys at the inn find his missing box? Did he know that the nasty Mr. Johnstone had stolen one of them? She signed and folded the paper and tied it with a ribbon. She didn't have a seal like Mr. Cameron's or Mr. Edward's, but a ribbon would keep it closed nicely. Thankfully Mrs. Cameron didn't mind the stop at Westminster on her way to London as it gave her an opportunity to hand out more pamphlets.

Every day after that, Emma eagerly waited for Mrs. Cameron's return. On the days she didn't go into London, Mr. Cameron arranged to have the letter delivered to Albert and for the messenger to wait for a reply.

After two weeks of daily letters back and forth, with Emma asking in each one when she could come to Westminster, a trip was arranged. Emma kissed Mrs. Cameron and the girls goodbye, assuring them she would be back for a visit. She waved to Francesca and the Twins as she ran to the waiting carriage carrying her bag packed with all of her possessions.

She sat tall, riding with Mr. Cameron into London. As they passed through the crowded streets, she had forgotten the stinky smells and the constant noise. At least, the covered carriage protected them from a shower of slops and other disgusting messes thrown out of upper windows. People hollered, some even thumped on their carriage as the wheels splattered mud and muck on them. Emma held her nose and gagged on the overpowering stench.

The instant they reached the Edwards' house, she scrambled out and raced up the stairs. Mr. Cameron followed and after many handshakes and confirming it was the right house, he took his leave.

With happy tears, Emma clung to her uncle and for the rest of the day, trailed after him like a puppy, holding his hand or climbing onto his lap. Albert had settled in the spare room and Mrs. Thorpe set up a cot in it for her. "This should serve you for one night."

She put her bag on the small bed. "One night? I'm staying forever."

"Of course, my dear. And we're happy to have you."

At breakfast the next day, Albert told how Mrs. Burke had made him hot mint drinks and how Mr. Burke found the missing box. Emma told him about the Cameron household and all the things she and the girls did together. The conversation continued in the sitting room as Emma chattered on about how nice Francesca was, and the look-exactly-alike Twins, and that Mrs. Hudson was a good cook.

He smiled. "You must miss them."

The next day and the day after that, Mr. Edwards had business in town and Albert had his books and writing to attend to. Mrs. Thorpe, busy making meals and taking care of the house, happily accepted a helping hand. Emma folded linen, watered plants, and cleaned a silver candle holder that held three candles. Her uncle also gave her his shirt full of crystals to unpack, and she spent the whole afternoon lining them up on a sunny shelf she had cleaned off for them.

On the fourth day, she knocked on the study door. Her uncle was always glad to see her, but he didn't like to be interrupted when he was deep into his thinking and writing. She knocked lightly again and opened the door a crack. His head was bent over the desk, a quill in his hand. She opened the door a little wider. "Uncle Albert," she whispered.

Except for his hand making a soft scratching noise, he didn't move. She stepped back and closed the door quietly. She could talk to him at mealtime.

Mr. Edwards, Albert, and Emma gathered for the late evening meal. Emma liked this time together, but by nine o'clock, she couldn't hold back the yawns. She'd been busy all day: banging the dust out of two carpets, mending socks the way Mrs. Thorpe showed her and cutting up a turnip for the stew.

As was their custom after the meal, they would take turns sharing the best thing they had done that day. Mr. Edwards had won a difficult case, and Albert had successfully found some much-needed information from one of his reference books. "What about you, Emma?"

She glanced at her uncle. "Well, I—"Her face brightened. "I learned how to mend socks."

"And did you enjoy that?"

She made a face. "Not really."

He lifted an eyebrow. "Would you like to visit the Cameron's for a while? You could go this weekend."

"Oh, yes. I would. They'll be missing me."

"Indeed, they will."

"But can you manage without me?"

Mr. Edwards put down his teacup. "We'll be fine. Don't you worry. Mrs. Thorpe takes good care of us."

"Can I come and visit you?"

Her uncle reached across the table and took her hand. "Of course, my dear. The same way you used to in Germany."

A cloud passed over her face, and she looked at her plate for a long time.

He squeezed her hand. "What is it, my dear?"

Fat tears fell from Emma's eyes, and she stared past her uncle into the distance. "I'm starting to forget what mama looked like."

He cleared his throat. "After supper, would you like me to tell you stories about when your mama and I were young and more about our adventures with the dragonfly?"

She gulped. "Yes, please."

"And you can visit your mama in dream time."

The next day, Emma and Albert settled into the carriage for their journey to the Cameron's. They agreed she would have regular visits to London, and Albert would visit Hollyhock as often as he could.

Chapter 30

At first, Emma asked about her Uncle Albert often and would write to him every day. As she grew more comfortable, she became less anxious. The letters dropped to twice a week and her visit once a month. He would get to Hollyhock as often as he could which averaged every six weeks.

She blended well in the Cameron household and grew healthy and happy living in the twelve-roomed house with a backyard that would easily fit three of Mr. Johnstone's squished-up house. Mother Cameron introduced her to the helpers who lived on the third floor. "We all serve in our own way, and we're happy to have helpers in our daily life."

Emma liked Francesca's husband, Giovanni Tonini, who helped Mr. Cameron. He always had Mr. Cameron's business clothes clean and ready for him every morning. As soon as the carriage left, Signore Tonini would change into work britches and a long shirt and help around the house. He'd let Emma help with polishing silver or straightening a tapestry that had slipped crooked. He had a yelly voice and at first she thought he was angry, but soon learned that was his natural way of talking. She liked to visit him in his carpentry shed attached to the stable and watch him repair a window sash or a picture frame.

That spring, he made her a whistle out of a willow branch with a small pen knife that Mr. Cameron had discarded when he'd bought a new one for sharpening his quill pens.

Every evening at ten minutes to six, Signore Tonini would change into his butler clothes and lay out Mr. Cameron's evening clothes. He and Signora Tonini—Francesca—lived in the west wing of the third floor with their own bathroom and a spiral staircase that wound all the way down to the kitchen.

Emma enjoyed getting to know everyone who lived in the house and always had stories to tell her uncle. She'd made good friends with Twin One and Twin Two and, like the others, ended up calling them simply Twin.

Mrs. Hudson, from Liverpool, made wonderful pies and Emma would help make the apple pie for her Uncle's visit. Mr. and Mrs. Hudson lived on the other side of the third floor. Their two grown-up boys had gone off for adventures in the New World far across the sea and Mr. Hudson spent most of his day in the livery stable.

He wore a special costume when he drove Mr. Cameron to work every morning and when he took the family to church but in the stable he wore work clothes when keeping the carriage oiled, and tending to his two horses, Irish and Mac. On fine days or special outings, he used the open carriage but Mr. Cameron preferred the closed one for his daily trips to London and back.

Emma loved learning and along with her regular tutoring, her uncle and Mrs. Cameron kept her well stocked with books. On every visit, he brought her a new one.

After morning lessons, the girls would race outdoors to play hoops, tag, or hide-and-seek. Beatrice and Catherine would groan when the Master tutor called them back, but Emma ran eagerly to her desk. Many an early summer evening, Mr. Cameron would find her reading under the apple tree while his daughters played with their dolls or spinning tops.

One evening at dinner, he announced to his wife. "I think Emma is reading too much. It's not good for her eyes." He buttered his bread. "After all, she only needs enough education to be a competent wife."

Mrs. Cameron slammed her spoon down, making her fork bounce. "My girls, and that includes Emma, will be fully educated." Her voice rose a notch higher. "There is no reason why women cannot be lawyers, doctors, or manage businesses as well—if not better—than men." She finished with a glower.

The Cameron girls paid no attention. They were used to their mother's outbursts but Emma smiled. *Mama would have liked Mrs. C.*

That night Emma had a dream about sitting on her mother's knee listening to her read the story of Ulysses and his adventures on finding his way home.

The next morning, Emma took out her dragonfly and stroked its back. "Thank you for bringing Uncle Albert back."

The years passed quickly with Mrs. Cameron busier than ever now that Cromwell had been declared the Lord Protector of England. She relentlessly protested against Old Ironsides and worked tirelessly to have Charles II take the throne. Further incensed when Cromwell prohibited Anglican services, she declared for all to hear, "How dare that dreadful man tell people how they can worship."

Emma, now a gangly eleven-year-old, would listen wide-eyed to the dinner time discussions.

Mr. Cameron would shake his head. "We need a strong Parliament. No King should be above the law and go about chopping off heads. That is too much power for one person. Even women fall under its lure. Look at Elizabeth—a queen who killed a queen."

After dinner, Emma would race to her history books and read how Queen Elizabeth signed the order for her cousin, Mary Queen of Scots, to be executed. *She must have been very angry.*

Beatrice and Catherine would groan when Emma came up to them book in hand, to read them a passage. More interested in boys, they chattered incessantly about them. At church, when Beatrice, now fourteen, would eye one she fancied, she would flutter her eyelids or giggle and act silly.

One Sunday afternoon, a boy with chipmunk cheeks and bulging eyes grabbed Emma in the hallway and leaned in for a kiss. She jerked her face away from his stinky breath and pushed him as hard as she could. He fell on his fat behind and laughed. He didn't even apologize for his outrageous behaviour.

That night as usual, Emma sat in her chair reading. Beatrice sat on the side of her bed, brushing her hair. Emma put her book down and watched Beatrice for a few minutes. "Why are you doing that?"

Beatrice kept sweeping the brush over her long hair. "Thirty-five. To make my hair pretty. Thirty-six. Boys like pretty hair."

Emma grimaced. "I don't like boys. They're stupid."

Beatrice grinned. "Thirty-nine—not all of them."

Emma grunted and opened her book.

"Forty-one. You wait and see. Forty-two, forty-three...."

Emma continued turning pages while Beatrice brushed all her way to a hundred.

Chapter 31

Years galloped by. On Emma's thirteenth birthday, Mrs. Cameron gave her a copy of *The Ingenious Gentleman Don Quixote of La Mancha.* She sighed. "I wish my two girls were as studious as you."

Sixteen-year-old Beatrice snorted. "Books are not gifts. I prefer a new frock or a necklace."

Emma, however, loved her books and spent hours pouring through them. Even Catherine, twelve, was bored with her constant yearning for more knowledge. "It's unnatural for a girl to want so much book learning."

But Emma continued reading. The stack of books on her dresser grew higher beside her old rag doll with its stuffing poking out from under its faded cotton dress.

She looked forward to her once a month weekend visit with her uncle. He didn't treat her like a child, and always asked her about the latest book she was reading.

One weekend he gave her Bishop Godwin's utopian tale, *The Man in the Moone.* They read it together, enjoying the part when its character, Gonsales, flies to the moon harnessed to wild swans.

She looked up from the book. "Do you think people will ever fly to the moon someday?"

"I like to think that anything is possible, but that seems beyond the realm of human endeavours." He put down his pipe, a new habit he'd recently acquired. "But, it's intriguing to imagine such a feat."

"At least he chose something that could fly."

"I wonder why he didn't choose birds that could fly higher? An eagle, for example?"

She laughed. "Now that's really make-believe to think an eagle could ever land on the moon."

At Hollyhock one afternoon, she had settled herself under a shade tree with Dante's *The Divine Comedy,* deep into it. Ralph Sanders, that annoying friend of Beatrice's, came into the yard and knelt on the grass beside her. She closed her book, stared into the distance and waited for him to leave. But he leaned over and put his hand on the front of her dress, an action neither divine nor comedy. She whacked him on the side of the head with the book and he yowled and stumbled off. A movement of the curtains in an upstairs window caught Emma's eye. The gauzy material fell back into place as Beatrice's face slid from view. *Did she tell him to do that?*

She closed her book, ran inside and bounded upstairs, eyes flashing. "Did you tell that horrible boy to touch me?"

Beatrice laughed. "Don't be so serious. Boys like to do all sorts of things to girls. And girls like it." She stuck out her tongue. "You may even get to like it."

Emma glared. "Boys are gross. I don't know what you see in them."

"You will one day." She winked.

"I don't know what all the fuss is about." She slammed the door, stomped downstairs and back to her tree and book. She had reached Dante's second circle of Hell, where lustful souls—without hope of rest—were eternally blown about by a violent storm. She shuddered. *I will not be tossed around by such desires. I will live a life of meaning and purpose.*

Although the Cameron house had plenty of rooms for the family and live-in helpers, the girls liked to share one large bedroom. Before Emma arrived, the two sisters slept in one bed but when a smaller bed had been brought in for her, Beatrice—pulling rank—commandeered it. Beatrice had also taken ownership of the new mirrored dresser where she would sit to do her nightly hundred times brushing task.

One evening, Emma looked up from her book and watched the monotonous movements for several minutes. "How can you do that for so long?"

She continued her rhythmic brushing. "I was wondering the same thing about you. How can you bear to read so much?"

Weeks passed, with Emma adding more books to her pile, especially after seeing her uncle. On her next weekend visit, after hanging up her cape, her uncle rushed to her. "Come and see what I have for you." He led her into the sitting room.

On the table lay a small book. She picked it up. *Utopia.* She sat down in the reading chair. "That's a short title."

He sat beside her. "The original title was much longer. *Libellus vere aureus, nec minus salutaris quam festivus, de optimo rei publicae statu deque nova insula Utopia.*"

Her eyes grew wide.

"Which translates to: 'A truly golden little, no less beneficial than entertaining, of a republic's best state and of the new island Utopia.'"

"Oh, my goodness. How would that even fit on the cover? And I hope it's in English. I read Latin more slowly."

"Yes. Newly published in English. I think you'll like it. It's a work of fiction by Thomas More about an imaginary island society who enjoys the utmost perfection in legal, social, and political systems."

She smoothed her hand over the leather cover and the gold tooling on the spine. "What does Utopia mean?"

"It's a new word coined by More to mean an imagined place in which everything is perfect."

"Mother Cameron would like that. She constantly works for a better society."

"More's descriptions are reminiscent of life in a monastery. Do you think a monastery or a convent is the only place where a perfect society could exist?"

"It would be easier with people whose beliefs are the same but I imagine they have arguments and conflicts as well." She tilted her head. "Do you think anyone will ever write about an imperfect society? They could call it un-topia or no-topia." Her face lit up. "I just made up a new word."

"You did. Topia is the Greek root word for place, so another name might be evil-topia or bad-topia. Or if we stay with Greek, you could call it dys-topia.

She laughed. "Who would ever want to write a whole book about a dystopia? And who would read it?"

He picked up his pipe, she opened her new book, and they settled into that warm and familiar place of each other's company.

Chapter 32

One evening, after Beatrice finished counting her hundred strokes, she put her brush down. "I have an idea."

Catherine pulled her nightdress down over her head and Emma, sitting in her reading chair beside the bed, looked up from her book. She'd been snatching a last few minutes to finish a chapter before extinguishing the lamp.

Beatrice continued. "Emma and I are the eldest, so we should share a bed. That way, we can talk about grown-up things."

Emma lifted her eyebrows. *Whatever would Beatrice and I want to talk about?*

Catherine finished yanking her nightdress down. "That's a jolly idea." She ran to Beatrice's bed, jumped in and pulled the blankets up to her chin.

Emma shrugged. She had been sharing a bed since she moved in, and it didn't make any difference to her which sister she slept with.

Over the next two weeks of their new sleeping arrangement, Beatrice did not offer any topics to discuss. Their interests were so divergent that Emma wondered what grown-up things Beatrice had planned to talk about.

One night a slim crescent moon heralded a new month. Emma blew out the lamp and sat in her chair for a stolen moment. She thought about her mother often: whenever she started a new book, always on her visits to her uncle, and sometimes for no reason at all.

That night, looking out the bedroom window at the sliver so bright in the sky, she remembered her mother telling her how a new moon meant new beginnings.

She closed the curtains, touched her dragonfly goodnight and crawled into bed.

All three girls were sound asleep when Emma awoke, startled. Beatrice had rolled against her with some force and had flung an arm across Emma's stomach. Emma lifted the arm, gave it back to its owner and closed her eyes. *She must have been having a nightmare.* A moment passed, and Beatrice's hand swung back on Emma—this time landing on her breast. Emma moved the roving hand away and turned over to face the outside edge of the bed. *She must be having a wild dream to fling about so.* The next morning, Emma didn't mention it, and Beatrice said nothing about dreaming.

Two nights later, it happened again. Emma moved Beatrice's hand away from her stomach twice, but when it returned the third time, she let it stay. It slowly moved up to her breast. Emma breathed in sharply. She should move it away, but this wasn't like when Ralph Sanders had touched her, or that smelly boy had tried to kiss her. That was gross, but this—this was different. Beatrice's hand moved gently over Emma's breast, and she gasped at the new and pleasant sensations that rippled through her body.

The next morning, Emma didn't breathe a word to Beatrice but she read a little less for the next few nights and retired to bed earlier. Three nights later, after several hours of sleep, she awakened with Beatrice's hand on her breast again. Her body, refusing to lie still, wriggled all on its own. The hand slid down her body, lingered on her stomach and continued its downward journey over the top of her thin cotton nightie. She held her breath. Another inch and—

A crash rang out, followed by a cry of pain. "Oww!" Catherine yelled. "Who put that trunk there?"

Emma jumped, and Beatrice's hand flew away.

"Are you all right?" Emma croaked.

"I banged my toe on the trunk. I forgot we'd moved it." She limped out of the room to the bathroom.

Emma's legs trembled. Beatrice had rolled to the far side and lay still. *What if she had woken up?* She took many deep breaths and finally fell asleep.

The next morning, neither girl remarked about any nighttime happenings.

Many times after church, Emma had seen Beatrice sneak off with boys and come back all flushed and silly. Beatrice would swear her to secrecy when she told her about letting boys touch her breasts and between her legs. "It feels so good."

That must be what Beatrice was dreaming about when she accidentally touched her in the night.

A week later, around three a.m., Emma woke up to a familiar hand fondling her breast. She had taken to wearing the nightgown that buttoned up the front, and that night she had left the top three buttons undone. Beatrice's hand roamed over the material until fingers slid into the opening onto bare skin. Emma's body tingled and she undid the rest of her buttons, opening her nightgown all the way. She pulled the material aside, and Beatrice's dreaming hand slid to Emma's bare stomach. It lingered there, light fingertips tracing circles. She held her breath and the hand drifted lower. She lifted her body, moving in rhythm while praying no one would wake up, especially Beatrice who would be astonished at what she was doing in her sleep. She pushed her fist into her mouth to stop herself from crying aloud and Beatrice's hand moved away.

Catching her breath, she fastened her buttons up to her neck and rolled onto her side at the far edge of the bed. It took a long time for her to fall asleep.

After moving to Hollyhock, Emma had been attending church every Sunday, and although she discussed many issues with her uncle, the topic of sex never arose. Mother Cameron followed the church's dictates that sexual love should only be expressed within the sanctity of marriage and not during Advent, Easter week, Lent, or feast days.

Emma wondered if God watched everybody in bed all the time. *Surely He had more important things to do? Like stopping wars and terrible sicknesses.* But she fell asleep before getting any answers.

Over the next few weeks, she looked forward to bedtime, but Beatrice had not had a dream for a while, so she took Beatrice's hand and placed it on her bare skin. After that, Beatrice seemed to have a dream every other night. One morning at breakfast after a delightful night encounter, Emma casually asked Beatrice how she'd slept.

"Fine. Why do you ask?"

"Oh, no reason. I wondered if you had any dreams last night?"

Beatrice looked off into the distance and put a finger to her chin. "Now, I remember. I had this delicious dream about Ralph. I dare not say what he was doing to me." She grinned. "I'll only say that I liked it."

Beatrice's sex dreams continued and Emma never minded being the recipient of their outer expressions. One night Beatrice rolled over, landing with her face close to Emma's. So close that in the next instant, she was kissing her on the lips and whispering, "Ralph, oh Ralph. Kiss me again." She kissed her once more and rolled away, leaving Emma pulsating with a new and delicious awareness.

She lay panting. *Should I feel guilty, letting her do those things in her sleep? Will God banish me to the second circle of Hell?* It was like sleepwalking really, only sleep-touching and kissing. Emma kept her nighttime secret to herself. She didn't even whisper it to her dragonfly when she tapped its wing goodnight.

On the evening of Beatrice's birthday, Ralph Sanders cornered Emma in the upstairs hallway. "You'll like this. Beatrice does." And he grabbed her between the legs.

Emma happened to be carrying a hefty book at that moment, and she swung it mightily on the top of Ralph Sander's head.

"Yowl." He staggered backwards.

Mrs. Cameron called out. "Is everything all right up there?"

"Oh, yes, Mother Cameron. Ralph just hit his funny bone." She walked downstairs, fuming. *How can Beatrice stand to have him touch her so roughly?*

The next Sunday, Reverend Powell preached a rousing sermon from the book of Genesis about how women were tainted by Eve's original sin. His bushy eyebrows made a fuzzy caterpillar over his blazing eyes as he pointed a shaking finger that seemed aimed right at her. His voice rose. "In order to curb women's insatiable desire, sex is strictly confined to marriage. And only for the purpose of reproduction." His finger waggled. "And every female, of any age, must guard against allowing any pleasure to take her over."

Emma shrank back in her seat. *Had God told on her?*

Beatrice's dreams continued as well as Emma's enjoyment of them, and Emma concluded that God might have changed his mind since writing Genesis. Something that good couldn't be bad. *How did God write anyway?* She must ask her uncle about that. It could be that the man or woman who wrote down God's words might have misheard them.

That Christmas, Beatrice announced her engagement to Ralph, which meant she would be leaving the house. Not just the house but her bed.

The day after Christmas, Emma asked Beatrice if she was concerned about her wedding night.

"What do you mean?"

"You know. When he puts—" she stopped.

"You mean when he puts his penis into me." She laughed. "He's already done it more than once, and it's most agreeable."

Emma grimaced. "It sounds gross. Why would anyone want rough hands touching you or have any part of some silly boy stuck in you?

Beatrice laughed. "Just you wait."

Chapter 33

Beatrice had a grand wedding and no doubt a grand wedding night while Emma tossed and turned in the bed by herself. Emma had grown into a beautiful young woman, and many young men showed an interest in her. However, she ignored them and with Beatrice gone, she returned with renewed vigour to her books. She had worked her way through *Dante's Purgatory and Paradiso,* and about his Beatrice, his all-abiding love, and how she guided him through Heaven. As she continued to read about his journey with his love, she longed for her own Beatrice and secret stolen nights of paradise.

The only education available for girls was needlework, a little music and social dancing. Classical languages and philosophy were thought to be unnecessary and harmful to a woman's weaker mind and to her marriage prospects. Although Mother Cameron supported the church's views about sex, she opposed the general belief that a woman's social life, as well as her morality, could be endangered by too much learning.

"Nonsense!" She would shout and inform anyone listening. "My girls will be educated."

Emma looked forward to the tutor's daily visit while Catherine moaned. "I hate conjugating Latin verbs. Boys don't care if I can do that?"

She also enjoyed her visits with her uncle and Mr. Edwards, where she would be assured to have an intelligent discussion. Sometimes she would only listen to their impassioned debates. Mr. Edwards would take the side that knowledge could be gained by the power of reason alone as espoused by Descartes, while her uncle would counter that all knowledge had to come through the experience of the physical senses, and he'd back it up by quoting Francis Bacon and Thomas Hobbes. But on her next visit, they would have changed sides and argue just as vehemently.

Even when she didn't fully understand their conversations, her Uncle Albert never told her how or what she should think. When she questioned if something was right or not, he'd say, "Think about it and decide for yourself."

On her very next visit she and her uncle had finished lunch and were on their last cup of tea. Mrs. Thorpe had already removed the other dishes and Emma brought up the subject of truth.

Albert put his cup down. "That is indeed a complex issue. One could simply say 'truth is what is in accordance with fact or reality'. But new facts arise and what is reality?"

"I hate it when you answer my question with another."

He laughed. "An appropriate question at the right time may well be the greatest gift. Remember, my dear, truths can change or move around like a sled on a slippery hillside. If you believe in your heart and from experience that something is true, then for you it is. Even if a hundred, nay a thousand scholars say the opposite.

"You sound like Don Quixote. He believed windmills were giants and an inn was a castle. That got him into a lot of trouble."

"Ah, one of my favourite books. There is more than humour to be gleaned from Don Quixote and his marvellous adventures. He went against what the physical world was showing him."

"What do you mean?"

"Don Quixote believed what he chose to and saw the world differently from the rest of society. He was brave enough to live according to his convictions."

"That would take courage."

"Indeed. It takes a strong person to do that. Perhaps he wasn't crazy at all. Perhaps he was a very wise man."

Emma wrinkled her brow. "You make me think, uncle, but sometimes my brain gets tangled up." She grinned. "But I like that."

"You look as if you have another question."

She took a breath. "Do you believe in magic?"

"That depends on what you mean by magic."

"Things you don't understand but somehow know."

"Give me an example."

"You'll think I'm daft."

"Try me."

"Sometimes, I think my dragonfly hears me and I hear it."

"There's much about the mind and consciousness we don't understand. I think it will be a long time before man discovers all the secrets—"

Emma frowned. "A woman could well discover some of them."

"Wha—oh, Emma. You know that man includes woman."

"I know it but I don't like it. Why does our language use one word to include the opposite? It doesn't make sense."

Albert opened his mouth to speak but she wasn't finished. "How would men like it if the word 'women' was used to include men?"

"Calm down. Language changes slowly as culture changes. You were born too soon." He pushed his chair back. "Let's continue on softer chairs."

In the sitting room, Mrs. Thorpe had just added another log to the fire. She brushed off her hands. "Land sakes, I've never heard two people talk so much. Would you like another pot of tea?"

Albert sat in his comfy chair in front of the fire. "That's a fine idea, Mrs. Thorpe. Thank you."

She left, and Emma sat in the chair beside him. On the third chair beside hers where Mr. Edwards usually sat, was a large black and white cat. She stroked its head. "When did you get a cat?"

"We didn't. It got us. It strolled in a couple of weeks ago, liked Mrs. Thorpe's scraps and never left. We put notices around, but no one claimed it, so there it is."

"What do you call him or her?"

"Black and White, and she's a she."

"Not a very original name."

"We thought it was perfect. She reminds us to consider both sides of an issue."

Emma patted it again. "She's a smart one, finding this house. Warm fire, good food, soft chair, and the unending rumble of words."

He laughed. "What were we talking about before you jumped onto your high horse?"

"Magic. Or things we don't understand. Like hearing voices in your head."

"Hmmm. Some would call that crazy. You know your mother and I received mental messages from each other."

"Yes but what about messages from an inanimate object like a pewter dragonfly."

Mrs. Thorpe came in with a tea tray. "You didn't have a sweet earlier, so I brought you some of my freshly baked lemon tarts."

Each warm bite made their hearts smile. Emma licked her fingertips. "Mrs. Thorpe should supply a wet napkin with these."

"Indeed." He took his handkerchief, wiped his chin and poured the tea. "So, you're talking to your dragonfly and it talks back."

"Are you teasing me?"

"Not at all. In fact, on the contrary." He added the milk. "I talk to many things—my pipe when I can't find it, and to a passage in a book and now to the cat."

She stirred her tea. "And do they answer?"

"I find my pipe quickly after I ask it where it is, and I appreciate or understand a meaning in my book better. And the cat? The cat definitely answers. I get a purr, a meow, a twitch of a tail, and sometimes a most curious look." He took a sip of tea. "I don't think it matters where the answer comes from—your own consciousness, another consciousness, or your imagination. It's still communication, and that's what's important."

"Thanks, Uncle Albert. I'm going to keep on talking to my dragonfly—and listening. It brings me great comfort."

Chapter 34

The next Sunday, Reverend Powell came to dinner at Hollyhock. He said the blessing and the first course had been served when Mrs. Cameron opened the conversation. "Kind sir, what do you think of the education of women?"

The intrepid clergyman did not hesitate. "Women do not much desire knowledge, having a soft and fickle nature. They have not the mind to be bookish. After all, the end of learning is to fit one for public employment, of which women are not capable."

Emma had placed a brimming spoonful of soup into her mouth and couldn't stop the ensuing splutter which stopped short of the good man's vest. She mopped up and Mrs. Cameron, with exaggerated slowness, set her spoon down.

She straightened her back. "Being a man of God, you undoubtedly know that Deborah, the Deliverer of Israel, was a learned woman who understood the Law."

The clergyman stared as Mrs. Cameron continued her litany. "In Chronicles 34, Chapters 20 and 21, King Josiah sent his priest to consult with Huldah, the Prophetess, who dwelt in a college." She emphasized the last word. Before the poor man could respond, she cited Minerva's Greek references and the nine muses. "The Sibyls could never have invented the Heroic, nor Sappho, the Sapphick Verses if they had been illiterate."

The befuddled man blinked and his furry eyebrows scuttled up his forehead. Had he any idea what Mrs. Cameron was raving about? Her torrent probably added credence to his belief that women should not be educated.

The rest of the meal finished with stretches of silence, mixed with polite words about the weather or the recent cost of lamb.

In October, Mildred's widowed sister, Millicent, took ill, and Mrs. Cameron rushed to her sibling's bedside in the country. It would be a good opportunity for the girls to receive practical experience of tending the sick, so she planned to take Catherine and Emma with her for an extended visit. Millicent lived in Woolsthorpe-by-Colsterworth, a small village in Lincolnshire County, nearly a hundred miles north of Hollyhock. Emma wrote to her uncle about her forthcoming adventure and packed her dragonfly but left Molly behind on her dresser. At fifteen, she was far too old for dolls.

They travelled all day by public coach and stayed overnight at an inn. Late the next afternoon, they arrived at the small farmstead on the outskirts of town, grateful to stretch their legs and let their thoroughly jiggled bodies calm down.

John, Millicent's seventeen-year-old son, greeted them and dutifully carried their luggage into the house. Catherine, now fourteen, acted like a silly ninny, giggling at his every word, and when he looked away, she'd pinch her cheeks giving them a rosy glow.

Emma glared. It should be the boys pinching themselves. Didn't nature make it clear it was the male's job to do the attracting? Just look at the peacock strutting its tail. *How did the human species get so turned around?*

Mother Cameron strode ahead. "Come along, Emma. Don't dawdle."

Emma followed behind John and a fluttering Catherine into the house. The thatched cottage had two levels, with pine furnishings rather than oak, and braided rag rugs covered the wooden plank floor. Lace curtains and crocheted doilies added to its warm invitation.

Auntie Millicent's firstborn son had emigrated to the new world, leaving John to help out. He spent more time drinking with his mates at the local inn than he did around the farm.

Emma sighed. *I hope I brought enough books.* She followed Mother Cameron and Catherine upstairs to the shared bedroom and unpacked her clothes. At least her tutor didn't treat her like an empty-headed female, as so many other men did. Thank goodness she had her uncle and Mr. Edwards, who were not only gentlemen but intelligent and knowledgeable men. *I'm going to miss our talks.* She placed her books on a designated shelf and her dragonfly on the bedside table.

Leaving Catherine shaking out her frilly frocks, Emma went outside to explore. In the back yard, unrestrained mint had scrambled all the way to a tall patch of Stinging Nettles, which would be collected for nettle soup or tea. Moss-covered flat stones offered clues of an ancient path leading to a dilapidated shed where the yellow flowers of St. John's Wort grew. Even though the garden had been neglected, nature supplied many useful herbs that she could use for poultices and healing hot drinks.

Emma liked a long read before bed and on the first evening settled herself downstairs to not disturb Mother Cameron and Catherine. Sitting by the flickering lamplight, she soon became engrossed in her book and did not hear John enter until he tripped over a footstool.

He lurched toward her. "Whatcha do-in'?" He grabbed the book out of her hands and flung it at the settee.

Emma's eyes flashed. "How dare you!"

He laughed, yanked her up and swirled her in dizzying circles.

"Let me go, you boor."

His smelly mouth sought hers, and she wrenched away, knocking him off balance. He staggered back against the door where she administered a kick in the place Beatrice said a man would suffer considerable pain. He fell howling to the floor, rolling about like an injured animal. Emma retrieved her book, blew out the lamp, and stomped upstairs.

She marched into the bedroom. Mrs. Cameron stirred. "Is everything all right, my dear?"

"I'm fine, Mother Cameron. Sorry to disturb you."

"I'm sure I heard a scuffle."

"It was nothing. Just an annoying gnat."

Chapter 35

The next morning, Emma woke early and walked west along the dusty road to gather wild camomile. At the lane of the next farm, she spied a young man hunched down at the side of the road. He appeared to be staring into a puddle of water. She walked up and peered down. *What's so entrancing?* A glint of sunlight sparkled off the surface. *Nothing unusual.* She bent closer and he looked up.

Emma smiled. "What are you doing?"

"You're blocking the sun. Please move aside."

She stepped back and sun flooded the water. She hunched down beside him.

He continued to stare at the puddle. "See how the light shines on the surface and how it bounces off different objects depending on where they are in the water." He spoke to her the way her tutor did.

"Why does it do that?"

"I'm not sure. But I'm going to find out."

The sun went behind a cloud, and the young man sighed. "I'm Isaac. Who are you?"

"Emma."

"I've not seen you around."

"I'm visiting my aunt, Millicent Spencer. She's ill, and my foster mother and sister have come to help out. Do you live here?"

He stood up, arched his back and wriggled his shoulders.

She waited. *How long had he'd been crouched over that puddle?*

"My mother and her new husband live here. They took me out of school to be a farmer. I hate farming."

"What do you want to be?"

"I'm a scholar and I have got to go back to school, or my head will burst from holding it all in."

"Holding all what in?"

"So many questions about how the universe works. What influence does sunlight have on water? What invisible substance holds the moon in the sky? There's so much to discover and understand."

Emma laughed. "You sound like me. You're lucky to be a boy."

"Why?"

"I can't go to lower school, let alone the University. I wanted to go to Oxford next year when I turned sixteen, but my tutor informed me that women are not allowed."

"What about Cambridge? That's where I want to go."

"I inquired there too." She shook her head. "There's nowhere I can study and it's most frustrating."

"You're the first person I've met around here who wants to learn. I'll teach you. It will help make this interminable farming tolerable."

"You'd do that?" She hoped he would not be interested in grabbing her body parts.

"Of course. What do you want to learn?"

"Alchemy."

His eyebrows shot up. "The study of alchemy is illegal. Punishable by death."

She met his stare and lifted her chin. "Are you going to report me?"

"On the contrary. Alchemy is one of my strongest interests. I have a crude laboratory set up in the shed behind the barn." He pointed to a large barn many metres from the farmhouse. "I'm trusting you to tell no one."

"It's our secret." They shook hands. "When I was a little girl, I overheard my mother and uncle talking about the mysteries of matter. It sounded magical."

"Maybe magic is logic not yet discovered."

"Maybe."

"Meet me at my lab after sundown."

Emma raced back to her aunt's farm with her basket half full of camomile plants. She burst through the doorway and ran into the sitting room startling Mrs. C and Aunt Millicent. She dropped her basket and words spilled out faster than a runaway horse. "I just met the most remarkable person. He's smart and he lives next door and he hates farming and he's going to Cambridge and he thinks women should be allowed to go too and I'm going to work with him." She stopped and caught her breath, her chest heaving.

The two women stared at her, eyes wide.

John scoffed. "He's always got his nose in a book or stares at things for hours and says he's figuring out how they work. He's stupid to think so much."

Emma's breathing had calmed down a little. "Well, I like him. I like boys that think."

Mrs. Cameron frowned. "I don't want you mixing with the wrong kind of people. I hear farm boys are rougher than city boys."

Aunt Millicent spoke up. "Isaac is a good boy. He's the stepson of Rev. Barnacle Smith. That boy must be 'bout seventeen by now."

Catherine perked up. "Seventeen? And his name is Isaac Smith?"

"No, he took his natural father's name even though his father died three months before he was born. The wee babe came too soon. So small he could've fit inside a quart mug of beer." She shook her head. "Even as a young lad, he never liked the Reverend."

Emma picked up her basket. "Well, he's smart, and I like him."

John smirked. "He asks the queerest questions that nobody can answer."

She tilted her head "I think there's someone who will answer them."

John plunked his fists on his hips and stuck his chin out. "And who is that, Miss Smart One?"

"He will." Swinging her basket, she marched to the kitchen. *Uncle Albert would like him.*

That night, she sat down and wrote a long letter to her uncle describing her meeting with a clever young man she'd met named Isaac Newton.

Chapter 36

Autumn turned to winter and every morning Emma would walk a mile to the make-shift laboratory behind the barn where she and Isaac would spend hours mixing up substances for their experiments. Isaac had attended the King's School in Grantham and Emma gobbled up every bit of knowledge he offered.

One late afternoon after an unsuccessful attempt at transforming a lump of lead into gold, she plunked her elbows on the table. "What are we doing wrong?"

Isaac, sitting on a stool next to her, stared at the unchanged stone in front of them. "That's not the right question."

"What do you mean?"

"The question is of utmost importance. It guides your mind." He raised a finger. "Besides, we didn't fail. Every result contains an answer. So even when it seems you've failed, it's really a chance to learn something." He picked up the inert lump. "Nothing is a total failure."

"I like that attitude. So what is the right question?"

"A more effective one is 'how?' or 'why?' or 'what happens if?' or 'what about that?' Rational investigation will uncover the inner workings of nature."

"You're not a farmer. You must go back to school."

"I agree and I think I have my mother convinced. She sees how miserable I am here."

Emma's mouth turned down.

"I don't mean here with you. My small laboratory is the only thing that keeps me from going mad. There's so much more I need to do."

"You will. I'm sure of that."

"Yes, I will. Meanwhile, let's see what else we can do." He went to another table strewn with charts, textbooks, and papers covered with mathematical formulae. "We live in a magical universe of invisible forces. To expose its secrets, we need only to keep asking, thinking, and experimenting."

Emma joined him. "I wonder what would happen if we add that." She pointed to a beaker containing a smelly sulphur mixture.

"Let's find out."

They spent the next hour absorbed in their inquiries, arriving at no useful conclusions. Isaac slapped his hands together. "We can continue tomorrow."

Emma helped tidy up, washing bottles and straightening scribbled papers. She gathered a pile of sheets up, stopped, and stared at them. "My Uncle Albert's papers."

"What did you say?"

"These papers. They remind me of helping my Uncle pack his papers into a box when we left Germany." She looked off in the distance. "It was a long time ago, but I remembered we had to hide them."

"That sounds interesting."

"My mother and uncle talked about alchemy. I remembered the word because it sounded funny, but I didn't know what it meant."

Isaac's face brightened. "Did they do experiments? Do you think they wrote their findings down?"

"I don't know but I wish we were closer to London to get them. I'll write to my Uncle right away."

"What about your mother? Won't she know?"

"My mother's dead. She died a long time ago from a sickness."

"Oh. I'm sorry."

She frowned. "It's curious but I don't remember her being sick." She moved the pile of papers to a corner of the table. "She was a healer. She could have healed herself."

"Some diseases are incurable. Three hundred years ago, The Black Plague killed half of London."

"That's terrible. I hope that never happens again."

"Unfortunately, the plague did come back. Thirty-three years ago and ten years after that."

"That was only twenty-three years ago." She shivered. "May it never come again."

He placed a beaker and a flask on a shelf. "Perhaps we shall be better prepared if it does."

She walked along the moonlit road back to her aunt's farm, plotting how to persuade Mother Cameron to leave for Hollyhock as soon as possible. Would she let her go alone? Maybe Isaac would come with her. Hungry for knowledge, he'd want to see her Uncle's writings and she trusted him with the contents. Perhaps such information would be helpful to his future studies.

Thoughts tumbled over each other and Emma quickened her step. Would her Uncle Albert's papers reveal some answers to their ongoing quest of unravelling the secrets of the universe?

Chapter 37

Mrs. Cameron didn't need much convincing. The next morning she listened to Emma's appeal and nodded. "Millicent has recovered and Catherine is bored. It's time we were back. We'll leave for London tomorrow on the first coach."

Catherine ran to the stairs. "Let's get packed."

That afternoon, Emma had a short visit with Isaac. His grasp of mathematics and precise way of explaining complicated ideas inspired her. He was deeply interested in studying the occult wisdom of the ancients, and she suspected he would be keen to see her Uncle's writings.

She returned in time for evening dinner and Catherine sidled up to her. "Are you sweet on that Isaac fellow?"

Emma looked at her dumbfounded. "Isaac? No, of course not. We're fellow explorers—explorers of knowledge."

She winked. "Oh, I bet that's not all he'd like to explore."

"He's a gentleman. Besides, he has a girlfriend in Grantham where he lodges closer to Cambridge. Her name is Katherine—with a K. She's the daughter of Mr. Clarke, the apothecary."

"Whatever you say."

Mrs. Cameron called from the dining room. "Come, girls, supper. We must be early to bed."

As soon as they arrived at Hollyhock, Emma wrote a letter to her uncle, which Mr. Cameron delivered the next day. Emma waited impatiently for him to return with an answer. She hoped the coming weekend would suit him and Mr. Edwards for her to visit.

When Mr. Cameron opened the door, Emma rushed up and he handed her the letter. She broke the seal and read quickly.

Catherine walked into the hallway. "What's that?"

Emma waved the letter at her. "I'm going to London this weekend." She ran along the hall and up the stairs.

Catherine followed close behind. "Can I go with you? I'd love to see London."

They reached their bedroom and Emma took a dress off a hook. "I must get Twin to press this fresh for travelling."

Catherine put her hands on her hips. "You're not even listening."

Emma looked up.

"I said, 'can I come to London with you'?"

"You'd hate it at my Uncle's house. All we do is read books and discuss them."

"What a silly thing to do in London." She plunked herself at the mirrored dresser and picked up a hairbrush. "You're no fun at all. I wish Beatrice were here." She started brushing and had reached fifty-nine strokes when Emma left.

In Westminster, her Uncle Albert handed her a sheaf of papers. "I think this is what you might be looking for."

Emma put them on the table in front of her. "Did you or mother write these?"

"Some of them. The ones on top I found in an old shop in London last year. I haven't had a chance to study them." He sat beside her. "Let's explore them."

Mr. Edwards came in and they invited him to join them. Many of the writings referred to Biblical text and contained the usual discussion any scholar might write.

Mr. Edwards took a handful of wrinkled sheets from the pile and smoothed the top one out. "Look here." He pointed. "What do those numbers and symbols on the top mean? I've never seen such before."

Albert peered at it. "Alchemists are notorious for veiling their writings in impenetrable jargon. Let's see what we can make of it."

Emma picked up the next page. "Maybe this will help." At the top was one word: Mycheal. "Does that mean Michael?" Further down the page were four letters, written three ways: sabe, beas, seab. She stared at them. "They could be anagrams."

Albert rubbed his hands together, "Indeed. Let's figure them out."

Mr. Edwards fetched pen and paper, and they re-wrote the letters in different orders looking for words.

Within seconds, they spoke in unison. "They all spell base."

On the next page, another four letters had been written: logd, dogl and lodg.

Emma manipulated the letters in her head. "Gold." She glanced at the word on the top of the first page. "And Mycheal is not Michael. It's Alchemy!" Her eyes lit up. "These papers are instructions on how to change base metals into gold." She looked at the men, her eyes dancing.

Albert gathered the papers and handed them to her. "Why don't you and Isaac see what you can do with these? I'm far too busy right now deciphering the hidden codes in the Bible."

"Isaac is interested in that too. He's written reams on *Revelations* and the *Apocalypse*. You must meet him someday." She took the papers from her uncle. "Thank you. I'm sure they'll help us in our search."

He crinkled his forehead. "What's your interest in gold? The government doesn't want people making gold and anyone who does, is lynched."

"It's not gold for gold's sake. It's about finding the right combination to transform not only minerals but also to purify the human soul, and to even cure illnesses with the same mix." She frowned. "Maybe we'll discover something that could have cured Mama."

Albert shook his head. "The cure to what killed your Mama would take a transformation in human nature and that is more difficult than finding the Holy Grail."

Emma's forehead creased into a washboard of lines. "What do you mean?"

The door swung open. "All right you three. Enough of this chatter." Mrs. Thorpe bustled into the room carrying a tray. "It's time to put those books away and have something to eat." She put the tray of hot buttered biscuits, gooseberry jam, teapot and cups on the table. "Mercy me. I've never heard three people go on so." She poured the tea. "Now eat up before you faint from all those words."

Emma arrived home late Sunday evening and a letter from Isaac was waiting for her. He wouldn't have received her letter yet. *What is his news?* She ripped it open. Henry Stokes, the master at King's School, had taken up his cause, earnestly trying to persuade his mother to send him back to school. She clasped the letter to her chest. *I'm so happy for him.* He'll be able to return to his beloved studies at Cambridge.

In her response, she wrote that she was glad he would continue his education and romance. She didn't tell him her own heart ached. *I wish I'd been born a boy.* She longed for education like a starving animal but the path of higher learning was forbidden to her. *My uncle says we decide who we'll be before our birth so why did I choose to be a girl who wants to learn*? She put her letter to Isaac on the hall table to be taken to the post, grabbed her cape and went to her favourite thinking place under the apple tree.

The girls she knew were only interested in finding a husband and Beatrice, happily married, was large with child. As far as romance went, the only boys she knew, other than Isaac, were uncouth and ignorant. Even in all those long days and evenings with Isaac, no stirrings of desire rose for her, and she assumed none for Isaac since he'd never approached her in that way. Maybe she was one of those women who liked women—a hidden topic only whispered about. Beatrice had told her of men pleasuring each other, and women with women. She sighed. *It's enough I'm forbidden to go to school. I don't need anything else forbidden in my life.*

Chapter 38

One early day in May, Mrs. Cameron rushed into the library, waving the morning news paper. "It's happened."

Mr. Cameron looked up from his book. "What are you raving about, my dear?"

She shoved the paper under his nose, but before he had a chance to focus, she grabbed it back and read. "King Charles has issued The Declaration of Breda, making certain promises in return for his restoration to the English throne."

She kissed her husband soundly on the bare spot on top of his head. "He'll soon be back from exile, and we'll have a king again. Long live England." She trounced out of the room humming a popular ballad.

The next morning on his way into London, Mr. Cameron read the latest bulletin. Parliament had passed a resolution "that government ought to be by King, Lords and Commons." He sighed a breath of relief. "England needs a Monarch, but no one person should have absolute power."

In celebration of his Majesty's return, a public holiday was declared, and Mrs. Cameron rallied all her helpers to prepare. Mrs. Hudson made batches of cakes and tarts. Francesca and the Twins decorated the house and backyard, while Signore Tonini carved 'Welcome King Charles' on a slab of wood.

On May 29, 1660, Charles II, on his birthday, entered London to great acclaim. Catherine begged to go into London to join the crowds gathered for the festivities of dancing, singing, and no doubt consuming copious amounts of beer, wine and gin.

Mrs. Cameron glowered. "That is no place for a young maiden. We will have a party right here."

Beatrice, Ralph, and the new baby Ralphy came for the occasion. Even Albert and Mr. Edwards joined in.

Everyone raised their glass to "Long live the King." Emma, now sixteen, said, "I hope this Charles will work with Parliament better than his father did. We don't want any more wars."

Mrs. Cameron lifted her glass again. "Indeed, but let us not talk of serious matters. The king is back and it's time for rejoicing."

And rejoice they did, throughout the day and far into the evening. However, Emma spent more time in the library with her uncle, Mr. Edwards, and Mr. Cameron than she did in the noisy sitting room or in the garden where the young people drank, danced, and laughed.

Several times, her uncle leaned over and whispered. "Why don't you go outside and join the party?"

And she'd whisper back. "Because they're silly, and they don't talk sensibly about important matters."

Catherine had been interested in boys since she was thirteen. Now that she was fifteen, her parents kept a tight rein on her and monitored her social engagements with care. She was still too young to walk out alone with a young man, no matter how much she begged. At church functions, Emma would accompany her as a chaperone, but Catherine would sneak off the moment Emma's attention shifted.

An hour later, when she'd tiptoe back, Emma would shake a finger. "You can't keep disappearing with some young man."

"We just hold hands and hug a little."

"Is that all you do?"

"Sometimes, we kiss." Her cheeks turned pink. "But that's all."

"Promise me that hand-holding and a little kissing is all you do."

"I promise."

They hugged and Emma prayed she would keep her word and her impulses under control.

That next Sunday, Catherine, in her best frock, ran into the library ready to attend an afternoon social hosted by the Parson and his wife.

"Emma, you're not even ready." She plunked her hands on her hips. "You can read when you're an old lady. Let's go."

Emma looked up from her comfy chair and put her book down. "Sorry, I forgot."

Catherine shook her head. "How could you forget *the* social event of the month?"

Emma changed her dress, pulled a comb through her hair and slowly followed a bouncing Catherine to the carriage.

The purpose of this monthly gathering was to introduce young people to each other in a respectable manner, and they all loved going to the Parson's house. The back garden's main feature was a large maze, and couples would get lost for hours behind its high hedges. The Parson and his wife were delighted that so many young people were interested in its foliage.

First, lemonade and sassafras were served to give time for greeting and meeting new friends. After that, in a very sort while, several couples, including Catherine with a new young man, would wander off to study the maze. A handful of shy girls and awkward youth remained, exchanging feeble comments. Emma, sitting in a corner chair, wished Isaac was there so she could at least engage in meaningful conversation. She glanced around the room and a piercing gaze met hers. The Parson's only child, a sturdy full-figured older girl, was smiling at her. Emma looked away, but a movement caught the corner of her eye. *She's walking toward me. What is her name? Helen?*

"Hello. You're Emma, I believe."

"Yes."

She stuck out a fleshy hand. "I'm Harriet, in case you forgot." She smiled, showing a neat row of small white teeth. Long dark hair, pulled back, framed her round face.

Emma politely lifted her hand, "How do you do."

Harriet took Emma's hand in hers and held it longer than necessary.

Emma rescued her hand. *She must think I'm someone else.*

Harriet sat down and chattered about inconsequential things: the weather, London fashion, who was travelling where and for how long. Emma answered in monosyllables and stifled a yawn.

The Parson's wife rang the bell, bringing the garden-lovers from the maze. They straggled to the house, straightening and brushing off clothes. Catherine, cheeks flushed, avoided Emma's questioning look.

On Emma's next weekend visit with her uncle, they'd finished the Sunday noon meal when he suggested they take a walk. A walk meant he had something serious to say. She put on her cape and for several blocks, neither spoke. As they neared St. James Park, she stopped. "You're not sick or dying, are you?"

He laughed. "No, I'm well. But I do have something to tell you."

She frowned. "You're not going back to Germany. I can't lose you." A flutter of anxiety rose in her chest.

He led her to a bench. "I am going on a trip but not to Germany. I'm going to France."

"France? Whatever for?"

He laughed again. "Even your old uncle is allowed time off for recreation."

"I thought books were your recreation."

"As much as I love books, I do get out now and then."

She waited.

"Do you remember Lord and Lady Everleigh?"

"No. I don't know them. Who are they?"

"Oh, that's right. You wouldn't know them. They're friends of a colleague you've never met." He crossed his legs. "The Everleigh's have invited me numerous times to meet their daughter."

"Do they live in France?"

"No. I'm getting to that. Several months ago, they asked me again to a weekend at their country estate. This time I got the strongest feeling I should go—or perhaps your mother was whispering in my ear. Lady Everleigh was eager to marry off her eldest daughter and I think she'd run out of bachelors."

"Please don't tell me you're going to France with a Miss Everleigh?"

"Emma, if you keep interrupting, you'll never know."

"Sorry." She clasped her hands in her lap.

"So I went to visit them but instead of being enamoured with their daughter, I met—"

She grabbed his arm. "Did you meet a new author or a scholar?"

He lowered his eyebrows and she pursed her lips shut.

"I met another young woman who was visiting from France with her parents. A Mademoiselle Charlotte DuBois."

"Is she a scholar?"

He smiled. "She is a beautiful, sensitive, smart and the most delightful woman I have ever met. Besides your mother and you, of course."

Emma's mouth dropped open. His face sparkled and she'd never seen that light in his eyes before. She frowned. "Are you in love?"

He took her hand. "Yes, I think I am."

"But you're so old."

He laughed. "A person is never too old to find love. When it happens to you, you'll know. It's the most delicious feeling in the world. Even better than uncovering the secrets of the universe." He looked at her. "Well, at least as good."

She stared at him, her mind running in circles. She'd have to share him now. And he was going away. A tear fell from the corner of her eye. "Are you going to live in France?"

He put his arm around her. "I'm only going for a visit. I'll write to you and I'll be back. I promise. I'm not leaving you."

She leaned against his shoulder. "I'm not ever going to fall in love."

Chapter 39

Two weeks later, Albert left for France and when the next weekend came for their usual visit, Emma curled up in her favourite chair to spend the whole day finishing the book he had given her. A minute before he'd stepped into the carriage he'd handed her Francis Bacon's *New Atlantis*. "Just because you're not allowed to attend university, doesn't mean you can't read about an ideal one." He'd meant well, but it was bittersweet reading.

On Monday, a letter arrived from Harriet. She was planning a shopping expedition to view the latest arrivals from Paris and would Emma like to join her? *Viewing new books maybe, but dresses?* She declined.

On Tuesday of the next week, Emma entered the sitting room and stopped short. Harriet was sitting in the new armchair next to Mother Cameron.

Mrs. Cameron looked up. "Look who's here, and she brought the most delicious almond cakes. Do join us, my dear."

Emma accepted a piece of cake and a hot mint drink she had introduced to Francesca. Mrs. Cameron and Harriet chatted on and on. *How can they talk so long about lace collars?* At least the cakes were good and Mrs. Cameron was an excellent hostess. Whether it was a barrister or a county clerk, she was always genteel and kept the conversation going. Emma swung her foot, tapped her fingers and her pasted smile grew weary. *What reason can I give to leave?*

Twin rushed in. "Come quick. Francesca and Mr. Hudson are in a terrible row."

Mrs. Cameron excused herself and hurried off.

Emma cleared her throat. "Have you read any good books lately?"

Harriet flapped a hand. "I am far too busy to be reading books." She held a plate out to Emma. "Do have another cake."

Emma put a hand on her stomach. "I've had quite enough, thank you."

Harriet, still holding the plate aloft, stared at Emma. "You have such lovely eyes. Shaped like almonds." Her gaze wandered around Emma's face.

Emma looked away. *Is my face getting red?*

"Are you aware of how beautiful you are?"

"I—er—not really." She glanced at the grandfather clock. The minute hand inched its way past the Roman numerals.

Harriet lowered her plate to the table. "I shouldn't eat any more cake. My father said I would make a good Ruben's model." She shrugged. "I found out later that was a polite way of saying I was plump." She smoothed her hand over her full bosom. "What do you think?"

Mrs. Cameron rushed into the room. "Sorry for the interruption. What did I miss?"

Harriet grinned. "I was just going to ask Emma if she would like to come and visit me."

Emma opened her mouth and closed it.

Mrs. Cameron patted Emma's knee. "That's a wonderful idea. She needs to get out more."

Harriet turned to Emma. "It's all settled then. Friday at two, I'm having a small gathering. You must join us."

Emma blinked at the two smiling women. "But—"

"That will be lovely," Mrs. Cameron continued. "I keep telling Emma she needs to have friends. She spends far too much time with books."

On Friday at one o'clock, Mrs. Cameron knocked once and stuck her head around Emma's bedroom door. "Remember Harriet's invitation for tea. It's a fifteen-minute ride and you don't want to be late."

Emma looked up from the paper on which she had been unscrambling anagrams. "Oh. Thank you. I forgot."

"I do appreciate you visiting. Her mother is so worried about her. She's twenty-four already and has no interest in getting married. She's even said she's happy being a spinster."

Emma put the paper down. "I can understand that. The boys I've met are gross."

"Oh, Emma. You just haven't met the right one yet. Why don't you wear your new summer dress? Maybe you'll both meet young men at the soiree. I'll have Mr. Hudson prepare a carriage."

Her footsteps receded and Emma stretched her arms over her head and wriggled her shoulders. *I guess it wouldn't hurt me to be a little more sociable.* She gathered up the strewn papers. *The Parson's grounds are beautifully landscaped and a walk would do me good.*

The Parson's wife greeted her and introduced the other young ladies present. Emma prayed for strength to endure an afternoon with five chattering women. As offensive as men were, at least they could speak of things other than hairdos or crinolines.

Harriet joined the group, spreading her arms in welcome to all her dear friends. A servant brought out honey cakes on fine china and green napkins.

Harriet sidled up to Emma. "The green almost matches your eyes."

Emma looked away. Why did women prattle such nonsense?

After an hour-and-a-half, the dull afternoon ended, and as was the custom among young women, they exchanged goodbye hugs and cheek kisses. Harriet kissed Emma on her right cheek but as she moved her face to the other side, she stopped short, and her lips landed on the side of Emma's mouth. A tingle sparked in Emma's body and she pulled away.

On shaking legs, she walked to the carriage. She hadn't felt that tingle for along time. Not since Beatrice and her night dreams. She climbed onto the seat and smoothed her skirt over her knees.

Two days later, a letter from Harriet arrived, suggesting a visit in the forthcoming week. Sitting at her desk in the library, quill in hand,

Emma chose her words for a polite refusal. Having finished her reply, she watched the drop of wax harden on the folded letter. *I had three good reasons not to, so why did I say yes?*

Mrs. Cameron walked in when Emma was arranging the carriage time with Mr. Hudson. She clapped her hands. "I'm so glad you're making new friends. Catherine met a lovely young man at the Parson's house and I have a feeling you're going to meet someone there too."

Four days later, dressed in a new frock that Mother Cameron had bought for her, Emma stood at the door of the Parson's residence. She let the peacock knocker drop with a clunk.

Harriet swung the door open. "Do come in. Excuse me answering, but the servants are off, and my dear parents are away for the day."

Emma walked in. "Am I the first guest?"

Harriet giggled. "Oh, my dear. You're the *only* guest—for our special time together."

Emma gulped and followed Harriet into the parlour. *How will I ever get through a whole afternoon of idle conversation with this dreadful female? Why did I ever come?*

Harriet steered Emma to the settee. "Sit here. I'll be right back. The water is on the boil for a new hot drink you simply must try."

A walnut chest with brass pear-drop handles faced her. A tapestry of a meadow scene with a winsome maid holding a child's hand hung above it. Two narrow windows let a little light into the dark panelled room. Emma sighed. *Maybe I can fabricate a headache and leave early,*

Harriet returned carrying a silver tray with a blue porcelain pot, two matching cups and saucers, and a small plate of poppy seed cakes. She placed it on a doily on the mahogany side table. "This is a new drink called China Tea. It comes all the way from the East India Company."

"Francesca mentioned something about black tea. Do you think it will catch on?"

"Oh, yes. Everyone is trying it." She sat on the settee beside Emma. "But we must let it sit to let the flavours infuse."

Emma cleared her throat. "You have a lovely house."

"People are surprised when they come here expecting a parsonage, but this house is not on church grounds or even owned by the church. My mother's family were well off and here we are." She smiled. "But enough of that." She touched Emma's sleeve. "What a lovely dress. Such soft material."

Emma drew her arm away. "Thank you."

Harriet picked up the blue teapot and poured a black stream into the cups. "Do try cook's special poppy-seed cake. It's most delicious."

Emma took a napkin and a piece of cake and nibbled on it while the tea cooled.

For the first twenty minutes, Harriet prattled on about nothing. Then she reached toward the table and her arm brushed against the front of Emma's dress. However, when she withdrew it, she moved ever so slowly and pressed it against Emma's bodice.

Emma sucked in a breath.

"What are you thinking, my dear?"

Harriet had not taken a piece of cake or refilled her tea. Emma averted her eyes. "Nothing of import."

Harriet moved closer, her thigh a whisper away. She lifted her hand and touched Emma's cheek. "You're blushing."

Emma stiffened and stared across the room. Curtains fluttered at a half-opened window. *This isn't like one of Beatrice's dreams. Harriet is fully awake.*

Harriet took Emma's hand in hers. "You have such soft hands."

The sheer curtain lifted with the breeze. Harriet's fingers lingered on Emma's hand and moved up her arm. She touched Emma's small amber pin which lay nestled between her breasts. "Such a pretty brooch."

Emma shrank back. "Thank you."

Harriet touched Emma's cheek. "Don't be shy. You must know I like you."

"I—"

Harriet leaned forward and kissed her lightly on the lips.

Emma stiffened and drew back. Harriet took her hand. "It's perfectly all right for ladies to kiss. I'm sure your mother kisses you."

Emma straightened up like an arrow. "My mother's dead."

"Oh, my poor dear. Of course. Mrs. Cameron told me. Come here." She gathered Emma to her, pulling her head onto her cushiony bosom and rocking her. "There, there, my sweet. You cry. I've got you. Harriet's here."

A half-hour later, Emma sat in the carriage for the fifteen-minute ride to Hollyhock. She shook her head. *What happened?* She hadn't had those piercing feelings about her mother's absence for a long time.

She looked out the window. *It was nice to be held and crooned to and kissed so lovingly.* But Harriet's kisses were not like her mama's. They were like Beatrice's—only more so.

Chapter 40

The evening after that first solo visit, Emma had a long talk with her dragonfly. She didn't know who else to talk to about kisses between women that were nothing like mother-daughter kisses. Her uncle was away, but she wouldn't have spoken to him about such intimate matters.

As open-minded as Mother Cameron was, Emma was sure she would be shocked at such goings-on. Maybe Francesca or the Twins would understand, but she was too embarrassed to approach them. However, her dragonfly listened as Emma vacillated about whether she should get involved with the Parson's daughter. Or any woman in the way that Harriet wanted. Such liaisons were strictly forbidden, punishable by gaol time or death. Not to mention shame and scandal for the family who has been so kind to her. She fell asleep with her dragonfly on her chest.

In the morning, she wrote to Harriet and accepted her invitation to come for tea again next week. Her hand shook as she pressed the seal onto the warm wax.

On that visit, and the week after, the intimacy between the women grew beyond girlhood dreams. Emma's shyness dropped away as she melted further into Harriet's warm embraces and loving touch. Soon she was going twice a week to visit her new friend, and Mrs. Cameron encouraged their outings, pleased that Emma was becoming more sociable.

One afternoon, the Parson and his wife came home early. When Harriet's mother went upstairs to tell her them about her day, she opened the bedroom door to find Emma dressed only in her shift.

Harriet rushed to her mother with a hug. "Emma was getting ready to try on one of my dresses to see if the colour suited her eyes."

"How lovely. I'm so happy you young ladies enjoy each other's company so much and are having such good times together."

She left the room and as soon as the door closed, Harriet planted a hand on Emma's breast.

Emma pushed her away. "She might return."

Harriet winked. "That makes it all the more titillating." She slid her other hand under Emma's shift.

Harriet's lavish attention captivated Emma, and she started looking forward to their daytime rendezvous even more than she had with Beatrice's nighttime dreams. *Something that feels this good can't be wrong.* She continued to ignore the priest's fire and brimstone sermons on the sins of the flesh.

In her uncle's last letter, he had written that he was staying in France a little longer. His month had turned into six weeks with no hint of his return. For once, Emma didn't mind her uncle's absence. Caught up in Harriet's spell of sexual ardour, for the first time in her life she was consumed with something other than books.

Catherine's sixteenth birthday approached and Mother Cameron fussed over the decorations for the party. Catherine's latest beau, Norman, was coming, as well as Beatrice, Ralph, and Ralphy, and, of course, Harriet.

Everyone scurried around preparing for the evening festivities. Twin came out of the kitchen with a full tray, and Mother Cameron stopped her. "Twin, are there still honeysuckles in the garden?"

"Oh, yes, ma'am. The vines have taken over the west wall. I'll fetch some." She, or maybe it was her sister, brought in an armful of branches and set them in vases.

At six, Beatrice, Ralph, and baby arrived. Fifteen minutes later, Norman's and Harriet's carriages pulled up simultaneously. When they entered together, Signore Tonini escorted them to the sitting room and announced them as a couple. Norman's seventeen-year-old face reddened, and Harriet hid a smile under her new scarf.

Catherine ran to Norman and took his hand. "This one's with me. Harriet is Emma's friend." She pulled a grateful Norman to the sideboard and handed him a glass of wine.

Mrs. Cameron rushed up, looking past Harriet but no young man was with her. "Come in, my dear."

Francesca and Twin One had the table set at seven, and with everyone gathered, Mrs. Hudson and Twin Two served mushroom soup followed by fish, braised vegetables and pigeon pie, with fruit cakes and honey biscuits for a sweet. At eight, the party withdrew to the sitting room.

Ralph fell into a chair, holding his stomach. "I couldn't eat another bite." However, he readily accepted a full glass of beer from Twin's tray. Beatrice took Ralphy upstairs to settle him to sleep.

At nine o'clock, Mr. Cameron left for bed and at ten, Mrs. Cameron yawned and excused herself. Ralph, who always needed more sleep, stretched and ambled upstairs.

Much earlier in the evening, Catherine had mumbled something about visiting a friend, and she and Norman disappeared.

Harriet went to fetch fresh drinks and Emma closed her eyes and leaned back on the settee, her head swimming with too much food and wine.

"Had any good dreams lately?"

She opened her eyes. A smiling Beatrice stood in front of her. Was it the wine or the question that made her face feel warm?

Harriet returned and held the drink out to Emma, who waved it away. "No more for me."

Beatrice raised her hand. "I'll have it." She took the glass and sat beside Emma.

Harriet glared at the interloper and pulled a chair up.

Emma turned to Beatrice. "Where's Ralphy?"

"Twin One or Two, or maybe both, are looking after him. Babies are extremely tiring, let me tell you." She shook her head. "The best fun about babies is making them. Too bad there's a consequence of such divine pleasure." She dragged out the word divine.

Harriet took a drink. "You can't stop people from doing it."

"That's for sure but I wish there was an alternative."

Emma glanced up. "What do you mean?"

"You know. Do something that would be as much fun but without resulting in a baby." Beatrice's gaze shifted from Emma to Harriet.

Harriet put her glass down. "It's late and my carriage is due."

Beatrice stretched out a hand. "Before you go, I have one more question for you."

"What's that?"

"Do you ever have sexual dreams?"

Emma blanched, glad Mother Cameron was not present to hear her daughter raise this topic of conversation.

Harriet answered. "Yes, I do. Quite enjoyable ones."

Beatrice turned to Emma. "What about you?"

Emma glanced away and crossed her fingers under the napkin. "I don't remember my dreams." *I hate lying. I hope my face isn't red.*

Beatrice grinned. "I used to have a lot of sex dreams before I was married. I wish I did now. They were so much fun. Almost as if I'd been awake." She directed a sly smile at Emma.

Emma trembled and looked away. *Had Beatrice been shamming sleep?*

Harriet put a hand on Emma's. "Are you all right, my dear? You've gone pale."

"Just too much wine." She stood up. "I really should retire."

"And I must take my leave. Good night."

Beatrice gave a little wave. "So nice to meet you."

Emma walked Harriet to the door and said goodbye with a quick peck on the cheek.

When she returned, Beatrice was still sitting there. "Good night, Beatrice. See you in the morning."

"Oh, I'll see you before then."

"What do you mean?"

"Ralph will sleep like a log and the twins have Ralphy." She grinned. "So I thought it would be nice if we sleep together. Just like old times."

"But—" *Does she suspect anything between Harriet and me?*

"But what?" She stood up and linked her arm in Emma's. "I've missed sleeping with you, and it's been months since I've had a full night's sleep without Ralphy howling."

They headed up the stairs. Emma quickly changed into her nightclothes and crawled under the covers. Beatrice removed her dress, shift, and undergarments and stood naked at the end of the iron bedstead. "Foolish me, I didn't bring my nightdress."

"You can borrow one of mine or Catherine's."

"I know it's naughty, but sometimes Ralph and I sleep with no clothes on." She walked to her old side of the bed, and with a big yawn crawled under the covers.

Emma lay rigid. Moments passed and neither moved. The memory of deliciously stolen nights circled Emma's head. *If anything happens, I don't have to tell Harriet.* She'd never told her about Beatrice's dreams and did not intend to. *Will Beatrice have the audacity to pretend she's dreaming?* She held her breath, waiting for an inviting touch.

Heavy breathing beside her changed to a snore. Emma let out her breath and turned on her side. Just as well. *But what will I do if she awakes later with a fake dream?*

They both slept soundly all night. Emma woke first, got dressed and brought tea to a groggy Beatrice. She placed the cup on the side table and a sleepy Ralph came in wrapped in a sheet. He grunted hello and crawled into bed beside Beatrice.

Emma looked over at Catherine's bed. It had not been slept in. She went downstairs and joined Mother Cameron in the parlour, where she was tending to the baby. "Where's Catherine?"

"She sent a messenger last night to tell us she was staying overnight at a girlfriend's house."

"I see." *She may be at a girlfriend's house, but where was Norman?*

Mrs. C picked up Ralphy and patted his back. "I'm so glad my girls have such respectable young women friends."

Chapter 41

Three weeks later, after church service on a bright Sunday afternoon, the parson and his wife were making a sick call in the country. A barking dog came upon them, frightening their horse, which upturned their carriage, tossing the parson headlong into a meandering stream. He lay in the water face down and drowned. The parson's wife was thrown to the other side where her head collided with a large rock. She lingered two days and succumbed to join her husband for their final reward in the great beyond. A parson from another parish filled in until a permanent one could be found.

Harriet recovered from the shock and dealt valiantly with the grief of her parents' deaths. Knowing they resided in their beloved Heaven, she looked forward to having the house to herself. The parson's wife had owned it, so it was now Harriet's and that, and a sufficient yearly stipend, fulfilled her requirements nicely.

She suggested Emma move in with her, and Mildred Cameron agreed that would be a good idea. "You'll be such a comfort to her until you meet your young men and get married."

Emma had mixed feelings the day she left the Cameron household —the only family she had known in England. Although she enjoyed Harriet's nighttime attentions, they shared no other interests, and she cherished her quiet mornings in the Cameron library. She was already missing her uncle. Of course, she wrote but it wasn't the same as visits, and she was starting to suspect he might become a permanent resident of France.

If only Isaac lived closer. They wrote, but it was not the same as the intellectual stimulation of a face-to-face discussion. He was at Cambridge now, not making any friends, and by his letters, he did not seem to want or need any. Emma was happy he was at school, and she told herself she wasn't envious. After all, envy was one of the deadly sins. Mother Cameron once quoted from Proverbs. "A sound heart is the life of the flesh: but envy the rottenness of the bones." But what did one do when your life's heart was to go to school?

The Parson house was closer to London, which meant more shopping and theatre. Emma would beg off the shopping but did enjoy theatre outings.

The afternoon after she moved in, the kindly old woman who lived next door knocked on the front door. Harriet opened it. "Come in, Mrs. Trent. How are you?"

The grey haired lady in a long grey dress held out a casserole dish. "I see you have a new resident."

Harriet invited her in to the sitting room and introduced her to Emma. With pleasantries over, Emma went to the kitchen and put water on for tea and brought back a plate with scones and strawberry preserves.

Mrs. Trent crossed her hands demurely on her lap. "I'm so glad you have company after your terrible tragedy of losing your dear parents."

Harriet patted her hand. "Emma has been such a comfort to me. We're just like sisters."

The grey lady glanced at the wall of family portraits, the tapestries and the leaded window panes. "And this is such a lovely house to entertain your young gentlemen friends."

The kettle rattled and Harriet rose. "Indeed. I'll make tea."

Living at the parson's house, Emma did not have as much time for her studies. Harriet liked to shop and eat out and be with her. She had taken over her parents' bedroom, and Emma had Harriet's old room.

Emma enjoyed having a place of her own and arranged her books and dragonfly within easy reach. Each woman had a large bed, and most nights Harriet would slip into Emma's room or Emma into Harriet's.

"I don't understand sex," Emma said one night. "How can one be so satiated and the next evening the body stirs and demands it again?"

"You don't have to understand it, just enjoy it."

The other activity they enjoyed was the theatre. The Puritans had objected to such frivolity, and they had been closed the whole time Emma had been in England. However, with Puritanism losing its momentum, the London theatres had reopened and now flourished, becoming a social highlight. Many young people, dressed in their finery, attended the latest new play. During the interval, men would look at Emma with interest, some even finessed an introduction.

One time Harriet yanked Emma away from a man who had approached her. Barely out of earshot, Harriet spat, "Stay away from men. They are disgusting and not to be trusted."

"He seemed to be a gentleman."

"They make you think that. Trust me, they only want one thing." She shuddered. "You must spurn any advances."

A memory of the rough and uncouth boys of her childhood passed through Emma's thoughts. "Of course. You're right."

Harriet plunked down on her seat. "I am. Now sit and enjoy the play."

Emma loved going to Hollyhock whenever she could and the next morning when Harriet left on one of her endless shopping trips, she hired a hackney carriage straight away. The usual morning rain had let up by the time she arrived and Mrs. Cameron greeted her with a big hug. "Come in, my dear. We'll have some of that new drink you like."

She removed her cape, and they walked to the sitting room. Mrs. Cameron looked around. "Twin, where are you?"

Twin popped her head around the door. "Right here, ma'am."

"Oh, it's you, Marie. Bring us that new China tea and some of Mary's poppy seed cake."

Twin scurried off. Emma sat on her favourite upholstered chair. "Mother Cameron, you're the only one who can tell the twins apart. How do you do that?"

"Ah, that's my secret." She winked. "Someday, I'll tell you."

"I'll keep you to that."

Mrs. Cameron sat in the matching chair and Emma asked, "So, what cause are you championing now?"

"Are you teasing me?"

"Not at all. I admire your courage, but there are so many people proclaiming they're right. How do you choose?"

Twin entered and put down the tray.

"Thank you, Mary." Twin left, and Mrs. Cameron tapped the lid of the pot. "We have to let it steep to bring out the full flavour. "What were you asking me?"

"About your latest cause. I hope you're not associated with those Ranters who protest in the nude?"

"Oh, good gracious no. They have such strange ideas." She leaned forward. "They actually deny the church's authority and proclaim that one can listen to the divine within. Can you believe that?"

Emma shifted in her seat. "Well, I—"

Mrs. Cameron went on. "They also preach that God is part of the universe and is in every creature." She frowned and shook her head. "Our pastor called that pantheism as if it was a dirty word."

"Similar beliefs are found in ancient books of Hinduism and in the works of many Greek philosophers such as—"

Mrs. Cameron raised her hand. "Stop. You read too much for your own good, my dear."

"I don't need books to know that I like the idea of listening to the divine within. What's wrong with that?"

Mrs. Cameron puffed up her shoulders and spluttered. "That makes God impersonal, and it doesn't allow for any difference between the creation and the creator. "

Emma wrinkled her forehead. "But if God is everywhere, He would be in every creature, including people. Wouldn't that make us all creators?"

Mrs. Cameron's mouth dropped open. "That is blasphemy and we'll speak no more of this." She filled one of the teacups and handed it to Emma. "How are you and your friend Harriet getting along?"

"Just fine." She took a sip of tea. *I do miss my uncle's discussions.*

A week later, Emma had begged off yet another afternoon shopping trip and immersed herself in her uncle's writings.

The door opened, and Harriet filled the doorway, her hands on her hips. "Are you still wasting time poring over those silly scratchings? I don't know why you bother your pretty head over such nonsense."

"Because it's important." *She sounds like the men who think women are imbeciles.* "And because I want to."

Harriet huffed out, slamming the door behind her, and Emma picked up another page.

Early the next morning, when Harriet was still asleep, Emma went to her own room to find the paper she had been studying the day before. Adept at anagrams and Latin, she easily translated *lapis philosophorum* into *Philosopher's Stone.* She had certainly come across the term in her alchemy readings.

Is it a real stone or some kind of elixir? Whatever it was, it was believed to have tremendous power. It promised to not only change base metals into gold, but also make people younger, and even offered immortality. Mysterious words like Golden Wedding Garment, Soul Body, and Living Stone fired her imagination, taking her beyond the mundane world of shopping, eating, theatre, and sex.

She read further. Some called it the Diamond Soul. Emma looked up. *Could the Philosopher's Stone help me experience my own spiritual connection?* Maybe it would open a pathway of communication with Mama? "I must see Isaac again. Together, we might find some answers."

Chapter 42

Harriet and Emma were happy, each in their own way. Harriet had found her mate and doted on her. Emma attended lectures wherever she was allowed, and her day enlivened when a letter from her uncle or Isaac arrived. She had planned to visit Isaac on the Cambridge summer break, but she wanted to go alone. She did not need the distraction of Harriet's constant attendance. Living with Harriet satisfied her body's desires, but her mind hungered for more stimulation.

One Sunday afternoon, she was reclining on Harriet's bed with a thick book. Harriet was sorting dresses at the wardrobe.

Emma looked up. "What do you think about Aristotle?"

"Who's he? A new dress designer?"

Emma sighed. "No, he was a Greek philosopher who wrote about the idea of the tabula rasa."

Harriet held a dress against her and tossed it at the foot of the bed. "I know not of what you speak. Such words garble my ears. I wish you'd not stuff your head with all that foolishness." She held up another frock. "What do you think of this one?"

"Oh, Harriet. How can you be so dense? Do you not think?"

"My darling. Don't get so upset over silly matters. We love each other. Is that not the most important subject of all?" She dropped the dress and stepped toward Emma with arms out.

She shrugged her off. "No hugs right now. I need mental input."

Harriet's mouth curved down. A moment later, she brightened. "John Fletcher's new play is opening Friday at Theatre Royal on Drury Lane. They call it a tragicomedy. Do let us attend."

Emma enjoyed the reformation comedies. "All right." She looked back at her book. "Tabula rasa is Latin for scraped tablet." The book flopped against her chest. "Do you think a person's mind at birth is a clean slate?"

"Whatever are you talking about?" She went to her bureau and opened her scarf drawer.

"Plato thought the human mind was an entity that preexisted in the heavens before being sent down to join a body here on Earth."

Harriet stared at her. "You speak such balderdash. It makes my head spin."

"Oh, Harriet. Do you not use that head of yours for anything but wearing hats?"

"I wish you'd stop filling yours with all that useless foolery." She turned back to her scarf drawer.

Emma closed the book. "It's common sense that we're born with a mind already primed. How else could men like Shakespeare, Jonson, and Marlowe write such brilliant plays?"

Harriet held up a blue scarf in one hand, and a peach coloured one in the other. "Which one do you like?"

"You're not even listening to me."

"You speak nonsense at which the clergy, I may add, would be most alarmed."

"A pox on the clergy." Emma folded her arms across her chest. "I will think what I like."

"The most important thing right now is what we're going to wear to the theatre."

"I don't care. You choose."

Harriet tossed the scarfs aside and took a yellow dress from the wardrobe. "I'll wear this, and you must wear your green one that matches your eyes."

A loud knock sounded on the front door. Harriet dropped the dress on the bed and went downstairs. She opened the door to their neighbour, who held a plate of freshly baked biscuits. "Mrs. Trent. How nice to see you again. Do come in."

"I can only stay a short while. There's always church business to attend to."

Harriet called Emma to join them and the short while stretched to an hour, which Emma endured while Harriet kept the conversation going with cheery chats about nothing.

The Grey Lady—for she wore no other colour—took a sip from her third cup of tea. "I haven't seen any gentlemen callers come to your door."

Harriet didn't miss a beat. She lowered her head. "I'm observing a year of mourning for my dearly departed parents." Her mouth turned down. "I'm sure you understand."

Mrs.Trent emptied her teacup. "Of course, my dear and that is admirable of you but don't wait too long to meet your life's mate. After all, it is a woman's duty to marry and have many children."

Theatre performances began in the afternoon to take advantage of the daylight. That Friday, at a quarter to three, Emma and Harriet wound their way along the narrow passages leading to the theatre's Bridge Street entrance. The building, a three-tiered wooden structure, held an audience of seven hundred. The glazed dome protected the stage, but with no roof over the seating area, people took the chance of being rained on. They threaded their way through a semicircle of backless benches covered with green baize cloth—each row a little higher than the next. Behind these, three galleries, divided into boxes ornamented with gold-tooled leather, rose in tiers where the gentleman and ladies sat.

Emma and Harriet settled into seats in the third row on a backless bench. When the first act finished, their legs and backs cried for a stretch. At this in-between time, friends called or waved to each other and gathered to discuss the first act or just chat.

In fifteen minutes, a young lad sprinted through the crowd, yelling the play was about to begin. Harriet dashed ahead to secure their seats, and Emma dawdled, thinking about the play's leading character.

The Lieutenant, capable of fighting ferociously was a hypochondriac. She smiled at the title's pun. *The Humorous*

Lieutenant, a play about a man whose medical humours were out of balance. *Whump!* She crashed headlong into a solid object, or it into her.

"Oh," a voice cried. A pair of arms encircled her, stopping her from toppling to the ground. "Are you all right?"

The tall man held her close. A wisp of lavender, or was it mint, drifted over her. His eyes the darkest blue she had ever seen. "I—I'm well, sir. You may let me go now." He did not wear a fashionable wig and his thick and wavy brown hair fell from under his hat to his shoulders.

"I beg your pardon, Miss." He dropped his arms, stepped back and with a flourish, removed his hat, making the feathers dance. "May I present myself?" He bowed. "I am William Johnstone, at your service." Even as he bent, his gaze did not leave her face.

Emma looked away, feeling a blush rising in her cheeks. *Who is this man, and why am I so addled?*

A well-attired man in a four-feathered hat on top of a white and curly wig stepped beside them. "William, are you coming? The play is about to begin." He grabbed his arm and pulled him away.

They took three steps, and the one who'd bumped into her turned his head and looked back. As the crowd swept the men away, a tiny smile jumped to Emma's lips.

She made her way to her seat, where Harriet had lifted her hand in a wave. *I wonder where they're seated. Not that it makes any difference.*

Harriet lowered her arm. "Who are you looking for?"

"No one."

A hush fell as the actors bounded on stage. A couple of times, Emma looked around as surreptitiously as she could. She slowly turned her head to the left and glanced along the row. A minute later, she looked right. She dare not turn around. *Why am I acting so silly? Who was he? He said he was William Johnstone.* She shivered at the mention of his surname. She would never forget that oily and disagreeable Mr. Johnstone, who had, so long ago stolen her uncle's box of books. She looked at the stage, reining in her wandering mind.

However, a few scenes later, she glanced up at the gallery boxes curving to the left. He was sitting in the front row, staring at her. She turned her head away. *Is my face red? I will not look in that direction again.* But her eyes had a mind of their own, and would meander off to the left. On one of her stolen glances, he was looking at the stage. He had a sculpted profile and strong chin.

Harriet nudged her with her elbow. "Stop fidgeting about."

Emma pulled her attention back to the stage. *Did his head move?* She stared straight ahead. *Is he looking at me?* She was glad she had on her jade-green dress and pearl necklace. Although her eyes faced front, her thoughts roamed elsewhere. *What is this strange feeling?* She gasped. She was acting like Catherine did around boys and when Beatrice would prattle on about Ralph. *But I don't like men. They're crude, rough, and gross.* She stole another glance to the left. Somehow she didn't think that lovely looking man, despite his surname, was any of those.

The play ended, and people crowded out. They made their way through the alley to the wider avenue where they would engage a carriage.

Harriet took her arm. "Are you acquainted with him?"

"Who?"

"Him." She tilted her head toward William, who was, at that moment, looking back at them. "That man keeps looking at you."

"He bumped into me at the interval."

"How rude."

"Oh, he was a gentleman. He stopped me from falling and apologized most graciously."

"Why are you smiling at him?"

"I'm not smiling. I'm being sociable."

The shorter dapper man with him had waved a carriage up.. William motioned for the other man to get in, and he followed. It was an open carriage, and as the driver guided the horse forward, William turned and looked back at Emma.

People brushed by, talking about the play and Harriet said, "I think you like that young man."

"That's foolishness. I just wondered who he was."

"Forget him. I suspect that he and his companion prefer each other's company. "

"What do you mean?"

"They are very discreet, as they have to be in public, but—" She lowered her voice. "There are men who love men, the way I love you."

Emma had heard about such liaisons. Her tutor was an effeminate young man who spoke with great devotion about his male mentor.

However, that subject was only whispered about in the most trusted of situations. Beatrice had also told her about men who desired men instead of women.

Harriet took her arm. "We're the lucky ones."

"What do you mean?"

"Women know what a woman wants, and besides, we have no worry about babies."

Emma remembered William's arms around her. *What would it be like to be with a man?*

Harriet tightened her grasp on her arm. "However, we have to be careful in public, especially men. In Germany, men who lie with men are burned with witches.

A swirl of dizziness came over Emma and a sharp pain shot through her head. "Do not speak of such things."

"What's the matter? Are you all right?"

Emma shook her off. "Talk of witches gives me a turn. I am sick with such thoughts. Never speak of witches or burning again."

A carriage pulled up, and Harriet got in.

Emma fumed. "It's monstrous and barbaric to burn or hang anyone. And I've read that most so-called witches were herbalists." She climbed in beside her. "And by whose authority is one kind of love considered good and another bad or sinful?"

The horse trotted over the cobblestones and Emma gradually calmed down from her curious outburst. Her thoughts drifted to William Johnstone. *Who is he?* When he had held her from falling over, albeit briefly, a cloak of closeness had surrounded her, like an old memory. *I know those arms—and those eyes. But that's impossible. I've never seen him before. How could I have any memory of him?* She looked out the window and stared at the passing scene without seeing it. *What if Plato was right? What if we bring memories from other lives into this one?* One might consider it a miracle to be born once, so why not twice, thrice, or a hundred times?

What if I've known William in another life?

Chapter 43

They arrived home, and no more was said about the evening or about the two gentlemen. Harriet prepared a meal while Emma busied herself with translating more of her uncle's papers. She wanted Isaac to read them, and rather than send the originals, she set out to make copies. It was laborious work, sharpening quills, painstakingly transcribing the deciphered anagrams, and adding additional notes. Her uncle had told her that many of his reference books were in the missing box. She put her quill down. *I wonder if William knows that nasty man?* It was a common name, but what difference did it make? She would probably never see William Johnstone again.

Three nights later, Harriet was especially amorous, and Emma found herself thinking of William. She closed her eyes, and when Harriet kissed her, William's deep blue eyes floated in front of her, and she imagined his strong arms around her. When she turned on her side to sleep, she lay awake for a few minutes, confused about entertaining such unfamiliar thoughts.

The next day she had an early breakfast alone and immersed herself in her work. She didn't see Harriet until mid-afternoon when they met for tea.

Harriet put the teapot, cups and a plate of almond cakes on the table. "You were quite the lover last night."

Emma squirmed. "You know I'm not comfortable talking about bedtime activities." *I dare not confess I had been picturing William in my mind.*

Harriet squeezed Emma's hand. "I'm so grateful you love me. I don't know what I'd do without you."

The next week end *Midsummer Night's Dream* was opening. Emma handed the notice to Harriet. "We must see that. It's one of my favourite plays."

On Saturday, they lined up early hoping to get a seat with a back. The theatre was filling fast and they found two seats in the first tier. The announcer came out on stage with his usual patter about what they were about to see.

Harriet whispered to Emma. "Why do they tell us the whole story before it is shown?"

"So we have the pleasure to see how the story unfolds and how they show it." She grabbed Harriet's hand. "Oh, good heavens!"

"What is it? What's wrong?"

She tilted her head to the left, indicating two men who were taking their seats. "Aren't they the two men we saw here last week?"

Harriet turned her head in that direction and gasped.

The men wore fashionable baggy breeches and short coats with copious ribbons tied at their neck. Ruffled long-sleeved white shirts blossomed forth from silk waistcoats. At the end of the wars, fashion had moved away from the military-style, now reflecting a more relaxed and peaceful look.

She frowned. "Pay no attention to them. They could be scoundrels."

It really is William. "They look respectable."

"You never can tell."

"What will be do if they approach us?" Emma's stomach did a little flip-flop.

"Ignore them. Listen to what the fellow is saying, or you won't know what the play's about."

At the interval, Harriet insisted they remain seated and lower their heads. However, out of the corner of her eye, Emma saw them stand and they were going to pass right in front of them.

Harriet stiffened. "Keep your head down."

They walked by right in front of them.

Harriet let out her breath. "That was close. We should change our seats."

"No. These are good ones." She got up. "I have to stretch my legs."

"Be sure those men don't see you."

Emma walked off and joined the crowd. The two men were just ahead.

When she got to the front area, she'd lost sight of them. Coming back she didn't see them either. Back in her seat, the warning bell sounded and the men came in a far opposite door.

The rest of the play went quickly and with the actors still taking curtain calls, people started filing out. The men went left and Harriet nudged Emma to the right exit.

Out on the street, the women waited for a carriage when a voice sounded behind Emma. "Excuse me miss. Did you drop this." He held one of Emma's gloves.

She turned and Harriet snatched the glove. "Come Emma. We must go."

The man with William tugged at his arm. "Come, the new coffee house will be packed."

William said to Emma, "Would you like to join us for an after-theatre coffee?"

"I've never tried that new beverage. I hear it's quite strong. From Turkey, I believe."

Harriet glared at William. "We do not know you gentlemen. Be gone and do not bother us."

William tipped his hat with a bow. "We are honourable gentlemen and only ask for your company to discuss the play over a cup of the coffee or tea if you prefer."

Emma turned to Harriet. "I would like to try that coffee drink. It's becoming popular and there will be a lot of people there.

Charles stepped up and removed his hat with a flourish. His curly white wig cascaded to his shoulders. He was a short man, or perhaps looked shorter beside William. "My dear ladies. We would be honoured to have your company for a short while."

William held out his hand to Harriet. "Gentle woman, have you never followed an impulse?"

"That is idle talk. I never have impulses."

Emma hid a smile. "There's no harm in a quick coffee and some lively discussion."

Harriet frowned. "Is it far?"

Charles took her arm. "Around the block." He stuck out his hand. "I am Charles Stanford and my friend. he gestured, is William Johnstone."

Harriet took his hand and shook it. "Harriet Brandon and my friend, Emma Lewis."

A short while became an hour, before the gentlemen flagged down a carriage to take the ladies home.

"We are fine by ourselves," Harriet said and climbed in.

Emma followed and the men tipped their hats goodbye.

In the carriage, Emma spoke first. "That was interesting. I've never heard so many people dissect a play so intently. Very stimulating."

"Hmmfph," grunted Harriet. "A lot of nonsense talk, if you ask me and why did you agree to meet with them next week?"

"Because a Ben Jonson's satirical play is coming."

"Are you sure it's not because of William's blue eyes?"

"Don't be silly. He means nothing to me." *I don't even know him.*

The next week passed swiftly. Emma was busy with transcribing her uncle's papers and Harriet tried her hand at millinery with the help of the woman in the hat store.

Saturday afternoon the women met their new male friends in front of the theatre and they found front row seats. The women sat in the middle, with a man at each side. Charles was about to sit beside Emma when William suggested that Charles would be more comfortable on the aisle seat.

After the play, they again walked a block to the fashionable coffee house and found a table for four. They ordered their coffee and discussed the play.

After a half hour Charles said, "Do you notice anything different when we are all together in a social setting? I noticed it was the same as last time we were here."

Emma shrugged. "We don't go to many social functions except the theatre."

"But do you ever get curious looks or people asking you where your young men are?'

Harriet grunted. "Oh we do get the latter. I get weary coming up with answers."

Charles nodded. "We get similar queries. Asking us where our wives are. And I, for one am tired of it." He paused. "William and I have a proposition for you to consider."

Harriet frowned.

He continued. "We have become more conscious of people's stares and possible suspicions when they see us so often together without the accompaniment of lady friends. We are physicians in training and wish no shadow of gossip, which could lead to dire consequences."

Harriet thrummed her fingers on her arm. "So you wish us to be your social companions to avoid the impression that you two gentlemen are lovers?"

Emma gasped.

"That is correct. I'm glad you deduced my meaning so swiftly. I pray you see the opportunity that as a team, we can be of aid to each other in our mutual interests of continued privacy."

Harriet unfolded her arms. "It may be a subject worth thinking about. I need some references from you."

"Of course. " He took a card from his waistcoat and handed it to her.

In the week that followed, Harriet made a trip to the hospital and to Oxford. At both places she was assured they were doctors in training with a fine standing and no record of any trouble.

The next Saturday, after an evening spent enjoying another reformation comedy, the four sat in the coffee shop.

Harriet stuck out a gloved hand. "We agree to be companions for a trial period."

Charles nodded. Strict and harsh laws were meted out to men and women who had carnal knowledge of the same sex. It was difficult to quash gossip, and if accused, one would be ruined, socially and economically, and, if proven guilty—burned, hanged, or drowned. He took her hand. "Fair enough."

Harriet picked up her cup. "We'll be social companions for propriety and safety's sake while continuing our personal lifestyles."

William turned to Emma. "Do you know an Albert Lewis?"

Emma turned her head smartly toward him. "He is my uncle. Why do you ask?"

"On the bottom shelf in my father's library, there are a number of books with the name *Albert Lewis* written on the flyleaf."

Emma was struck dumb. *My Uncle's books! The stolen box. That horrible Mr. Johnstone.* It was true. That unpleasant and disagreeable person *was* William's father. Her brain fought to integrate two impossible truths. How could a man like William have a man like Mr. Johnstone for a father? *But the books. They're there.*

Harriet touched her arm. "What's wrong my dear? You've turned white."

"I—" She took a deep breath and looked at William. "Many years ago, after my uncle fell ill, I rode with your father to London. I was a child, but I remember when I arrived at my steward's home, a box of books was missing."

William's eyes lit up. "My father must have found them."

Emma kept her face blank. *I can't believe that nasty man is William's father.*

William put down his cup. "I will ask Father about the books and you can retrieve them."

"Do you see your father often?"

"No. We've had a falling out. He doesn't approve of Charles. I've not seen him for some time."

"Perhaps it would be better for me to call on him unannounced." *If he has advance notice he could hide them.* "I am happy to go alone to save you any embarrassment."

William smiled. "That's probably a good idea. If he sees me it would only irritate him, but I'll be right behind you in case he tries to deceive you."

Emma frowned. "He is most disagreeable but he can't deny the books are not my uncle's with his name written inside."

"True. But I'll still be right behind you."

"I'm not afraid. He may be a thief but I suspect he is a coward too." She lowered her eyes. "Excuse me talking about your father that way."

"He's not my real father."

Emma's eyebrows went up and the heaviness in her stomach lifted. Why did it matter to her who his father was or wasn't? *Of course, I don't care.*

William continued. "I was a foundling, presumably an orphan and left on the steps of a monastery. The kind monks took me in and I lived there till I was nine. Mr. Johnstone visited one day, looking for rare books, when he apparently took a liking to me and offered to adopt me." He shrugged. "He said he needed a boy to run errands and do gardening, both of which I did neither."

Harriet smiled. "How fortunate for you."

"He tended to my every need, some I didn't know I had, and introduced me to the right path."

Emma picked up her coffee cup. She looked into his blue eyes. *Is he one of those empty-headed men? At least he won't be grabbing at my personal parts.*

He continued. "I'll be glad to show you where the house is."

"Thank you. I could never have found it."

"It's been a couple of years since I've been there, but Father doesn't like change, so there's a good chance the books are in the same place."

Charles spoke up. "Why don't we all go? After Emma collects the books, we could dine out.

Chapter 44

Arrangements were made for their first outing on the following Friday evening. They would make a quick stop at Mr. Johnstone's house and after that dine at a fashionable downtown restaurant.

Emma became more and more nervous as the day approached. She desperately wanted to recover the books, but the visit needed to be a surprise to give the man no time to clear the shelf. Friday arrived and the women were dressed in their theatre going clothes. Harriet had insisted she pay Emma's and her expenses. In public, the men would pay, and in private, perhaps every fortnight, they would tally up, and Harriet would reimburse them.

William and Charles arrived promptly. The women climbed into the carriage and sat opposite the men. William rose and took Harriet's hand. "May I? It would be prudent if we pair off."

She stood up, and they changed seats so that William now sat beside Emma and Harriet beside Charles. No one objected to the arrangement. What difference would it make how they paired off? It was all a sham, but Emma's stomach fluttered with unexpected anticipation.

No one spoke as the horse joined other carriages on their way into London's crowded cobbled streets. A gentle rain fell as they wound through narrow passageways. When they reached the tall house squashed between two others, Emma's stomach flip-flopped. This time from apprehension. She gulped as William called to the coachy to stop.

He jumped out and helped her down. "I think I should come in with you."

"No. You said if he sees you it would set him off in a foul mood. I'll be all right."

Their carriage was blocking other carriages and coachmen yelled for them to move on. William called to the driver. "Take it around the block." He and Emma walked to the front door.

She lifted the brass knocker and let it fall. *I'm not eight-years-old. I can do this.* The door opened, and Nathan, the old servant of eleven years ago, faced her. William stood at the side out of sight.

"I am here to see Mr. Johnstone."

"Is he expecting you, Miss?" His voice wavered.

"No. I met him long ago."

"Come in. I will see if he is available."

Emma followed his unsteady steps.

He indicated a room on the left. "Please wait here."

She hadn't been in that room when she was last in that house. She stepped in. Three walls of bookshelves. *So many books. Has he read them all?* A fireplace, with no fire, was to the right of an oak table, on which stood a lamp, a silver inkstand and two quills. And there was the two-shelved bookcase on the side wall below the front window exactly as William had described. She took a step toward it, eyeing the bottom shelf.

An oily voice spoke from the doorway. "How may I be of service, Madam?"

She turned to face him. "Mr. Johnstone. You may not recall me. You were kind enough to transport me to London many years ago."

His hollow eyes remained blank.

"My uncle had fallen ill, and you picked me up at the doctor's house."

He frowned, and a greasy string of hair flopped over his brow.

"From there, you took me to Mr. Edward's and—"

"Are you Emma Lewis?"

"I am she, and I believe you have my Uncle's books."

"Your uncle?" His eyes narrowed to slits.

"Albert Lewis is my uncle. When you took me to Mr. Edwards, you forgot to leave a second box containing his books."

He frowned. "I remember. Was he not your father?"

"No. My uncle."

"I know nothing about a box of books."

In two steps, Emma was at the bookshelf. She pointed to the bottom shelf. "Those look like my uncle's missing books." She bent down and put her hand on one. "And I suspect his name is written inside." She pulled it out and turned her head to look at him.

He had stepped closer and in his raised hand, he held the fire poker.

She moved back, but not fast enough. The blow struck her arm and ribbons of pain shot to her shoulder. The book dropped and she clasped her elbow.

A writhing face leaned over her. His voice stone-cold. "Do not touch those books." His sunken eyes darkened and with a menacing glint, he swung the fire poker over his head.

"No!"

The poker blurred toward her, and she fell unconscious and bleeding onto the faded oriental rug.

Chapter 45

The front door slammed open, followed by swift footsteps. Mr. Johnstone swung around, poker still in his hand. William rushed into the library. "My God, Father! What have you done?"

Frederick Johnstone stared at William. His eyes wild. "What are *you* doing here?"

"What am *I* doing? What are *you* doing?" He knelt beside the fallen Emma. "I know you hate women but this is outrageous."

"She was an intruder about to steal what is mine."

William leaned over her slumped body. A pool of blood spread around her head, matting her hair. He put two fingers to her neck. Her pulse was weak. "Quickly, send Nathan for Doctor Preston."

Nathan, the manservant, had followed William and stood in the doorway. Mr. Johnstone spoke in a dry, even voice. "There's been an accident. Please fetch the doctor."

Nathan hurried out and William carried Emma to the couch in the living room. "I need cloths and water. I must clean the wound and stop the bleeding."

Mr. Johnstone, the poker still in his hand, stood where he was.

"Make haste, Father. Get me some clean cloths and water."

Nathan reappeared. "I sent a lad for the doctor. I will get water, young master." He left the room and, in a moment, returned with a basin and clean towels draped over his arm.

By the time Doctor Preston arrived, William had cleaned and wrapped the wound.

The doctor checked her over. "She'll have a nasty scar on her forehead. That is if she lives."

William grasped the doctor's arm. "What do you mean? She must live."

"She's lost a lot of blood, but I'm worried about inward bleeding." He examined William's bandage.

"Excellent, William. You have learned your lessons well. You'll make a fine doctor."

He was still pale. "Thank you, sir. It's more difficult when it's one you know."

"Ah, yes." He looked at the limp figure on the couch. "We have to wait now and let nature take its course. The body has amazing healing properties, and with God's grace, we pray she'll recover."

Harriet burst into the room with Charles close behind. "Oh, my heavens!" she shouted. "What's happened?" She ran to Emma, knelt down and stroked her cheek, "My darling, my poor dear." She glared at the circle of men. "What has happened here?"

William and the doctor exchanged glances. Neither had seen what happened.

Mr. Johnstone stepped into the room. "I had just picked up the poker to tend to the fire when Miss Lewis tripped and hit her head."

Harriet's eyes narrowed. She pointed to the poker in his hand. "Why is there blood on the poker you hold?"

"I must have dropped it in my haste to help the poor woman."

William frowned. *He lies.* Should he expose this man who had changed his life? The man who had loved, nurtured, and educated him. If Emma died, it would be murder. *She cannot die.*

Harriet's eyes shot daggers at Mr. Johnstone. She turned to the doctor. "Can she be moved? I want to have her home so I can tend to her needs."

The doctor shook his head. "She should rest quietly for twenty-four hours." He felt her pulse again. "It is steady but best to leave her right where she is." He took the lap throw that Nathan handed to him and covered her. "William is qualified to attend her through the night. I will come by in the morning."

Harriet put her hand over Emma's limp one. "But I must stay. I cannot leave her."

The doctor touched Harriet's arm. "You can do no good for her now. She needs rest and quiet. Better you go home and pray." He looked at Charles. "Your young man can take you home. Don't worry. Come back tomorrow."

Harriet straightened her shoulders. "I will be back at first light." She shot a piercing look at William. "Take good care of her."

"I will, madam. Indeed, I will."

Nathan showed them out, and William pulled a chair beside the couch. His father was gone. *Where was he?* The books! Nathan came back into the room, and William jumped up. "Watch Miss Lewis for a moment. There's something I have to do." He raced into the library.

His father, kneeling on the floor at the bottom shelf, was rapidly stuffing books into a wooden box.

"Father, what are you doing?"

He glared at William. "Keep out of this. It's not your business."

"I think it is. A young woman of my acquaintance has been injured under suspicious circumstances. I know she was here to fetch those books, which I understand are her property."

He sneered. "Didn't I teach you to never consort with women? They are evil and will put a spell on you." He grabbed another book. "Do not meddle in my affairs. These books are valuable and will bring a substantial price at auction."

"You will not sell them. You will pack that box, and I will take it for Miss Lewis."

His face twisted. "Miss Lewis." He spat the distasteful words out. "You know not of what you speak."

"I know that each of those books has Albert Lewis's name on the flyleaf."

The two men's eyes locked. Mr. Johnstone took another book off the shelf and placed it into the box. William stared at him. The older man turned back to the shelf and took another book and another. He stopped and slammed the lid over the full box.

"Thank you, Father. I will have that now."

"No."

"If Miss Lewis dies, I will be sure a thorough investigation is carried out." He pointed to the bloodstain on the carpet and the splatters on the rounded edge of the bookcase. "There is nothing sharp on which Miss Lewis could have hit her head to have caused such an injury, and the grate is cold, so you were not attending to a fire."

The older man's lips twitched, and his eyes blazed. He pushed the box toward William. "Take the bloody books." He stood up and puffed his thin chest out. "But know this. I shall change my will on this very night. You will get nothing." He lifted his pointed chin. "Do you understand? Nothing."

"I want nothing more from you, Father."

"Do not call me father. I am not, and have never wished to be, your father." He strode from the room, leaving the packed box and his adopted son behind.

William hoisted the box and returned to the sitting room. He sat on the chair closest to Emma, where he could guard her and the box all night. Nathan brought him a plate of bread and cheese, a pear and a glass of wine. It wasn't the fine dining he had planned for that night but to his surprise, it tasted delicious and with her at his side, he wanted nothing more.

Nathan returned and took his plate away. William wiped Emma's brow and checked the bandage. The bleeding had stopped. *Thank goodness.* She was breathing steadily, and her pulse was getting stronger. He prayed her brain had not been hurt. There was still so much to learn about the human body. Thank God Dr. Harvey had discovered how the heart pumped blood through the body. William was only fourteen when he had the honour of meeting him—a year before the great man died—but that short visit had inspired him to become a doctor himself.

He put his feet up on the edge of the box. If he fell asleep, he would be alerted if anyone dared try to move it. How could his Father do such a thing? He shook his head. *I know he's greedy for wealth. The sole purpose for his well-stocked library was for its monetary value.* He's probably not read one book in it.

He checked Emma again, leaned back, and drifted into sleep.

Chapter 46

In the middle of the night, William awoke with a start. One boot had slipped off the box. He turned his head. Emma was looking at him. The moon shone through the window, and her jade eyes sparkled with life. He caught his breath. *Thank you, God.* He continued to gaze at her. He had seen those green eyes somewhere. A long time ago. In the same moonlight. He gasped. She was the girl who had slept in the guest room so many years ago.

She spoke first. "You're the boy."

"And you're the girl."

"The boy I saw here eleven years ago. The orphan boy who came to do gardening."

He'd never done a speck of gardening in his life. "Yes, I am he."

They stared at each other, transported back to when they were children and had gazed deeply into each other's eyes and had never forgotten. *How strange to see her again in the very same house.*

He touched her hand. "How do you feel?"

"My head is throbbing and I'm hungry. Otherwise, I feel fine."

"Hunger is a good sign. I'll get you some food."

He went to the kitchen and brought back a tray. She sat up and enjoyed the bread, cheese and grapes.

He pointed to the box. "Your books are safe."

"Thank you."

"I'll take them and you home in the morning."

When she finished eating, He took the tray and put it on a side table. "I'm glad you're well."

"I am too."

The moon was bright that night. Emma tried to shake off the feeling that she knew this man. But where could she have met him? She would have remembered. Perhaps it was a dream. A fairy tale dream of an imagined long ago love.

He looked at her, wishing she were a man. He knew how to love a man, and he would have liked to love her.

She looked at him, wishing he were a woman. She knew how to love a woman, and she would have liked to love him.

They fell asleep, and the moon continued its nightly journey through the black colander of stars. Anyone seeing it at that moment would swear it smiled.

In the morning, William changed the blood-soaked bandage for a fresh one. He sat beside her while she ate a light breakfast.

Harriet arrived in a flurry, her hair unruly and face pale. "My dear. How are you?"

"I am well. Do not worry."

"Your beautiful forehead. You'll have a nasty scar."

"It won't be my first."

William stood up. "She was fortunate."

Harriet stiffened. "You call that fortunate to be nearly killed by a madman over a box of old books." She glared. "We must leave now. The carriage is waiting. I will take care of her."

"She should rest for the next few days."

She bristled. "I'll be sure she is well looked after."

Emma finished her last mouthful of egg and was still holding her fork when Harriet thrust an arm around her. "Let me help you up."

"I can walk, Harriet. Don't fuss." She put the fork down.

"Let me at least take your arm, my dear." She linked her arm in hers, and they walked to the front door.

Emma turned and almost bumped into William, holding the wooden box. "Oh. I was just going to ask you to bring that."

"I must have read your mind."

Harriet hurried Emma through the doorway. "Come along. We must get you out of this dreadful place."

William carried the box to the carriage and secured it on the seat beside the driver. They pulled away. He waved and stood there for a moment. Did he imagine she'd looked back?

He said goodbye to Nathan and left without seeing his father. He had been taught to honour him and be grateful for what he'd done for him.

He hailed a Hackney carriage and climbed in. *But I can never forgive him for endangering Emma.* How could anyone do such a dastardly act?

The next afternoon, William and Dr. Preston checked in on Emma. Harriet sat close by.

The doctor patted her hand. "You're doing very well, my dear. The wound is healing nicely."

Emma didn't mention that she'd prepared a herb poultice to draw and hold the skin together. The scar would be minimal. She also drank several cups of camomile and vervain tea.

"You've lost enough blood so there's no need for further bleeding."

She grimaced at the barbaric medical procedure and motioned to the tea tray. "Will you stay for tea?"

"Yes, that would be—"

Harriet stood up. "I'm sure the gentlemen have more important duties to tend to. Come this way, sirs." And she rushed them out.

That evening, Emma lifted the lid off her uncle's box. She took the first book out.

Harriet walked in. "What are you doing? You need to rest."

"I'm fine, Harriet. I'm not sick. I just got a bump on the head."

"I don't want you to strain yourself, my love."

"I'm not an invalid." She opened the book.

"One would think those silly books are more important to you than I am." She put her hands on her hips. "What do you want with those musty old things anyway?"

Emma glanced at a flyleaf and picked up another book.

Harriet grunted and swept out of the room, banging the door shut behind her.

The pile grew higher. Indeed, Albert's distinctive signature was on every book. In his last letter, he'd said he would be returning soon. He'd been away far too long. *What has he been up to?* "I must write to him immediately about finding his missing books."

Most of them were arcane volumes or folios with copious notes, diagrams, spells and recipes. Precisely what she and Isaac needed for their further research. She ran her fingers over a hand-written parchment. *It must have taken hours to create such beauty.* On the top of the page was a single Arabic word *alchimia—the Egyptian art.* She was grateful for the many hours she'd spent studying ancient languages. The early Arabs had made significant contributions to alchemy, emphasizing the mysticism of numbers, and the quantities and durations for processes. Her heart quickened. "I must copy this out for Isaac right after I write to Uncle."

She sat at her desk with quill and paper so absorbed she did not hear Harriet enter with the tea tray.

"You do have to eat, my love." Harriet set it down. "Put that aside and have some cake."

Emma stretched her arms, wiggled her fingers and reluctantly left her desk. For the next hour, she endured Harriet's chatter about hats, and the latest dress colour. Meanwhile, her mind tugged at plans of seeing her uncle again and getting together with Isaac.

"So, what do you think?"

Emma jerked. "Pardon?"

"I said, 'our new acquaintances, William and Charles, would like to take us to dinner this Friday.' Do you feel up for it?"

"This Friday?" Her mind swirled with numbers and formulas, but William's name had pushed them aside. "Yes, I would like that."

"Good. I'll let them know. Now it's time you rested. Enough of those smelly books." She picked one up. "Time to put them away."

Emma frowned. "Leave them, please."

"I was only trying to help." Her lower lip quivered.

Emma sighed at Harriet's *poor-neglected-me* pose. "It's just that there's something important I have to read. Give me another half hour, and I'm all yours."

"Promise?"

"Yes."

"I'll hold you to that. We'll have a lie down when you're finished."

To Harriet, sex was the answer to everything. As soon as she left, Emma went back to her desk and looked at the thick book on top. Her mind drifted. *Stop thinking about that man. He means nothing to me.* She shook her head and opened the book where she'd placed a marker. *And I'm sure I mean nothing to him.* She liked to read aloud. Hearing the words was like a great teacher speaking to her. "Alchemy is an ancient path of spiritual purification and transformation. Through images, one can expand one's consciousness, developing both insight and intuition."

The image of William surfaced again. She took a moment to refocus. "Steeped in mysticism and mystery, it could initiate dreamlike symbols with the power to alter consciousness and connect the human soul to the Divine." *Perhaps not all men are uncouth and crude.* She shook her head again. *What is wrong with me?* It must have been that bump. She wasn't thinking straight.

Harriet opened the door. "Enough of that boring reading. Come to bed."

Emma sighed and closed the book. As she readied for bed, a face with brown wavy hair and dark blue eyes danced in her mind.

Friday arrived and by seven, Emma and Harriet, coiffed and dressed in their finery, awaited the arrival of their new gentlemen callers. Fashion-conscious Harriet happily wore her latest new dress with the low neckline revealing more of her ample bosom. She also preferred to wear a periwig which was faster than curling her own hair. Emma's walnut curls hung to her shoulders and her pale blue dress showed off her white skin.

Emma tugged at the front of her dress. "Is this too low? It was only a few years ago we were wearing dresses up to our neck."

"You look fabulous." Harriet frowned. "It's a good thing these men aren't attracted to women."

Emma tilted her head. "What do you mean?"

Harriet put on a glove. "They'd be all over you." She pulled on her other glove. "I see how men look at you." She sniffed. "At least being seen with our gentlemen escorts will stop the gossip and whispering."

That night they'd planned to go to a popular restaurant which would stifle any idle rumours, and their once-a-week outing to the theatre or opera would squelch any other further suspicions.

In the carriage, William took his seat beside Emma, leaving Harriet and Charles as a pair. The evening went well. In public, the women took the men's arms, and everyone was attentive and charming. They laughed gaily and interchanged glances and innocent touches. Any onlooker would think they were two couples having a night out and Emma had to admit she did enjoy the pretence.

Chapter 47

Emma awoke early the next morning. The air sparkled with excitement. The night before she had received a letter from her uncle that he had arrived home. It had been nearly a year since she'd seen him. *How can time fly by so fast?* She had so much to tell him. Letters were fine, but some things had to be said in person. She threw off the blanket and got ready for the day.

At breakfast, Emma broke the news to Harriet. "I'll be spending the weekend at my uncle's. I need to take his books to him."

Harriet dropped her fork. "You can't do that."

"And why not, pray tell?"

"A new play is opening this afternoon. I told Charles we'd be going."

"But, we went out last evening." *It would be nice to see William again.* "You can go with Charles, or we can see the play on a weekday."

Harriet frowned. "You know they're in Oxford during the week. Your uncle can wait for his dusty old books."

Emma shoved her plate away and stood up. "I am going, and that's it." She stalked off.

"Come back. I didn't mean to insult your precious uncle or his—" But she had already left the room.

The carriage pulled up in front of Mr. Edward's house. She scrambled out and bounded up the steps.

Albert met her at the doorway and grabbing her in his arms, he swung her in a circle. "You've grown up on me!" He held her at arm's length. "Have I been gone that long?" He hugged her again, and they walked into the house and along the hall.

She stopped short. "Your box!" She ran to the front door and yanked it open.

Albert followed her. "What box?"

She turned to him. "Your books! Your missing box. I found it."

The coachy walked up the front steps with the box. "You left this, ma'am."

A flustered Albert gave the man some coins. "Thank you for delivering my two most cherished treasures."

The man left and Emma stood in the hall with her hands on her hips and a twinkle in her eye. "So, I am no more to you than an old box of books?"

Albert carried the box into the sitting room." Oh, I'd say you must be worth at least two."

She followed him in. "Only two?"

He put the box down and hugged her again. "I've missed you."

"I've missed you too. I wondered if you were ever coming back. I have so much to tell you."

Mr. Edwards walked in and greeted her with a bear hug. "It's been far too long, young lady."

They sat down, and Mrs. Thorpe came around the corner, hands a flutter. "Land sakes. You've grown. It's been so quiet around here, and now we have you both back." A quick hug, and she left to make her special lamb stew.

The afternoon passed swiftly. Emma wanted to hear everything about his trip and what he and Charlotte had done. In her many letters, she had told Albert she had moved in with Harriet and about meeting the brilliant young Isaac, but he insisted on more details. She talked a lot about Isaac but not much about Harriet and nothing about William except he had attended her head injury.

Albert waggled a finger at her. "You should have waited for me to fetch the books."

"I probably should have, but once I knew where it was, I had to get it as soon as possible." She put her hand on the top of the box. "I felt responsible that wretched man had kept it."

His eyebrows shot up. "You were only eight years old. You did a magnificent job, and you looked after me when I was sick." He hugged her. "Your mother would be so proud of you."

She gazed past his shoulder and through the window. A bluebird landed on a branch of the maple tree, making it sway. "That was such a long time ago."

They swapped stories well into the evening until Mrs. Thorpe announced supper. Mr. Edwards joined them in the dining room, and between mouthfuls, the conversation continued.

The next day after breakfast, Albert rearranged some book shelves to hold his newfound books. Emma sat cross-legged on the floor. He opened the box and found a book containing a pack of loose papers. He pulled them out and handed them to her. "Have a look at these?"

On the first sheet, the word *alchimia* was written in large letters. She looked up. "Did you know that Alchemy dates back to ancient Egypt?"

"Indeed. Egyptian alchemists used their art to make alloys, dyes, perfumes, cosmetic jewelry and to embalm the dead."

She looked at him fondly, glad he hadn't given his whole life over to love. She pointed to a book he'd just taken out. "That one was most enlightening. I copied some parts to show Isaac."

"You seem quite taken with this boy. Do I sense a romance?"

She stared at her uncle. *Romance? What is he talking about?* "Oh, no. Isaac and I are study partners. And he's much smarter than I am."

"Don't underestimate yourself. You have a good mind."

"Thank you, but lately, my brain seems to be elsewhere."

"What do you mean?"

She sighed. "I find it hard to concentrate on the words. My thoughts roam off."

"Perhaps it's from that nasty bump you got when you fell."

She hadn't told him the details about her head injury. She didn't want him or Mr. Edwards insisting she charge the horrible creature. She wanted nothing more to do with him. "Perhaps."

He put a book onto the shelf. "We don't have to discuss Alchemy right now."

"But I want to. It's such a fascinating subject." She glanced at the paper in her hand. "Imagine taking a piece of lead and changing it into gold. It would eradicate poverty. Everyone would have a house to live in and plenty of food."

"Yes. But some people quest for gold for selfish reasons." He stretched his shoulders. "Time for a tea break. Let's move to more comfortable seats."

Mrs. Thorpe was happy to make tea, and she had just at taken a pan of lemon tarts out of the oven. "You sit yourselves down. I'll be right in."

They moved to the upholstered chairs in the sitting room in front of a low burning fire. For several minutes they watched the flames flicker and dart around a lazy log. Mrs. Thorpe brought in a lovely tray with fresh lemon tarts and steam rising from the tea.

Albert continued from where he'd left off. "One can also approach Alchemy from a spiritual perspective. To purify oneself by eliminating the *base* material of the self to achieve the *gold* of enlightenment."

"Isaac is very spiritual. He said the universe is an outpouring of the Divine, and I think he's doing a good job of wrestling its secrets out."

"It sounds as if anyone can, he will."

"I believe he will. We read more of the *The Emerald Tablet* where it says, 'as above, so below' but with spiritual alchemy, one could think, 'as within, so without.'"

He smiled. "I don't think there's anything wrong with your brain."

Emma continued. "The protestants have proclaimed one can experience God directly without the intervention of the clergy." She looked up. "Maybe alchemy is another way to the Divine Source."

They spent the rest of the morning poring over the paper and referring to several books until Mrs. Thorpe interrupted with lunch.

Chapter 48

On Sunday, they finished breakfast, and the conversation turned to more personal matters. They sat at the dining room table drinking tea, while Mrs. Thorpe cleared the rest of the dishes away.

Emma refilled her cup. "You were in France for a long time. How did a month turn into a year?"

"It's easy when you're with the one you love."

Emma plunked her cup down. "You've waited this long to tell me that?" Her eyes flashed. "Are you going to marry her?" She held her breath. *Is he going to live in France?*

"Yes, Emma. I *am* going to marry Charlotte." He took her hand. "When your mother died, I never thought my heart would mend. And if it hadn't been for you—" He squeezed her hand. "You gave me a reason to live."

Tears welled in her eyes. The feeling was mutual. Her uncle was her only family, and she nearly lost him once. "Does this mean you'll be moving to France?" She held her breath.

"We talked about that, and she appreciates what you mean to me. We'll live in France for six months and in London for six."

She let her breath out. "I can't wait to meet her."

"You will. And soon. We've set the date—in France. In one month. We want you to come, of course."

"One month! So soon. I guess not. You've been gone forever."

"And bring a guest. There is plenty of room at the DuBois estate."

Mrs. Thorpe came in and picked up the empty teapot. "Would you like a top-up on those tea leaves?"

Albert laughed. "Let's have a fresh pot, Mrs. Thorpe. We'll take it in the sitting room."

In comfortable chairs, Albert tilted his head. "So is there anyone special in your life you'd like to bring to the wedding?"

She lifted the woollen tea cozy and lid off the pot and briskly stirred the leaves. The spoon rattled.

"I'm sure there's plenty of young men interested in you."

She replaced the lid and its warm cover. *What would he think if I told him everything about Harriet?*

"Or perhaps a young woman?"

Emma glanced away. "Harriet and I are—good friends."

"There's nothing wrong with that. We can't help who we fall in love with."

"Oh, I don't love her." She stopped. "I mean—I—I don't know what I mean."

Albert took her hand. "You're young. Give it time, and it will work itself out."

"I'm so confused. I thought I hated men. Boys are so uncouth and vulgar, and when Harriet—well, I assumed this was who I was."

"And is it?"

"I don't know." She glanced down. "When William bumped into me at the theatre, something woke up in me. Like an old memory."

"William? Ah yes, the young man who bandaged your head."

"You remembered his name when I told you about that?"

"I'm your mother's twin brother. I know you better than anyone. Your voice changed when you first said his name, and again just now."

She lifted the cozy up and peered under as if to discover a hidden secret. "It must be ready." She poured two cups and handed him one. They sipped quietly for a few minutes.

She let out a long breath. "I don't know what to think—or do. My mind and heart are in a whirl. Why would I have such a reaction to a man? When he is close to me, I tremble like an egg in hot water."

Albert laughed. "That sounds like love to me."

"But how can I love him. I hardly know him."

"Perhaps you knew him in a past life. Or a future one. Depending on how you believe in reincarnation."

She put her cup down. "That did cross my mind. I've read Plato and thought I understood all about that."

"Words do not teach. Experience does."

"I'm shocked. You love words."

"I do. Words can inform us, guide us and influence us, but experience is the real teacher."

"I see we've both made changes in our lives."

That evening on the way back to the Parson's house, thoughts marched through Emma's head. *I know I should invite Harriet to come with me to France.* She looked out the window. A light rain pattered on the glass. *I wonder if William has ever been?* The wheels rumbled over the cobblestones. *That's impossible. I couldn't ask him.* She gazed out the window again. *Harriet would go wild if I even suggested he go with me.* The rain slowed down to a drizzle. She would be home soon.

In another ten minutes, the carriage pulled up. She ran to the side entrance where Harriet greeted her with a scowl. "You stayed long enough. I thought you said you'd be home for supper."

Emma shook off her cape and hung it up. "You know how it is. We got to talking."

Harriet crossed her arms. "Am I ever going to meet that elusive uncle of yours?"

They walked into the kitchen, and Harriet put on the kettle. Emma got out cups and saucers. "Did Mrs. Trent bring any more treats?"

Harriet pointed to oatmeal biscuits. "She popped in yesterday."

Emma took one. "How would you like to go to France?"

"Did you say France?" Her face lit up. "Anywhere close to Paris?"

"Is ten minutes by carriage close enough? My *elusive* uncle is getting married next month, and—we're invited."

Harriet slapped a hand over her mouth. "The fashion capital of the world." She shook her head. "How wonderful. When do we leave? I must get new clothes. We'll go shopping first thing in the morning."

Harriet prattled on while Emma poured bubbling water into the pot. *I wonder what William would have said if I'd asked him?*

Chapter 49

The next morning Harriet left early for shopping. It was late afternoon when she returned, her arms full of parcels.

Emma looked up from her book. "Why are you buying clothes when you can get them in Paris."

Harriet ripped open the first parcel and shook out a full-skirted dress with long sleeves. "I can't go to Paris looking like a country bumpkin." She held it up.

"Did I tell you I'm going to go to my uncle's next weekend to help him look for a house for him and Charlotte?

Harriet laid the dress over the back of the settee. "You can't go on a weekend. It's the only time Charles and William can come to the theatre with us. And Romeo and Juliet is opening. You said you wanted to see that."

Emma had read the play and did want to see it performed. "All right. I'll go to my uncle's on Monday, but I'll stay for the whole week. We have to buy furnishings as well."

Harriet opened the next parcel and pulled out a blue silk scarf. She shook it out and wafted it in front of Emma. "I bought you a present."

Emma caught it, letting it slide in ripples over her hand. "Thank you. It's beautiful." She draped it around her shoulders. "I'll wear it to the theatre on Saturday."

"Aren't you going to save it for Paris?"

She lifted it to her face, pillowing her cheeks in clouds of silk. "No time like the present."

Friday came quickly. All week, Emma had looked forward to seeing the play. However, as they left the theatre, she fumed. "How dare they change the ending to have them live happily ever after."

Harriet, walking beside Charles, turned to her. "It's only a play. What's the difference?"

Emma stopped short, making the couple behind them veer around her and William. "What's the difference?" She put her hands on her hips. "You don't mess with a Shakespeare play or anyone's. It's how they wrote it and we should respect that."

Harriet took her hand. "Don't get yourself into a muddle. Come along. I heard of another one of those new coffee cafes has opened."

On Monday morning, Emma took a hackney carriage to Westminster. She and her uncle would need to find the right house for him and his new bride.

Albert did not want to live in overcrowded downtown London, so they kept their search to the west end. On the second day, they found a recently vacated three-story stone house on the Thames only three blocks from Mr. Edward's house. They walked in, and Emma stood in front of the row of windows in the sitting room. "You can watch the boats go by."

"Do you think Charlotte will like it?"

She spun around. "How could she not?" She spread her arms wide. "Four bedrooms, three bathrooms, a dining room, a huge kitchen, and this lovely sitting room."

He bit his lip. "But is it big enough?"

Emma's mouth made an O. "Big enough? Uncle Albert, how many rooms do you need? And isn't this going to cost a lot?" Her uncle had always lived frugally. This was a new side of him.

He grinned. "Charlotte's home in France is quite large, and we'll need a spare room for when you come to visit." He waved a hand. "As far as money goes, don't worry. I have an inheritance from my parents, collecting interest until I needed it."

Emma's mouth dropped open again. "You mean you could have been living in your own house or flat all these years? Why have you lived in one room at Mr. Edwards?"

"I liked it there. It was close to St Paul's Churchyard and the booksellers, and Mr. Edwards was a formidable debater. Not to mention Mrs. Thorpe's cooking."

She smiled. "What will you do without her lamb stew and lemon tarts?"

"Charlotte has written to her sources in London to find her a day cook, a housekeeper, and a maid. And Mrs. Thorpe is writing out her recipes."

With the house secured, they spent the rest of the week going to furniture makers choosing chairs, settees, a mahogany sideboard, oak tables, and beds to be moved in. The large four-poster bed would be the most challenging item to maneuver up the carved staircase.

At the end of the week, weary from the unaccustomed flurry of furniture buying and arranging for movers, they sat in Mr. Edward's sitting room waiting for one of Mrs. Thorpe's soups.

Emma looked up. "I have a question, Uncle Albert."

"What's that, my dear?"

"If you and mother had an inheritance, why didn't my mother return to England after my father was killed? Why did you go to Germany?"

"That's easy to answer. At that time, Civil War was raging in Britain, and it wasn't a safe place to be." He grimaced. "However, Germany wasn't so—."

Mrs. Thorpe entered with fragrantly steaming bowls and a plate of bread. "Here you are. Eat up."

Tantalizing smells of onions, garlic, cardamom, and cumin mixed with tangy roasted vegetables and fried chicken swirled around them. They dug in and didn't speak until their bowls were empty.

Emma patted her stomach. "Mrs. Thorpe's famous soups should be called stews."

Albert put his spoon down. "I'll miss Mrs. Thorpe's cooking."

"I hear the French are rather good cooks."

"Indeed, they are." He poured tea and took a sip. "Your own inheritance will come into effect on your twenty-first birthday."

"My inheritance?"

"From your mother."

Emma wrinkled her forehead. "I assumed hers went to you."

"Oh, no. That was set aside for you. It's not grand, but over the years, the interest has grown. In a couple of years, you'll be an independent woman with a healthy yearly income."

"Were your parents rich?"

"They were comfortably well off. Our mother's family, your grandmother, owned a good chunk of land in north Wales, and when she died shortly after your grandfather, it went to Anne, the first born." He lifted his teacup in a toast. "But your mother, being who she was, insisted it was to be shared between us."

Emma cut the pound cake and spooned custard over it. "Do we still own the land in Wales?" A little shiver passed through her. She handed the plate to Albert.

"Oh, yes. Over the years, Mr. Edwards has been collecting and managing the funds from the tenants."

"I'd like to visit someday."

Albert stuck a fork into his cake. "Yes. Let's do that. It's in Holyhead." He looked up and squinted. "I think there's even an old castle on the land."

Chapter 50

The weeks sped by. Albert moved into his new house and bought another bookcase. Harriet continued to shop for the trip to France.

Emma packed her travelling bag, mostly with clothes, but she couldn't resist putting in at least two books. Much to Harriet's annoyance, she liked to read every night and most of the time Harriet fell asleep waiting for her to finish. Emma picked up the pile of books from her bedside table and tumbled them onto the bed for sorting. Her dragonfly toppled onto the quilt. She gasped and held it to her chest. "Dragonfly. I've been ignoring you, or you've been hiding on me. Of course, you must come to France." She kissed it and placed it securely into her travel bag, sliding it between her new nightgown and the blue silk scarf Harriet had given her. "You'll be comfy there, my friend."

On the next afternoon, Harriet, dressed and ready for the Opera turned in a circle in front of Emma who was curled up in a chair reading. "What do you think?"

No response and Harriet yelled, "Emma."

Emma jumped and looked up. "What?"

Harriet fumed. "Sometimes you infuriate me."

"What did I do?"

"When you stick your nose in a book you ignore the whole world around you. I was showing you my new dress."

"Very pretty."

"Is that all you can say? It's one of the newest arrivals from Paris."

"Why did you buy it here? We're leaving for France tomorrow where we'll be a ten-minute carriage ride from Paris."

"I want to arrive looking as if I belong." She poked her hand through the beaded handle of a small embroidered purse trimmed with white lace.

"I suppose the purse is Parisian as well?"

"Of course. Are you ready? Charles and William will be—." The door knocker clattered. "They're here." She ran downstairs.

Emma, already dressed, put her book aside and went down. She entered the hall on Harriet's words. "—and we'll be gone for three whole weeks."

Charles tapped his cane against a buckled boot. "Oh, dear. What will we do? Othello is opening next weekend."

Harriet opened the door. "You'll just have to get along without us." She stepped out.

William held Emma's cape and slipped it over her shoulders. "We'll miss you."

Emma grasped the door frame to steady herself. *Did his hand linger for a second on my shoulder?*

Early the next morning, Albert arrived in a covered coach for the first leg of their journey. He and Emma would not be travelling in an open wagon as they did ten years earlier. They settled onto a padded seat and Harriet sat opposite with a stack of boxes piled beside her. The trip would take six days—two to get to Dover and across the Channel to Calais and four days through France to the DuBois home.

By mid-morning, the mist had lifted, and after a tea break, they continued on. It was early evening when they approached Sittingbourne, the half-way point where they would stop for the night. A small inn on the right displayed a swinging sign with the head of a dog and bull painted on it. As they passed by, Emma whispered to her uncle. "I wonder if Mrs. Burke is still there?"

"Mrs. Burke? Oh yes, that was the place. Do you want me to have the driver stop? We could stay there tonight."

"No. I don't want to remember that time. And I don't think the rooms would suit Harriet."

Harriet looked up. "What are you two mumbling about?"

Emma squeezed her uncle's arm. "Just an old occurrence that happened a long time ago."

In Sittingbourne, the coach pulled up to The Lyon Inn. They stretched and climbed out, and the driver assured them he would look after their parcels and luggage.

They signed in and headed upstairs to freshen up before supper. Albert led the way. "Did you know that Henry V stayed here on his way back from the Battle of Agincourt?" They continued along a hallway. "And Henry VIII stayed here twice." He stopped at his door.

Harriet opened the door opposite. "Maybe we'll sleep in the same bed that a king did."

The next morning at breakfast, Emma asked where the name Sittingbourne came from.

Albert put his teacup down, eager to add another piece of history. "It's a Saxon word meaning 'the hamlet by the bourne or small stream.'"

Harriet spread peach preserves on her toast. "It's certainly a busy spot now. We took the last table for breakfast."

He continued. "Its popularity rose after the murder of Tomas Becket, and pilgrims would flock to Canterbury Cathedral. Chaucer also mentions Sittingbourne as a stopping point in The Canterbury Tales."

Harriet held her toast aloft and gazed at Albert. "How do you keep all that information in your head?"

Emma grinned. "You'd be surprised at what information he keeps."

Harriet shrugged and took a large bite of toast. They finished their breakfast in silence and resumed the trip to Dover.

The weather promised a comfortable voyage and the crossing was smooth. On arriving at the dock, Albert made inquiries and was directed to a Captain Mercier where M. DuBois had arranged for a private vessel to transport them across the twenty or so miles stretch.

Harriet settled inside the small cabin, but Emma and Albert left their bags and went outside to lean on the rail. Sailors hustled about, pulling ropes and calling to each other. Gulls squawked and soared over their heads as vast sheets of canvas unfurled.

The wind whipped Emma's hair about and flapped at their capes like an impatient child. She held her hair off her forehead and leaned to her uncle's ear. "It doesn't smell as bad as I remember."

He pointed to a large ship with billowing black sails, its decks crowded with cargo. "I'll bet that one does."

They joined Harriet inside and enjoyed tea and sandwiches, and small sweet cakes dipped in chocolate. The sailor serving them called them Madeleines. Harriet discovered another cabin with a cot, and she was happy to be rocked to sleep for a few hours.

The ship docked at Calais with plenty of time before the sun set. They disembarked, and took a few moments to regain their land legs, when they received another welcome surprise. A young lad in scarlet and gold livery approached and led them to a two-horse covered coach again sent by the M. DuBois. He took care of their bags as they settled onto the wide upholstered seats fitted with curved metal springs to lessen the shock of wooden wheels bouncing over rough roads. The liveried coachman and lad also carried firearms, assuring safe passage and protection from untoward highwaymen.

Taking the reins, the driver started them on the longest leg of their journey. Since their last trip, more inns lined the popular route, and two horses moved faster than one. The first night they stayed in a convent and the next two in well-appointed inns with excellent food and soft beds. Any payment offered by Albert was refused. Although they had food and rest breaks throughout the day, both for the horses and themselves, it was a tiring journey.

Harriet, rubbing a hand on her bent back, hobbled into the last inn. "Just show me a bed and don't wake me for ten hours."

On their fourth and final afternoon, the driver slowed and carefully passed a large oncoming passenger coach drawn by four horses. Six or perhaps eight people crowded inside while more rode in an open basket attached to the back. Two men sat on the roof, holding tightly to luggage and handrails. Emma leaned out the window at the lively sight. One risky fellow lifted his hand and waved.

She leaned back in her seat. "We must thank M. DuBois for the excellent transportation."

Their coach slowed, and the horses turned onto a wide path of hard-packed earth, which instantly offered a smoother ride. Albert peered out the window. "You'll soon be able to have your ten hours of rest."

Harriet stretched. "Thanks be to our dear Lord. I'm so tired of this constant moving. I'm sure I'll sit for a whole week."

Fifteen minutes later, the path became cobblestones, and the horses stopped at a wide iron gate with a large curved metal B affixed in the centre. The lad jumped down, opened the gate, and the coach moved through. He closed and latched the gate and jumped back on. The landscape opened to fields of grapevines.

Harriet's mouth gaped. "You didn't mention they made wine."

Albert laughed. "They don't. They own the land, but monks at a nearby monastery cultivate it and make the wine. Of course, the DuBois family has an unlimited supply."

In another ten minutes, hooves clicked on tile and came to a stop. Albert stepped down and helped Harriet down. She gasped. "What is this place?"

A rambling structure stood before them. It looked as if the architect couldn't make up his mind or perhaps many architects had put their hand to it. Different sized additions clung to the original two-story fieldstone house. On the right of the main building, rose four stories of various styles, meeting together at a gabled roof. On the left, three levels became two, changed their mind and grew back up to three again. Wood, stone, marble, and slate fought for attention.

Albert shrugged. "Did I tell you that Charlotte lived in a unique house?" He reached up for Emma. "With a large family."

She took his hand and stepped down. "They must need a map to find their way around."

A woman with blonde curls to her shoulders ran out and down the broad stone steps. She rushed to Albert, who scooped her into his arms. "And this is Charlotte."

She hugged Emma. "I've heard so much about you." She flung her hand toward the bold, yet warmly beckoning building. "Welcome to La Maison DuBois.

Chapter 51

Four hundred years ago, La Maison DuBois had been a simple hunting lodge in the woods. Over the centuries, each DuBois added levels, wings, parlours, bathrooms, nurseries, and passageways to create a sprawling maze of living quarters. A mixture of building styles, from circular turrets to Gothic spires, offered an architectural feast. Some might call it a nightmare. Italian marble columns met a mason's fieldstone walls, and a manicured green terrace rolled into a massive vegetable garden at the bottom.

The present DuBois family consisted of a healthy and active mother and father, twelve robust children, a spinster sister, two sons-in-law, and three grandchildren. In addition to nursemaids, cleaners, housekeepers, gardeners, cooks, bakers, carpenters, caretakers, stable boys, and drivers.

At dinner the first night, the family gathered in the main dining hall around a very long harvest table. Only the two eldest children, Marcel, a priest and Noelle, a nun, were absent. Charlotte, twenty-six, and her siblings, every two years apart ending with ten-year-old Adele, solemnly sat with hands in prayer position. The husbands of two married daughters and their three children, ranging from four years to a babe in arms, sat at the far end beside Madame DuBois's older sister, Agnes.

M. DuBois lifted his hand for silence, said a short blessing, and finished with bon appétit. The clamour of eating and talking began.

Emma's head spun with the barrage of names. She read French well, but with ears not attuned to such fast speech, the bevy of excited voices overlapped each other. At intervals, M. DuBois would rap a spoon on a metal dish demanding quiet. Even the baby would hush, however, the respite was short. First, a whisper, then a giggle, or a question to the visitors and before they answered, another question would tumble forth, followed by a hubbub of raised voices. Within minutes, much ado about everything had escalated to new heights.

That evening—Jeanne or maybe it was Louise—led Emma and Harriet through a maze of hallways in the direction of what was called the north-east wing and opened the door to an amply furnished room: two bureaus, a double wardrobe with mirrored doors, two high-backed wooden chairs, two single beds piled with overstuffed pillows and duvets, and a small side table beside each bed. A large table held a basin, a jug, and a stack of towels. The girls dashed kisses on Emma and Harriet's cheeks, and with a quick, "Breakfast at seven," they scampered away.

Emma put her bag on a bed. "I hope they'll come for us."

Harriet climbed onto the other one and flopped onto a cloud of feathers. She lay back with an arm behind her head. "My goodness. I didn't think the food or the talking would every stop."

"I've never heard so much French spoken all at once. And so fast."

Harriet groaned. "Can you imagine having a dozen children."

Emma pulled her covers back. "Most women have eight to ten children and half of them die before they're five. This family was obviously blessed."

Harriet grunted. "I would call it cursed."

"That's a terrible thing to say. Haven't you ever wanted to have children?"

"Never. And I hope you never want any."

Emma pulled her nightdress out, put her dragonfly on the table beside her bed and went to the washbasin.

The next two days, a melee of people, food, and wedding preparations filled the hours. Madame DuBois was delighted Charlotte had finally found her helpmate and could now get on with giving her more grandchildren.

Harriet, eager to see Paris, hinted broadly as to when and how this could happen. The two older brothers, Pierre and Andre, twenty-four and twenty-two, willingly agreed to take their fetching young guests into the city to visit a new coffee house.

After dinner, the boys called for a carriage. Pierre snapped up the seat beside Emma, leaving Andre and Harriet sitting together opposite them. He pointed to Emma's beaded purse in her lap. "Keep a tight hold of that." He nodded to Harriet's small bag, which hung from her shoulder on a braided cord. "And yours, especially. Beggar children are trained to cut those strings and run off before you know it."

Harriet frowned and grasped her purse. "Oh, dear. Is Paris as crowded as London?"

Andre laughed. "I haven't been to London, but Paris streets are narrow and covered with a foul-smelling soup of mud, garbage and horse droppings. Don't worry. We won't be walking far."

They stopped at a bustling coffee shop and after that an all-night cafe for a light snack and wine. On the way home, Harriet dozed and Andre attempted a song, but at the end of a slow and wavering chorus, he slumped and flopped his head onto her shoulder.

Emma smiled. It was a good thing Harriet was half asleep, or she would have shoved his male head far from her.

The carriage reached the DuBois gate, and the horse made its way along the cobbled path to the house. Pierre inched closer to Emma. "Did you have a good evening, my dear?"

She leaned away. "It was certainly noisy and crowded, but the coffee was good."

He took her hand and kissed it. "I would like to kiss your rosy lips." He swayed toward her, stopping inches from her face. "But I promised father I would be a gentleman." He gazed into her eyes. "And a gentleman always asks permission first." His voice ended with a question mark.

Emma froze. Pierre was a gentleman with soft hands. He was not rough or crude like the silly schoolboys. *What would it feel like to have him kiss me?*

Hooves clattered on paving stones around the circle and the carriage came to an abrupt stop, jerking the passengers about.

Emma gathered her purse and tapped Harriet's knee. "We've arrived. Wake up."

The foursome slowly disembarked. A stumbling Andre and a smiling Pierre bowed, thanked their companions for a lovely evening and staggered to their own rooms. The women followed a maid up the stairs and through the maze of winding halls to theirs.

The next morning, sharp raps on the door and giggles through the crack woke them up. Adele and Louise poked their heads around, speaking over each other. "Time to get up." "Breakfast in five minutes." "Hurry up." "Follow the yellow ribbon." More giggles, and they disappeared.

Emma and Harriet washed, dressed, and cautiously opened the door to an empty hall. Harriet glowered. "How will we ever find our way to the dining room?"

"This way." Emma pointed to a yellow ribbon tied to a wall sconce.

At each turn, another yellow ribbon marked the way. In one passage, it took some keen observation to discover the tip of yellow peeking out from behind a portrait. When they reached the main hallway, they followed the babble of voices, clanking dishes, and a baby's howls.

By late afternoon, everyone was dressed in their finery and a line of carriages waited at the entrance. The bride and groom would travel in separate carriages to the local church. Although Emma and Harriet stood beside each other in the line, Emma was hustled into a carriage and it took off leaving Harriet to ride with Aunt Agnes and two of the children.

She settled in her seat, surprised at who her companion was.

Her uncle took her hand. "I've hardly seen you since we've arrived and I wanted a moment with you."

"I'm glad it's you who arranged to whisk me away. I was afraid it might have been Pierre."

"Afraid? Does he frighten you? Has he made untoward advances to you? If so, I'll—"

Emma laughed. "No, nothing like that. Afraid is too strong a word. Perhaps curious or wondering, but I'm sure you didn't haul me in here to discuss Pierre."

"You're right." The carriage pulled through the gate and turned onto the main road. He waited till it straightened out. "I love Charlotte dearly, but I wanted to assure you that you'll always come first in my life."

Emma gulped back the lump in her throat. "Oh, Uncle Albert. You are a dear to say that and I love you so much, but I won't hold you to that. Anyway, you've always said that hearts are big enough to embrace many loves, each with its own special first place."

He squeezed her hand. "You're a wise girl to listen to your uncle."

"Indeed I am. And someday, I hope to find a love like yours and Charlotte's."

"I never thought it would happen to me and when it does for you, you'll know. Be true to who you are and follow your heart. It may take you onto a few side paths or bumpy ones along the way but every step is the way. Every moment is the right one to lead to the next as long as you keep checking in with your heart."

"I think Mama used to say something like that."

"She did. She'd say, 'Live every moment because now is the only time we have'."

The carriage turned a corner and pulled up to the chapel. She leaned over and kissed him on the cheek. "Thank you. I love you."

He hugged her and the carriage door swung open. A young lad in crimson livery stood with his hand up. Emma climbed down, followed by Albert. A quick hug and he was led off to the side of the chapel while the carriage behind unloaded.

Harriet rushed up. "I thought you'd left me. Don't ever do that again."

More people crowded up and everyone made their way inside. The church was soon packed with family, friends, and neighbours. Since they'd arrived, Emma hadn't had much alone time with her uncle. The

DuBois family loved him and there was always someone at his elbow, pulling him this way or that on some crucial mission. She would always cherish that short carriage ride.

The vows were said with glowing faces and she touched her dragonfly in her pocket. *We'll follow our heart, dragonfly. Let's see where it leads us.*

Back at the sprawling house, a gargantuan feast followed. Never-ending platters of food streamed from the kitchens: thick onion soups, scalloped potatoes, mushroom garlic chicken, fish and veal with rich, creamy sauces and hot white bread. The monks had also supplied an assortment of soft and hard cheeses made specially for the occasion. After a petit intervalle to rest the stomach, bakers presented platters of marzipan cakes, sugar tarts, and puff pastry with whipped cream. Concurrent with the cornucopia of food, bottles of red and pink wines flowed from the well-stocked cold cellar.

At the end of a long and boisterous evening, Emma stood on the front balcony, blinking back tears, and waved at the departing carriage. Albert and Charlotte had made their escape from the adoring crowd and were on their way to a secluded hideaway.

A voice sounded in her ear. Pierre stood beside her with a handkerchief held in his hand. "Do not cry, Mademoiselle. There is no greater happiness than true love."

She accepted his offer and dabbed at her eyes. "I am happy for them."

He took her chin in his hand and gently touched his lips to hers. She neither responded nor turned away. He pressed more firmly and put his arms around her. A long and sweet kiss, tasting of wine.

He took her hand. "Mademoiselle Emma. My room is close by."

"Too close for me, I'm afraid." She turned and walked inside to make her way through the maze to find the room she shared with Harriet.

Chapter 52

The next morning, Agnes and Harriet were ready for a trip to Paris. Even at fifty, Agnes was still sprightly and keen on fashion. She had been a fine seamstress and knew which shops to frequent. Harriet made a final plea to Emma. "Are you sure you don't want to come?"

Emma shook her head. "Madame DuBois is going to show me Albert's and Charlotte's quarters. I'll see you later."

Harriet turned to the older woman. "Come, Agnes. We have shopping to do."

Adele was happy to show Emma to where her mother was waiting.

Madame DuBois kissed Emma on each cheek. "Good morning, my dear. Did you sleep well?"

"Very well. After so much food and your splendid wine and soft bed, it was easy."

"Come. Our carriage awaits."

"Can we not walk to their quarters?"

"It is only a ten-minute walk but I thought you'd like to see more of the grounds first."

Emma patted her pocket where she'd placed the dragonfly that morning. It reminded her that even though her Uncle had left with the woman he loved, he was still a part of her life.

The tour took over an hour—through the vineyards, past a large vegetable garden bursting with tomatoes, peppers, kale, spinach, cucumbers, and melons. They continued past herb gardens, flower gardens, outbuildings, stables, sheds, and row upon row of grapes. Madame DuBois waved at the people working on the land—some in brown monk's robes and others in peasant grey. Almost coming full circle, they slowed at the stables which housed thoroughbreds and the workhorses.

Madame DuBois ordered the driver to stop as a magnificent chestnut stallion was being led to the exercise paddock. "Young King Louis loves the races, and we are honoured to stable his horses."

Emma raised her eyebrows. "Does he not have his own stables?"

"He has some land adjacent to ours. It's also an old hunting lodge called Versaille. He uses it as a getaway from Paris, but rumours say he plans to add stables, gardens and more buildings. He's quite enamoured with theatre and dance." She smiled. "I wouldn't be surprised if he builds a grand palace there one day."

From there, it was a short ride to Albert's and Charlotte's new home. The driver pulled up to a two-story fieldstone building, landscaped with flower gardens and a covered courtyard.

Madame DuBois stepped down. "We had the old stone grange fixed up for them. It was part of the original farm."

They walked along the curving path to the carved front door. Madame DuBois took an iron key from her pocket and opened it. Emma grinned. "My uncle will love it."

On the right of the entrance hall was a large sitting room with a ten-foot stone fireplace. A row of windows opposite flanked a door that opened to a covered courtyard surrounded by flowers and low bushes. Two stuffed armchairs faced the hearth, and bookcases, already half full, reached the roof beams on both sides.

The kitchen was fully equipped. Under a cloth napkin, on the pine table, lay a plate of freshly baked rolls and a pot of marmalade. A teapot, waiting to be filled, sat nearby.

Emma picked up the tin of tea leaves. "Does a leprechaun or a kitchen fairy live here?"

"I had a maid bring a little something over for us."

Emma made tea, and they sat outside in the courtyard protected from the light rain that washed over the slates. She filled the china cups. "Thank you, Madame DuBois, for showing me this. I can envision my uncle here." Tears erupted, and she lowered her head.

"Oh, my dear. Don't cry. He is so happy."

"I know. Please forgive me. I am selfish."

Madame DuBois patted her hand. "You will find your true love, my dear." She put her hand to her chest. "I feel it here in my heart."

Emma touched the dragonfly in her pocket. "Do you believe there is a special person for everyone?"

The older woman reached over and took Emma's hand. "We French believe in love. You may love several special people on your way to finding the one that makes your heart sing, your breath sweet, and your body dance. Be yourself and when love falls over you, grab on and don't let go."

The Paris shoppers arrived home weary and weighed down with parcels. Harriet opened a hatbox and modelled the latest fashion of headgear. With feathers dancing, she lifted the lid off another box. "And look at this." She pulled out a long dress with the new slit sleeves that showed another colour of material underneath. "And the skirt also has slits to show a petticoat of matching colour." She spread it out. "I got one for you. Let's try them on."

They followed Louise up the stairs and through the maze of hallways to their room. Harriet, still wearing her feathered hat, dropped an armful of boxes onto the bed. "This is the best time I've had all week. Agnes is so much fun. We could have talked forever." Her face flushed.

Emma raised an eyebrow. "Should I be jealous?"

Harriet flapped her hand. "Don't be silly. We only went shopping." She took off her hat and circled the rim with a fingertip. "Well, we did stop for a drink of wine." She looked up. "That's what people do in Paris."

"I'm glad you had a good time."

Harriet laid the hat into the round box, tucking an errant feather in place. "Speaking of jealous. It's I who should be jealous."

"What do you mean?"

She snapped the lid on the box. "Pierre has been panting after you since he met you. He couldn't keep his hands off you in the carriage."

Emma frowned. "He was only being attentive to his sister's guest."

Harriet folded her arms across her chest. "He didn't get bold with you, did he?"

"Why would you ask that? You know I don't like men." *The kiss was rather bold.*

"It's a good thing we're going home tomorrow." She sighed and turned to the pile of boxes on the bed. "However, it would be nice to spend more time with Agnes." She went to a suitcase beside the wardrobe. "Come, we have to get packed."

After a mountain of hugs and kisses from the DuBois family, they climbed into the carriage and started on the long journey home.

The next four days dragged on. Harriet was in a foul mood, yelping at every bump in the road, groaning at the dust or the rain and every two minutes asking if they were there yet. The inns they stayed in were either too hot or too cold, or the food was terrible.

By the time they arrived at Calais and boarded the ship, Emma was ready to throw her overboard. For the entire voyage, however, Harriet stayed in the cabin groaning and heaving.

Emma leaned on the rail as she had done with her uncle on the way over. She was happy for him. *Am I as happy with Harriet?* She stepped back from a sudden spray of ocean, and watched the water slosh off the deck while more incoming waves crashed and curled over each other. *Pierre was sweet. The kiss was enjoyable but—the same as a Harriet kiss.* Two seagulls swooped by, squawking with loud cries. *Did I think a man's kiss would be different?* The seagulls swerved past again. *Any silly thought I had about William was just some aberrant notion.* The ship dipped sideways and she grabbed the rail. *Anyway, he prefers men. He means nothing to me.* A giant wave surged high over the side drenching whatever it met. She gasped as the cold saltwater poured down her face, over her body, and filled her shoes.

206 Gloria W. Nye

Chapter 53

More or less settled after their trip to France, Emma and Harriet resumed their weekly dates with William and Charles. One Saturday afternoon, after the curtain closed on Monteverdi's *Orfeo,* they took a carriage to a popular public drinking locale where it was fashionable for young people to gather. Harriet was especially happy wearing her Paris hat. They found a table and put in their order.

Charles opened the conversation. "Did you enjoy the opera?"

Emma preferred symphony concerts. "It was most enjoyable, and you?"

"Oh, yes. I adore opera."

The conversation halted while drinks were served. William picked up his glass. "Charles and I have been thinking. This social arrangement seems to be working for all of us. Would you agree?"

Harriet picked up her glass. "Quite satisfactory, I would say."

"We thought so and wondered—for convenience and propriety sake—if you would be interested in making it more permanent?"

Emma glanced at him. "What do you mean?"

Charles touched a finger to his temple. "William and I had a stroke of genius. We thought it would be a brilliant idea if we were married. That way, there would be absolutely no gossip, and we could live our lives more easily, coming and going as we please."

Harriet spluttered into her glass. "Married? You mean I marry one of you?"

Charles quickly added. "Yes, but it would be in name only." He shuddered. "No consummation."

"I should say not." Harriet grimaced, and Emma's eyes opened wide. The two women looked at each other and Harriet lifted her shoulders. "What do you think?"

Emma opened her mouth, but William spoke. "I think it's a good idea. In name only, of course."

Harriet's brow furrowed. "I've never thought to marry, but I love Emma, and this arrangement would make our relationship appear even more socially acceptable." She nodded. "That is a brilliant idea, Charles. I say, yes."

Emma gripped her glass and stared into the dark liquid. A tremor moved through her body. Marriage was for life, even if it was a sham. *I can't give my word unless I mean it.* She looked up. Three pairs of expectant eyes stared at her.

Harriet touched her hand. "My dear. Marriage would mean we could live together without fear of public shame or punishment."

Charles added, "You know how our kind is shunned. There is a high risk we can be prosecuted and killed."

Harriet patted her hand. "It really is the best thing for us, my dear. Do say yes."

She looked into William's deep blue eyes, and a word popped out of her mouth. "Yes."

Charles slapped his hands together. "I will make arrangements for a double ceremony. Is a fortnight too soon?"

Harriet jerked her head toward him. "Indeed, yes. Far too soon. The banns must be read over three Sundays. And we have to find suitable attire, plan the food, send invitations. It must look proper."

"A month it is then. Now who should marry who?"

William shrugged. "It doesn't matter, but since we've been seen out many times as couples, we should stay that way. I will marry Emma."

Charles raised his glass. "A toast." William and Harriet raised theirs. "To marriage."

Emma's hand shook as she picked up her glass.

The proclamation of the intended marriages was posted, and the next Sunday at lunch, they sat around a table in the Parson's house and discussed where they would live. The men were reluctant to leave their fashionable residence on St. Martin's Lane, and Harriet did not want to leave her childhood home. Emma didn't offer any ideas on living arrangements; however, it was agreed that no one wanted to live in the traffic-clogged polluted city.

Charles lifted a hand. "I am not moving to some suburban slum."

William put down his fork. "We could go to Westminster near the king's court at Whitehall."

Charles perked up. "That would be droll. How ironic to live our lives under the noses of the aristocracy. Especially since many of them enjoy similar lifestyles as ours."

Emma sat silent while the three of them bandied about which house and where. The thought of being married to William took more of her attention than where they would live. *It will mean I am his wife, but not his wife.* The room grew quiet. She looked up at three expectant faces staring at her. "Oh, sorry. My mind was elsewhere. What did you say?"

Harriet sighed. "We agreed the west end was the best locale. It's a convenient distance from the city where we can enjoy the nightlife—"

Charles added. "When William and I have completed our studies at the university, we can set up our own medical practice there."

Harriet patted her hand. "So, what do you think?"

Emma blinked. "I wasn't listening."

William spoke up. "We talked about how it would take time to find a suitable residence with separate quarters to house two couples, so we agreed to live here at the Parson's house."

Harriet squeezed Emma's hand. "I can have my parent's rooms opened in the east wing, where you and I can be private."

Emma pulled her hand away, interlaced her fingers and made a steeple with her index fingers.

Harriet grunted. "For heaven's sake, Emma, what is wrong? This is the best arrangement for all of us. Say yes so we can proceed."

"I—I don't know." She glanced at William and down at her plate. "Yes."

Harriet and Charles clapped their hands, picked up their wine glasses and clinked them.

Emma glanced at William. His dark eyes shone back, and she flicked her gaze away, her heart pounding.

The next day they met with Reverend Duggan. He spoke solemnly on the indissolubility of marriage and emphasized the primary purpose was procreation. He quoted biblical texts, establishing the patriarchy, which undergirded the definition of such a union.

Harriet interrupted his litany. "Do you mean I have to forfeit ownership to all my belongings? Including my house?"

The good reverend bobbed his head. "A woman is likened to the moon with no light of her own, but a reflection of the sun—her husband. A husband may not only beat his wife, but all that the wife hath is his; all goods, her chain, her bracelets, her apparel belong to him."

Emma stiffened. *Such nonsense.* Mother Cameron would have apoplexy thinking that anyone could believe or live with any such law that kept women under their husbands' domain.

The reverend continued. "The law impinges three estates of life for women." He held up three fingers and tapped each one in turn. "Unmarried virgin, wife, and widow. A woman is under the control of her father or guardian before marriage and, after that, fused with her husband, and they are legally one person."

Emma pushed her chair back. "We need to discuss a few matters first."

Rev. Duggan's eyebrows shot up, deepening the etched lines in his forehead. He looked at the men.

William stood. "Exactly what I was going to suggest."

Five minutes later, the foursome was sitting at a secluded table in a nearby restaurant.

Emma spoke first. "Why does any woman get married? She gives up everything."

Charles placed his folded gloves on the table. "You get security and love and—"

Harriet snapped, "I already have that. I don't need a man for it."

"But how else can we safely continue with our lifestyle?"

Talk halted while drinks were served.

She took Emma's hand. "It is a sacrifice, but I see no other way."

Emma took a large swallow of wine. *What am I getting into?* Maybe she should become a nun and leave all physical pleasures behind. She took another mouthful.

Charles plunked his glass down. "There's no other way. It really is the ideal arrangement."

Harriet stood. "I agree. Come, Emma. Everything will work out."

Emma emptied her glass. "I'm still not sure." One glove lay in her lap, and she bent over to pick up the other one.

At that exact moment, William also bent down to retrieve it.

Their heads bumped, and both cried out.

He rose, her glove in his hand. With a bow, he handed it to her. "Many pardons, m'lady. I will do my best to be a gentle husband to you." He held out his hand in an invitation to stand.

She rubbed her head, but a smile creased her lips. "I'm not hurt. Just a little stunned." She took his hand.

He squinted. "Did I cause that mark on your forehead just now?"

Harriet stepped up. "No. That's an old scar from childhood right beside the one when your father tried to kill her." She put her arm firmly in Emma's and pulled her forward. "Let's go. The reverend is waiting."

Back in his office, arrangements were made to join the four in holy matrimony. The reverend droned on and Emma rubbed her head where it had collided with William's. The red spot covered a tiny scar made so long ago—a scar she didn't remember getting in Germany. But she was fully conscious now. Or was she? *Have I lost my mind?* A part of her was telling her to walk away from this travesty, but another more insistent part held her fast to her chair.

Chapter 54

The month passed quickly, and the date for nuptials loomed. Harriet insisted she and Emma buy new garments for the special occasion. Laces, bows and ribbons were the styles for men and women, and Emma chose a simple pale green dress with a pointed bodice and slit sleeves that showed white lace underneath. A periwig of curls covered Harriet's straight hair, giving her a softer look.

Emma had written to her uncle and he and Charlotte changed their plans so they could attend. They arrived a few days before the wedding and had settled into their new house in Westminster. Late that same night, Emma went for a short visit but ended up retiring to the spare room that Albert insisted on calling Emma's room.

The next morning, she arose early but it wasn't until the clock chimed ten that Albert and Charlotte came downstairs. After hugs and cheek kisses, Charlotte headed for the kitchen, insisting she would make English tea. "I have to learn your customs."

Albert and Emma made their way to the sitting room, where Emma sat in one of the upholstered chairs in front of the fire. Albert sat in the twin chair beside her. Neither spoke for a moment and when they did, they both started at once.

Albert laughed. "You go first."

"I was going to say how beautiful this house is, but I also wondered if you missed your bachelor quarters at Mr. Edwards."

"Not at all. He's not far away, and I certainly plan to visit him every time I'm in London. And of course, I have to introduce Charlotte to Mrs. Thorpe's stew."

"She'll love it." She crossed her legs and swung her foot. "I am glad you've found love."

"I never thought I could be so happy married to Charlotte. We're close enough to her exuberant family but we still have our privacy." He smiled. "I could live in a cave with her and be as happy."

Charlotte came through the archway, holding a tray with teapot, cups and saucers. "I let the water boil. Have you told her?"

Albert took her hand. "I wanted to wait for you."

Emma looked from one to the other. "Wha—" She gasped. "You're having a baby." She leapt up and hugged Charlotte and her uncle. "I'm so happy for you."

Charlotte sat on the settee, holding Albert's hand. "We wanted to tell you in person."

"When?"

Albert smiled. "He, or she, will be our Christmas present."

For the next hour over tea and biscuits, they talked baby plans and caught Emma up with the latest news from France. She shared what plays she and Harriet had attended.

Charlotte jumped up. "Oh, I nearly forgot. I have a gift for you." She ran from the room and returned with a small box. A silver bow spilled over the lid.

Emma tugged at the ribbon. "I should have one for you." The bow fell loose, and she lifted the lid. A small silver dragonfly lay on a puddle of silver chain. "Oh." She held it up.

Charlotte leaned forward. "Albert told me about your dragonfly brooch, and I thought a necklace would be something you could wear every day. Perhaps starting with your special day."

Emma hugged her new aunt. "I love it." She blinked back tears. The dragonfly was a replica of her pewter brooch. "But—"

"It was a conspiracy. When you were visiting, Louise borrowed yours from your room, and Andre, who's a bit of an artist, drew a likeness so we could have one made."

Emma held it to her chest. "Thank you. I will wear it forever."

Charlotte stood. "And now, I'm going to leave you two to talk. I have unpacking to do."

Emma stood for a hug and two cheek kisses. "Thank you again."

"You are most welcome. I hope you're as happy as we are." She picked up the tray and left.

Emma sat back in the big chair and looked down at her new necklace, coiled on her palm. "Did you know about this?"

"It wasn't my idea, but when I heard of it, I thought you'd like it."

They sat in silence for several minutes. Albert spoke again. "Are you happy, my dear?"

She stared at the object in her hand, her head bent.

"I was surprised to hear you were marrying."

She covered her face with her hands. He leaned over and put his arm around her. Her tears came, and he handed her a handkerchief.

She blew her nose. "Oh, Uncle, I don't know what to think or feel. I'm so confused."

"Marriage is a huge step. One of the biggest in one's life."

"I know. That's why I'm so confused."

"Do you love him?"

Emma looked into her uncle's eyes. "I'm supposed to be Harriet's love and yet—I have feelings for William. Feelings I don't understand."

"Love is like that. It can turn you upside-down and in-side-out all at the same time."

"But he loves Charles."

"Then why is he marrying you?"

Emma snorted. "Well, he can't marry Charles, and I can't marry Harriet. So we—or rather they—planned this sham wedding so we could all live together and love whom we wanted."

"And whom do you want to love?"

Her voice rose in volume and timbre. "That's what I'm talking about." She raised both hands. "I don't know."

Albert went to the sideboard. "I think this is a good time to open a bottle of Maison DuBois wine."

He brought back two goblets and handed her one. "I can't, and even if I could, I wouldn't tell you what to do." He sat down. "But whatever you decide, I'll support you."

She took a large mouthful and sighed. "I feel like a character in one of Mr. Shakespeare's plays."

He lifted his eyebrows. "Which one? Juliet? Ophelia? Surely not Lady Macbeth?"

She grinned. "None of those. Somewhere, he must have written about a woman confused about her sexuality or perhaps out of her mind. Maybe it is Ophelia."

"Every one of us is unique, and yet we are all one. That's the paradox."

"I'm not in the mood for philosophy, but I do feel better talking to you. I wonder what mama would say?"

"She would say 'follow your heart.'"

"The trick is to hear what your heart is saying."

Chapter 55

Too soon, the day was upon them. Caught in the whirlwind of dressing and hairdos, Emma had no time to ponder any further. This wedding was happening, like it or not. She fastened her new necklace securely and patted the dragonfly at her throat. *Why do I feel thrust along by some inevitable force?* She shook her head, but no clarity or answers came.

Harriet rushed in. "Are you ready?" She took Emma's arm. "It's time to go."

She bustled her into the carriage which whisked them off to the chapel. Friends and family dressed in their Sunday best filed in. Charles's brother came, but William's estranged father was absent. Albert sat in the front row with Charlotte, and the Cameron clan filled the two rows behind them.

The couples stood at the front of the church while the vicar made his pronouncements for the Solemnization of Matrimony. "Dearly beloved friends, we are gathered together here in the sight of God, and in the face of His congregation, to join together these men and these women in holy matrimony, which is an honourable estate, instituted of God in paradise in the time of man's innocency, signifying unto us the mystical union, that is betwixt Christ and his Church."

Emma stood on William's left. Her knees quivered, and her heart raced. *What am I doing here? I should turn and run.*

The vicar droned on: "—and is commended of Saint Paul to be honourable among all men, and therefore is not to be taken in hand unadvisedly, lightly, or wantonly, to satisfy men's carnal lusts and appetites, like brute beasts that have no understanding." He glared at William and Charles, and back at the book he held. "But reverently, discreetly, advisedly, soberly, and in the fear of God, duly considering the causes for which matrimony was ordained."

A civil ceremony would have been quite adequate, but Harriet insisted on a church wedding with plenty of witnesses. "There must be no whispers of forbidden liaisons."

The vicar continued listing the reasons for marriage, and as he did, Emma added her own mental postscripts.

His voice boomed out. "One, the procreation of children."

Emma's face remained neutral. *No chance of that.*

"Secondly, a remedy against sin and to avoid fornication."

Too late for that. We're already deep into sin.

"Thirdly, for the mutual society, help, and comfort that the one ought to have of the other, both in prosperity and adversity, into which holy estate these four persons present come now to be joined.

At least we're following one of the reasons, even if it's not with the person we're marrying.

"Therefore, if any man can show any just cause why they may not lawfully be joined together, let him now speak, or else, hereafter, forever hold his peace."

The church was quiet. Although the vicar called for any man to speak, a wild desire rose in Emma. *I should stop this farce now.* The impulse bubbled to the surface, and when she opened her mouth, the vicar turned and looked squarely at her. His voice boomed. "I require and charge you, as you will answer at the dreadful day of judgment, when all the secrets of all hearts shall be disclosed, that if either of you," he shifted his eyes to William, "Do know any impediment why ye may not be lawfully joined together in matrimony, that ye confess it. For be ye well assured that so many as be coupled together otherwise than God's word doth allow, are not joined together by God, neither is their matrimony lawful." His eyes pierced through Emma.

She gulped. The vicar's words had cut into her heart. *Did he guess the truth?* Lifting her chin, she met his gaze. She was not ashamed of love and would not be browbeaten. A long silent moment hung in the air. The vicar's eyes bulged, daring Emma to faint in submission.

When she did not, he turned and repeated the same dire words to Charles and Harriet. Harriet winked at Emma.

Emma gasped as she remembered a secret Harriet had told her about a cleric who had gone to her father for advice concerning a delicate issue with another man. Was the pious vicar standing in front of them that same cleric now spouting dire words of warning?

The vicar turned to William. "William Johnstone, wilt thou have this woman to thy wedded wife, to live together after God's ordinance in the holy estate of matrimony? Wilt thou love her, comfort her, honour and keep her, in sickness, and in health? And forsaking all other, keep thee only to her, so long as you both shall live?"

William took her hand and looked into her eyes. "I will." His blue eyes glistened in the candlelight.

The vicar looked at Emma. "Emma Lewis—"

She stared into William's eyes. The sounds and sights around her faded. Ripples of an ancient memory lapped at her awareness—a recollection of doing this washed over her. A time when she had stood before that same man—

"—so long as you both shall live?" The vicar stared at her.

The church fell quiet. Waves of waiting filled the air.

Emma's heart skipped a beat, and she said the words she had uttered centuries ago to the same spirit of this man who now stood in front of her. "I will."

William spoke in a clear, strong voice, following the vicar's lead. "I, William, take thee, Emma, to be my wedded wife, to have and to hold from this day forth, for better, for worse, for richer, for poorer, in sickness, and in health, to love and to cherish, till death us depart, according to God's holy ordinance, and thereto I plight thee my troth."

It was Emma's turn. "I Emma, take thee, William—" The words embraced the same intent echoed from a deep and enduring past. "—and thereto, I plight thee my troth." *Who is, or was this William person, and why does this feel so right?*

William took the ring from the prayer book and slid it on Emma's finger. "With this ring, I thee wed, with my body, I thee worship, and with all my worldly goods I thee endow. In the name of the Father, and of the Son, and of the Holy Ghost. Amen."

Emma remained still, but an inner part of her spiralled into another time and place and a wave of everlasting love welled up inside her. Her knees buckled and William tightened his hold on her hand.

The vicar continued. "O eternal God, creator and preserver of all mankind, giver of all spiritual grace, the author of everlasting life, send thy blessing upon these thy servants, this man and this woman, whom we bless in thy name, that as Isaac and Rebecca lived faithfully together, so these persons may surely perform and keep the vow and covenant betwixt them made, whereof this ring given and received is a token and pledge, and may ever remain in perfect love and peace together, and live according unto thy laws, through Jesus Christ our Lord. Amen."

He placed his hands over theirs, looked out at the congregation and boomed. "Those whom God hath joined together, let no man put asunder. For as much as William and Emma have consented in holy wedlock and have witnessed the same before God and this company, and thereto have given and pledged their troth, either to other, I pronounce that they be man and wife together. In the name of the Father, and of the Son, and of the Holy Ghost. Amen." His hands sprang off theirs.

The newly wedded couple lowered their clasped hands, but William did not let go.

The vicar turned to Charles and Harriet and repeated the litany with them.

Emma hardly heard a word. Her mind swam with those she had just spoken to the man who now held her hand so firmly it shook. *Why is he gripping it so tightly? For appearance' sake?*

The vicar stopped talking, and people clapped. It was over, and later they would sign official marriage certificates. They left the church to joyful shouts of friends and family and made their way to the church hall and tables laden with food and drink.

Mrs. Cameron was the first to rush up to Emma. "I'm so happy for you, my dear. William is a fine young man."

Beatrice was again large with child. She leaned over and whispered to Emma. "If you get tired of him—or Harriet—come and visit me."

Emma glanced away. Did Beatrice guess the marriages were a pretence? Did she regret marrying and having children? At least no children would come from this union despite the vicar's insistence of it being the main reason for wedlock.

Albert and Charlotte had to leave early, and quick kisses and hugs were exchanged by all. Albert gave her a final hug. "You look lovely." He whispered at her ear. "Remember, you can't go wrong if you follow your heart."

The party finished, and at the end of the long day, a carriage took the foursome to the Parson's House. It was late when they arrived, and everyone was weary.

Charles flopped onto a chair. "That was an ordeal."

Harriet groaned. "I thought the vicar would never stop talking."

Emma took off her gloves. "Would you like a cup of tea?" She didn't want to retire yet.

Charles grunted. "Tea? Are you daft woman? I've had too much wine to follow it with tea. I only want to bed." He leered at William. "And not with my newly married wife."

Harriet laughed. "This will be a wedding night to remember." With a motion of her hand, she indicated where the men should go. "You two can take Emma's room."

Charles took William's hand. "Come, William, to bed we go. Goodnight, ladies."

Harriet grabbed Emma's hand. "And the ladies to theirs."

Emma let herself be led down the hall. She glanced back at William the same moment he turned his head to look at her. *It's not supposed to be this way.* Was that her thought or his?

Harriet set her periwig on the dresser and they prepared for bed, replacing their new finery with long night shifts.

Emma did not want Harriet's hands on her but could hardly beg off on that special night. "My dragonfly!"

"What about that old thing? '

"I need to get it from my room."

"You can't disturb them now."

"But I need my dragonfly." She ran out the door. Charles, in his nightshirt, was heading away from her to the privy. At least she would not find them in bed. At her closed door, she put her ear to it. All was silent. She knocked lightly. Was he in bed already?

Slowly, she pushed the door open. Standing before her stood a startled William.

Stark naked.

Chapter 56

Emma froze. She gasped and spun away, took two hasty steps and stopped. She edged her way backwards and, turning her head ever so slightly, spoke over her shoulder. "I—I came for my dragonfly."

"Your what?"

The picture of him remained etched in her mind. "My—my dragonfly. It's on my bedside table."

"A dragonfly?"

Footsteps padded over the wooden floor, then silence as his feet met the rug by her bed.

"Ah, here it is."

Soft footsteps came toward her. She stuck her arm behind her, palm open. A hand cupped hers and laid something hard onto it.

She curled her fingers around its wings. "Thank you." She fled from the room and charged down the hall. Stopping breathless at Harriet's door, she put one hand on her chest. She didn't know what prompted her to look, but she glanced back up the hall. William's head was poking around the door frame, looking back at her. She burst into Harriet's room.

Harriet jumped. "What is it?"

Emma slammed the door and leaned against it, her chest rising and falling.

Harriet ran to her. "Oh, my God. What's the matter? What happened? She put her arms around her and patted her back as if comforting a child.

They stood for a few minutes as Emma caught her breath.

She pushed away. "I'm fine." She went to her side of the bed and put the dragonfly on the table.

"Then what was your fright, my dear? Did he try to touch you?" Harriet looked ready for battle.

"No. It was nothing really. I was just startled to see him." She wished Harriet would be quiet or at least change the subject. She needed time for private thinking. Beatrice had talked about men's equipment and what it did, but until that moment, she'd only imagined what *it* must look like. Seeing him fully naked was shock enough, but the amazing part was how *it* grew and stood up. And by the look on his face, he seemed surprised as well. She burrowed under the covers and lay on her side, facing out.

Harriet doused the lamps, crawled into bed and cuddled up behind her. "It's our wedding night."

Emma tensed. They had been married that day but not to each other. *What a strange situation.* The brides sleeping together in one room and their lawful husbands in another.

She did not respond to Harriet's touch, and Harriet rolled away. "That's all right, my dear. You're tired. We have the rest of our lives together."

The next morning, Emma didn't come down for breakfast until the men had left. Harriet had already moved most of her clothes to the freshly painted west wing. Her parents' belongings had been packed up and sent to the poor house. The women now had their own separate area with its own entrance at the side, which led to a small private sitting room. Upstairs was their bedroom and bathroom, and downstairs in the main house, the couples would share the kitchen and dining room.

Emma sat down to a piece of toast and marmalade to have with her morning tea.

Harriet walked over with a pan of scrambled eggs. "You have to eat more. Have some of these."

Emma put her hand up. "No. I'm not hungry."

"Too much excitement yesterday, I guess." She slid the eggs onto her plate. "That was quite a performance for us all." She put the pan onto the stove and sat down. "I thought I was in a play."

Emma finished her tea. "I'm going to move my things from my room while the men are out."

"Good idea. I'll be up soon."

Emma took her clothes over to the new wing and was in the bedroom, arranging books when Harriet came in.

She held an armload of hats and placed one of them on a shelf. "I was thinking I should have another kitchen built, so we don't have to eat with them."

Emma placed a book on the shelf beside the bed. "We usually eat at different times. I don't think it will be a problem."

Harriet put the last hat on the shelf and stuck her hands on her hips. "Why do you need books in the bedroom? Isn't it enough you have so many in our sitting room?"

"You know I like to read every evening before I go to sleep." She put another book in place.

Harriet harrumphed. "Yes, and half the time I fall asleep before you even get into bed.

The house situation worked well with its two separate areas each with its own entrance. The side entry led to a parlour where the parson would have seen parishioners, and it suited the women perfectly, leading to their own private sitting room. The front door, which the men used, led to the main sitting room and a separate staircase. Each couple could come and go independently. They had carefully set up each sitting room, so it looked like a man and a woman lived there.

When visitors came, Harriet and Charles would welcome them at the parson's entrance and usher them into the smaller sitting room where Charles's pipe-stand rested on the sideboard.

Emma and William's entrance led to the main sitting room where a sewing basket and a half-finished piece of embroidery lay on a side table.

Harriet grumbled about the women's sitting area being too small, but the stairway at that end led up to the larger bedroom and newer bathroom, which she liked.

Acquaintances from the church thought it charming to see such close couples and "wasn't it fortunate they could spend so much time together." Perhaps one or two suspected the truth, but at least the outer appearance was socially acceptable. It was no one's business who slept with whom or did what with whom in the privacy of their home.

The foursome settled in, living separately as they had before their marriage vows. When a visitor was expected or when the garden gate squeaked, Emma and Charles would trade places to play their assigned roles as a proper couple.

As an extra precaution, they had set up a simple string and bell system, which they used to signal each other if any one of them heard the gate creak announcing an unexpected guest on their way to the door. By the time they arrived, the appropriate couples would be suitably paired and ready to greet the vicar or whomever.

Mrs. Trent, their next door neighbour, made it a habit to drop in at unannounced times. She would stand at the door with a titter and a casserole. "You must try this new dish. I can give you the recipe. I'm sure your dear husband will like it."

The next time she came to the main door. For privacy reasons, the couples did not employ live-in servants. The gate squeaked and Emma skirted over to the men's sitting room. As usual, Charles and William were in London all day. She opened the door. "Come in, Mrs. Trent. You're just in time for tea." Emma was well versed now in the expected social graces and she led her to the sitting room.

"And how is your dear husband? Is he a full-fledged doctor?"

"Almost. He and Charles are completing their studies at St. Bartholomew's Hospital in London."

Mrs. Trent sat, and Emma went to the kitchen. The kettle had been simmering, and she was back promptly with a small tray. While they waited for the tea to steep, Emma picked up her stage prop of embroidery.

Mrs. Trent lifted an eyebrow. "Are you still working on that handkerchief, my dear? You were at the same place last week when I visited."

Emma fumbled for an answer to give the neighbourhood busybody. She was not fond of needlework and only pretended to do the piece Harriet had started for her. "Er—yes. I have been having trouble with this particular stitch. Perhaps you could show me?"

Mrs. Trent was happy to assist the young bride in her wifely skills, and she would undoubtedly let everyone know how indispensable she was to these two young women starting out.

After that visit, Emma was sure to have a fresh piece of embroidery set out for Mrs. Trent's perusal.

Chapter 57

Weeks passed, and the couples relaxed in the security of the new arrangement. One night Emma woke up in the wee hours of the morning with the recurring image of William standing naked. As much as she was comforted by Harriet's softness, like a mother's cushiony bosom, she wondered what it would be like to have a man's strong and muscular arms around her. *Not any man's—William's.* She shook off such silly flights of fancy. *William loves Charles. And Harriet and I are happy. There's nothing more I need in my life.* She got out of bed and went to the kitchen for a drink of milk.

She sat at the table, two hands around the glass and thought of other things. She had only seen her uncle once since the wedding, and now he and Charlotte were back in France. He spent more time there than in England, but she was happy for him. She took a drink. She missed Isaac too. Corresponding with him and sending him copies of her uncle's writings wasn't enough. She longed to work on experiments with him. Charles and Harriet concluded it would be nonsense for her to have a lab of her own in the house and reminded her that women did not do such things. William did not object, but both Charles and Harriet insisted it was untoward. People would think she was a witch, and they had enough to contend with protecting their sexual preference. *It's been far too long since I've seen Isaac.* "It must be at least a year."

"Did you say something."

Emma startled and gripped the slippery glass. "William, what are you doing here?"

He sat down. "I couldn't sleep and I hear milk is good for insomnia." He poured himself a glass full from the jug.

She grinned. "You're the doctor."

"I hear you're known for your remedies and herbal concoctions."

Emma flashed a furtive look to him and, in a conspiratorial whisper, said, "Oh, yes. I can mix up a brew or potion for any ailment you can come up with."

He raised his eyebrows. "I think you really mean that."

"My mother was a herbalist and taught me a little. The rest I've learned from books."

"I've been reading Culpeper's book on herbs. Many doctors are using them now. We've found wintergreen is effective for pain."

"It's about time."

"Culpeper has linked each plant with a sign of the zodiac, which some doctors don't believe is useful at all."

"What do you think?"

"It's fascinating to contemplate that planets and stars might influence life on earth."

"It's good to keep an open mind." She took a drink of milk. "A friend of mine, Isaac, is quite knowledgeable about the zodiac. You must meet him."

"I'd like that."

Neither spoke but the silence wasn't awkward.

He took a drink. "I've heard that warming the milk helps too."

"I'll try that next time."

They put their empty glasses into the sink, said good night, and Mr. and Mrs. Johnstone walked to their bedrooms up separate staircases to opposite ends of the house.

Chapter 58

That summer, Mildred Cameron and Catherine planned a holiday at Aunt Millicent's. Beatrice, Ralph, and young Ralphy who was toddling, were visiting Ralph's parents in Liverpool and Mrs. Cameron invited Emma and William to join them for two weeks.

Emma accepted, and at tea time when she told Harriet that she and William might be going away together, Harriet's face turned red.

She slammed her spoon down so hard the dishes shook. "You can't go away with that man. I won't allow it."

"Calm down, Harriet. I haven't even asked him yet."

"Well, you're not going to. It's an outrageous idea."

Emma bristled. "Don't tell me what I can or can't do."

"But—"

"It's natural that Mother Cameron would invite me and my husband to accompany her."

Harriet sneered. "Husband. You're not his wife. You're mine."

"I'm not talking to you about this anymore. I'm asking William to come with me." She pushed her chair back and stalked out of the kitchen.

In less than five minutes, she returned. Harriet looked up.

"He can't leave at this time."

"Did you really ask him?"

Emma sat in her chair and glowered.

"Well did you?"

"No. I just asked how busy he was for the next few weeks."

Harriet lifted the teapot. "Would you like more tea?"

Emma shook her head. "I'll talk to Mother Cameron. I'm sure she'd be pleased if you came instead."

Harriet grinned. "And I'm sure William and Charles won't miss us a bit."

A week later, packed and ready to go, Emma tucked her dragonfly into her purse. "Time for a country holiday, my friend."

Aunt Millicent greeted them with open arms and happy to meet Harriet. Her son John lived in the city now, so an old widow friend lived in with her as a helper. She apologized for the lack of room and beds, which meant doubling up.

Harriet hastened to say it would be satisfactory if she and Emma slept together. "We're like sisters."

Mrs. Cameron and Catherine took the other bed. However, being in the same room, Emma and Harriet would not partake in any nighttime interaction. Emma didn't mind. She mainly wanted to focus on seeing Isaac and working on her uncle's recipes.

He only had two weeks away from his duties at Cambridge. The busy young man was obsessive about his work in alchemy, biblical prophecy and religious disputations. Emma, keenly interested in his work in alchemy, admired his ability to think so profoundly and to come up with such original ideas. She'd never met a person like him. He too, thought it nonsense that women were not allowed in the universities and agreed the academic life would have suited her: arguing till dawn, nose continually in a book or mucking about with chemicals and smelly substances in a lab.

A week after they arrived, Emma received word Isaac was at his mother's farm next door. She picked up two books, patted her pocket where she'd placed the dragonfly that morning and told the ladies she'd be gone for the day. She ran out before Harriet could protest.

In the lab, Isaac looked up from the table. "Did you bring your uncle's book?"

"And hello to you, too."

Isaac stared.

"I've missed you." She put down the books. "How have you been?"

He opened the first book. "Fine." He moved his finger down the table of contents.

"How are things with you and the chemist's daughter?"

"I'm far too busy with my experiments to be experimenting with love." He pulled a loose sheet of paper from the book and held it up. "It seems your mother wrote some of this."

"My mother?"

"The style of writing changes and at the bottom is a signature, *Anne Lewis*. You did say that was your mother's name?"

"Yes. What does it say?" *How did I miss that?*

"She writes about Aristotle's four basic qualities: hotness, coldness, dryness, and moistness. Fire is hot and dry, earth cold and dry, water cold and moist, and air hot and moist."

"What does that mean?"

"Every metal is a combination of these four elements, therefore, the transmutation of one metal into another could be affected by the rearrangement of its basic qualities."

"How could that be done?"

He grinned. "That is precisely what we will attempt to discover." He picked up another loose page and read. "A substance called 'al-iksir' may mediate the change."

"That's Arabic. The word 'elixir' is derived from it." She looked at the page. "Al-iksir is a dry red powder made from a legendary stone." Her face brightened. "The Philosopher's Stone."

"If anyone discovers the Philosopher's Stone, it will be I. It's the key to how the basic elements of the physical world combine and act on each other." He furrowed his brow. "We can make an amalgam from mercury and another metal, treat it with sulphur, and we'll have red powder."

For the next half hour, they measured, mixed, stirred, and added several corrosive salts before heating it. The mixture bubbled up.

Emma put down an empty beaker. "What shall we test it on first?"

"What about an ordinary stone?" He took the tongs and immersed a small clean garden stone into the thick, burbling stew.

"How long should we leave it?"

Isaac glanced at the paper. "There's no mention of time. I would say overnight."

Emma agreed. "I will return at first light to inspect it with you."

"We have enough of the mixture left. We should try it on several metals." They filled six small bowls with the mixture and placed a piece of silver, copper, lead, or iron into each one. "I wish we had some pewter for the last bowl."

The last one containing their magical mixture sat on the table beside sheets of paper and bottles of coloured liquids. Emma touched the bump in her pocket. Despite scientific curiosity, she did not want her precious dragonfly dropped into that murky substance. She hesitated. *Or should I? Pewter may be the perfect metal.* Anything could happen. It could be distorted out of shape. It could dissolve completely. Or—it could change to gold and the elixir for eternal life.

Isaac lifted an eyebrow. "What is it?"

"I have some pewter."

"Well, put it in."

She drew the dragonfly out of her pocket.

"It looks very old."

"Yes." With a shaking hand, she held a wing and poised it over the bowl.

"Go ahead."

She took a deep breath and lowered the dragonfly toward the odiferous mixture.

Chapter 59

The tip of the dragonfly's wing hung a breath away from being plunged into the potentially lethal mixture.

She jerked her hand back. "I can't do it."

"What's the matter?"

"I will not put my dragonfly in there."

"But we have no other pewter, and it could be changed to gold. It would be more valuable."

"It cannot be more valuable than it is now." She tucked the dragonfly back into her pocket. "It's the most precious article I have."

"No matter. We have done enough for today."

The next morning, Emma rose early and got dressed. Harriet rubbed her eyes. "Where are you going at this God-forsaken hour?"

"Go back to sleep. Isaac and I have important work to do."

Harriet groaned. "I didn't come to the country to have you spend all your time with that queer fellow."

"He's not queer. He's a genius, and I'm privileged to be his friend."

Harriet wrinkled her forehead. "What's gotten into you? You've been acting so strange lately."

"What do you mean?" She put on a light jacket, her dragonfly safely stowed in a pocket. "I have to go." She blew a kiss to a frowning Harriet and ran out the door and down the stairs.

Isaac was already in the makeshift laboratory. "Ah, there you are."

One by one, they slowly lifted a pocked or misshapen piece of metal from the bath. None was gold.

Emma leaned on the table." Maybe the Philosopher's Stone has never meant the search for physical gold."

Isaac drew his brows together. "Yes, indeed. There is that thought."

"Maybe the ultimate quest is to eliminate the base material of the self and achieve the gold of enlightenment."

"Or eternal life."

She picked up a nearby book. Archaic symbols decorated the cover."My uncle and I have discussed this book at length."

Isaac glanced at it. "*The Emerald Tablet* of Hermes Trismegistos."

She opened to the first page. "That which is above is like that which is below, and that which is below is like that which is above."

He nodded. "As we discover more about the physical universe, it takes us deeper into the Divine. The Bible holds many undeciphered secrets." He hesitated. "I can say to you what I would only utter to a handful of people. The Holy Bible is more than a literal tale. It's stories and parables are metaphors for consciousness."

"My uncle and I have discussed that very thing."

Isaac tapped the cover. "The Bible has many references to life everlasting or eternal life."

"Wouldn't it be strange if we're searching for something we already have?"

The two heretics smiled and sat silent for a moment. Isaac shifted in his seat. "I have to return to Cambridge on the morrow."

"Oh, no, we have more work to do."

"I'm sorry you're not allowed into the university. You have the mind of a scholar, and it should make no difference that you're a woman."

She shook her head. "I think I was born too soon. I hope that someday women will be educated as they wish."

"I agree. It is a waste."

She sighed. "At least I've been able to work with you."

"It's good for questing minds to come together. What else do you wonder about?"

Emma stared into the distance. "Many things. I wonder why we are here and why people die when they do."

"There is so much to learn."

They sat in a comfortable silence each with their own thoughts. After a moment, Emma said, "I had a thought the other day when I was sitting under the apple tree in my Aunt's yard looking forward to early fall russets."

"What was that?"

"You'll think I'm foolish, wondering about such things."

"Never. Wondering and imagining are the avenues of discovery. Tell me."

"I wondered why apples always fall to the ground. Why don't they fall up or sideways?"

"That's a good question. I'll give it some thought."

"Maybe they want to fall down."

He laughed. "You think that apples have volition?"

"Not like we do. But everything has or is some kind of consciousness. Even stones."

"Perhaps, but I think there are some basic physical laws of the Universe, like one that makes things fall down and not up."

"That may take many lifetimes to discover."

"I'll do my best in this one." He rubbed his chin. "Hmmm. Maybe the air has consciousness and is pushing everything down."

He left the next day for Cambridge. Emma said goodbye, and walked back to the house, head hung low. *What am I going to do for the rest of the summer? I've read all my books and now Isaac is gone.*

When she got back, Mother Cameron met her at the door. "I'm sorry my dear, but we're leaving for home first thing in the morning."

"But—"

"I know you want to spend more time with that young man, but I'm tired of hearing Catherine's whining. All she can talk about is Norman this and Norman that. Now come along. We need to pack."

Emma followed her upstairs. "Who's Norman?"

"Gracious, Emma. For a smart young woman, you do miss things. She met him last Easter at the church picnic. You were there. I think."

"Was he the young man who came to her birthday party?"

"Yes but Catherine's wish is not the only reason I want to get back. I'm concerned about Beatrice."

"Isn't she in Liverpool with Ralph and Ralphy?"

"I thought so but I just received a letter from her that she didn't go. Being eight months with child, she didn't feel like the long trip. If you ask me, I think she wanted some quiet time in her old room."

"I can understand that."

"She assured me that Mrs. Hudson, Francesca, and the twins have taken good care of her. But I can't help but worry."

Early the next morning, the coach trundled up the lane. Mother Cameron called up. "Come along girls. Don't tarry. It's a long ride."

Harriet followed Emma down the stairs. "Maybe I'll see you more when we're home. You spent far too much time with that horrid Newton man." They walked out. "All he does is work and think and do nasty experiments. He has no life at all." She climbed in.

Emma sat beside her. "That is his life."

Harriet crossed her arms. "Hummpff."

Chapter 60

On their return to Hollyhock, a devastated Beatrice met them at the door throwing herself on her mother, crying hysterically. Through sobs and stutters they learned the terrible news. She had just found out that her husband and firstborn had succumbed to scarlet fever.

Mrs. Cameron took her distraught daughter upstairs. Harriet grabbed Emma's arm. "We should leave right away. There's nothing we can do." They had only come in for a short rest before continuing home to the Parson's House.

Emma pulled away. "Are you mad? I cannot go. You go if you like." She threw her bag on a chair. "I need to get something." She ran in a couple of minutes with a handful of lavender and chamomile blossoms.

Harriet stayed, but the next morning, she waited impatiently for Mr. Hudson to return from taking Mr. Cameron to his London office.

The minute he walked in the door, she pounced. "Hudson, we need you to take Emma and me to the Parson's house as soon as possible."

"Yes, ma'am, but I will have to hitch up Mac. Irish needs a rest."

Harriet glowered. "It's only a fifteen-minute journey. Can you not take us right away?"

"No ma'am. London is a stressful place for a horse, and Irish needs to rest."

"All right, but be quick about it."

A half-hour later, he announced to Emma that Mac was ready and the carriage waiting.

She had just finished breakfast. "Ready? For what?"

Harriet rushed into the room. "To take us home, of course. Come along. Our clothes are still packed."

Emma put down her cup. "I'm not going. I have to tend to Beatrice."

"You've done enough. Your mother and the help are here. Come along."

"I'm not going." She poured herself another cup of tea. "You go. I'll join you when I can."

Harriet stamped her foot. "But you must. I need you."

Emma narrowed her eyes. "Beatrice needs me more. Now go."

Harriet huffed. "Sometimes, you are impossible." She stalked out.

Emma stayed a week at Hollyhock and then another. Harriet wrote several times, begging her to come home, but when Beatrice's baby came early, Emma informed her she would be staying for yet another two weeks.

The next Sunday, Harriet appeared at the door, supposedly for a short visit, but ended with her pleading Emma to come home. Emma held her ground and Harriet left in a huff.

Mother Cameron met Emma in the hallway. "Come in and sit, my dear. Mrs. Hudson has made lemon tarts from the recipe you gave her." She took her arm, and they went into the sitting room where tea and tarts were laid out.

"I'm sure Harriet is only concerned for you. You must miss your husband." She poured the tea, handed her a cup and touched her arm. "How are you and William?"

Hearing his name, Emma's hand shook. She grasped her cup with two hands, steadying herself. She had missed him. *I'm being foolish over a man I barely know.* Wrong word choice. She had seen him bare. She looked up. "Everything's fine. He's busy with his final studies at Oxford and at the hospital. I—I don't see him as much as I'd like."

"I understand, but Beatrice is much better now and the baby is doing well. You know you're welcome to stay as long as you want. This is always your home, but maybe it's time you went home to your husband."

Emma took in a deep breath. "I'm sure you're right. And I'm happy Beatrice is tending to her new daughter so well."

Mother Cameron patted Emma's knee. "It's high time you had a little one of your own."

Emma left the next morning, Hudson pulled the carriage up to the Parson's house.

Harriet ran out. "Come in." She took one of Emma's bags and started walking toward hers and Charles's side entrance. She stopped. "What am I doing?" She laughed and turned to the main door. "You live here." Hudson brought the rest of her things into the front hallway.

Emma hugged him. "Thank you, Hudson. And thank Irish for me."

He tipped his hat. "My sure."

Emma waved as he drove away. William's cape hung on a hook in the hall. She put her bag down and Harriet snatched it up. "I'll help you take your belongings to our quarters."

The next day Mrs. Trent, their relentlessly nosy neighbour, knocked on Emma's door. Emma had heard the gate creak and she arrived at the door in time. The men were in London as usual, and Mrs.Trent was charmed that Harriet could join them for tea and cake.

She waggled a finger. "When are you two going to have babies? You've had plenty of time." She tucked her chin into her neck and peered over her spectacles. "Why haven't you?"

Emma glanced at Harriet. *Did the intrepid Mrs. Trent suspect anything? Perhaps the half-finished pieces of embroidery hadn't fooled her.*

Harriet donned her best wifely face. "The good Lord hasn't blessed either of us yet."

The men arrived home late that evening and had just finished eating when Harriet entered the dining room and requested an immediate group meeting.

Charles picked up a wine bottle. "You go ahead, William, I'll bring the drinks."

Harriet and William joined Emma in the sitting room where they sat in comfortable chairs in a half circle in front of the fireplace.

Before supper, Harriet had prepared the grate with stacked paper and kindling. "Let's have a fire to take the chill off." She picked up the small tinder box, took out the flint and steel and struck one against the other. A shower of sparks fell to the charcloth in the bottom of the box.

Emma jerked and pulled her feet under her chair. "Be careful."

"Oh, for heaven's sake. I've lit plenty of fires. I know what I'm doing." She blew on the cloth, setting the sulphured tip of a wooden splint on fire and then touched this fire-stick to the paper. The paper caught, passing flames onto the kindling and a fat dried stick on top. The burning stick tumbled out onto the hearth, taking the flaming paper with it.

Emma screamed. "Fire, fire." She pulled her knees to her chest and cowered in her chair like a caged animal.

William kicked the stick back into the grate and stamped on the paper just as Charles came in, carrying a tray of filled wine glasses. "What's all the commotion?"

Emma, her face a mask of fear, stared blindly at the rising flames now safely contained. Charles and William exchanged a glance. William frowned. When they did their practice sessions in Bedlam Hospital, they had seen faces like those on people who had lost their wits.

Harriet rushed to her side "Emma. "All is well. There's no danger."

Emma's wide, glassy eyes remained locked on the flames. Her hands, held tightly around her knees, shook her whole body.

William snatched two glasses and dumped wine onto the fire. It crackled and sizzled out. "The fire's gone."

Charles put the tray down. "Was that necessary?"

William glared at him. "Yes."

Emma blinked. A wisp of smoke rose from the blackened soggy paper and dripping sticks. She blinked again and looked at the three alarmed faces in front of her. "I—I—." She slumped into a faint.

Harriet caught her from falling off the chair. "Emma. Emma." She turned to the men. "What's wrong with her? What happened?"

William stepped over. "I don't know." He felt for a pulse and frowned. He bent over, his arms out.

Harriet grabbed his arm. "What are you doing?"

"I'm taking her upstairs to her bed. She needs to rest."

"Oh. Yes. That's a good idea."

She followed him up where he laid her on the bed. She pulled the quilt up over her. "I'll see to her. You can go."

William looked down at the sleeping Emma. He put his hand on her forehead, brushing her hair back as he did.

Harriet frowned. "Thank you, William. I can manage."

"Of course." He turned and left.

The next day, no one mentioned Emma's strange reaction to the fireplace incident. Harriet watched her closely all day but Emma acted as normal as ever. That evening in bed, she leaned back on her pillows reading a book.

Harriet sat at her dresser brushing her hair. "I didn't know you were so afraid of fire."

"What do you mean?"

"Last night you nearly jumped out of your skin by a little fire and you fainted."

"Did I? I don't remember."

"What? You must remember. It was only last night—"

"I'm tired. I want to go to sleep." She closed her book, put it on the table, and turned on her side. "Goodnight."

Two days later, Mrs. Trent dropped in again, and like the last time, asked if they had any news to share about a coming 'blessed event' and reminded them again for the umpteenth time. "It's a Christian woman's duty to give her husband children."

That evening Harriet cooked a roast and invited the men to eat with them. After supper, they would resume their meeting of the previous evening that had been interrupted by Emma's queer turn.

The meal went smoothly, and everyone enjoying Harriet's culinary efforts. Charles filled their glasses with his new French champagne. "I love those bubbles." He lifted his glass. "To what shall we toast?"

William lifted his. "How about the return of our good wives from their country holiday and midwife duties?"

Charles laughed "Why not?" He bowed his head toward the women. "To our devoted wives. Welcome back."

They all drank and Harriet plunked her glass down. "You may well laugh at our play-acting, but I have called this meeting for a reason."

Emma hadn't looked directly at William since she'd been back. *I'm not avoiding him on purpose. Am I?*

Harriet continued. "Speaking of midwife duties, we've been asked more than once why we're not with child yet."

The men stared at her.

Harriet shook her head. "It's most disconcerting when Mrs. Trent voices such inquiries as she did again his morning. We all know how her stories can travel, and we don't need any more gossip she might entertain. It's an impossible situation."

Charles said, "We could take in an orphan child. There are plenty of those around."

Harriet grimaced. "No. That would not work. It might even make people more suspicious."

William took another drink.

Charles tapped his glass. "There's only one solution."

Three faces turned to him.

"One of you must have a child."

Harriet lifted her chin. "I will not lay with a man for any purpose."

Three heads turned to Emma.

She gulped. "Surely, there must be something else we can do to allay wagging tongues."

Charles shook his head. "Other than move away from each other, I see no other way."

Harriet gasped. "We cannot live apart." She turned to Emma. "My dear, you must have a child. You only have to do the sex part once, and we'll all be present to support you."

Charles cleared his throat. "Who will father the child?"

William spoke up. "I will. I mean, I should. Since I'm the husband." He didn't look at Emma. "The child should resemble me rather than Charles." Had he forgotten his father's strict orders to never touch a woman's private parts? Even Brother Francis had hammered that into him. Both men had taught him the pleasures of a man's personal attention, something no woman could ever offer.

Charles clapped his hands. "Then it's decided. Thank you, William, for sacrificing yourself. No offence Emma, but I would not deign to do such an act with any woman."

Chapter 61

The next evening, William and Charles, wearing robes over their nightshirts, stood in the doorway of the women's bedroom.

Emma and Harriet lay on top of the bed covers. Emma wore a light shift, and Harriet had on a thick flannel robe over her sleeping gown, which she held closed at her neck.

William took a hesitant step into the room. He didn't look at Emma. *Was she as nervous as he? Had she ever done this with a man?* As a doctor, he knew anatomically all about women, and that his penis would not fall off as Brother Francis had warned him.

He stumbled to the bed, removed his robe and lay down awkwardly, his body less than an inch from hers. Charles kept his robe on and climbed in beside him, pushing him over two inches. Emma didn't move when the whole side of William's body touched hers. His thin nightshirt did not block the heat radiating from her body, and he drew his breath in sharply. They lay like four sticks on a grate, lined up for ceremonial burning. No one spoke. The bed would barely hold three bodies, let alone four. Harriet and Charles teetered on the outer edges.

Harriet's tone attested to the nasty chore. "Let's get this over with."

No one moved. William liked sex but had only done it with men.

Harriet blurted. "Well, do what you do to—activate that thing."

William flinched when Charles touched him. He stared at the ceiling, but his loins stirred and his nightshirt lifted. He knocked Charles's hand away.

Harriet cried, "All right. Do it and be quick about it."

Emma stared at the ceiling. Harriet reached over and pulled her gown up, exposing her lower body—a mound of soft hair nestled between smooth and rounded thighs.

William gasped and Harriet barked. "What are you waiting for? Just do it."

Would that damnable woman be quiet? William lifted his nightshirt and knelt astride Emma. Harriet opened the top of Emma's gown. A cream curve of a breast appeared. His hand moved toward it, but Harriet's hand covered it first. Emma arched at her touch, and William's ready member brushed against her.

Harriet scowled. "Hurry up. Be done with it."

For God's sake, woman. Shut up. William's mind, body and heart scrambled for consensus and a tremendous desire rose within him. At that moment, he looked at Emma. She was looking at him, and her lips moved ever so slightly in what he would swear was a tiny smile. She raised her body to him and he slipped easily into her. His breath stopped. *Good God!* She moved with him. Soft, but surprisingly strong, they fit so well. He cried out and fell on top of her quivering body. Her arms gripped him, his face dangerously close to hers. Her hot and quick breath caressed his cheek. *Dear God, what just happened? She's so soft and yielding.* Her half-opened lips—so close to his. Less than an inch away. A half-inch. A quarter—

Harriet's strident voice broke the spell. "Enough. It's done. Get off. Go now."

He stared at Emma's shining face and smiling eyes. Her hands tightened on his back. She looked as if she wanted to be kissed—and not by Harriet.

Chapter 62

He held her gaze and lowered his face.

"Get off her." A bellow from Harriet and a blow to his head pushed him against Charles, nearly knocking both of them off the bed.

William shook his head, his ears ringing, and his thoughts swirling. *What was I thinking? What was she thinking?*

Harriet yanked Emma's nightgown down.

Charles rolled off the bed. "Let's go. The deed is done."

William didn't move away from the soft creature alongside him. His body trembled as his mind scurried one way and another.

Charles grabbed William's arm and pulled him to the edge. "Come along. What are you waiting for?"

William shook him off. "I'm coming."

Harriet snorted. "You've already done that." She swung her arm up like a sword and pointed to the exit.

He stood, put on his robe and slowly walked across the room. He stopped at the doorway, turned and looked back at Emma. She had a curious expression on her face. *Is she as astonished as I?*

Charles yanked at him. "Come along, man."

William grabbed the doorjamb and stumbled out.

Harriet stroked Emma's sweating brow. "How awful for you."

Emma held back an irresistible smile. *Not awful. On the contrary.* Her body throbbed, his hot breath still on her cheek. She never dreamt sex could be so—. *So full. So exciting. So surprising.* He wasn't rough like those boorish boys. His soft lips had been so close to hers. *Was he really going to kiss me?* She trembled.

Harriet smoothed Emma's hair off her forehead. "You're flushed. Let me get you a drink of water." She went to the sideboard and filled a glass from the jug. "You poor thing, having that man all over you." She returned to the bedside. "Don't worry. You won't have to go through that again."

Emma shrugged with a what-could-she-do-look. "If I must, I must." *I can't tell her I wouldn't mind.* She wouldn't understand. *I don't understand myself.* She had never been attracted to men sexually. Aside from sweet Pierre, the ones that had approached her had been crude and loutish—their leering and smelly breath unpleasant. William was not like that. A whirlwind of thoughts and feelings spiralled through her mind and body. Thoughts and feelings she must put aside. *My life is set with Harriet, and William is with Charles.*

In the following week, the men worked long hours fulfilling their practice requirements at the hospital. They ate before the women were up and late at night after they had retired. Emma caught sight of William once, and he was so bleary-eyed, he could hardly speak. Often, either one of the men or both would stay overnight at the hospital.

A fortnight passed, and the men managed a day off. At midday, Emma called everyone together. They sat around the table with tea and biscuits, and she told them her menses had started.

Charles frowned. "Oh, no. What are we going to do now?"

Harriet made a distasteful face. "They will have to do it one more time."

Emma cleared her throat. "Please do not talk about me as if I'm not present."

William put up his hand. "And me too, I may add."

Charles ignored them and addressed Harriet. "Maybe you and I should do it."

"Are you mad? I don't know how poor Emma stood it."

Charles grunted. "She was not standing if you remember."

Harriet frowned. "It's not something to joke about."

Emma poured milk into her teacup. Her hand shook ever so slightly. "What are we going to do?"

Harriet groaned. "As awful as it is, you'll have to go through it one more time."

Charles winced. "I'm afraid so."

Emma stirred her tea rapidly and took a deep breath. "If we have to, we have to."

William's cup jiggled as he placed it on the saucer. "If we must, we must."

Charles shifted in his seat. "I could sacrifice myself, I guess. Do you want me to do it?"

Emma and William spoke at the same time. "No."

William followed quickly with, "I mean, I've done it once, and I would hate to put you through that ordeal."

Charles touched his arm. "I thank you for that. I did try it once, or at least a woman tried with me. I was a lad of fourteen, and despite her experience, it didn't work. It was only when her husband joined us that things got interesting. After that, I stuck to men, so to speak."

Harriet glowered. "No man is ever doing that to me. Just let one try."

William looked at her fierce face. *I certainly wouldn't try.*

Charles sugared his tea. "Harriet and I appreciate you both for enduring such an act but rest assured we'll be there to help you through." He squeezed William's arm. "It's a good thing I was there, or you probably couldn't have performed."

Emma's and William's glances coincided with each other, and they swiftly looked away.

Harriet frowned. "It's too bad there's not a more civilized way to make a baby. It's so barbaric that a man and woman have to couple."

William shrugged. "Oh well, since that's the only way, we'll just have to do it." He picked up his cup. "And keep doing it until we make a baby."

Harriet's eyes opened wide. "Dear God in heaven. I hope not more than one more time."

Emma lifted the teapot. "Tea, anyone?"

Chapter 63

Over the next few days, William grew more confused. Whenever he thought of the forthcoming event, his body responded—most alarmingly. *What's happening to me?* He lay with Charles as usual, but something had changed. A new appetite had been whetted within him and he looked forward to tasting the forbidden fruit again. What was Emma thinking? Was she disgusted with him? They had hardly seen each other since that night, and neither had spoken of it. *How did she feel? Was it the first time for her with a man? Did she like it? Did she want more?*

The appointed evening arrived and they gathered for a late supper. Charles took extra care with the meal—roast duck with orange sauce and baked potatoes with fresh chives.

Was that to make the evening as pleasant as possible? Or to keep his mind from the coming event. Everyone was nervous.

"You've outdone yourself, Charles," said William.

"First class," said Harriet.

"I loved the potatoes that way," said Emma.

Harriet put the dishes into the sink and joined the others in the sitting room. They sat in front of a low fire, sipping glasses of French red wine.

"How do you like this new wine?" asked Charles.

"First rate," said Harriet.

Emma and William emptied their glasses first. She crossed one leg over the other. In less than a minute it was swinging. William held the stem of his wine glass, spinning it back and forth.

Conversation dried up and Harriet plunked her glass down. "We might as well get this over with. Come, Emma. We'll get ready."

The women went to their staircase and the men to theirs.

In their bedroom, William pulled off his clothes and went next door to the bathroom. Charles put on his nightdress and robe and sat in the chair. In ten minutes, he went to the bathroom and opened the door. William was sitting in a full bathtub. Charles lifted an eyebrow. "What are you doing?"

"I usually wash before bed."

Charles raised his eyebrows. "Not a full body wash. Anyway, you have a chore to do before you go to bed and you don't need to bathe for that."

William picked up the bar of sweet-smelling soap Charles had bought him and lathered his whole body.

Charles frowned. "Don't use all the good soap up. You don't have to wash for her."

In the women's bedroom, Emma removed her clothes and stood naked.

Harriet handed her a thick cotton night shift. "Put this on, silly."

Emma put it on the bed. "I want to wash first." She went to the adjoining bathroom.

Harriet followed. "Wash for him? Why? More likely, you would wash after the disagreeable act."

Emma turned on the taps and stepped into the tub as the water-filled. "I want my body clean to receive a child." She took the cloth and rubbed her skin with the new lavender soap Harriet had bought for her.

"And you're using the good soap! Such a waste."

Emma trembled at the thoughts of William touching her again. Throbbing inside her. Having his hot liquid fill her. She caught her breath sharply.

Harriet looked up. "Are you all right?"

"I'm fine. The water's cold."

Back in the bedroom, Emma chose another nightdress—one with lace trim that opened down the front. She tied the ribbon at the top.

Her small, uplifted breasts held the material away from her body as it fell to her ankles.

Harriet walked over, clamped her hand on the thin fabric over Emma's breast, and kissed her hard on the lips.

Emma stiffened. Harriet could be rough at times, sometimes as rough as the men she'd warned Emma about. William wasn't rough. He was gentle and sweet when he touched her. She turned away and walked toward the bed.

Harriet frowned. "What's the matter?"

"Nothing. I just want to prepare my mind." She lay on the bed, her heart thumping.

"I understand. I hope it won't be too distasteful for you. But, I'll be there."

An outrageous thought darted into Emma's brain. What if Harriet and Charles were not there? What would it be like to be alone with William and have him do all the things that Harriet did and more? William fit so well with her. Her body quivered.

There was a knock on the door.

"Come in." Harriet lay down on the bed beside Emma. "Don't worry, my dear. It will be over soon."

Not too soon, I hope.

The door opened, and the men entered. Charles wore his usual long nightshirt under his robe, but William's robe revealed bare legs beneath his, and a bare chest at the neck.

Emma shivered. *Is he naked underneath?*

Charles pursed his lips. "Let's get this over with."

William strode to the bed. "I know what to do. I won't need your help, Charles."

Charles's eyebrows went up. "But how will you get aroused? A mere woman cannot do that for you."

William stood at the side of the bed. "Oh, of course not." As he gazed at the soft creature lying there, his loins stirred. Her light shift had fallen open at the top, showing a sliver of enticing skin. He removed his robe and stood naked before them.

Harriet gasped. "Have some decency, man. We do not wish to see you like that."

Emma flicked her eyes up to his chest. *What is that wine mark on his skin?*

William climbed into the bed with Charles close behind. He did not lay down beside Emma as before. His member stirred without Charles touching him. He knelt over her and her shift fell all the way open. He smothered a groan. He wanted to kiss her stomach and breasts and all of her and never stop.

She looked at him. Not a look of disgust, dislike, or boredom. She looked as if she wanted to be kissed all over. He moved closer and the delicious sensation of sinking into heaven engulfed him. Emma's body rose to meet him. Their bodies merged, moving as one. In a starburst of ecstasy, he fell heavily on top of her.

Harriet shouted. "All right. It's over. Get off her." She tugged at his shoulder, but he didn't move.

Charles pulled at his other side. "William. You did the deed. It's finished. Let us be away." He yanked harder, jarring him.

William lifted himself off this dear sweet soft being. She gave a small cry of alarm. Her arms still held him and she looked deeply into his eyes. He hung over her, suspended in time, holding her gaze. Words formed in his mind. *I love you. I only want to be with you and no other. No man, nor any other woman. Only you.*

She heard and silently replied. *I love you, dear William, with my heart, soul and body. Only you.*

And he heard her voice as if she had spoken aloud.

Chapter 64

William continued to gaze into her eyes, his heart thumping. He touched his lips to hers. She held his head and opened her mouth to receive him. The kiss did not stop.

"What are you doing!" A loud shout and a mighty push from Harriet jarred them apart.

Charles yanked him away. "It's time we left." He pulled William from the bed and handed him his robe. "Cover yourself. We must go."

Harriet's face twisted. "How dare you!" Her face was livid, and her hands shook. She snatched Emma's gown closed, grabbed the quilt at the bottom of the bed and pulled it up to her neck.

Emma blinked. *I kissed him. I kissed him in front of Harriet and Charles.* She let out her breath. *And I didn't want to stop.*

Charles pulled William to the door. When they reached it, William shook Charles' hand off and stood perfectly still for a moment. He squared his shoulders, tightened his sash, and stepped out.

Harriet stroked Emma's cheek and pushed damp hair away from her brow. "That insufferable cur. How dare he kiss you."

Emma's face was still flushed. *Did she not see that I kissed him back? What should I say? What can I say?*

Harriet patted Emma's shoulder. "Never mind, my dear. You'll never have to go through that again. Even if you don't conceive, we'll find another way. That man must never touch you again."

She said nothing. She couldn't explain to herself, let alone to Harriet. *Did I imagine I heard his voice? Heard him say he loved me, and did I say the same to him?*

Harriet spoke again. "Come, I'll wash you, and we'll be together."

"No, I'm fine." Emma rolled over, turning her back to Harriet. "I want to sleep." She did not want to wash William off her. She never wanted to wash again. She licked her lips, tasting him, and her body throbbed with a new sweet desire.

"All right, my dear. I understand." Harriet curled herself along Emma's back and put an arm across her. "Sleep my darling, and forget this ever happened."

She would never forget that night, and with Harriet's body pressing against her, she thought not of Harriet but William. *What will he say when next we meet?*

Since that night of sexual intercourse with William, Emma buried herself even more in her books and pleaded tiredness to avoid lovemaking. She was fond of Harriet and did not want to hurt her, but sexual desire for her partner had waned. She desperately wanted to know how William felt. Was he just experimenting? Was a future even possible with William? She shivered at the thought of having him love her. *Is this how man-woman love feels?* Had she ever really loved Beatrice or Harriet?

It had been several days since the event and William and Emma had not even glimpsed each other. He was extra busy at the hospital, and she immersed herself in sorting a pile of books.

She settled into one she had been wanting to re-read and curled up in the big comfy chair in the sitting room. After reading the same page for the third time, she shook her head and went back up to the top line. The front gate creaked. *This isn't Mrs. Trent's usual visiting day.* She put her book down and ran along the hall to the main sitting room. She had just picked up the handkerchief with its half-finished edging and the door opened.

William filled the frame. She gasped. *He was to be in London the whole day.* He looked drawn and tired. "William."

They had not seen each other since their monumental meeting three nights ago, and she did her best to keep her voice steady. "You look tired. How was your day?"

He sat down and pushed his hair off his forehead. "The days are long. I do what I can, but today I needed to leave early. I was no good to anyone."

"They expect too much of you."

He gazed at her, and she resisted the impulse to reach out and touch his hand. Neither spoke for a long moment. A wave of ripples surged through Emma's knees and up her body. She was glad she was sitting.

He leaned forward. "I—I—"

"What is it?" She willed her body not to lean toward him but her body moved anyway.

He made a fist and pounded on his knee. "I think I love you, and I don't know what to do about it."

She covered his trembling fist with her hands. Her whole body sizzled. "I think I love you too."

They stared at each other.

She spoke first. "What are we going to do?"

"I know only one thing. I want to be with you always. As your real husband and not a puppet for society's sake."

"And I wish to be your wife. Your real wife, forever." She smiled. *I have fallen in love with my husband.*

They rose as one and flowed into each other's arms as man and woman, husband and wife. He had bathed at the hospital and he smelled fresh and new. She kissed his ear, his cheek and found his lips. Their tongues searched, sending waves of desire through their bodies. Emma groaned and pushed her hips against his hardness. She wanted only one thing to quench the thirst inside her.

The side door opened and crashed shut. "What is going on here!" Harriet dropped her packages and planted her hands on her waist. "What are you doing?" Her glare shot daggers at the tightly embraced couple.

Chapter 65

Flushed and flustered, the lovers broke apart, but William's arm remained around Emma, and she didn't move away.

Harriet scowled. "Emma, come here. What is this beast doing to you?"

She shook her head. "Harriet, it's not what you think."

"I know what's happening. He's forcing himself on you, and I'll have none of that."

He put out a hand. "Harriet, I love Emma."

She gaped, her eyes wild. "*You* love her! You cannot. You love Charles, and I love Emma. That's the way it is." She strode to Emma and grabbed her arm.

Emma stood firm. "No, Harriet. It's my wish too. I love William."

Her eyes grew even wilder and her face twisted. "You can't love him. You love me."

Emma pried Harriet's hand off. "I do love you, but now as a friend." She squeezed her hand. "I love William."

Harriet yanked her hand away. "You can't. You love me. You must." Tears swelled in her eyes, and she turned away. In the next moment, she swung back with a ghastly grin. She gestured to the chairs, and spoke in an over-controlled voice. "Let's sit down and discuss this. I'll make tea." She turned swiftly, stumbled over her fallen parcels, and ran from the room.

They sat down, and Emma gasped. "What have we done?"

"We've done what we had to. We've found each other and we'll get through this."

"But I don't want to hurt her. And what about Charles?"

"I spoke to him last night. He knows. He was upset at first but there are plenty of men who pine for his affections."

Harriet, her face cheery, returned with a tray of biscuits and three cups. She put it down as if offering it to a neighbour who had stopped in for tea. "The water's on to boil. I do hope you like the almond cakes. I bought them for Mrs. Trent's visit but…" She trailed off, losing her bravado for a moment.

She pulled a chair up, clasped her hands in her lap, and looked at them like a Sunday school teacher about to give a lesson. "Now, what's all this silly nonsense about?"

William answered. "It's not nonsense, Harriet. We love each other, and we want to be together."

"But Emma and I are together. We can still be that way. We can make a variety of arrangements."

Emma's raised an eyebrow. "What do you mean?"

"We can trade partners now and then." She scowled. "However, I have no wish to bed with Charles. Perhaps on the nights you are with William, Charles and I could invite special friends in."

Emma's mouth dropped open. "What you suggest is preposterous. I will not be a party to any such arrangement." She took Harriet's hand, and her voice softened. "My dear, things have changed. I still love you but not as a lover. I want to be William's real wife now. I want to live with him."

"But you cannot. You live with me. I will not let you go." Harriet pulled her hand out of Emma's. "The water must be boiled by now. We'll talk no more of this until you come to your senses."

She sprang up and dashed from the room, stepping over the unopened parcels scattered about on the oriental rug that her parents had bought her.

Chapter 66

That evening, all four dined together. Finally, at dessert the topic was addressed. Like some enormous creature, its silent presence had filled the room since they'd sat down.

Charles started. "We have to discuss what will be done."

Harriet waved her hand. "No need for that. We're fine. Things can continue as they have."

Emma placed her fork beside her plate. "How can you say that? Things have clearly changed. When will you face that?"

Harriet glared. "Never. I will never accept that you don't love me."

"Harriet, I do love you, but it's different now. I love William."

"Why can't you love both of us? There are many that love a man and a woman."

"I'm sorry, Harriet. I cannot. I don't mean to hurt you, but I love only William."

That evening, the couples went to their usual beds, but neither touched their partners. Harriet did not speak as she undressed for bed, and she turned her back to Emma when she got in.

The next morning, Harriet left early saying she had shopping to do in town.

The men left for the hospital, so Emma had the day to contemplate her new life. She longed to be with William, to love him and know him. To learn all about him and to share herself. Would she move in with him or he with her? And how would that work with Harriet and Charles so close? That would be impossible. *William and I will have to relocate. Find our own place.* It would be hard on Harriet, but a clean break would be best for everyone.

The morning passed quickly and it was late afternoon when the front door handle rattled. She had prepared what she would say to Harriet and hoped she could make her understand that life was not over and that she would meet someone else. The door opened, but it wasn't Harriet.

"William!" She rushed to him.

He flung his arms around her, and they spun around until dizziness overcame them, and they fell into a jumble on the settee. He covered her face with kisses, and she laughed like a child on Christmas morning.

The door swung open with a bang. Harriet stood squarely in the doorway. In her right hand, she held a beautifully crafted, gold-trimmed lady's flintlock pistol—pointed straight at Emma. Her face twisted with rage. "If I can't have you, no one will."

Chapter 67

Harriet lifted her arm, holding the fully cocked pistol steady and ready to fire.

She would only have one shot before she had to reload—time enough for either of them to rush her and secure the gun. A well-aimed shot, however, could kill one of them first.

Emma gasped. "Harriet, what are you doing!"

William stretched his arm out. "Harriet, put the gun down."

Harriet's eyes flashed from William to Emma but she held the gun steady. "Goodbye, my love."

Time stretched to a standstill as milliseconds counted down. Her finger tightened and she started to squeeze the trigger.

William willed his muscles to move—to push him through the thick and unyielding molasses of space between him and Emma.

The mainspring clicked as he strained to lift his arm and press his torso forward inch by inch, fighting to force his way closer to her.

The ball of lead moved through the barrel toward its target just as he broke free of gravity and flung himself over Emma.

The bullet tore into his back and an ear splitting explosion ripped through the air. The recoil of the gun yanked it from Harriet's hand. She stumbled backwards, covering her ears and choking as the smell of rotten eggs met her nose. Emma screamed and threw her arms around a limp William.

Charles raced in, hands over his ears. He kicked the pistol away as if it were a venomous snake. "Are you mad, woman?" He pushed her into a chair and ran to the bleeding William.

Emma clung to him with wet sticky hands as he slowly slumped to the floor, his blood soaking her dress, and his weight pulled her down. "William! William!" *You can't die. Not now.*

Charles knelt and lifted him off. "Move aside. Let me see where the bullet struck."

Emma, her ears still ringing from the blast, slithered out from under but remained at his side. Blood flowed from his back below his shoulder.

"The bullet seems to have missed vital organs. Fetch some cloths. I have to stop the bleeding. It's a damn good thing I left early myself today."

She pulled her skirt free, brushed past a dazed Harriet and ran out. When she returned a moment later with an armful of towels, Harriet was gone. The gun still lay on the floor in the corner. Charles had ripped William's shirt off and was pressing it against the wound. Emma dropped the towels at Charles's feet. William groaned.

She knelt beside him. *He's alive. Thank you, God.* "How is he?"

"He'll live, but the bullet must be removed. We have to get him to the hospital. Can you find a carriage?"

Emma raced to the hall, threw her cape over her bloodstained dress and flung open the door. She ran into the street, waving her arms. No carriages. She ran up to the high road and turned the corner. A large hansom carriage came toward her at a steady clip. At that pace, it probably had a passenger. Lifting her arms high, she ran onto the road in front of the horse's path. The animal reared, and the driver pulled the coach sideways to a crooked stop. Emma ran around to the door and grabbed the handle. The driver, reins in one hand, raised a bludgeon in the other. "Away with you."

"I mean no harm. I need help." She swung the door open.

A finely dressed woman grasped the edges of the seat. Her feathered hat bounced with the rocking of the carriage.

"Please, we need your carriage. My husband has been shot."

The coachy leapt down and grabbed Emma's arm. "Be gone."

The lady inside lifted a silk-gloved hand. "It's all right, Harold. The young woman needs our help." She extended her hand. "Come in, my dear, and show us the way."

She jumped in. Her feet touched carpet. "Thank you, madam. You're very kind."

"Nonsense, my dear. It's times like this when one's mettle is tested." She held her head high. "Which way?"

Emma leaned out the window and called directions. The carriage moved on, and Emma sat back on the thick velvet seat. *This lady is a real Lady.*

As if hearing her thoughts, the lady said, "I am Lady Worthington and glad to be of service."

The carriage pulled up to the house, and on order from Lady Worthington, Harold, the burly driver, followed Emma inside. He lifted William like a baby and carried him out with Emma and Charles close behind. The bleeding had subsided, but the makeshift bandage around his chest had already soaked through, wetting the clean shirt that Charles had slung over his shoulders. Harold placed him onto the seat, and Emma climbed in beside him. "Charles, please find Harriet and assure her she has killed no one."

He put his foot on the step. "I should come with you."

"We'll be all right. Someone must stay with her."

"Go quickly." He slammed the door, and the carriage moved into the street, gaining a fast pace.

Lady Worthington took a soft woollen blanket from the seat beside her and offered it to Emma. "Poor boy. Whatever happened?"

Emma put the blanket over William's lap. "An unfortunate accident with a firearm. He'll be all right once the bullet is removed."

Lady Worthington leaned across and patted Emma's hand. "I'll pray for his full recovery, my dear."

"Thank you." Beatrice's words rang in her head. *'The rich and gentry are snobs. They look down on everyone.'* Ironically, Beatrice desired to be rich and adored like them. This regal lady wore an ermine-trimmed cape opened at the neck, exposing a glittering array of emeralds and diamonds. Beatrice would be surprised at how kind and gracious this rich lady was. A lady who did not fret about the bloody hands that had mucked up her satin and velvet-lined carriage.

Lady Worthington gestured toward William. "What is that red mark on his chest?" She pointed below the bandage. "It doesn't look like blood."

Emma touched the mark with her finger. "It's not blood."

The woman leaned closer, and Emma opened William's shirt to expose a wriggly shaped A below his heart. It looked as if a child had scribbled it on. *That's the mark I saw when—*

The woman gasped. Her face turned white and she covered her mouth with a gloved hand.

Emma closed his shirt. She would ask him about it later.

Lady Worthington blinked rapidly and fumbled with the opening of the satin purse she clutched in her lap. With a shaking hand, she took out a white silk handkerchief and covered her face.

Emma reached toward her but pulled her hand back.

With head bowed, Lady Worthington dabbed at her eyes. After a few long moments, she straightened up, carefully folded her handkerchief in half and in half again, placed the small square into her purse and snapped it shut. "Please forgive such a display."

William groaned, and his head flopped onto Emma's shoulder. She pulled the blanket up and covered the mysterious mark on his chest. "Hold on, my love. We're nearly there."

Chapter 68

The swiftly moving horse soon reached the hospital. At the door a nurse helper called for a stretcher and William was lifted out of the carriage. Emma turned to the woman. "Thank you, Lady Worthington. How may I reach you to repay you for your kindness? At least for the cleaning of your coach."

She took Emma's hand. "No need for that, my dear, but please come and see me at Larks' Nest Abbey. I wish to speak with you."

Emma stepped down and rushed after William. *Whatever could Lady Worthington have to say to me?* She ran alongside the stretcher. *I should have brought some healing herbs.*

An attendant stopped her. "There's been a boarding house fire. You can't come in. It's a madhouse in there."

"But he's been shot and—"

"We know William, and he'll be well cared for." He ran off.

Emma stood for a few moments and turned back to the street. Lady Worthington's coach was gone. A hackney carriage pulled up and let a couple off. She climbed in and settled herself for the ride home. *Thank you, angels, for sending Lady Worthington's carriage.* A niggling thought nudged her. There was something about that woman, apart from her stature and jewels. *Her eyes looked familiar.*

An urgent thought pushed its way to the front of her brain. *Harriet! Did Charles find the gun? I should have picked it up.* Would Harriet do anything foolish? What if she tried to kill herself and botched it? The ride took forever as thought after thought galloped through her head.

She arrived at the house, and Mrs. Trent, skirt flapping, hurried up. "Oh, my dear. We saw William taken out. What happened? Mrs.

Stevens said she heard a shot." Mrs. Trent's eyes were alive with anticipation of gleaning a new piece of notorious gossip.

"All is well, Mrs. Trent. It was an accident. There's nothing to worry about." She brushed past, holding her cape over her bloodstained dress. At least Mrs. Trent had not reported any more shots. She waved a cheery goodbye to her inquisitive neighbour, reassuring her with smiles and finger waves, and rushed to the sitting room. *Where's Harriet? I pray she's come to her senses.*

The gun was gone. So was Charles, but a note lay on the hall table. "Harriet is resting and I've headed to the hospital."

William's blood, so red as it drained out of him, had dried a dark purple on the settee and rug.

She hung up her cape, took a big breath, and walked up the stairs to the bedroom. The room where so much love had taken place. The love, which had been snatched from Harriet.

Harriet sat on the bed, a pillow propped behind her. However, Emma's relief was short-lived. Harriet held the shiny new pistol in her right hand—her index finger curled around the trigger. Was the gun fully cocked? Emma had heard of half-cocked guns going off and causing damage to the shooter as well as the intended victim. Sometimes they even blew up in a person's hand. She took a cautious step forward. "Harriet, don't be foolish."

A blotchy face framed tear-swollen eyes. "Stay back. I don't want to hurt you."

"Give me the gun." She stretched out a wavering hand.

With a macabre smile, Harriet twisted it one way and another. "It's such a pretty little thing. Don't you think?"

"Harriet. I know you don't want to hurt anyone. Please do not do anything you'll regret." She took another step forward.

"Stay there." She pointed the gun at Emma. "I'm trying to decide who to shoot—you or me."

"Harriet, please stop this. Put the gun down. I don't want either of us shot. I love you."

"Oh, you love me, do you? So much so that you are running away with that—*man*." Her lips curled as if tasting something repugnant. "How could you? After all we've been together."

"Harriet." She took another step and spoke gently. "There are many kinds of love, and you will love again." She reached the foot of the bed and put her hand out. "Please give me the gun before someone gets hurt."

"You don't think I'm hurt?" Her voice rose. "What's a little bullet added to that? It would put me out of my misery. I have nothing to live for now." She pressed the pistol against her temple.

"No, Harriet. Please." Her voice broke. "Don't do this."

"You're right. It's better I shoot myself in the heart." She moved the small gun and pointed it at her chest. "It's already broken. What more harm can one small bullet do?"

Emma inched her way up the side of the bed.

"Don't come any closer." She pressed the gun deeper.

Emma stopped and planted her hands on her hips. *It's a risk but maybe I can shock her into some sense.* "All right, you silly woman. Shoot yourself. See if I care." She held her breath.

Harriet frowned. "I knew you didn't care. I might as well die."

Emma glared, hoping her act would work. "I agree. Just die. Get it over with. If you're in so much misery, that would be the best thing to do." *Dear God. Make her put it down.*

Harriet's eyes flickered and tears glistened. "You're so mean. Did you ever love me at all?" She waved the pistol in the air.

They stared at each other.

Emma wanted to step forward but didn't dare. *Don't do it, Harriet.*

An enigmatic smile creased Harriet's face. "I have made up my mind about whom I will shoot." She pointed the gun.

Chapter 69

Harriet held the pistol steady and pointed at her heart. Her mouth a humourless line. "It's the only way."

Emma's knees shook, but she spoke in an even voice. "Then do it."

"You're feigning. When I kill myself, you'll be distraught, not only because I'm dead, but—." She pushed the barrel hard against her chest. "Because my death will be *your* fault." Her voice rose. "You'll be remorse with guilt!" Her finger quivered on the trigger. With blind speed, Emma flung her hand at the side table, grabbed the closest object and threw it at the gun. It hit squarely, knocking it from Harriet's hand. Both objects clattered to the floor.

Harriet clutched her hand. "Ow."

Emma lunged onto the bed and grabbed Harriet's hands. "Shooting yourself or anyone is not the answer."

Harriet wrenched her hands away and cupped one over her thumb. "My life is over, and you can't stop me from ending it."

"You're right. If you're determined to kill yourself, so be it. But it's a foolish act. The love you have for me is inside *you*, not me. You *will* love another."

Harriet snarled. "I don't want to hear platitudes from some book you've read. It's *your* fault I feel this way. You've ruined my life."

Emma crossed her arms. "That is the most preposterous thing I've ever heard. You're an intelligent woman. I expect more from you."

Harriet pouted and Emma spoke softly. "Each of us is responsible for our *own* life. I'm not inside your head or heart to tell you how to think or feel." Harriet's jawline softened a little, and Emma took her hands in hers. "You're a loving person. You have plenty of love to give."

"But not to you."

"Not in the way we have. But I will always love you."

With a grunt, Harriet pulled her hands away and rubbed her reddening thumb. "Did you have to throw it so hard?"

Emma stood up. "Why don't you get some sleep. I'll bring tea up later."

She turned on her side and pulled the covers over her head.

Emma tiptoed around the bed. No sense leaving the pistol. The object she had thrown lay beside it. *My dragonfly!* There was a new nick on the wing where it had hit the pistol. "I think we might have saved a life today, Dragonfly. Thank you."

Charles returned from the hospital after eleven. Emma heard him come in and leaving a sleeping Harriet she ran to the men's quarters. He assured her that William was doing well. The bullet had been removed and had hit no vital organs.

Emma fell into a chair. "Thank God."

Charles hung his cape up.

"Charles, you must be hungry. I have a casserole and tea made. Come into the kitchen."

"I'm not hungry, but I would like some tea." He followed her and slumped at the table while she poured tea for both of them.

He didn't look at her as he stirred in milk and sugar. "We have to talk about our living arrangements."

Emma touched his hand. "Charles, I'm so sorry."

He drew his hand back. "Don't be sorry for loving William." His voice broke. "He's an easy man to love."

"But I've hurt you and Harriet. I never meant—"

"Love hurts sometimes. But the hurt is always worth it." He lifted his cup as if making a toast. "Whenever and wherever love finds you, you have to let it in."

Chapter 70

The next morning, Emma wrote to Lady Worthington at Larks' Nest Abbey. She thanked her for her kindness and offered to pay for the cleaning of her coach.

William remained in the hospital for a week, during which time, Emma, Harriet, and Charles had several long discussions. They concluded that Emma and William would have to move out. Neither Charles nor Harriet wanted to have their ex-partners at such close quarters.

Emma arranged to have her and William's belongings moved to Hollyhock, where there was plenty of room and would serve them until they could make their own plans. It wasn't much farther from London for his work, and he would need some rest time before returning to his duties.

Harriet, meanwhile, had concocted plans of her own. She wrote and invited Beatrice who had remained at Hollyhock with baby Phoebe, to visit her at the Parson's house. Beatrice welcomed Harriet's personal attention and thought it a brilliant idea that she and Phoebe move in. Mrs. Trent was delighted to hear a baby was coming to live next door.

Charles had no immediate plans for a new companion. It would be hard enough for him to see William at work. However, as time healed William's physical wound, so it would heal Charles' heart.

Hudson picked William up from the hospital and took him directly to Hollyhock. Charles didn't accompany him.

Mother Cameron warmly welcomed William into the household and Francesca showed him to his and Emma's newly furnished quarters. Mrs. Hudson fussed over him and made steaming pots of chicken soup. His injury was healing nicely with the help of Emma's comfrey poultices. The twins helped, but only after Emma assured them she was not a witch.

Emma wrote to Harriet every other day, but it was two weeks before she received a reply. She was relieved to hear that Beatrice and baby had settled in and Harriet was happier. Also, Charles was entertaining a few gentlemen callers and was smiling again.

Emma and William enjoyed their days and especially nights in their new quarters at Hollyhock. Mrs. Cameron remarked that she'd never seen Emma so happy. "Nothing like a close call to bring a couple together."

They'd been there for three weeks when Mr. Cameron arrived home from work with a folded card Harriet had delivered to him. He gave it to Emma. "This was sent to you at the Parson's house."

"Thank you." She turned it over. An emblazoned W lay etched in a puddle of crimson wax. She ran upstairs and burst into the sitting room. "William, look at this." She waved a letter at him.

He pulled his face back. "What is it?"

"It's a thick letter or a card. A fancy one."

"I can see that. Who's it from?"

"I don't know." She looked at the wax mark. "Just the initial W."

"Why don't you open it?"

"Good idea." She broke the seal and opened up a page of vellum. "It's from Larks' Nest Abbey. An invitation from Lady Worthington."

"Who?"

"Lady Worthington. The lady I told you about who took you to the hospital." Her eyes flashed along the lines. "Oh, my goodness."

"What is it?"

"She wants us to come and visit."

"Whatever for?"

"She doesn't say." She read aloud. "We would be pleased if you and your husband would come for tea a week Wednesday at 4:00 pm." Emma looked up. "R.S.V.P. Larks' Nest Abbey. "

William laughed. "Maybe they're going to present you with a cleaning bill."

She wrinkled her brow. "I remember now. In the carriage, she said she wished to speak with me."

"That's strange. What about?"

"I have no idea." Her face brightened. "Wait a minute. She asked about the mark on your chest and after we saw it was the letter A, she took a queer turn."

He frowned. "You don't think——. Do you think she might know something about my birth parents?"

She grabbed his hand. "Oh, William. She might know someone who knows someone who knows about a baby born with a scraggly A on his chest." She waved the letter. "She might lead you to your real parents. Or at least give you some information about them."

William took the letter and folding the sides in place, made the cracked W whole again. "Next Wednesday at 4:00. We must reply right away."

Chapter 71

At three-fifteen on Wednesday, Emma fussed at the ribbons on her neckline. She wore her dragonfly necklace that Charlotte had given her. "Does this dress suit me? Should I wear my evening cape? Am I showing too much?"

William put his comb on the bureau top. "You look beautiful. I like this new fashion of lowered necklines. More of you to see." He kissed her lightly on the lips.

"Don't mess me up." She ducked away.

"You don't mind me messing you up every night."

She smiled. "That's different."

They arrived at five minutes to four and followed a butler down a long hall covered with portrait painting. In the grand sitting room, tall windows filled one wall with glass doors that opened onto a courtyard surrounded by birch trees and hedges. Groupings of giant clay containers, overflowing with red and yellow flowering plants, circled the outside seating area. The magical glow of a late afternoon sun spilled into the room, infusing and illuminating everything it touched.

The butler bent his head. "Please be seated." He gestured to a quartet of matching white wicker armchairs arranged in an arc. A low round mahogany table sat in front of them, on which lay a circular lace cloth and a bowl of freshly cut yellow roses.

Emma sat on the silk-covered cushion and removed her gloves. William sat beside her. "What a beautiful room," she whispered.

In a few minutes, Lady Worthington entered and extended her hand. "Thank you for coming."

William stood, took her hand and kissed the back of it.

She smiled. "You are in better shape now, I see."

"Indeed, Madam, and I thank you for your kind assistance."

Emma stood and Lady Worthington turned to her. "So nice to see you again, my dear." She motioned with her hand. "Please sit. Tea is coming. I do like to catch the late afternoon sun. This is one of my favourite rooms."

Emma sat and motioned to the window. "You have a lovely garden."

"My husband and I are fortunate, and we are grateful for our lives."

William cleared his throat and leaned toward her. "Excuse my boldness. Emma told me you were taken aback when you saw my birthmark, and I must ask. Do you know anything about my birth parents?"

"I like a direct man. Yes, I do know something about your birth parents."

William gasped, took Emma's hand and held it tightly.

Two maids walked in. One carried a large oval tray, with a silver tea service and four delicate bone china cups and saucers. The other, a large plate of scones and strawberry preserves which she placed on the table.

"My husband will join us shortly." She poured three cups of tea and added sugar and milk as requested.

William picked up his cup. "Please tell us what you know."

She looked past him, fixing her gaze beyond the window. "Many years ago, I knew a young woman named Sarah Midhearst. When she was fourteen, she fell hopelessly in love." She glanced at Emma. "A true Romeo and Juliet love except they were from friendly noble families so it wasn't a feud that tore them apart. They got pregnant, and to avert any breath of scandal, she was whisked to Switzerland on an extended holiday where she had her baby. Her lover David visited when he could, and they loved their little boy—the little boy who was born with a pink letter 'A' scrawled on his chest." She hesitated. "They called him Arthur."

William's hand shook as he placed the teacup on the tray. Emma took his hand, and they listened to the words they never thought they would hear.

Lady Worthington continued. "In two years, it was time for their marriage. They left their young son in good hands and planned to return in six weeks and bring him back to England as an orphan child that Sarah had grown fond of." She hesitated, and now her hand shook when she picked up her cup. She put it down without taking a sip. "However, six weeks later, when Sarah and David went to fetch their son, he was not there. David's father, a very strict man, thought it best for everyone that the child be removed. That way, the young couple could start their life fresh with no hint of scandal for their noble families."

Emma squeezed William's hand. "That must have been difficult for your friend, Sarah."

Lady Worthington looked up. "Yes, it was terrible for Sarah and David. They returned to England with broken hearts. The years passed, and they had two more children, a girl and a boy, but they never forgot their firstborn son. The tiny baby with an A on his chest."

William gulped. "Did they ever try to find—their son?"

"They searched every orphanage in England and Europe and concluded that strict orders had been given and someone paid well to keep the child hidden from any inquiries." She hesitated. "They finally gave up but held him always in their hearts."

A tall, distinguished gentleman came in. Lady Worthington lifted a hand. "May I introduce my husband, Lord Worthington."

Lord Worthington bowed, took Emma's hand and kissed it. William stood, shook the proffered hand and resumed his seat. Lord Worthington sat beside his wife and took her hand. They exchanged a long look.

She turned her attention to William. "My husband's name is David and I am Sarah."

Chapter 72

Emma gasped. William opened his mouth and leapt to his feet. His legs trembled as he gazed at his newfound parents. Lady Worthington opened her arms, and William dropped to his knees and put his head on his mother's lap. Lord Worthington put one arm around his wife and his other over his son. Mother, father, and son sobbed and Emma pulled out a handkerchief for her own overflowing tears.

After many long moments, Lady Worthington lifted her head and dabbed at her eyes. "Little did I dream that a wild young woman risking her life to stop a galloping horse would bring my son back to us." More tears welled up.

Emma looked into Lady Worthington's eyes. Those same eyes she saw in the coach when she held a bleeding William. *They were William's eyes.*

William sat cross-legged on the rug in front of his parents, his hands still holding theirs.

Lord Worthington wiped his eyes and blew his nose. "Get up, my boy."

William shook his head. "I never want to leave you again."

More tears from everyone and Lord Worthington cleared his throat. "For twenty years, we've prayed to find you and it took a gunshot to bring us together."

William rejoined Emma and sat beside her. "It's no wonder you couldn't find me. I wasn't taken to an orphanage."

All eyes looked at him. "I was left in a monastery in Germany. At the time of Henry's Dissolution of the Monasteries, a small group of Benedictine monks fled from England. They were granted use of a derelict building in Lamspringe to carry on their order."

Lady Worthington put a hand to her chest. "We visited orphanages in Germany but never knew monasteries took children in."

"As a rule they don't. This one was in an isolated area, and a Brother Francis took me under his wing."

Emma took his hand. "I lived in Germany until I was eight. I wonder how far away we were from each other."

"I left when I was nine when a traveller enticed me away."

Lord Worthington leaned forward. "What do you mean?"

"A Mr. Johnstone, on a search for rare books, became my adopted father. He told me that he loved me the minute he saw me and with a substantial donation and a promise that he would take good care of me, he whisked me away." He took a deep breath. "Brother Francis didn't want me to go and I didn't want to go either. We cried a long time on that cold and rainy day."

Lady Worthington took William's hand. "My dear boy."

"Oh, don't feel sorry for me. I was well looked after in London. My new father educated me. He didn't beat me, he supplied tutors and paid for medical school."

"He must have loved you very much."

"In his own way he did." He paused. "I believe he did his best."

His mother nodded. "I wonder why they called you William rather than give you a name that started with A."

"Brother Francis said the A was a mark of the devil. I think that was also part of the reason they let me go. They rubbed sand on it and all kinds of burning ointments but nothing removed it."

Emma squeezed his hand. "I'm glad they didn't succeed. You would have been a monk and we might never have met. And you would have never found your parents."

"They attempted to make a W out of it with two upward slashes but the cuts healed without leaving a scar."

Lady Worthington gasped. "My dear boy. How terrible for you."

"The monks were kind and Brother Francis especially so."

Lord Worthington lifted his head. "How about we call you William Arthur? William Arthur Worthington." He stood up and put his hand on William's shoulder. "Stand tall, my son. You're home." They embraced for an endless moment.

Lady Worthington broke the silence. "Would you like to meet your sister and brother?"

A young woman and young man tumbled into the room as if they'd been waiting for a prompt.

Tears and laughter flowed as William Arthur met Margaret and George. A week earlier, they had been told the story, and shock had turned to curiosity with many questions.

Margaret threw herself at him in a hug. "I've always wanted a big brother."

George shook his hand. "And I've never wanted to be an Earl. You can have it. I'm an artist."

William's eyebrows shot up. "Things are moving too fast. I'm only a doctor."

Lord Worthington laughed. "I'm planning to live a long life, so no need to worry about that."

For the next hour, Emma joined in with five people acting decidedly un-English. Such boisterous and uninhibited emotions had never been heard in those Abbey halls.

Supper was served in the main dining hall where they all sat at the far end of the twenty-four-foot-long table, swapping stories of their lives and bringing everyone up to date. They finished eating and retired to the family sitting room with more comfortable chairs and talked far into the night.

Margaret, eighteen, was engaged to be married. George, sixteen, was enrolled at the École des Beaux-Arts, run by the Royal Academy of Painting and Sculpture in Paris. Emma said he must meet her uncle and his wife.

Midnight chimed and Lady Worthington invited Emma and their newfound son to stay the night. "We have plenty of room."

Margaret jumped up. "Please stay big brother. I'll have Marion open the Blue Room for you." She ran off.

Emma shrugged. "We'd like to but we're expected at Hollyhock. They'll worry if we don't arrive home."

Lord Worthington stood. "Do not fret. I'll arrange for a driver to take a message. William—" He looked at his son. "Write a note, and both of you sign it, so they know you're not kidnapped."

George showed Emma to the desk where she wrote a short note to Mother Cameron that they were safe and sound. The sharp quill slid smoothly over the delicate paper embossed at the top with a curly W.

Margaret bounced into the room. "All set. Marion is finding night clothes for you. The Blue Room has its own bathroom, and she's putting out chewsticks for you."

An hour later, washed, teeth cleaned and dressed in long silk nightshirts, they lay in a grand four-poster under a mountain of feather comforters. Green velvet curtains surrounded the bed in a warm cocoon.

Emma giggled. "I feel like a princess in a storybook."

William let a long breath out. "I feel like—I don't know what I feel like. This whole evening has been incredible." He put his hands behind his head. "I used to dream my parents would find me, but once Father took me in, I gave up." He put an arm around her, and she cuddled in. "In all my fantasies, I never dreamt of having such distinguished parents. But I don't think I want to be an Earl. I've only ever wanted to be a doctor."

"Can you not be both?"

"I don't know." He kissed her lightly. "But if I ever am an Earl you'll be a Countess."

" A countess. I don't know about that."

" Well, one thing I know for sure. I'm your husband and that I'll be no matter what else." He kissed her again and they were soon immersed in their favourite nighttime activity.

Chapter 73

In six scurried weeks of activity, a crew of designers, artists, carpenters, and cleaners, transformed the unused summer house on the Worthington estate and Emma and William moved into their new home at Larks' Nest. A housekeeper came in every morning to clean the ten rooms, and a cook made their afternoon tea and supper. On Sundays, they joined the family for their evening meal but Margaret would often drop by, and she and Emma became good friends. Emma loved the old herb garden and spent hours bringing it back to its full splendour. She dug out barrels of weeds and encouraged the cooking, healing, and other aromatic plants to flourish.

A driver and carriage was assigned for their private use, which William, now back at work, appreciated.

Harriet and Charles remained living in the Parson's house, continuing their role of a happily married couple. No one could replace William in Charles's heart but his new companion, Richard, an up-and-coming barrister, brought new happiness to him. Richard came to the house for dinner several times and Mrs.Trent was happy to babysit, so Beatrice could join him and Charles and Harriet on a night out. She was so glad to see the young widow having another chance at love. Beatrice was pleased to live at the Parson's house and have the love and support of Harriet and she fully understood the unique living arrangements. After a well designed public "courtship" she and Richard were married, thus filling the place of Emma and William.

It turned out that both Beatrice and Richard had a liking for either sex and unbeknownst to Harriet or Charles, the newlyweds honoured their wedding vows by enjoying a conjugal afternoon when Charles was at work and Harriet, shopping.

Mother Cameron was content that Beatrice had found a new love . She did miss her other daughter Catherine, who with her new husband Norman, had relocated to the colonies of New England across the sea. Happy that two of her daughters were settled, she still fussed that Emma had not yet been blessed with child.

Emma wrote long letters to her uncle about William and their new family, the house, the herb garden, and the latest book she had found. She and Isaac also continued to exchange letters from Cambridge which he loved so much. She stopped writing, and leaned back, touching the soft feather end of her pen to her cheek.

The whiff of further education still stirred her soul, but the sting of defeat had lessened. She read voraciously and attended lectures at Oxford whenever guests were allowed. Usually she was the only woman present. However, she also loved being a real wife to William, supporting him, nurturing him, working in the garden and trying out new meals. Maybe being a scholar wasn't her destiny. *Does anyone ever really know who they are? Perhaps it takes a lifetime or two to figure that out.*

She dipped the quill into the ink pot. *Maybe no one ever does. Maybe there's no definitive answer. A person is simply who they are at that moment.*

She finished her letter, let the ink dry and folded it over. William's vermillion wax stick lay on the desk but she preferred the natural colour of beeswax. Tipping the candle, the drips made a puddle of warm wax. Three choices of seals lay before her: an ornate W, a replica of the scrawled A on William's chest, and a very fancy E. On her last birthday, William had gifted her with her own seal copied from an illuminated letter of an old manuscript. She pressed it into the golden wax. "I am, and that's enough." *Anyway, whatever definition I put on myself, or another puts on me, is temporary. What I am is eternal.*

The bright noonday sun shone through the library window, warming her face. Could she be any happier?

That afternoon Emma took a carriage to Hollyhock, delighted to find Beatrice had dropped off Phoebe. Mrs. Cameron bounced the baby on her lap. "When are we going to hear yours news that a little one is on its way?"

"I'm quite happy right now without a baby to look after. I've seen how much work they take."

"Oh, but they're so worth it. You wait."

On the ride home, Emma's thoughts turned to her own mother. She wrinkled her brow. *I was only eight when Mama died.* The carriage bumped along the rutted road. *We were cutting vegetables in the kitchen.* She looked out the window and stared at the passing scenery without seeing a leaf or a bird. *I had my doll Molly on my lap and I'm filling a bowl with carrot rounds.* She closed her eyes. *People yelling. Mama grabbing my hand. We're running—.*

The carriage jerked, knocking her sideways, wheels creaking and splashing, hoofs pounding. Rain thundered on the fabric roof. She shivered and gathered her cape around her shoulders. It would be past teatime when she got home. *I must have maid prepare a good meal for William.*

The rain had let up when they reached the summer house. She hurried inside, shook off her cape and turned to hang it up. William was standing stark naked in the hallway.

"William, what are you doing?"

His face was grey and drawn. He grabbed a cloak from the rack and pulled it around himself. "I just got in myself."

"Why are you naked?"

"I removed all my clothes outside and left them in the rain. Then I waited until the rain poured well over me."

My husband has gone mad. She took his hand and they walked to the kitchen. "Come. I'll make tea and find a towel for you."

She guided him to a chair and handed him a towel. She grabbed another one and rubbed his hair.

He stopped her. "Emma. Sit down. I've not gone mad."

She pulled up a chair and sat down. "What is it? You look scared."

"I am scared."

"William. What is it? You're scaring me."

He took a long breath. "The Bubonic Plague has hit again."

"But it's been over for thirty years."

"Yes. and twenty before that. There is no rhyme or reason when or why it emerges. All I know is that it has."

"God save us."

Chapter 74

He shook his head. "For the last few years, there have been reports of it in parts of the continent. Ships coming in from infected ports were quarantined, but that didn't stop it from reaching England."

"What's causing this dreadful disease?"

"If we knew that, we could be more effective in controlling it. Some blame emanations from the earth, or from sicknesses of livestock, or even to the number of moles, frogs, mice or flies." His cape fell away, exposing a bare leg.

"At least you were right to wash. It seems the sensible thing to do."

"My worse fear is that I'll bring it home to you. Perhaps I should stay in the city while this thing rages."

Emma grabbed his hand. "No. I will not have that. Do you think I could stay here, not knowing if you were dead or alive? No. No." She shook her head. "Now that warm weather is coming, we'll have hot water and a clean set of clothes waiting for you outside." She kissed him lightly. "We can't have you wandering around naked as the day you were born."

Every day after that and for the rest of the month and into June, one of the maids would set out a tub of warm water, soap and towels in the side courtyard with clean clothes ready. He would deposit his worn clothes into a vat of water and lye soap where they could soak.

It was worse than they imagined. Hundreds had already died especially in the dock areas outside of London, where poor workers crowded into ill kempt districts. Emma pleaded with William to let her go with him. "I can bring herbs and—"

"No. I know you want to help, but the conditions are appalling. There's no sanitation. Open drains flow through the streets. The cobbles are slippery with dung, rubbish and slops." He shook his head. "The muck buzzes with flies, and the stench makes you gag. The sight of people with seeping boils and open running sores, dying painful and grotesque deaths will remain etched in your brain forever."

From the beginning of June, Lord and Lady Worthington, Margaret, George, and all the Abbey staff never left the grounds. Every evening they heard the latest news from William and each time, the report grew worse.

"The Privy Council Committee is investigating ways to prevent the spread of this horror. Some alehouses in affected areas have been closed, and the number of lodgers allowed in a household has been limited. A quarantine system has been set up, and any house where someone has died of the plague is locked up and no one must enter or leave for forty days."

Lady Worthington nodded. "That seems like a good idea."

"Unfortunately, it doesn't protect the remaining inhabitants who either die of plague or starvation. "

"That's terrible," said Margret. "Can't food be delivered to them?"

"No. A plague house is marked with a red cross on the door and the words, 'Lord have mercy upon us.' A watchman is assigned to stand outside." He threw up his hands. "Not only that. The searchers are changing the cause of death to consumption. No householder wants their house to be marked a death house, and even the Parish Clerks are covering up cases of plague on their official returns."

"Who are the searchers?" asked George. "And why are clerks covering up the number of deaths?"

"Searchers are men who walk around London searching for the dead. They carry a white stick to warn people of their occupation. They live apart and must stay inside unless on duty. As far as changing the records, the clerks don't want their district listed with an abundance of plague deaths."

Lord Worthington shook his head. "Such times we live in. How do you know so much?"

"At the hospital, we hear all the news, and I see it when I'm on duty in the streets where I'm obliged to diagnose and report sick persons."

"Oh, no." Emma cried. "I hate to think of you in the midst of all that."

He took her hand. "It is terrible. But I'm sure the packet of herbs you hang about my neck every morning is helpful. At least it keeps my nose happy."

Margret held up a small packet of herbs wrapped in linen and tied with a ribbon. "Everyone is wearing a nosegay now. My friends and I are making some for you to take to the hospital."

Letters from France reported the same ugly stories. Albert, Charlotte, and family were safely ensconced in the house of DuBois. They had plenty of wine and food to eat, and when a maid or driver returned from the outside, they were required to follow a strict cleansing procedure before entering.

Harriet, Beatrice and baby had fled to Aunt Millicent's. However, Mother Cameron insisted on remaining in the city, helping wherever she could.

In July, King Charles, his family, and his court left for Salisbury. Other nobles and those who could afford to, found refuge in their country homes. Some poorer people left the city but it was not easy for them to abandon their accommodation and livelihoods for an uncertain future. Before exiting through the city gates, they were required to show a certificate of good health signed by the Lord Mayor, and these became increasingly difficult to obtain.

When the numbers of plague victims rose, people living in the villages outside London resented the exodus and refused to accept townsfolk from London, with or without a certificate. The refugees who were turned back had to travel across country and forced to live rough on what they could steal or scavenge from the fields. Many died in wretched circumstances of starvation and thirst.

When worry of William's safety crowded Emma's thoughts, she talked herself out of it, knowing no good would come from such dire ruminations. She would picture him strong and well, going through his day with fortitude, no matter what horrors faced him.

The Lord Mayor of London, the aldermen, and other city officials stayed at their posts but businesses closed when merchants and professionals fled. Nothing could be seen but wagons and carts with goods, women, servants, and children, or coaches filled with people who could afford them, all hurrying away. Only a few clergymen, physicians and apothecaries remained to cope with the growing number of victims. As the numbers mounted, burial grounds became overfull, and pits were dug to accommodate the dead. Drivers of dead-carts travelled the streets calling "Bring out your dead" and bodies were piled on top of each other in an unruly mound. When the authorities became concerned that the number of deaths might cause public alarm, they ordered that body removal and internment be done only at night.

William told Emma more than he did the rest of his family. "I saw Dwight and Mildred Cameron today. She was helping with burial details, and he was keeping some fires burning."

"Fires? What for?"

"They keep them burning day and night in hopes it will clean the air. Any substance that gives off a strong odour—pepper, frankincense, or hops—is burned to ward off the infection. Everyone is encouraged to smoke tobacco, especially young children."

With too many victims and too few drivers to remove the bodies, they stacked them against the walls of houses. The plague pits became mounds of decomposing corpses. In one parish, a great hole was dug near the churchyard, fifty feet long and twenty feet wide. Digging continued by labourers at one end while the dead-carts tipped in corpses at the other. With no room for further extension, they dug deeper until groundwater reached twenty feet. When finally covered with earth, it housed over a thousand corpses.

William brought back such dismal report with little hope, he stopped going up to the Abbey each evening. The toll showed on him, and Emma begged him to stay home. "You've given enough over these past months. You must take a rest yourself."

William lay on the bed, bone-weary and face drawn. "If only we knew more about this wretched disease, we might be able to stop it or at least abate it."

Emma sat beside the bed and held a cool cloth on his forehead. "You're doing everything you can. I only thank God and the Goddess and every deity or nature spirit that you are alive." She even asked her dragonfly and if it had any magical powers, to keep her husband safe.

He shook his head. "Some think the disease might be linked to domestic animals and the City has ordered a cull of dogs and cats."

Emma frowned. "I just hope the dogs and cats aren't keeping down the very pests that might be the causal link."

William sighed. "Dear God. If we only knew—." He closed his eyes and fell into a much-needed sleep.

Trade and businesses dried up and the streets were empty of people except for the dying and the dead-carts. So many wretched, sick people covered with foul-smelling, running sores.

The villages around London supplied food. However, denied of their usual sales in the capital, they left vegetables in specified market areas. They negotiated their sale by shouting and collecting their payment after the money had been submerged in a bucket of vinegar to disinfect the coins.

Deaths crept to a thousand persons per week, then two and by September, seven thousand. It was a mystery why some died and others not. Every night Emma awaited William's return, praying he would, and when he did, she prayed he was not afflicted.

Cooler weather arrived but that did not arrest the rampaging horror, and he spent even longer hours in London tending to the sick and frightened. If the plague did not get you, the terror of it did.

One evening, Lord and Lady Worthington came to the summer house, and with Emma, again begged William to stay home. "You've done your share."

He shook his head. "I'm a doctor. I'll take one day off and then I have to return."

Emma handed him another cup of tea.

He wrapped his hands around the small cup. "This contagion is not only physical. Rampant fear doesn't help."

"I remember my mother saying that fear could kill more people than the disease did."

"I have wondered why more doctors are not afflicted."

Lady Worthington patted his shoulder. "Probably because you're too busy or too tired to be afraid."

William sighed. "There could be truth in that."

By late autumn, the death toll in London and suburbs slowed until, in February 1666, it was considered safe enough for the King and his entourage to come back to the city. With the monarch back, others began to return: The gentry came in their carriages accompanied by carts piled high with their belongings. The judges moved back from Windsor to sit in Westminster Hall. Trade recommenced, and businesses and workshops reopened. London soon became the goal of a new wave of people flocking to the city to make their fortunes.

People prayed the coming summer would not bring a further outbreak. Nearly a hundred thousand people, a fifth of London's population, had died of the cursed disease.

Emma's uncle wrote that he and Charlotte and family were well, but were sad that Aunt Agnes has succumbed. She had gone to Paris, and didn't come back to infect the family. Also, one of the DuBois maids had snuck out to meet her lover. When they were discovered together, they were isolated in an outbuilding with food brought to them. They died in each others arms and the building burned.

The family and staff at the Abbey had been careful, and all were safe. However, one of the carriage drivers who had left to volunteer his services in London never returned.

The daily newspaper printed an official list of deaths. William brought the paper home each day, and Emma would slowly slide her finger down the columns.

She sat at the kitchen table, the paper spread out. A moment later, she tore at it, crushing the sheet in her hands sobbing. "No. No."

William ran over. "Who?" He pried the crumpled paper out of her fists. The second name in the 'C' column was a Mrs. Dwight Cameron of Hollyhock House.

She collapsed and he held her as long as she needed, whispering soothing words. When her sobs lessened to whimpers, he carried her upstairs to the bedroom. He took off her shoes and covered her with a blanket. That was the second time she'd lost a mother. She'd never spoken much about her birth mother. Only that she'd died of a sickness. She would tell him more when she was ready.

Mr. Cameron had been frantic when his wife never returned after three days. She often stayed over but would let him know if she did. He made further inquiries and eventually learned that her abandoned purse had been found in the volunteer's room of a small makeshift hospital. When she never claimed it, she was presumed dead, probably dying in some common dwelling while taking food to victims. With so much confusion and fear, she too was left to die, and buried in a mass grave along with the people she was helping.

Mr. Cameron had a granite stone engraved with her name and placed in the honeysuckle garden at Hollyhock. Emma and William joined him, along with Beatrice, Harriet, and baby Phoebe to remember the woman they all loved. Francesca, Signore Tonini, the Hudsons, and the Twins contributed memorable Mrs. C. stories along with all the others. Many tears filled the afternoon—tears of sadness mixed with bursts of laughter, which quickly turned to tears again.

Prolonged goodbyes brought more tears and Francesca handed Emma a parcel. "A few months before the terrible epidemic started, Mrs. C. and I were clearing out closets, and she wrapped this bundle up for you. She wanted you to have it."

"Thank you, Francesca. I'll open it later."

On the carriage ride home, Emma stared out the window.

William took her hand. "Are you all right, my darling?"

"I am, sitting here with you." She squeezed his hand. "Promise me you won't die. Ever."

"I promise."

She leaned her head on his shoulder. "Thank you."

Chapter 75

On the first weekend in September, William stayed overnight in a small inn outside of London after working late at the hospital. He often stayed over so Emma wasn't worried when he didn't return on Saturday night. She looked forward to his midmorning arrival on Sunday.

On that Sunday morning of September 2, 1666, William woke early, stretched his arms and rubbed his eyes. He looked forward to getting home to Emma and enjoying a lazy day with her.

He finished his second cup of morning tea when he overheard two maids talking about a fire and he called to them. "Is there a fire somewhere?"

One turned to him. "Nothing to be alarmed about. It's only a small blaze in Puddin' Lane."

Fire could mean burn injuries. Perhaps he should head over to the hospital. He joined a few others who had stepped outside. In the distance, a red glow lit the sky, and black smoke billowed from the downtown core. He frowned. *That doesn't look small.*

The innkeeper shrugged. "I'm sure the firemen have it in hand."

William had seen enough of the inner city—its overcrowded warrens of narrow, cobbled alleys, all a fire trap ready to explode. People used cheap building materials of wood and thatch for roofs, even though such materials had been prohibited for many years. Overhanging upper floors, typical of the six or seven-story timbered tenement houses, projected across alleyways. A fire could easily jump from building to building where these jetties met.

The red patch in the sky grew larger, higher, and it seemed to be moving closer. *That's no small fire.* He turned to the innkeeper. "I have to get to the hospital."

"Come round the back. I have a wagon."

The horse was already hitched and William climbed up beside the innkeeper. At London Bridge, the packed row of houses on the bridge blazed.

The innkeeper shouted. "That's bad. Very bad. There are six hundred tons of black powder stored in wooden barrels in the Tower of London."

William grasped the side of the rocking wagon. "I thought that was declared a death trap."

"It was. Way back."

"Why wasn't it cleaned up?"

The innkeeper tightened the reins as the horse shied from the intense heat. He turned the frightened beast away from the river to roads adjacent to the raging flames which were rapidly eating their way from house to house. People, with armloads of bundles, or pushing overloaded carts, crowded the streets. Mothers ran, clutching screaming infants. Children stumbled after them, grasping at a mother's flapping skirt with one hand and holding a squirming pet or a bedraggled doll in the other. Most were running to St. Paul's or toward any place thought to be a safe house.

William frowned. *How long would any of those locations be safe?*

The innkeeper turned the wagon onto a main street where the fire had not yet reached. He pulled up when a fire wagon and an angry group blocked their way. William jumped down, and pushed his way through the crush of yelling men. Around the scrambling firemen, and three policemen, a crowd of irate citizens were hollering and waving their arms.

The parish constable, his face streaked with sweat and dirt, yelled over the din. "We have to pull the adjoining buildings down to stop it from spreading."

A stocky man pushed forward, his jaw stuck out. "My house is not burning. You can't take it down."

The Fire Marshall hollered. "It's the only way to stop it."

A carriage drew up, and the Lord Mayor, Sir Thomas Bloodworth, stepped out.

The red-faced Fire Marshal approached him. "Your Lordship. We must demolish the adjoining houses and you're the only one, other than the King, to give permission."

The Mayor looked left and right. No buildings were on fire on the street on which he stood.

"Well, your Lord? Give us the word. It must be done! And quickly."

"Er. Well—I." His eyes darted back and forth. "I cannot do that until I locate all the owners."

The Fire Marshal threw up his hands. "You don't need the owner's permission. You're the Lord Mayor, and you have the right. For the safety of this city, you must—"

Sir Bloodworth announced, "I cannot. Anyway, it's not that big."

William stepped over. Rumours flew that Bloodworth had been appointed Lord Mayor, not for his capacity for the job but because he would answer in the affirmative. Maybe that was true but William spoke up. "Sir, this is a hard decision, but it's the right one." *Have courage man.*

Sir Thomas, his face pink, took a quick breath and turned to the desperately waiting firemen. "Tis not much of a fire." He waved a hand. "Why, a woman could piss it out." He brushed by the men, climbed into his carriage and left the scene.

William rushed on to the hospital. So far, surprisingly few people had been brought in with burns. Even though the fire was spreading at an alarming rate, people had managed to keep ahead of it, leaving their houses in time. However, rescue teams could not get to the old and infirm. Those who could not move would be incinerated in their tinder box dwellings. William went back out into the packed streets where dangerously high winds had risen.

By midmorning, any attempts at extinguishing the raging inferno had been abandoned. Londoners poured out of their homes in a mass exodus, carrying what possessions they could. Thousands jammed the streets, laden with bundles or pulling carts through narrow lanes away from the advancing blaze. Firemen and carriages could not get through as greedy flames rapidly consumed adjoining houses on its way toward the paper warehouses and flammable stores on the riverfront.

A smoke-streaked William joined a line of neighbours and firemen passing slopping leather buckets hand to hand in a valiant attempt to douse the flames but it was like a small boy peeing on a volcano. A fireman ran up. "It's no use. It's coming too fast." He turned to the frantic owner. "Save what you can and get out." The crackling roar of hot wind punctuated his command.

William made his way through the melee to nearby St. Paul's Cathedral. Handcarts, piled high, and weighed-down pedestrians carrying their few precious goods, swarmed the streets. Some headed toward the city gates and some to St. Paul's already packed with people and their belongings. Its wide surrounding plaza and thick stone walls formed a natural firebreak and hopefully a safe refuge. By the time William reached it, it was crammed full of rescued goods, and its crypt filled with tightly packed stocks of the printers and booksellers from nearby Paternoster Row. A wooden scaffolding, previously set up for repairs, rose tall on one side. Samuel Pepys hurried up to William. They had met at a social event many months earlier. The man was forever jotting notes in a small book.

They shared a quick handshake, and Pepys waved his notebook. "Terrible, terrible. I have been on the river and through the city. It's devastating. People have stopped trying to put it out and are taking flight." He shoved the fat notebook into a pocket of his waistcoat.

William shouted. "The mayor has fled the city."

Pepys shook his head. "I heard that. He's a weak, indecisive man." He bent and picked up something an old woman had dropped—a small pack of letters tied with a faded blue ribbon. He handed it to her and she tucked it into her bundle and, with watery eyes, disappeared in the crowd of St. Paul's.

"Samuel, you know the king. Is there any way you can get word to him? He's the only one who can save London now."

"The king is well aware of this horror. He's being summoned as we speak."

More and more people crowded in, arms full, carrying what they could. William frowned. "God, give us hope."

They said their goodbyes, and William passed a young couple clinging to each other as they struggled through the crush of people. "Emma! My God. I've got to let her know I'm safe." He reached the street where carriages and people on foot pushed on. A young lad on horseback wound his way through the melee. William waved him down.

Yes, he knew Larks' Nest Abbey and he would take a message. William had no paper or quill, but the lad could deliver a verbal message to Emma Worthington, wait for a reply and deliver it back to the inn.

He gave the boy a shilling and hit the rump of the horse. "God be with you." The lad set off, urging the beast through the scrambling crowd.

By Sunday afternoon, eighteen hours after the alarm had been raised in Puddin' Lane, the fire was a raging storm, creating its own weather. The chimney effect drove a tremendous uprush of hot air above the flames. Jettied buildings narrowed the air current, leaving a vacuum at ground level. Some thought the resulting strong inward wind would put the fire out, but it added fresh oxygen. The turbulence created by the uprush made the wind veer erratically, moving both north and south of the main easterly direction of the blowing gale.

On that same fateful Sunday morning, Emma was busy with her maid, Isabel, preserving fall fruits. The russets made a fine jam, and the lemons and limes a superb marmalade. She could have left this chore to the household staff, but she enjoyed filling the shiny jars. It was early afternoon when they finished.

The clock chimed two. William was not back yet. A trickle of concern crept into her thoughts. *Where is he? He should be back by now.*

She threw on a cape. *Maybe he left a message at the abbey.* Halfway up the lane, a horse galloped up. The rider pulled to a stop in a swirl of dust. "Are you Emma Worthington?"

"Yes." She waited while he caught his breath.

He puffed the words out. "I have a message—for you—from William—He said to—to wait for an answer."

"What is the message lad?"

"He said to say—all is well."

"Is that all?"

The lad steadied the horse. "He was busy at the time. Oh, he said not to worry."

Emma frowned. "Come to the house. You can rest your horse and have tea while I write a reply."

He followed her to the Summer House. Martin took the horse to water and brush it down, and Isabel made tea and put out biscuits. Emma went to the library and jotted a quick note asking when she could expect him.

In the kitchen, the driver bent close to Isabel. "Don't tell your mistress, but London is on fire. It's a terrible mess, but the man didn't want her to worry."

Isabel gasped. "I should tell her."

"No. Don't. I promised him I wouldn't."

Emma came back with the letter, the seal still hardening. "Are you sure my husband is not hurt?"

His eyes opened wide. "Oh, yes. ma'am. He said to say all is well. That's what he said."

Emma held the letter aloft and looked at him. "Are you sure all is well?"

"Oh, yes, ma'am. Indeed. That's exactly what he said." He took a biscuit. "Very good biscuits. Thank you."

Chapter 76

William worked through the whole of Sunday and far into the night. Injured people continued coming in, either from burns or falling timbers, while the fire grew dangerously close to the hospital doors. At two a.m., an insistent gentleman took his arm and guided him outside to a carriage. William staggered into it and instantly fell asleep.

A long time later, he awoke with a start. Flickering flames from a small fire in the grate darted shadows across the dimly lit room. *Where am I?* "I have to get back to the hospital."

"Rest a while longer, sir. My man will take you back."

An elderly gentleman sat opposite in a padded armchair in a well-stocked library.

William looked around. "Who are you? Where am I?" He pushed himself up on one elbow. He was on a cot bed set up in front of a tall bookcase.

"I am Lord Westerfield, and you are at West Fields, a few miles from London."

"But—"

"No buts. You must rest, or you'll be of no use to anyone."

William lay back. The man was right. If he did not take care of himself, he would become a victim. *But I must send Emma a letter to reassure her.* "I need to get a message to my wife."

"There is pen and paper on the desk and you can send it in the morning post. It will arrive the same day."

"Thank you." He finished the letter and sealed it with his signet ring. It was all he could do. Or was it? Emma had told him about mental talk and how messages could be sent and received between people who were especially close. He wasn't sure how to do it, so he cleared his mind the best he could and imagined Emma in front of him. *Green almond eyes—long curly walnut hair with hints of red flashing through—and that special Emma smile.* He lay back on the day bed and fell into a deep sleep.

The next morning, William woke with a start as the first rays of sun glimmered through the orange and red stained-glass windows. He jumped off the cot. *I have to get back to London.* Lord Westerfield stopped him at the door. "I have plenty of room here to take in injured people if the hospital is at its capacity."

"Thank you. That will be a big help."

"I'll send a messenger to the hospital to deliver supplies and nursing care. Meanwhile, my housekeeper will prepare some rooms."

William climbed into the carriage and with a wave he set off.

The 18-foot high Roman wall enclosing the city put the fleeing homeless at risk of being shut in the inferno. With the riverfront on fire and the escape route cut off by boat, the only exits were the eight gates in the wall. Near-panic scenes erupted at the narrow gates as distraught refugees frantically crowded to get out with their bundles, carts, horses, and wagons making it near impossible for a horse and carriage to get back in. William called to the driver that he would go on foot, and he leapt from the carriage and headed first to the General Letter Office in Threadneedle Street, where all the post for the entire country passed through. A rubble of smoking bricks and scorched beams lay where the building once stood. He would have to find another messenger to take his letter to Emma.

The fire was still out of control but King Charles had stepped up and declared a state of emergency. Overriding city authorities, he put his brother James, Duke of York, in charge of operations. James set up command posts around the perimeter of the fire, pressing men of lower classes into teams of well-paid and well-fed firefighters. This visible gesture of solidarity from the Crown was intended to cut through the citizens' misgivings about being held financially responsible for pulling down houses. But by the time orders came directly from the King to "spare no houses" the fire had devoured hundreds more, and the demolition workers could no longer get through the crowded streets.

Confused and irate citizens raised their voices, yelling that the papist or the Dutch, or the French had started the fire on purpose.

William shook his head. *Why did some people need to assign blame? And with such wild and unfounded accusations.*

He left the post office and headed for the hospital. On the next block, a burly blacksmith, holding an iron bar high over his head, stood over a cowering man. With a howl, he smashed the heavy bar down.

William sprinted over as a woman, screaming in French, ran to the wounded man. The weapon had glanced off the side of his head, but the blow could have killed him. The blacksmith had fled and William carried the injured Frenchman into his shop—his wailing wife right behind.

"Lock the door," he commanded. "There are others too ready to blame."

He dressed the wound as best he could. "As soon as he comes round, get out of here. You're in the line of this raging firestorm. You must leave as soon as you can."

She scurried about packing a bundle, her eyes wide with fright.

Back on the street, William pushed through the swirling mob, elbows and parcels crushing against him. He was glad that Emma was safely at Lark's Nest. She was so afraid of fire and this would devastate her. He had one more stop to make before going to the hospital. He'd not seen Father in over a year, and that was only for a brief meeting in the presence of a lawyer. At that time, William had been duly informed that Mr. Frederick Johnstone had not only disinherited him but, from that moment, disowned him. He had been ordered to change his surname and desist using the name of Johnstone. That had been no problem. By then, William was already officially and legally William Arthur Worthington the third. He did not hate the man he called Father. He'd received a good education, and after meeting Emma, he did not regret a moment of his life for what he had now.

Winding his way through the sea of people, he reached the Johnstone residence. It was still standing, but it too would soon fall like the thousands before it. William opened the door. Nathan, carrying an empty wooden box, rushed along the hall.

William stepped in. "Nathan."

He stopped so swiftly he nearly tottered over. He dropped the box and wrung his hands. "Master William. So good of you to come." He waved a hand toward the open door of the library. "He's gone off his head. You must do something."

William put his arm around the old man. In some ways, he had been more of a father to him than Frederick Johnstone. "What is it, Nathan? How can I help?"

"He's gone mad. He's ordered all the books to be loaded into the carriage." He pointed a shaking finger toward the half-opened library door. "In there."

William strode into the room.

The man, who had been his father for so many years, pulled a handful of gold-trimmed leather books from a shelf and crammed them into an already overflowing box.

"Father, what are you doing?"

A harried face looked up. "Get out. I am not your father. You are nothing to me. Be gone from my sight." He reached to another shelf.

"You must get out. Leave the books. There are too many to carry."

He shoved another fat book into a box. "Nathan is packing the carriage."

"The streets are jammed. You'll never get through."

"I must save my books. I have buyers for them."

"They're not worth your life."

"What am I worth without the money they will bring?"

"You're delirious." William bent down and took his arm. "Come with me."

"No. Leave me." He shook him off and turned back to the bookcase.

William stared for a long moment. "As you have it, but I'm taking Nathan with me."

"Take him. You've taken everything else from me." He dumped a pile of books on top of an overflowing box.

William looked at the man who had changed his life. A half dozen boxes, haphazardly packed, surrounded him. Books impossible to save. The fire would eagerly eat each page, and for Frederick Johnstone, it would be like pound notes burning. His money, his cherished money would be gone, and since he loved money more than life, he would probably die with his burning books.

William leaned over and took his arm again. "Let me help you up. Come with me to safety."

In a flash, the frenzied man grabbed the poker and swung it back. "Get away from me. You just want my money."

William tightened his grip. "Father, please."

"Let me go." He swung the poker at his once beloved son.

William ducked to the side, and the poker smashed onto a book ripping into its cover.

His father howled. "Look what you made me do." With shaking fingers he tried to push the edges together. "My book. You hurt my precious book." Strands of stringy hair fell over his forehead.

William backed away and stood for a brief moment. "Good bye, Father." He looked at the man moaning and rocking a book in his arms. He turned swiftly and strode to the front door. "Come, Nathan."

The flustered manservant followed William out, and they walked into the street to join the desperate throng on their way out of London.

Chapter 77

For the rest of Sunday, Emma's attention kept wandering to William and the cryptic message he had sent. *Why didn't he take the time to write a letter?* She slept fitfully that night and woke early Monday morning. Her skin itched, and her foot swung whenever she sat down, which wasn't for long. She'd jump up, go to the table to get something and forget what she went for.

Something's wrong. She closed her eyes and took in a long breath and imagined William standing in front of her. As she brought him into view in her mind's eye, her heart beat faster. *He's in trouble.* She opened her eyes. "Chaos all around him." She forced herself to remain calm and closed her eyes again. *A mass of humanity moving forward, pushing, pressing to escape. The air thick with fear and panic. And smoke. And fire!*

A noise broke her focus. She opened her eyes and ran to the window. A horse and rider galloped up to the house. By the time Emma got to the front door, Isabel had opened it, and the rider was shouting. "A bad fire. Very bad. All of London is aflame."

At the word fire, Emma started to shake. She slapped her hands to her chest, closed her eyes and took in several long slow breaths. *Breathe. Just breathe. I'm safe. All is well. Keep breathing.*

Isabel touched Emma's arm. "What is it, madam?"

Emma jumped and stared at her maid, her eyes wild "William's in London. I must go this minute."

The rider steadied his horse. "It's madness to go into the city. Hordes are leaving. It's not safe."

Emma's eyes glistened with a fierce light. "I must. My husband is there. I need to find him."

"Madam, it is utter folly to enter London. I implore you. Wait here till he comes back."

"Do your ears not work? I must go. " Her head throbbed and a deep constricting pain pounded against her ribs. *I can't lose William. The fire will burn him.* "I have to go," she cried. "I must, I must." Her eyes flashed as if lit from some burning force deep inside. "I'll fetch my cloak. Isabel, tell Martin to get a carriage ready. Now."

She raced upstairs and scrambled into travelling clothes: a sensible dress, her sturdy walking shoes, and a long cape. Halfway out of the bedroom, she stopped and rushed back to her dresser. "Come with me, Dragonfly. Give me strength and help me find William. We have to save him." She pushed it deep into her pocket and flew out of the room.

Martin pulled the carriage up. "Are you sure of this? It's insanity to go into the city now."

"I must go. Immediately and fast."

"It's too dangerous, and we'll have trouble getting in with so many people coming out."

"Then go as close as you can. I'll walk the rest of the way." She climbed onto the seat and the obedient horse moved away from the Abbey grounds, and headed towards a fiery London.

As the carriage rattled along, she took a big breath, while her mind ran in circles and her palms sweat. The sensible part of her rationally told her it was mad to go to London, and reminded her she was terrified of fire. But a higher terror drove her on. A fiercer part screaming from deep within erupted and obliterated all reason. *I can't —I won't lose William.*

They got as far as Southwark by the Thames. People, pouring out of the city, blocked further passage with their carts and stuffed carriages. She jumped down. "I'll walk from here."

Martin leaned over. "Please, Madam. Do not go any further. It's too dangerous."

Her grown-up part answered. "I'll be fine, Martin. I'll go to the hospital. He's probably there." She disappeared into the throng of humanity, fighting her way against the wave of panic and the cries of her younger, terror-stricken part. *Fire kills.*

After several blocks, she broke free of the crowd and turned to the doors of St. Bartholomew's. A flurry of activity met her. She stopped a Sister carrying an armful of bandages. "William. Have you seen him? Is he here?" Her words came fast and breathless.

The Sister, dark circles under her eyes, peered at her. "William?"

"William Worthington—Johnstone-Worthington. He's a doctor. Have you seen him?"

She frowned. "I don't know. I have work to do." She stepped away and stopped. "Wait. He was here yesterday. I haven't seen him today."

"Is Mr. Stanford here?" *Maybe Charles knows where he is.*

"He is somewhere helping with the evacuation."

"What? What's happening?"

"This hospital is in direct line of the fire and it's moving fast. You would be wise to get far away. I have to go." She rushed down the hall.

Emma stepped back. *Where's William?* Her eyes lit up. Mr. Johnstone—his father. *It would be like him to go there.*

She raced out of the hospital and stood on the edge of the surging crowd. *This is madness. I'll never find that tall, squished house.* The name of the street popped into her head. *Thank you, angels.* She ran to a constable for directions.

He shook his head and yelled over the noise of the crowd and the roar of the approaching wall of fire. "You can't go near there. That street is long gone." He took her arm. "You'd best move on, madam. For your own safety."

She moved in the direction he'd indicated, blending in with the mass of humanity, then turned and pushed her way back through the crushing horde. Her eyes wild. Searching but not seeing. Pressing at all odds against the impossible. *I must find William. I have to save him.*

The crowd thinned and she moved faster. Still far from that horrible man's house. *He may not even be there,* Her mind scrambled for direction but blind fear kept reason at bay. A single unceasing thought drove her forward. *Save William or die trying.*

She rushed around a building where a line of volunteers were passing sloshing buckets hand-to-hand. The line stretched from the river, over the road and ended at a burning house. Emma stopped short. *William.* A woosh and a flash of flames shot high into the air. Black smoke billowed out and her throat and chest burned. She bolted toward the crackling heat and with a great cry, threw herself onto the steps, clawing and scrambling up the burning sticks of wood. "Mama, Mama. I must save Mama."

The man closest yelled, dropped his bucket and grabbed her off. Her dress was on fire and forehead bleeding. He held her fast, smothering the flames, but she was hysterical—kicking, screaming and scratching at him. "Mama, Mama." The next instant, she went limp and slumped in his arms.

Chapter 78

William held Nathan's arm as they made their way up the narrow cobbled street. He had to find a hackney carriage for the old man. "Wait here." He led him to a door stoop. "I'll be right back."

At the next road, he spied an empty carriage and waved it over. After paying tenfold the regular price to go to Larks' Nest, he settled him in and handed him the letter. "Give this to Emma and tell her I'm all right. I'll be home as soon as I can."

William made his way to the hospital, winding through less crowded back streets. When he arrived, a carriage with a Head Nun and two nurse helpers with supplies had just left for West Fields to set up an emergency medical centre. Many people had been injured battling their way through the crammed gates. Broken bones, sprained ankles, and bloodied heads were more frequent than burns. William entered the hospital—its hallway crowded with patients waiting to be taken to safer locations. As soon as he told the assistant Sister he'd been to West Fields, he was assigned to be the officiating doctor there. A wagon and driver pulled up to the front and nurses and assistants helped the injured out.

William rushed up to a doctor who had his arm around a man with a bandaged leg. "Charles. Are you all right?"

A bleary-eyed Charles blinked. "Are you? You look terrible."

William took the man's other arm and walked out with them. "I'm going back with the wagon to West Fields. Will you come?"

"No. Some patients can't be moved. We have to pray the fire doesn't reach here."

They settled the man in the wagon and Charles turned to go, but stopped. "Sister Marguerite mentioned a woman was here looking for you."

William stared. "A woman? Who?"

"She didn't say." He looked around. "Here comes Sister Marguerite now." Charles hurried back into the hospital.

It couldn't have been Emma. She intensely feared fire. *Surely she's at Lark's Nest. Or is she?* He greeted the nun and asked who the woman was asking for him.

"She didn't give her name but I can describe her."

William listened and blanched. *My God, it was Emma.* His mind raced. *Where would she go? Where is she now?* He staggered and grabbed onto the side of the wagon. *Get hold of yourself. You can't go running about like a wild man. She's a sensible woman. She'd go home and wait for a message.*

The nun took his arm. "Are you all right?"

"I—yes." He shook his head. "I have to go to West Fields now." He climbed up beside the driver and they pulled into the crowded street. *Where are you Emma? Where did you go?* The wagon wound its way to a city gate. *Surely she would go home. Dear God and all your angels. Take care of her.* As soon as he could he would send another message to her but a niggling feeling kept gnawing at him that she wasn't at the abbey.

At West Fields, the driver was directed to the main house. He pulled up and William jumped down and helped unload the injured. The nurses and house staff had made up the large ballroom with cots, blankets, and medical supplies at the ready. William checked each patient and gave instructions for splints, salves or bandaging. As he finished with each one, the sense of urgency that crept around his thoughts, grew stronger and more insistent. *I must get back to London. I must find Emma.* Finally he finished and strode to the front door where a carriage was waiting for him. *I'm coming Emma. I'll find you no matter what. I won't leave London without you.*

The volunteer fireman held the crazy woman who had thrown herself onto the fire. "She needs medical attention. Bartholomew's isn't far. I can carry her there." He strode off, leaving the valiant bucket-line the task of trying to save a doomed house.

At the door of the hospital, a nurse helper stopped him. "We're not taking any more patients but if you wait here, another wagon will be along soon to take her to West Fields."

"When? I can't leave her here. She's unconscious and badly injured. She could die."

" I don't know. It depends on—."

"I can't wait." He hurried to the street. A carriage with one passenger had stopped in the slowly moving traffic. He ran to it. "Please help. This woman needs a doctor. Can you take her to West Fields?"

"I can do that." He opened the door.

The man lifted her in, and with Samuel Pepys's help, they laid her on the other seat. "Thank you, sir. I need to get back." He closed the door and ran off and the carriage slowly made its way toward West Fields.

When they arrived, they were directed to the nearby Coach House where two more rooms had been made into a hospital ward. Emma was taken in, and Mr. Pepys returned to a fiery London to continue his historic scribbles.

William swung open the front door with one intense thought. *I must get back to the city. I have to find Emma.* He took a step and a footman ran up to him. "Doctor, three firemen were just brought in. They need your help."

"I didn't see any new patients come in."

"They were taken to the Coach House, down the lane and around the corner." He ran back inside.

William slammed his fist onto the edge of the door. "Damn it. I can't do this. I need to find my wife." He raced down the lane. *Wait for me, Emma. I'll find you.* The lights of the Coach House guided him, and he rushed in.

An examining room had been set up in an alcove off a larger room where four cots had been placed. One fireman had been carried in, the other two walked with help. William quickly attended to them, cleaning their burns and one man's wrist was broken from a falling beam. All three were exhausted and choking from breathing in acrid smoke. He left them in good hands with Sister Maria and two maids from the main house.

Finally, he could get out and head back into London to find Emma. There would be a carriage at the main house. Nothing would stop him now. He strode along the hall. A long library table had been set up to keep records on patients. No one was there. *Was it Monday or Tuesday?* His mind dashed about in a muddle, thoughts jumping about. He grappled onto the most important one. *I have to get out of here*. He took three steps past the table, stopped and backed up. Were his eyes fooling him? *Is that what I think it is?* His heart leapt. A dragonfly brooch lay on the corner—Emma's brooch. He picked it up and looked around. A maid came out of a doorway carrying a basket of clothes and linens.

"Excuse me, miss." He held it up. "Do you know where this came from?"

"It fell out of my basket when I took clothes out to be washed or discarded. I don't know which garment it came from."

"Are there more patients here?*"*

"Yes, sir. They were brought in earlier."

"Are there any women patients?" His heart beat faster. Emma's dragonfly was here. She had to be here too. *Dear God, make her be alive.*

"Yes, sir. Three." She pointed to the door she had just come from.

He raced to it and swung it open. Moonlight shone over five cots. The first two were empty. On the next a mass of black hair poked out from under a blanket. In the one beside it, a quilt hid her hair, but her bulk far surpassed Emma's. At the last one, his legs went weak. She lay on her back, eyes closed, and her forehead wrapped in bandages. One cheek had a nasty scrape. Her hands and arms, bandaged to the elbows, lay on top of the comforter. He sank to his knees beside the cot. *Oh, my darling.* He leaned his head on her shoulder. *Thank God you're alive.* He was asleep in less than a minute, the dragonfly still clutched in his hand.

He awoke with a start. *Where am I?* He was on his knees, slumped over a cot with one arm across the bed's occupant. He blinked and rubbed his eyes. *Emma. She's here. She's safe.* A fullness swamped his body. *Thank you.* He stood up slowly, stretched his arms and shook his legs awake. She hadn't moved all night. Her arms were in the same position and her eyes still closed. *Who first attended her?* He tucked the dragonfly under the blanket on her chest and walked out.

In the hall, a young man, probably a footman or gardener pressed into the duties of a clerk, sat at the table.

"When was Emma Worthington brought in?"

"Who?"

"Emma Worthington. My wife. I've just come from her room. She's with two other women."

He shuffled papers around. "Sorry, sir. We didn't know who she was. She was unconscious and I think stayed that way while Sister Marie tended her."

"Where is she now?"

"Who?"

Confound that man. "Sister Marie."

"Oh." He looked around as if she might pop out at any second. "I think she's with the firemen."

"Thank you." He strode along the hall to where he had gone the night before.

They were sitting at a table eating oatmeal porridge. One hoisted a large teapot and began filling cups. "Ah, Mr. Worthington. Our saviour." He put the pot down. "We sure needed that sleep, but we have to get back."

"Go back? Is that damnable fire still raging?"

The other fellow spoke up. "Word just came it's under control, but individual fires are burning themselves out and we have to monitor them. They could burn for days."

William shook his head. "Three days is long enough for any fire."

The fellow with a splint on his wrist grimaced. "Three days! You mean four. It's Wednesday."

"Dear God, help us." He frowned. "What about St. Bartholomew's?

Another fireman spoke up. "It was a close call but the good Lord spared it."

"Thanks be to that." He looked around. "Have you seen Sister Marie?"

"I'm right here." A round-faced nun entered with a plate of toast and a jar of red jam.

She put the plate on the table, and she and William walked into the hallway. The news about Emma was not good. She had come in unconscious and had remained that way.

She touched his arm. "The clerk just told me. I am sorry. We didn't know she was your wife."

"She didn't respond even when you washed and bandaged her?"

She shook her head. "Nothing, I'm afraid."

"How bad are her burns and the head injury?"

"The burns are superficial. She was lucky a man saw her throw herself onto the fire, and her head—"

"Throw herself onto the fire?" *Good God, what was she thinking?*

She shrugged. "That's what the man who brought her in said. That she had run right past a man, screaming something."

William scrunched up his brow. "What was she screaming?"

"Apparently something about saving her mother."

He frowned. "I'll check on the other patients and be right back. Keep an eye on her and inform me the second she wakes."

"Yes sir."

He strode down the hall and out the door to the main house.

He checked his patients quickly, rushed back to the women's room and met Sister Marie in the hallway. She shook her head. "No change."

William rubbed his forehead. "I met Thomas Sydenham in Oxford —a brilliant and innovative doctor. He spoke of a condition called coma. Have you ever seen that?"

"No, I've not heard of such a thing."

"It's where a person can be unconscious for several days, weeks, or even longer."

"We'll watch her closely. Have you eaten?"

"I'm not hungry."

"You look as if you haven't slept or eaten for days. You have to look after yourself for when she wakes up."

"I'm fine. I slept last night and I'll eat soon." He turned and entered the room where Emma lay still and silent.

Chapter 79

Emma slept all that day, the next night, and all the next day. William had sent a fast horse with a messenger to his parents that he was safe and looking after Emma. He spent most of his time on a chair beside Emma's bed, either talking to her, holding her hands, which were healing nicely, and leaving her dragonfly on her so as soon as she woke up, she would see it. He wasn't a praying man but the words found their way out. *Please, dear Lord, save her. Bring her back to me.*

Another two days crept by. William rubbed her legs and arms, turned her or held her and rocked her like a baby. He refused another doctor's suggestion of bleeding her. They tried putting strong smelling substances under her nose, but garlic, cinnamon, rotten eggs, tobacco, coffee, and marmalade had no effect. Water, warm tea, or strained chicken soup was dribbled into her mouth. Her swallow reflex accepted some, but most ended up on the towel he held under her chin.

By the fifth night, William was witless. During those long days, he had slept in fits of an hour at a time, determined to be at her side when she awoke. He ate little and paid no attention to the dire predictions of fellow doctors. Another doctor had been brought to West Fields to cover for him. Sister Marie suggested Emma might do better at home, and he agreed that being in her own surroundings might encourage her to wake up. Arrangements were made to convey her to the Abbey the next day. Medically there was nothing more they could do.

Late that afternoon, after a ten-minute nap, he opened his eyes and looked at his wife's closed eyelids. *Emma, please come back to me. I can't lose you.* The anguish in his heart had grown deeper with every day that passed, tearing his life into meaningless pieces. He took several long breaths. *I have to stay strong.*

He stroked her brow and pushed her hair off the gash in her forehead. It had scabbed over but would leave a white line parallel to the smaller one at her hairline. *I don't know what else to do.* He took the dragonfly off her blanket, held it in his palm and stared at it. *If only you could help.* He kissed the dragonfly and lightly put his lips to Emma's, lingering for only a moment, like a butterfly on a blossom.

He lifted his head and gasped. *Did her eyelids flutter?* He held his breath and stared. *Yes. They did.* After several blinks, her eyes stayed open. Tears sprung to his. "Emma, Emma." He held back the urge to yank her into his arms and smother her with kisses. More tears fell as he smiled as broadly as a baby recognizing its mother.

Her voice was a whisper. "William." She took a deep breath. "What happened? Where am I?"

He took her hand. "You had a bit of an accident. Apparently, you fell onto the fire. Thank God, someone was near and pulled you off."

She crinkled her brow. "My head hurts."

"You hit something sharp and got a nasty cut. You're going to have another scar." He put the dragonfly into her hand. "But you're all right now. Now that you're awake."

"Have I been sleeping long?"

"For a little while."

"I'm hungry."

After a bowl of soup, custard and three pieces of toast with jam, she leaned back onto the pillow, half sitting up and holding a cup of tea in both hands.

William sat in the chair beside her bed. "Do you remember what happened?"

She was quiet for many moments. Tears slid from the corners of her eyes and down her cheeks. "I remembered the man coming to the house telling us that London was burning. I knew you were there and I was afraid." She gazed into the cup. "Afraid to go and afraid not to."

She looked into his eyes. "I had to find you." She reached a hand to him.

He took it and squeezed it gently. "What happened next?" He didn't know the aftermaths of this coma thing but perhaps it would be good for her to talk about it.

"I remember getting into the carriage and then nothing until I was standing in front of that raging fire. It was like a dream and I was living in it."

"What do you mean?"

The cup shook in her hand and he took it from her. She wiped her eyes with the edge of the bed sheet. "It was more than a dream. It was as real as waking life." She stared straight ahead, her eyes focused on nothing. "My mother did not die of a sickness."

He frowned. "But that's what your uncle told you."

"He didn't lie. She did die from a terrible sickness. The sickness of ignorance, prejudice, and fear." Her eyes remained focused inward. "My mother and I were making soup. We ran but they grabbed Mama and dragged her away. I tried to save her—" Her voice broke.

"My darling. You don't have to tell me."

"I need to say it out loud but it's not a pretty story." She stared at the blanket for a long time.

"Would you like another cup of tea?"

"Yes. Bring the whole pot."

As William kept her cup filled, she related the gruesome tale of an eight-year-old witnessing the capture and burning of her mother. Of her frenzied struggles to save her and being snatched away by a grief stricken uncle, and terrorized by a brute who almost broke her neck. He did not interrupt and when she paused, he asked no questions.

She put her cup on the side table and took William's hand. "When I heard you were in London in that terrible fire, I had no choice. A frenzy rose in me, and I was compelled to find you or die in the attempt."

"You nearly did."

"My angels looked after me." She smiled even as tears fell. "My mother was with me. She's always been with me. And the dragonfly. It's been my talisman and my connection to her and to—"

"To what?" He handed her the dragonfly.

She held it to her chest. "I don't know. I think other women have held it and gotten strength from it." She looked at it on her palm. "It has many tales to tell. Tales of courage, power and purpose."

He covered his hands over hers and the dragonfly. "Then I'm grateful to it, and I'm eternally grateful you didn't stay asleep." He kissed her again lightly on the lips.

"I'm not a fragile piece of china. Kiss me properly."

And he did.

The door opened. "Oh, excuse me." Sister Marie turned to go.

He waved her in. "Come in. Emma's just finished a large pot of tea."

"And before that, I ate enough for three people. It felt as if I hadn't eaten for a week."

The nun walked up. "You haven't."

"You mean I've been lying here asleep for a whole week?"

"For five long days. It seems you had some catching up to do."

She nodded slowly. "Yes, I certainly did."

Chapter 80

There was much jubilation on Emma's return. The family and staff were joyous to have her back, safe and healthy. Albert, Charlotte and baby Edward were on their way from France and would arrive in two days. Emma was eager to meet her new cousin but also wanted to talk to her uncle about that time in her life so long ago. When he had risked his own life to save her and how he'd cursed the fiend who'd held her so tightly she couldn't breathe.

Lord and Lady Worthington treated her as their own daughter and insisted she rest, but Emma assured them she'd had plenty and was ready to do what she could to help in the aftermath of the Great Fire.

The final battle to quench the inferno was won by two factors. The strong east winds had died down on the Tuesday night, and the Tower of London garrison used gunpowder to create firebreaks to halt further spread eastward. The light rain that had fallen a week after also helped extinguish the last of the blazes. However, it would take many weeks for the coal in cellars to burn out.

The devastation had been massive and the talk never-ending. William's younger brother, George, read the official list posted. "Over thirteen thousand houses gone, eighty-seven parish churches, forty-four Company Halls, the Royal Exchange, the Custom House, St Paul's Cathedral—"

Emma gasped. "Not the cathedral. But the booksellers and all their books!"

George continued. "Not just their books. People brought piles of their own, thinking they would be safe. The Worshipful Company of Stationers had loaded the crypt with books and paper." He shook his head. "Diarist John Evelyn wrote. 'When the roof collapsed it smashed through to the crypt beneath and everything burnt with exceptional ferocity.'"

His sister, Margaret, spoke up. "The heat must have been intense. Witnesses said the stones in the cathedral exploded like grenades." She held up a bulletin printed off a hastily set up press. "The offices of the London Gazette went up in flames, but we're starting to get a little news."

George went on with his litany of destroyed sites. "The Bridewell Palace and other City prisons are gone, the General Letter Office, and three western city gates—Ludgate, Newgate and Aldersgate." He lowered the paper. "The officials figure the monetary loss is over ten million pounds."

Emma frowned. "What about the loss of life?"

William answered. "Surprisingly, the deaths counted were few, and most of the injuries were from falling timbers, minor burns, or breathing in too much smoke." He shook his head. "However, we don't know how many souls were incinerated in their own homes—the old and infirm. We'll never know. The fire was fed by not only wood, fabrics and thatch, but oil, pitch, tar and turpentine, not to mention all the gunpowder stored in the riverside district."

George added. "It was so hot it melted the steel lying along the wharves and the iron chains and locks on the City gates. That's two or three thousand degrees!"

Lady Worthington raised her hand. "I think we've talked enough of this. Let us not add any more words to the suffering."

Margaret waved her paper. "But listen to this. Evelyn also wrote: 'The acres of lead on the roof of St. Paul's melted and poured down the streets like a river, making the pavements glow with a fiery redness.' That must have been hot."

Emma shook her head. "It's like Hell had come upon us. First, the plague and then that unspeakable fire."

The butler entered and announce lunch was served, and the family made their way to the dining room. Lord Worthington offered the blessing. "Bless, O Father, Thy gifts to our use and us to Thy service for Christ's sake. And for what we are about to receive, may the Lord make us truly thankful and keep us always mindful of the needs of others. Amen."

It didn't take long for conversation to resume. Emma started. "Thinking of being mindful of the needs of others, what about the mass of people who fled. Where are they?"

Lord Worthington had news of that. "There are reports of two hundred thousand people of all ranks and stations lying in the fields towards Islington and Highgate beside what they could save."

William had spoken to Pepys the day before. "Samuel visited Moorfields, a park north of the city, where he saw a great encampment of homeless refugees. He was horrified at the numbers of distressed people in tents or makeshift shacks, clutching their small parcels of miserable good. Many without a rag or any necessary utensils, bed, or board and reduced to extreme misery and poverty."

Emma shook her head. "That's dreadful. What can we do?"

William put down his soup spoon. "I don't know. Word is that the distressed Londoners, even in their hunger and destitution, have their pride, and will not ask for one penny for relief."

Lady Worthington frowned. "That's nonsense. We must help."

Emma put up her hand. "I think I might know a way."

When Albert and Charlotte arrived with their son there was constant handing of the infant around until everyone had their turn. Finally Charlotte rescued him and retired to a quiet room.

Albert wanted to hear all about Emma's plan, but first they had to tell news from France. Even though feelings between France and Britain were strained, King Louis had made an offer to his aunt, the British Queen Henrietta Maria, to send food and whatever goods might aid in alleviating the plight of Londoners.

As happy as everyone was to hear that, Albert added, "The King also made no secret that he regards the fire of London a stroke of good fortune for him."

George had attended school in France and the unrest between the two countries was evident. "The Sun King believes the fire has reduced the risk of French ships in the Channel and the North Sea being taken or sunk by the English fleet."

Lady Worthington turned to Emma. "I would rather hear what Emma can tell us about her project to help the proud and starving refugees."

Albert looked to his niece. "What are you planning?"

She pulled out a large sheet of paper covered with drawings and figures and spread it on the table. "It's not complete, but we've made a start."

For the next hour, she explained her ideas for a school to be built on several unused acres of the Abbey grounds. "And not only the school—the children will also need a place to sleep and eat. So an adjoining building with dormitories will go here." She pointed. "The project will provide work for masons, carpenters, cooks, bakers, caretakers, gardeners—"

George frowned. "Isn't that going to cost a lot?"

"Indeed." She pulled out another sheet, a smaller one with columns of figures. "Now that I have my inheritance, there are more than adequate funds to not only build it but I've set up a trust fund in perpetuity."

Albert smiled. "You may have been stopped from going to school yourself, but nothing can stop you from building your own."

She slapped the architect's drawings. "I'm not only going to build it, I'm also going to teach in it." She lifted her head. "And it will be for boys *and* girls and the girls will not be taught needlework and household management. Their mothers can teach them that. They will learn Latin and mathematics along with the boys." A silent expression of 'so there' hung in the air.

Charlotte clapped and others joined in, cheering and congratulating her.

Albert looked across the room, caught her eye and winked.

She smiled back. *Maybe I'll invite Isaac to be a guest speaker.*

Chapter 81

Time passed too quickly and Albert and Charlotte were preparing to return to France. William was at the hospital, and Margaret, after assuring Charlotte that Edward was well looked after, stole her away to do some shopping.

Albert and Emma took their tea and the teapot into the library. They sat in front of the fire and she took a sip. "This reminds me of so many wonderful days with you and Mr. Edwards."

Albert nodded. "I do miss those days but I make sure I see him every time we're in London."

"You were both so fortunate that your houses survived the fire."

"Yes, the angels looked out for us that day. And for you too."

She looked up at him.

He reached over and took her hand. "William told me about your injuries encountered in that terrible fire and the memories it unearthed. Is there anything you want to ask me?"

She was quiet for several minutes. "While I was seemingly asleep for those five days, I was far from asleep. Something had loosened in my head and terrible scenes flooded back, filling my vision." She shook her head and her voice broke. "My mother—I tried to save her."

He squeezed her hand gently. "Your mother was a wise and brave woman. She did not suffer physical pain. She left her body the instant you were safe."

Emma nodded. "Yes. Mama came when I was in that 'sleeping' state and comforted me." She looked up at her uncle. "You saved me that day, and despite your own unbearable grief got us to England and safety. I've never thanked you for that. For being mother, father and mentor all these years."

He smiled. "It has been my life's pleasure to watch you grow into the woman you are now."

She kissed his cheek. "Thank you, Uncle Albert for saving my life. I guess we won't know why we had to experience such an atrocity until we get to the other side."

He nodded. "She never left us you know."

"I know. She left me her dragonfly which gave me the courage to never give up and to be the best I could be. I've tried to do that."

"You have done that and more. I'm so proud of you." He picked up the tea pot. "Refill?"

She held up her cup. "Nothing like a good hot cup of English tea."

He filled his cup and tapped it to hers. "To many happy days ahead."

Months passed with Emma engrossed in a myriad of plans and schedules on completing the school and the boys' and girls' residences. She'd also devised a plan for a farm garden. This would employ many workers and supply food for thousands of homeless families struggling to rebuild their lives while living in tents and shacks in fields outside of London. It would take years for the city to restore itself but it was a start. A new law stated that every house and structure had to be made of brick or stone, and if a wooden one went up, it would be immediately torn down.

Emma also had flower beds planted around the summer house, supplying many hours of work for needy labourers. Rows of hollyhocks at the front, and honeysuckle and wisteria at the back. On the east side, she designed an extensive herb garden based on monastery plans she found in books. Sage, chamomile, cumin, comfrey and other healing plants were the first to go in. Nathan, now an official member of the household, eagerly tended the flourishing gardens. He was an old man now, at least sixty, and used a cane to get around. Emma fondly remembered meeting him when she was eight and again when she'd collected her uncle's box.

Harriet, Beatrice, and Phoebe—now an inquisitive four-year-old—loved to visit Emma in her new house. Their own living arrangements at the Parson's House worked well for them and the two men. However, they were considering moving to Hollyhock House, as it would also be close enough to London to suit Charles and his new gentleman friend, a banker. Mr. Cameron had kept all the staff on, but he missed his wife and children and looked forward to having Beatrice and her new family close.

Emma agreed it would be a fine idea for everyone. "Why not offer the Parson's House as a refuge to families who have no place to live?"

Harriet looked at Beatrice and back to Emma. "That's what we'll do. Father and Mother would've loved that."

Two weeks later on a visit to Hollyhock, Emma helped the women unpack their clothes and personal items. "What about the furniture?"

Beatrice put her brush and comb on top of her old bureau. "Oh, we left it all. We have all we need here." She looked over at Harriet, who was stacking hats on a shelf. "But we'll bring our fourposter."

Harriet winked. "Definitely."

Francesca walked in holding Phoebe's hand. "We have a little girl here wondering where her mama is."

Phoebe ran to Beatrice. "Look what Twin One gave me." She held up a poppy seed cookie.

Beatrice laughed. "I remember Twin baking those for me. I think it's time for a tea break."

The three women sat on the back veranda as Twin One—or perhaps Two—pushed Phoebe on the swing that Mr. Hudson had made for the Cameron children, Beatrice and Catherine, so long ago.

Emma turned to Beatrice. "Did your mother ever tell you her secret about the twins?"

"Secret? No, what secret?"

Emma sighed. "She was the only one who could tell them apart. She knew which one was Marie and which one, Mary."

Beatrice shrugged. "I'll guess we'll never know."

Emma took a sip of tea. "We could ask them."

Beatrice laughed. "Catherine and I tried that. They just smiled and walked away."

Later that evening, Beatrice tucked Phoebe into her new bed. She'd already had three stories—or perhaps one story told three times —and a second drink of water. After the final goodnight kiss, she looked up at her mom. "What happened to Twin One's finger?"

Beatrice wrinkled her brow. "What do you mean?"

Phoebe looked at her mom with those all-knowing eyes of a four-year-old. "You know. She's only got half a baby finger on one of her hands."

Beatrice's mouth dropped open. "I don't know how that happened." She kissed her daughter's cheek again. "But let's not mention it to Twin One. She might be sad about it."

"All right, mommy. Good-night."

"Goodnight, my dear one."

Chapter 82

The next morning, Emma tackled the job of rearranging her vast collection of books into categories. The library shelves held a variety of subjects loosely grouped together and sometimes she'd have trouble finding a particular book she wanted. Sorting them turned out to be a distracting job. More than once she'd discover a book she didn't know she had and of course she simply had to stop and dip into it.

At mid-morning, Nathan brought her a cup of tea.

She looked up. "Is it that time already?"

He put the cup on the table. "That looks like a very old book."

"It is indeed. I don't remember seeing it before."

"Perhaps, it was one of Mr. Edwards'."

"I think you're right."

Mr. Edwards' house, although dangerously close to the fire, had suffered no harm. From that day on, he'd immersed himself in sorting out his own massive library and had given Emma several special ones he thought she would like.

She smoothed her hand over the leather cover. "It's a rare book— hand-written and illustrated four hundred years ago. *A Medicinal Herbal*, by a Margret Silverson, Holyhead, Wales. I thought the first book on medicinal herbs was Culpeper's. I must show William."

"I'm sure he'll be interested." He nodded and shuffled out.

She picked up her cup and took it and the book to the window seat overlooking the herb garden. *It's interesting that my grandmother left me some land in Wales—and in Holyhead.*

She put the cup on the window sill and opened the book. On each page of parchment, an illustration of a herb had been drawn, along with its name, its uses, and the various ways to prepare it. She brushed a finger lightly over the drawing of a flowering Lavender plant and on that warm summer day a chill fell over her.

She turned to the last page and her heart skipped. She held her breath for a long still moment, her hand over her triple-beating chest, as she gazed at the gold and indigo blue illustration of her dragonfly.

When William returned that evening and before he'd removed his cape, she ran to him with the book. "What do you think?"

He moved the page away from his nose. "Are you sure it's the same dragonfly?"

"Absolutely. Look at those tiny markings on the wings. There's no dent where I threw it at Harriet and the scrape which has been there since I've had it." She looked at the dragonfly in her hand and back at the illustration. "It is. It's the same one. It's my dragonfly."

He shook his head. "As strange as it sounds, I think you're right."

"And the book is four hundred years old. The author, Margrett, must be the dragonfly's first owner."

"As soon as I wash and change and eat and have a little rest, I'll have a closer look. Speaking of rest, how are you doing?" He put his hand on her large and rounded stomach.

She covered his hand with hers. "I'm doing well. The baby is lively and eager to join us."

"It won't be long. Are the midwives arranged?"

"Yes. They moved in yesterday and are settled in the west wing."

He kissed her cheek. "Do you think it's a boy?"

"I know you want a boy, but this one's a girl. The next one will be a boy."

He lifted his eyebrows. "You sound pretty sure of yourself. How do you know such things."

"If you don't know me better than that by now—"

He laughed and hugged her. "That's another reason I love you. You're a woman of mystery and you continue to amaze me."

Chapter 83

The next afternoon, Emma sat at the front window in the sitting room. Birds and squirrels argued while the skirts on the pink and purple hollyhocks danced in the breeze. On her lap lay the brown paper parcel she'd found on a bottom bookshelf. Why she'd put it there, she didn't know, but she remembered that Francesca had given it to her after Mother Cameron had died. At that time, she was not ready to open it.

She pulled the pink ribbon off the package that Mother Cameron had tied and unfolded the layers of papers. When the last one fell away, tears sprung to her eyes.

Her old fabric doll Molly—one eye wonky—lay on the sweater that Otto's wife had made for her from her mother's shawl. The doll was well-worn with a rip in one seam and the braids straggly. "It won't take much to fix you. I'll have you cleaned up in time for—" She stopped. "No. I'll fix you up, but you'll live on my dresser." She placed it on the window sill. "I'll make a new Molly for my baby."

She lifted the woollen sweater and held it at arm's length. *It's too small for me now.* She brought it to her cheek and the delicious aroma of Mother Cameron's cedar chest flooded her.

"I know what I'll do." She stood up and something fell to the floor. It was the striped sash that Otto's wife had made to hold the sweater together. "That is certainly a riot of colours." She rolled it up and put it on her doll's lap on the window sill. "I'll find a use for you." She went upstairs and passed midwife Ellen, who asked how she was.

"I'm fine. I just need something from my sewing basket." She took out a pair of small scissors and on her way downstairs another idea fluttered in. *The sash would brighten up my beige dress. Or I could cut it into five-inch pieces and make bookmarks.* She smiled to herself as she imagined Mother Cameron's stringent protest. *You can't cut knitting! It will unravel.* "Don't fret, Mother Cameron. I'll sew up the ends most carefully."

She sat down again in the special chair that Nathan had made for her. He'd remembered how his mother used to walk back and forth, rocking his baby sister in her arms. Last month, he took two curved pieces of wood and affixed them to the bottom of Emma's chair legs. After a few false tries and much sanding, he perfected the curves and a secure way to attach the legs. The housemaids thought him daft. A person could get their toes caught in such a contraption.

Emma took her dragonfly out of her pocket. Since she'd found that ancient book with her dragonfly drawing in it, the dragonfly was never far from her.

She picked up the garment and rocking back and forth, snipped away each tiny sewn stitch that held it together. As each one fell, a tear fell with it. So many stitches and so many unshed tears.

Slowly, the sweater transformed into a shawl. She buried her face in it filling her nose with the memory of her mother's herbal soups. She closed her eyes and saw her mother's smile and heard a whisper. *I have never left you, my darling. I sent you William to love.*

After a long moment, she took a deep breath and dried her tears. She wrapped the shawl around her shoulders and, holding it across her chest, breathed in hugs of warm cedar and sweet honeysuckle.

An almighty kick bounced the dragonfly on her lap. She put her hand on it, holding it steady over her rounded stomach and her baby's beating heart. "Your name will be Margrett, my little one, in memory of the dragonfly's first owner. And your second name is Anne, after my dear mother.

On Nathan's moving chair, in the rays of a smiling summer sun, she rocked back and forth. The dragonfly bounced again. "Rest easy, my daughter. We'll be starting on our new adventure soon enough."

Thank you for reading
The Forbidden Path

I hope you enjoyed it as much as I did writing it. I laughed and cried along with Emma as she grew into the woman she became.

It would be a big help to me if you would leave a review at amazon. Either .com or .ca or both if possible

Reviews can make or break an interest in a book and we Indie writers depend on them to help browsers decide if a book would be a good read for them.

If you've never left a review it can be tricky to find where you do that. First, to find the page where this book is listed, search: **The Forbidden Path-Nye.** It's a good idea to put the author's name in case there are other books with the same title. Once there, click on the book's name or cover which will take you to the product page. From there you scroll down, past a couple of rows of book covers, till you see Product Details on the left. Scroll past another row of books, and then on the left again, you'll see 'Customer Reviews' and a sign under that 'Review this product.' Under that is a box: 'Write a Customer Review'. Click that and it takes you to the review page

Thank you for taking the time to do this.

P.S. If you don't have an account at Amazon, I would love it if you would send me a review about your experience reading **The Forbidden Path** and your permission to put your comments on my author's page, and my web site. You can send it to me at gloria@gloriawnye.com or visit my authors website at www.GloriaWNye.com

Coming Next:
Book 4 in the Dragonfly Series

More adventures with a new heroine as the dragonfly comes into her life to help her overcome obstacles and find her own power and true love.

If you have read the first three Dragonfly books, you'll know that each one stands alone, with the identical dragonfly being the link that joins all the women in their journeys. However, you will probably have noticed the parallel between Margrett in Book 1 and Cynthia in Book 2, suggesting a strong reincarnation connection.

There is a similar pairing of the women in Books 3 and 4 as well. Madison in book 4 will meet many of the challenges that Emma did in this book. The title of book 4 has yet to emerge, but visit my website at www.GloriaWNye.com for news about that. I am looking forward to a late 2021 release.

About the Author

Gloria W. Nye is an award winning author, receiving several prizes and acclaim for her short stories from various writing festivals: Elora Writers' Festival, Eden Mills Writer's Festival, and Sharon's Words Alive Literary Festival. Several of her stories have been shortlisted at the Writers' Union of Canada Contests.

She is a retired special education teacher, living in Southern Ontario by a wide river among several thousand trees where she writes and paints.

Acknowledgements

Writing is a solitary (and rewarding) experience but bringing a book to its fruition and then to the marketplace takes many helpers and I couldn't have done it without the following.

First and foremost, my sister, Alberta. Not only an avid reader—she regularly whips through three books a week while living an active life—she is an excellent writer and I trust her instincts as much as I do mine. She is also a professional film maker (edits to a quarter of a second!) and creates beautiful and effective book trailers. Thank you, thank you, thank you.

Thanks, Marilyn Kleiber, aka J.M. Tibbott, author of the Pridden Series. In our small but dynamic River Writers Group, your editing critiques have been invaluable to me, pulling me out of stuck plot points and wandering side stories.

Thank you, Rose Kubik, my number one fan. Your enthusiasm for my books lift my spirit. I am so delighted that you enjoy my stories.

Thank you my dear friend Ruth Cunningham, whose poetry touches deep within one's soul, taking your breath away one moment, and making your heart sing the next.

A writer needs first readers, and I am blessed to have a great group to give me their honest opinions before a book is launched. Your comments are important and I appreciate your time and attention. Thank you Barbara McKell, Iris McQueen, Debbie Gopsill, Alberta Nye, Marilyn Kleiber, Barbara Heagy, Mary Ann Moore, and Lynda Noyle. Thanks Lynda for your first hand experience with flintlock pistols. Who knew they smelled like rotten eggs when shot?

Thanks to my to creative team: Robin Johnson at Robin Ludwig Designs, for designing yet another perfect cover for the third book in the Dragonfly series.

Myton_music at fiverr for your original music composition for the book trailer.

And to the artists at Shutterstock, Pixaby, Upsplash and Istock, for photos for the cover and book trailer, thank you.

Many thanks to the support team at MailerLite, especially Maria, Claudia, and Matias, who guided me through the tangle of landing pages and an automated mailing system so I can easily communicate with my readers

We indie writers/publishers are fortunate to have so much online help with the complicated and sometimes frustrating maze of marketing: Thank you to David Chesson, the Kindleprenaur guy, and to Mark Dawson and Rob Eager for your guidance and expertise in this ever growing field.

Thank you Janice Hardy for helping me bring my writing craft to another level.

And speaking of writing, I am forever grateful to Marie Davis Zimmerman, my first editor. Your gentle editing pulled the writer out of me, and your belief in me gave, and continues to give me the courage to keep doing what I love doing most.

Seeing my grandchildren, Ricky, Jake and Genessa, in person was limited this past year of 2020 and I appreciate their ongoing support, and for sending pictures and videos of baby Claire taking her first steps.

Lastly and mostly, to my daughter, Melanie. You started it all. There would have been no books without you. Thank you for choosing me to be your mom. Your birth turned me from a forbidden path and set me in the right direction. It brings me great joy to see you continuing to grow and expand into all you are meant to be. Thanks for being you. You inspire me.